Tyler Anne Snell lives  same-named husband, the... 'lions' and a burning desire to meet Kurt Russell. Her superpowers include binge-watching TV and herding cats. When she isn't writing thrilling mysteries and romance, she's reading everything she can get her hands on. How she gets through each day starts and ends with a big cup of coffee. Visit her at tylerannesnell.com

Katherine Garbera is a *USA Today* bestselling author of more than 100 novels, which have been translated into over two dozen languages and sold millions of copies worldwide. She is the mother of two incredibly creative and snarky grown children. Katherine enjoys drinking champagne, reading, walking and travelling with her husband. She lives in Kent where she is working on her next novel. Visit her online at katherinegarbera.com

Also by Tyler Anne Snell

Small Town Last Stand
Search for the Truth
The Deputy's Secret Double

The Saving Kelby Creek Series
Uncovering Small Town Secrets
Searching for Evidence
Surviving the Truth
Accidental Amnesia
Cold Case Captive
Retracing the Investigation

Also by Katherine Garbera

Price Security
Bodyguard Most Wanted
Safe in Her Bodyguard's Arms
Christmas Bodyguard
Find Her
Relentless Pursuit

Discover more at millsandboon.co.uk

AGAINST THE CLOCK

TYLER ANNE SNELL

COLTON'S BLIZZARD GUARDIAN

KATHERINE GARBERA

MILLS & BOON

All rights reserved including the right of reproduction in whole or in part in any form. This edition is published by arrangement with Harlequin Enterprises ULC.

This is a work of fiction. Names, characters, places, locations and incidents are purely fictional and bear no relationship to any real life individuals, living or dead, or to any actual places, business establishments, locations, events or incidents. Any resemblance is entirely coincidental.

Without limiting the exclusive rights of any author, contributor or the publisher of this publication, any unauthorised use of this publication to train generative artificial intelligence (AI) technologies is expressly prohibited. HarperCollins also exercise their rights under Article 4(3) of the Digital Single Market Directive 2019/790 and expressly reserve this publication from the text and data mining exception.

® and ™ are trademarks owned and used by the trademark owner and/or its licensee. Trademarks marked with ® are registered with the United Kingdom Patent Office and/or the Office for Harmonisation in the Internal Market and in other countries.

First Published in Great Britain 2026
by Mills & Boon, an imprint of HarperCollins*Publishers* Ltd
1 London Bridge Street, London, SE1 9GF

www.harpercollins.co.uk

HarperCollins*Publishers*
Macken House, 39/40 Mayor Street Upper,
Dublin 1, D01 C9W8, Ireland

Against the Clock © 2026 Tyler Anne Snell
Colton's Blizzard Guardian © 2026 Harlequin Enterprises ULC

Special thanks and acknowledgment are given to Katherine Garbera for her contribution to *The Coltons of Dark Canyon* series.

ISBN: 978-0-263-42021-0

0226

Printed and Bound in the UK using 100% Renewable Electricity at
CPI Group (UK) Ltd, Croydon, CR0 4YY

AGAINST THE CLOCK

TYLER ANNE SNELL

This book is for Doc Ernest and her retirement. My favourite background character who has popped up in almost every story I've written is finally passing the torch to her daughter. For readers who caught on, just know she's on a private beach somewhere with a very handsome man at her side and an extremely yummy drink in her hand.

Chapter One

Rose Little didn't want to talk about it. No way, no how. She wanted to stay tight-lipped, closemouthed, quiet as a mouse.

The man, wearing a nice button-up shirt with a skinny tie and holding a business card he was trying to Houdini into her hand, was begging that she do the opposite.

"We don't mind paying for the story," he said, not for the first time since he had met her outside the coffee shop. "We just want an exclusive so it can reach more people. Don't you want to share your good deed with the world?"

Rose didn't know which annoyed her more: the reporter trying to cash in on her two minutes of fame or the fact that he'd chosen to do so on her off day. Normally she would be wearing her deputy's uniform and her McCoy County Sheriff's Department badge but right now she had on a good pair of jeans and an old sweatshirt that was multicolored, faded and always comfortable despite outside annoyances.

Off days were rare for a department so small. They were even more rare for the smallest of that small.

Rose loved her work.

She just wasn't a fan of bragging about it.

"Doing a good deed is enough for me," she said, stepping around him on the sidewalk. Her car was in the lot behind the business complex. It seemed that the reporter didn't mind the extra few yards to it. He got into line next to her, unfazed.

"Oh, of course, of course," he said. "I'm not trying to say you did it for the fame or anything, I'm just saying that this is truly inspiring and a really good comment on courage in the face of danger. It's not about you getting recognition, it's about creating hope for others."

Rose was the first person to admit that her last name was unfortunately a very accurate description of her physically. Rose Little was petite. Only an inch over five feet, she could put on a Halloween costume and go trick-or-treating as a child without anyone suspecting she was actually a thirty-two-year-old woman.

Most times it didn't bother her—she had spent years becoming mighty despite her size—but walking alongside the reporter, she found their height difference to be annoying. She wanted to frighten him away with what her colleagues at the sheriff's department called her scary eyes.

Green little daggers that let whoever was on the receiving end of them know that they had managed to get on the diminishing side of her patience.

But Rose couldn't do that to this man. Not only did he keep his attention ahead of them, he was a full foot or so above her. She would have to grab him by the collar and pull down to really level him out.

And she had a feeling Sheriff Weaver wouldn't be a fan of that.

So, she settled for a verbal attack. Passive but pointed.

"I don't see how what I did would inspire hope for others. Not many people find themselves trapped in that kind of situation every day."

The man rounded the street corner with her.

He was shaking his head.

"The point isn't the people, it's you," he said. "Not many people would have risked their lives like that. You were a hero, saving the day by yourself and doing it like you were in an action movie. I mean, you've seen the video, right? It went viral for a reason. The entire country is talking about—"

Rose could see her car in the distance. She didn't want to see the man anymore.

"Listen—" she stopped to face him "—I get that this is your job and that there's a lot of people who might eat a story like me up even though it's been months, but I don't want to make this a big deal. Because it wasn't, really. I didn't do it for fame or fortune or comments. I did it because it needed to be done. So it was nice to stroll with you, but this is where that ends."

Rose wasn't entirely heartless. She'd been born and raised in Seven Roads, Georgia, and had spent a majority of her life in most of the same spots since. She knew there was a Southern etiquette, and she tried to practice some with the reporter to help the rejection go down easier. So she held out her hand for a shake, thinking that was it.

The man took her hand, only to push forward his own agenda.

She felt the business card against her palm before she could stop him.

He smiled big, taking the rejection with stride.

"I'm sure you'll change your mind," he said. "And when you do, call me at this number."

Rose watched as the man retreated as fast as he had popped up. It left her a little dumbfounded. She had expected a lot more buzzing. She slipped his card into her pocket—she wasn't going to litter—and went to her car, glad for one less annoyance for the day.

That lack of annoyance didn't last long.

Her car started lurching and the check engine light went on before she could make it back to the house. Rose was glad it had at least waited to act up when the reporter wasn't around. He would have no doubt eaten it up had he seen her car—*the* car from her "daredevil rescue"—was having issues.

"There's no way I'm letting anyone get wind of this," she told herself aloud. She patted the dashboard. "Don't worry. We'll get you fixed, keep avoiding reporters, and eventually everything will die back down. They'll find another story more exciting than me, and we can keep on living our lives without the world caring."

The car didn't talk back but it did shudder here and there as she changed direction toward the only mechanic in town.

Rose didn't blame it one bit.

She should have taken it to the shop after everything had happened.

However, life had become…a lot after what she had done. Not just from reporters. The town of Seven Roads held gossip longer than grudges. Five months later, she still was stopped on occasion at the grocery store to chat about it.

Sure, Rose could admit what she had done was a little more than what some might have. And yeah, she had potentially saved several people by putting her own life on the line.

But…she hadn't been able to save everyone.

It was a fact that so many seemed to gloss over from the word jump.

Rose's hand tightened around the steering wheel.

She knew the truth, no matter how indifferent the rest of the world seemed to be about it.

A world hadn't ended with a bang but a whimper.

And she seemed to be the only one who had remembered the sound.

Now all she could do was hope for the quiet again.

JAMES KELLER WAS having a pretty decent day so far.

The old Maxima he had been having trouble with was done, fixed, paid for and gone. The same went for the engine issues with an even older Buick and Mrs. Jones's usual oil change and tire rotation. James had even dealt with Mr. Donahue's impromptu drop-in for a stay-and-chat session.

He had updated James on the neighborhood's latest news, given his opinion on his grandkids' current obsessions, and gone as far as to bring up his recently divorced daughter Layla again.

"Now that she's dropped that baggage of that sorry husband of hers, I'm ready for her to get a nice, good guy who knows value when he sees it." Mr. Donahue had given a pointed look over to James at this. "Someone who runs their own business because he's a good son and an even harder worker."

James had nodded along with the sentiment but hadn't taken the bait. While he did indeed run Keller Auto, the only mechanic shop in Seven Roads, to help his father, he didn't want that, his work ethic, or Mr. Donahue to be why he reentered the dating pool. He had exited it for good reason two years beforehand and wasn't sure dating or marriage was in the cards in his immediate future. Something he had told the older man a few times before. But, as with a lot of folks in Seven Roads, James's thoughts on the subject didn't seem to matter much.

So, getting Mr. Donahue to leave the shop without much fuss had been a feat. One that, along with his shrinking to-do list, had contributed to his good mood.

A good mood that was still holding in place when an unscheduled job drove up into the dirt lot that surrounded Keller Auto.

A good mood that stayed mostly strong when he realized who was behind the wheel.

A good mood that only slightly wavered when the driver got out with an expression that looked ready to turn everyone else to stone.

Deputy Rose Little, the wild card of Seven Roads, walked up to James in the garage bay with absolute purpose. Her small frame was an odd contrast to the set of her brow and gaze. James wasn't a longtime local, but he had been told quickly that Rose wasn't someone you could judge by appearances.

And that was before what had happened outside of the hospital's research annex a few months ago.

James reined in the urge to think Rose looked particularly cute today, with her dark hair done up messy and wearing a fluffy, colorful sweater, and instead put down his notebook to greet her.

Or, rather, listen to the greeting she threw his way.

"I would have called but my car started struggling a few minutes ago. The engine light came on too. I thought it would be easier to just drive it here while I still could." She thumbed over her shoulder back at her car. "Do you have time to look at it?"

As far as James knew, Rose didn't exactly know him. He'd never had a chance or need to talk to the deputy before. But that didn't mean he didn't know of her tendency to rush in first, ask questions later. The hospital annex situation was the most sensational story yet.

Not that it was just some story. One of the people she had saved had recorded the whole event and posted it online. Then it had gone viral.

Some worshipped her, some praised her simply. A spare few blamed her. Some said she had done too much in an attempt to get some attention.

James knew *of* Rose—not who she really was—but he doubted her heroics had been for glory.

Rose Little had rescued a busload of people from a terrifying death, all while narrowly avoiding the exact same fate. James had watched the video too—who hadn't in Seven Roads?—and didn't need to have been there in person to understand just how close she had come to losing her life.

If she had done that for fame and glory only?

Well, then she probably would have greeted him with her name first, her problem second. As it was, she was standing there looking expectantly at him with a small scowl across her face.

James wiped his hands on his coveralls from habit and nodded.

"As it happens, I'm having a light day, so I can take a look now." He gestured toward the open bay behind him. "Drive it in and I can get started."

Rose gave one curt nod and did as she was told.

James watched, noting the car drove okay, but there was a sound he couldn't place as it moved. He was running through the possibilities when Rose appeared at his side. She explained what had happened and did a brief rundown of the car's history.

It was an older model but had been mostly rebuilt by her over the years.

Which told James that what she had done during her rescue hadn't just been luck.

She was good with cars.

"My dad was in a wheelchair a lot when I was a kid, so I became the one in charge in our family for everything car-related since middle school," she said, as if hearing his thoughts. "Whatever is tripping this thing up, it wasn't because of an error on my part at home. There shouldn't be any problems on the maintenance side."

James eyed the tires.

She must not have missed the move. She sighed.

"The tires have recently been replaced," was all she said.

If she was expecting him to ask about the research annex, she didn't show it. James respected that. He didn't bring up anything to do with her job and instead focused on his.

"You can wait in the main building while I take a look if you want," he offered, grabbing a light. When she didn't budge, he added, "Or you can hover here."

He worried it sounded snarky the second he said it, but Rose didn't take it the wrong way. She nodded and stayed put.

If she had been an attention seeker, he thought that would extend to him. Talking his ear off, regaling him with her own glory. As it was, he forgot she was there at all until a few minutes later into his check.

"Do you have a maintenance record?" he asked. "Or did you do most of it yourself?"

At this, her resting scowl woke up.

"I did the maintenance I could myself but kept records for both my own work and when I had to get a new transmission put in out of town once. The records for both are in the glove compartment. I also have a running log I keep at home if that doesn't work for you."

James raised his hands in defense.

"I'm sure what you have is fine." He had been at the hood but now moved around to the passenger's-side door. He opened it and leaned over for the glove box.

This was a move he had done countless times in his career.

Lean over, reach for the glove compartment handle, open and take out what he needed. All while never even touching the seat.

But, for whatever reason, James did something slightly different this time.

He sat down on the seat before reaching out.

That was where he messed up.

That was where their problems began.

Because no sooner had he lowered his weight onto the fabric than three things happened almost at the exact same time.

There was a *click* sound.

Followed almost immediately by the feeling of something shifting below him.

Then, as his brain and body both processed what he was hearing and feeling, the third thing happened a breath later.

Rose Little grabbed his wrist and, despite her small size, she said something in a voice so commanding and quick that James couldn't help but listen with every fiber of his being.

"Don't move a muscle."

Chapter Two

The space between a good decision and a bad one was, according to Rose's late grandmother, only as long as the finger that wags.

"People sure aren't as self-aware as they should be," she'd told a younger Rose once. "Most don't know they're doing wrong until someone is yelling it at them. You know, wagging that finger in their faces. Especially us Little women. We're so dang confident in ourselves that we need a good person to tut at us from time to time. To show us we might have made a choice we shouldn't have. Or, we're barreling toward one we should avoid."

Grandma Little had then lovingly looked at her husband, sleeping next to her hospital bed, and smiled.

"Just make sure the finger wagging at you belongs to someone worth listening to or else it's just some silly nilly wasting your time judging you."

Rose was staring at James Keller's coveralls, smelling car oil and sweat off him and the garage around them, and knew she didn't have the time to wonder whether or not he was someone worth letting judge her choices.

Mainly because of the bomb strapped beneath the man's hide.

"I'm going to have to ask you to elaborate on that *don't move* command," James said through a terse line of his mouth. To his credit, he moved very little while delivering the request.

Rose was careful not to move too much herself, worried that he might subconsciously mimic her, but there was no easy way to answer.

So she didn't mince her words.

"I think there might be an explosive under the seat. One you just triggered by sitting down. That was the click I heard and, I'm guessing you felt something beneath you too?"

He didn't nod but he did confirm.

"I felt something like a click."

Rose looked down.

There was no easy way for her to look under the seat, even with the door open. Not without the man moving for her. Even while sitting, James was undeniably a big man. Tall, tall and taller with legs that matched his stature inch for inch. His knees almost touched the dash and, had he not sat down at an angle, there wouldn't be any space between at all. Despite Rose being the very opposite in size, she couldn't see a way for her to get around them to look beneath the seat. At least, not without moving him.

And *if* she was right, that could spell a big ol' *boom* for both of them.

"A bomb," James said flatly. "You're saying I'm sitting on a bomb."

Rose tore her eyes up from his legs and the floorboard. He kept his gaze forward, his head not moving at all.

"I can't get a good look from here," she said. "I'm going to try and look under the back of the seat. Hold on."

Rose wasn't going to let a second slip by without some

kind of action tied to it, so she did as she said and opened the back door behind him as gently as possible. James's voice carried easily to her despite his lack of movement while speaking.

"I know you're law enforcement and all, but how familiar are you with explosives? Is that even in your list of skills?"

Rose wasn't about to fault the man for doubting her abilities. Mainly because he wasn't exactly wrong to be skeptical. She stepped back, kneeled outside of the car and then angled her hands and head into the empty floorboard with more care than she had ever put into peeking at anything before.

She didn't respond until after the top of her head was lifted off the floor mat once her peeking was done.

She went back to standing next to the stationary mechanic a few seconds later, hand hovering near her back pocket where her phone was currently residing.

"I've just done some cursory training but, no, I'm nowhere near an expert in explosives. But I think we should probably stop talking and not move until I call in some backup to see what they say."

"Is there something really there? A bomb under the seat?"

Again, it wasn't like Rose could fault the man for asking.

She pulled her phone out and brought up the sheriff's number directly beneath her finger.

If the mechanic had been someone else, someone showing a lot more fear than he was, Rose would have put on her gentler verbal gloves. But there was something sturdy-feeling about this James Keller. Rose trusted in his sense of self-preservation.

So she stayed blunt.

"I'm about ninety percent certain it's an explosive with a pressure plate. One you triggered, and are keeping from going off by sitting on it. Shift your weight too much and it'll detonate. But I can't see enough of it to be absolutely sure about any of that. So I'm going to call in the right people who do have the skills to figure it all out."

The line of his jaw got mighty tight at that. For a second Rose worried he would nod. Instead, James Keller gave her a terse one-word.

"Understood."

Her finger hovered over the call button but her mind was sticking to the why of it all. If there was an explosive beneath the seat, why? Who did it? Why the passenger's side and not the driver's?

The call started, the ringing loud enough that it echoed slightly in the garage around them. It would have carried more had the bay they were in not had a door wide open to the outside. No sooner did she have the thought they were lucky to be alone in the shop than dirt kicked up in the distance at the road. A beige truck was driving into the lot. The windows were tinted enough that she couldn't see who was inside.

"Someone's pulling up," Rose said, already taking a step back. "I'm going to tell them to leave and be right back. Is that okay?"

Rose's priorities had stacked in an easy order the second she heard the click beneath James.

Keep the civilian safe.

Remove James and the bomb without anything and anyone taking damage.

Two simply stated goals.

Now they shifted to make room for another.

Keep civilians from getting into danger.

Then the other two priorities on repeat.

If James had his own list, he showed that they at least synced up on this want. James Keller was nothing if not impressive. He gave her another one-word answer.

"Go."

Rose hurried out of the bay while the call continued to ring. Her mind went on dual trains of thought as she decided to call the sheriff's department directly next, while also thinking of what she should say to get the mechanic shop's customers out of danger without causing a town-wide panic.

She had never been a nifty talker like other people in her department—Deputy Collins could talk someone into oblivion yet seemingly manage to never annoy said person—but Rose believed tact might be needed here. If only a little. Dealing with this situation, whatever it may be, would be a lot easier if all of Seven Roads didn't drive up after the news undoubtedly spread like wildfire.

The truck stopped a few yards off, almost where she had stopped to talk to James when first arriving, when another vehicle drove up behind them and into the lot. It was a lot smoother than the first, older truck with its dents and rust. This one was an upkept black 4Runner with dark tint that matched the first.

Rose slowed her gait. The call went to voicemail in her hand. She didn't hang up. The 4Runner stopped next to the old truck.

Sheriff Weaver's voice was low as his to-the-point, prerecorded message asked the person calling to leave their details. He promised to call them back after.

Rose watched as neither driver exited their vehicles.

If the thing beneath the passenger's seat wasn't a bomb, that would be a great—and embarrassing—misunderstanding. She would hear about it for days, weeks, probably the occasional comment through the years. The sheriff wouldn't say much—he was a quiet guy, like their only detective, Darius, was—but Price and the few other deputies in the department? They would use the incident in good humor as long as the situation had an opening for it, like older brothers teasing a sister.

It would be annoying for Rose.

However, if she wasn't wrong? If someone had planted an explosive in her car—*the* car—then that changed everything.

It gave her a bad guy with bad intentions.

A bad guy who probably wouldn't just lurk in the shadows if their handiwork found its way to a mechanic's shop, of all places.

A bad guy who might bring backup.

Still, Rose stopped walking and gave the two vehicles a look of reproach.

Maybe they were simply friends or from the same family, coming to the mechanic's shop for oil changes or tire rotations at the same time. Maybe they weren't getting out yet because they were on their phones or not even paying attention to the woman standing a few yards away, phone in hand and staring.

Maybe—

The beep of the sheriff's voicemail stopped her from going down the question rabbit hole.

Instead she let her gut talk.

"I'm at Keller Auto and I think we're about to have a big problem."

The truck's driver's-side door swung open.

It was a good thing she was already running.

The gun that aimed her way sure didn't give her much time to do anything else.

THE DAY HAD taken a turn. There were no ifs, ands or buts about that. James had gone from a quick workday and right into an unbelievable nightmare.

Was he really sitting on a bomb?

Who even did that anymore?

At least in some place as tiny and mild as Seven Roads, Georgia?

But you're in Wildcard's car, he reminded himself no sooner than he'd questioned the why of it all.

Wildcard Rose wasn't some tiny little name in a tiny little town anymore. At least, she hadn't been in the past several months. She was the deputy who had made national news with a viral video of rescue that had been movie-worthy.

Not all attention would be wholly good, right?

But that also didn't mean her getting targeted with an explosive beneath her car seat was the next, logical step. Her passenger seat to boot.

Maybe it wasn't a bomb. Maybe it was a prank or something else that reminded her of the same kind of explosives that were in movies like *Speed* and *Lethal Weapon*.

Maybe we're just overreacting and this will be one heck of a story to tell Dad and Mr. Donahue later.

James mentally nodded his head to himself—he wasn't chancing movement just in case, regardless of how impossible it seemed to be sitting on a pressure plate was—and decided this would just be an inconvenience. One he would have to endure a little longer.

It was a weirdly calming thought.

One he held on to with great effort as a gunshot tore through the air behind him.

The sound was an explosion all its own and, having involuntarily reacted by jumping slightly, James thought for a moment that *he* had been the one who had exploded. His hands had moved up in front of his chest, like he was ready to fight the sound, but as far as he could tell, nothing else around his personal area had changed. Explosion or otherwise.

He registered the fact that it must be a gunshot a second after.

James wasn't a stranger to the sound, but he couldn't understand why he'd heard it here of all places.

It only made sense that Rose had been the one to fire the shot.

A breath later and the woman in question was at his side again. However, there was no gun in her hands.

"How do you shut the bay door?" she asked. Her breath came out in a pant but there was power behind the words. It pulled an answer from James before a question.

"There's a chain on the left side next to it. Yank it and it'll fall."

She was gone before he finished.

"Don't move!" Her warning came only a few seconds before the familiar clank of the chain James had pulled slowly and with caution over the last several years sounded. He braced himself for what he assumed came next.

James couldn't see it, but he sure heard and felt the metal garage door slam into the concrete floor beneath it.

"Does it lock?" Rose yelled out to him.

Again, he answered without wasting a moment.

"A latch in the middle! The bar secures into the ground!"

James could only see the back wall of the shop. Pegboards with tools, a workstation that doubled as a counter that ran the length of the wall, and the only door and its one way to access the never-used traditional front of the shop. The door that led into the office was to his left, out of sight, and to his right was the only other engine bay with its track clear and pit matching the one Rose's car was sitting over now.

Which meant he had no idea what had gotten the woman more stressed out than the potential bomb beneath his seat.

It must have been enough to have her feel more comfortable locking herself in with a bomb.

After he heard a quick movement somewhere behind the car, James finally had to do what any normal person might in this situation.

He finally asked some questions.

"What's going on? Did you just shoot at someone, or did they shoot at you?"

He could hear Rose talking but realized it wasn't at him. The urge to turn in his seat was so intense his muscles tightened to resist. He was about to ask again when the small woman managed to fill the entire space next to him in the doorway.

She was empty-handed still.

But she wasn't panting anymore.

In fact, Rose Little looked frustratingly calm.

Which made what she said next even more wild.

"I have some good news and some bad news."

Chapter Three

Rose was sweating. Her heart was racing and there was a hitch at her side. There was also blood on her right hand, something she only noted after trying to wipe some of the sweat off her palms in preparation for what happened next.

Blood, sweat and tears—not that she was crying—didn't do much up against bombs. Or guns. Or men who appeared at a time that was too coincidental to not connect to the former, seemingly with no problem using the latter.

Yet in all the quick chaos, there was one thing that surprised her the most.

James Keller hadn't moved.

At least, not enough to count.

Rose hoped their luck stayed true through this next part.

"The good news is, we don't have to wait a while for the experts to show up before we move you," Rose continued from her earlier statement, not giving the man room for a response. This time, though, she did pause a little as she looked at the space between the open car door and the concrete pit of the bay next to them.

James used the pause well. He got right to the point. "What's the bad news?"

Five feet, give or take, Rose decided of the distance. She moved to the spot she thought was directly between the two points of interest and bent her knees slightly. Then she went through an imagined motion of pulling something from one side to the other.

It might work.

"The bad news is we don't have to wait for the experts to show up before we move you," she answered.

James said something but Rose's attention split again. At the far side of the room the door she had blocked shook violently. The men had realized she had locked the bay doors. Now they were trying to come in through the office.

Rose kept her voice as still as the surface of a lake but even she could tell there were definitely about to be ripples in it.

"How deep is the pit beneath this car?" she asked.

"The service pit? This one is around five feet five inches with the wooden floor in."

"And the one next to us?"

James was quick.

"Six feet. There's no floor in it."

The opening didn't seem as wide and there were metal tracks for the vehicles in the way of those four feet. The closest track to them might be a problem.

But it wasn't like they had many other options.

The door across from the garage started to take more damage. The men were ramming it with something.

Rose realized it was time to get very specific with her new mechanic friend.

"I don't have my gun and there's at least two men with

their own trying to come in. They're going to make it in before backup gets here. I can't defend you and I can't leave you, so I'm going to move you instead."

Rose was actually thankful that James couldn't turn to look directly at her. She guessed his expression wouldn't be kind. Instead, he parroted her intentions with notable grievance.

"You're going to move me?" he asked. "Doesn't that mean that if I'm on a bomb, that bomb goes off? No offense, I'd rather you leave me than blow me up."

Rose got close to him, no need to bend over too much given her short height.

"We're not going to blow you up. We're going *to hope* that there's a small delay between you leaving the seat and the explosive going off."

"So what if there is? We'll still get the blast right after."

He couldn't see it, but Rose thumbed over her shoulder.

"Not if we jump into the service pit. The concrete should—" Rose was cut off by a noise she had been hoping not to hear.

A gunshot.

In this context, an impatient one.

It looked like their mystery combatants were getting frustrated. Though she had no idea why.

Either way, Rose had to wrap this up.

Now.

"We're going to jump into the service pit behind me and hope that covers us," she said.

James's jaw was a hard line. She could see sweat had already formed along his neck. The effort of not moving was a lot more taxing than most people might think. A bead of sweat rolled down the side of his face as he said *no*.

"You leave," he added. "If there's a delay then I can make it to the pit myself. You run out the back now."

His words were surprisingly resolute.

Rose was more so.

"You're too tall and you've been cramped in there for too long, so you're probably going to lose time just trying to stand and get out," she said. "You need momentum as soon as possible. So I'm going to give it to you."

Rose wrapped both of her hands around James's arm that was closest to her. It wasn't enough to trigger the weight shift, but it was enough to get James to slightly turn his head finally.

His eyes were a mix of green and brown. There seemed to be some gold in there too, blurring the line between.

It was nice.

"You don't need to do this." His voice was deep and low but sounded louder than the men trying to break down the door.

"But I am," she said. "Now, I'm going to count to three and on the word *Go* we're going to throw ourselves as fast as we can into that pit."

James was silent for the briefest of moments.

"What if there's no delay and this thing blows sky-high the second I'm off it?" he finally asked.

Rose knew it wasn't a smiling occasion, but she couldn't help it.

"If that happens, then I promise you, we won't know it."

The gravity of her words probably didn't have time to sink in. Or, maybe they did. Whatever weight they held for James, he seemed to make a decision after that.

It timed almost too well with the toolbox and chair that

had been propped against the office door finally clattering to the ground.

They were now at the true now or never.

Those hazel eyes with their gold in-between hardened. "On *Go*," he said.

Rose nodded.

Then she counted down from three.

JAMES'S ADOPTION HAD been a quiet one. He had been seven and in foster care for three of those seven years. He'd known his biological parents, but in the last little while had grown to think of them more as simply people he visited once a month in a small room at the department of human services. If anything, it was his social worker, Ms. Bell, that he had grown a deep attachment to over the course of their time together.

So when her sister had offered to take him in when adoption was finally put on the table for him, James had felt some excitement. He would still get to see Ms. Bell all the time.

It was a silver lining that he clung to through his parents' rights being terminated, through his visits stopping, through the rocky year of waiting for the courts to catch up to him, and even when he told the judge he was ready to be the legal son of the Keller family.

They were good, nice people and he would have a good, safe home.

But then Ms. Bell went and moved out of state for her husband's job.

It was only as they watched the moving truck pull away that the then-seven-year-old James thought he finally understood what a sinking feeling in one's gut really felt like.

A part of him felt like he had given up his biological mother for the maternal love of Ms. Bell, only to realize that, at the end of the day, she had been doing her job.

Now the job was done, and Ms. Bell had moved on in both the literal and physical sense.

At nine years old, James's new sinking feeling came from the intense and sudden worry that he had made a wrong choice somewhere along the line. That, even though he knew he hadn't actually had many options, he had still somehow misstepped.

And now everything had changed and there was no going back for a redo.

That feeling had grown and stretched as James had grown and stretched as he got older. It was still there sometimes, a lurking worry, but not as it first had been. Then, as he had reached the age of thirty, he realized it had become more of an ache. An echo. He could get to *it* but it didn't often get to *him*.

However, for the first time since he was a child, James felt that sinking feeling come back to life, strong and loud.

That helpless fear that he'd made the wrong choice and now the world was forever changed for it.

The pain registered first but he couldn't place exactly where it was on his body. It all hurt. He hurt everywhere.

He wasn't lying down but he wasn't on his feet either. He also wasn't sitting. He was, instead, lopsided.

James blinked a few times. An almost overwhelming sense of nausea turned in his stomach. That was when he realized what he had been hearing since opening his eyes.

Ringing. In his ears.

And that was it. No other sounds.

Just pain and ringing.

What had—

All at once the car, the bomb and then the gunshots pounded through his memory. Then the confusing world around him started to make sense.

He had made it to the bottom of the second service pit. Despite the distance, despite the bomb's blast, despite the men banging their way through the garage to them. Unbelievably, James had made it.

His gaze was pitched up and there he saw one of the metal tracks they used to service the vehicles overhead. It was still above but warped and bent, not completely intact anymore. That might have had something to do with the giant-something partially lying across it.

It was part of a roof—the Keller Auto roof—and past that he could see a strip of sky.

It was a startling contrast. One that finally pushed James even closer to reality.

The rest of the details finally sharpened.

There *had* actually been an explosive beneath the car seat, and it *had* gone off. Debris was all around the pit and the smell of smoke and burning things was so heavy it clogged his nostrils. There was no telling how badly the rest of the garage was damaged but the pit itself had actually held. At least, it had kept its structure. The debris still falling was an issue. James caught a burning something next to him on the ground. It was paper, small, but actively on fire. On reflex he palmed it out.

The movement hurt, but not because of the flame.

There was a weight on his side, and it had taken until now to notice it.

That sinking feeling nagged again.

The most important detail inside the service pit had come last.

Rose Little did in fact seem little. She was a deadweight lying against him, her back to his side, head pressed against his rib cage. Her hair was splayed out across her face and only the downward turn of her lips could be seen through it. James couldn't remember how they went from the car to six feet down, but Rose had obviously taken a bigger blow than he had.

"Deputy Little?" Her name came out warbled and wrong against the ringing in his ears. James used the hand that had palmed out the small paper fire a second ago, unable to worry about the soot it had left behind, and gently held her face against him.

Rose wasn't moving.

James shifted his weight slowly, holding her, until they were both sitting up.

He called her name again, but the woman remained slack against him.

He couldn't tell if she was breathing—there was too much going on around him—so he moved his fingers to her neck.

Then he held his breath.

What felt like a lifetime stretched between nothingness and then a beat.

Her pulse.

James wanted more confirmation. He sidestepped any modesty and placed his large hand spread out against her chest.

He held his breath again.

Then felt hers go out.

If James wasn't currently forming a human cage around the woman, he would have let relief wring him out. Instead, he gave the deputy's body a cursory look.

There were no protruding bones or obvious and alarming injuries as far as he could tell. Her clothes had seen better days, and she was somehow missing a shoe, but there wasn't anything that spelled immediate issues.

Well, other than the fact that she was out cold.

And they were in a pit in the ground of a burning building.

Then there was the whole *men with guns* business.

Had they been in the blast or far enough away like them that they had survived?

James was seized by a coughing fit. He kept Rose tight against him until it passed.

She had said backup was on the way but he couldn't just sit and wait for them.

James winced into that pain he couldn't exactly pinpoint and slowly pulled them both to their feet. Rose definitely wasn't faking her condition. She was a rag doll in his arms as he stood to his full height. He stepped on debris and over clutter, holding Rose against him like a groom ready to walk his bride through their bedroom door.

Flames and heat and smoke and pain danced around them.

Holding her was easy. Getting out might be a different story.

James took one quick look down at the slack face resting against his chest.

Wildcard Rose Little looked relaxed, peaceful even.

"I can't defend you and I can't leave you."

James nodded and spoke his resolve, even though he and the woman he was holding couldn't hear his words.

"Don't worry. I'm not about to leave you either."

Chapter Four

Rose didn't wake up until the next day. To be more exact, she didn't wake up until early the next morning. So early that the darkness outside of the hospital window threw her for a moment.

Not as much as the overwhelming pain that went through her head the moment her brain seemed to connect the dots around her.

Beeping machines. Something in her arm. A bed. Not her clothes.

Hospital.

She wasn't dead.

She was in the hospital.

Rose didn't have the time to take comfort in that fact before nausea bowled her over. She might have realized where she was but that didn't mean she was fully oriented. She jolted up, covered her mouth and looked over the side toward the window, hoping that there was a trash can to catch what was about to happen.

There wasn't.

There was, however, a takeout bag.

It appeared like magic right where it needed to be just as the pain in her head came from her mouth.

There wasn't time to feel self-conscious about it either. She couldn't spare the time to worry about the hand that touched her back as it happened or the low rumble of the voice behind the action.

"I did the same thing," he said. "Just don't be like me and refuse the pain meds when they offer them the first time."

The hand was heavy and warm and stroked a small path there on her back until the waves of nausea finally stopped. Then the warmth was gone, along with the bag. A tissue found its way to her next.

Rose wiped at her mouth and let a shaky breath out.

A doctor she hadn't seen before took the bag she'd just gotten sick in and headed out to the hallway without another word. He was back a few moments later.

Rose took the remote attached to her bed and pressed a button to adjust the bed until she was sitting upright. She leaned back and sighed as the man mimicked the lean on the couch next to her. He met her eye when both had settled, and smiled.

"Now that you're awake, I have some good news and some bad news."

James Keller looked like he was the bad news. His hair was tousled, maybe wet, his face was bruised, and there was a split in his eyebrow. It was a crack above a stare that felt kind and patient and unbothered. There wasn't an IV attached to him and he wasn't wearing a hospital gown like Rose, but she could see he was wearing loose sweats and a baggy T-shirt. He was probably bandaged somewhere. She thought there might have been a wrap of some kind on his wrist. But she also wasn't on her A game and the lighting wasn't the best. There was a lamp on in the corner and backlights around the machines, but the overhead light was off.

The clock read 3:00 a.m.

She noted James was wearing slippers, not full shoes. Was he a patient still?

He arched an eyebrow at her obvious inspection.

She fought to focus back on what he said.

"Good news and bad news, huh?" she repeated.

He nodded.

"Are we a good news first kind of lady or a Band-Aid rip off kind of gal?"

Rose didn't have to think on that long at all.

"Rip it off."

James clasped his fingers together. He rested his hands on his lap, a picture of relaxation. Which made his words quite the contrast.

"The bad news is, you were right about the bomb," he started. "I don't know the details—I'm assuming you'll find out more and faster than me—but from what I've been told it was attached beneath the passenger's seat, and I really did trigger it by sitting on it. The sheriff came in here all hot about it and said he has some experts doing their job to figure everything out and that they'd update me when they had an update. But, again, I'm sure you'll get more than I will, considering you're the law. And, well, it was also your car."

Rose had already figured that she had been right about the bomb. If only for the fact that she'd woken up in the hospital in pain. And the next morning. The blast or the fall must have knocked her out. The last thing she remembered was pulling James.

After that, not a thing.

"The good news?" She had a lot more to ask and say but that seemed to be the better to aim at.

James undid his hands to point a finger gun at her.

"The good news is, you were right about the bomb."

It was Rose's turn to arch her eyebrow in question.

James explained with a smile.

"Most people would have thought they were jumping to conclusions and not some character in an action movie. But you jumped and landed right on the truth." His smile fell. He sobered a little. "Your sheriff said that if you hadn't acted as fast as you did, there were a few separate times we both probably would have bitten the dust. So, good news that you were right, and you acted when you did. And thank you for that."

Rose heard the sincerity.

She had heard the same before.

It made her…uncomfortable.

She smiled to be polite and gave a little nod.

That nod took her smile and rattled her pain back to the forefront.

James's eyebrows knitted together.

"I saw the nurse in the hallway earlier. She said the doc will be here in a minute but let me see if I can't hurry him—"

Rose waved her hand to cut him off.

"I'm okay," she said, pushing through a wave of nausea and hoping her statement was true. "I'm concussed, right?"

James didn't look convinced, but he did nod.

"You have some bruising too. Oh, and two stitches on your leg. I didn't see it but the nurse had me look away while she checked so I think it's probably high up there."

He paused while Rose did a quick inspection.

Sure enough, there was a bandage on her upper thigh and hip. Right where her underwear should have been.

Good on the nurse for having James turn away.

Though it did pose a question Rose hadn't thought to ask about yet.

"You've been here since earlier? Why?"

A look Rose couldn't place passed over James's expression and tugged the corner of his lips down. He seemed to think carefully before he answered but it was simple enough.

"They said no one else was coming."

An uncomfortable heat climbed up Rose's neck and started to slide onto her cheeks. It wasn't embarrassment—she wasn't embarrassed at her lack of emergency contact—but it wasn't all gratitude either. Instead, she had traveled back five months prior to the same hospital but on a much different floor.

She was staring at a doctor, seeing her lips move as she spoke, but all Rose could focus on was the body covered by a sheet behind her.

Derrick Tillman hadn't had an emergency contact either.

And because of Rose, he would never need one again.

"Hey, don't go getting all weird about it." James's words broke through the memory with surprising ease. Rose let her gaze refocus on the man. He waved a hand as if wiping it away. "I have a thing about hospitals," he continued. "When I was a kid, I woke up in one alone and it really did a number on me. Now I try to make sure that it doesn't happen to others if I can."

He dropped his hand and snorted. There he was, playing nonchalant again. Casual and cool.

So very far from what Rose was currently feeling.

"But you did save my life," he pointed out. "The least I could do was keep you company to say thanks."

It was true, she supposed. He was there because he was thankful. Because he felt indebted.

Rose didn't like either feeling.

She tried to smile into the new discomfort and play it off.

"Well, thanks, but next time don't worry about me," she said. "I don't mind waking up alone. If something was really wrong, though, I'm sure the sheriff would pop in to check up on me. It's just a hazard of the job."

James rolled his eyes. Actually rolled them like some annoyed teenager. Yet, the look was oddly intriguing on him. Like a massive man being called Tiny. He was at odds with his own image. Rose couldn't help but give him a questioning look in return.

"I've never been in this situation before, but I think you're really underselling the whole saving us from a bomb thing," he said. "Most people would probably have already filled this room up with flowers and cards and would be trying to name their kids after you. I think waiting for you to wake up to say thanks is way less than you should get."

Rose felt that heat again, moving up her neck.

Again, it wasn't embarrassment, but she couldn't quite figure out the feeling.

Instead, she tried to match the man's casual attitude with her own.

"I don't do what I do for praise." She sighed. It hurt. She certainly was going to be sore for several days. "If I wanted flowers, I'd buy them myself. If I wanted a kid named after me, I'd have my own and name them myself too. Helping people is the job. I shouldn't be doing it in hope of getting something in return."

After the bus incident she had seen the room full of flowers, heard the cries of gratitude, and undying promises to return the favor. Rose understood wanting to thank someone who had helped them, but to do so much and stretch that gratitude out... Well, it made her skin crawl.

Did that mean she wanted James to leave now?

She wasn't sure.

His eyes seemed to find something in her expression that was interesting enough. His gaze didn't leave her as he opened his mouth to say something, but the door opening to her left stopped him.

It was the doctor—someone Rose was more than familiar with. He had a nurse with him, and he looked caught between a man doing his job and a father about to scold a child for doing something reckless.

This was what she was used to, this was what she wanted.

No special treatment, just treatment.

Rose didn't speak to James again after that. Not in as much detail as before at least. Somewhere between the doctor summarizing her injuries and talking about what happened next, James left.

After the doctor and nurse had gone, Rose looked at the spot where he had been sitting. She closed her eyes after a while.

The next time she opened them, sun was peeking through the slit in the blinds over the window. Someone was taking up the same space, but it wasn't him.

Deputy Price Collins had his phone in one hand and a coffee in the other. He grinned when he saw that she was awake.

"Even on her off days, Deputy Little manages to set the world on fire," he said in greeting. "When I say you could have your own TV series, I'm not at all exaggerating."

Rose didn't mean to, but in the moment, all she could think about was the man who had sat there before, smiling at her.

Then, she wondered where James Keller was.

Then she wondered why she had wondered that at all.

THE MAIN MECHANIC at Keller Auto might have survived the explosion but the shop itself hadn't been as lucky.

James fiddled with the bandage on his forearm before dropping his hand deep into his coverall pocket. There was no reason to wear what he normally worked in, since the building in front of him could no longer be considered a building. Or, at least, a safe one.

The explosion had been small, he was told. Minor compared to what most thought of when the word *bomb* came into play. That was the only reason why he and Rose had survived at all. It had been a targeted attack, meant to decimate the vehicle it was hidden in.

And the people sitting inside.

"On top of that, I'm not sure the person who made it knew their stuff. I'm told it was *sloppy*," the sheriff had said at their last conversation earlier that day.

Sloppy had almost been enough.

For the building, it surely had been.

Keller Auto had stretched across the middle of a two-acre lot and was just over 4,000 square feet, shop, lobby and office included. Most of that space had been the two bays themselves.

Now the building had been halved. The first bay had exploded, and the second bay had gone down in the aftermath. The lobby and office hadn't suffered from the impact but the small fires that had broken out had eaten through most of the former. The fire department's hoses had brought on the final damage, water destroying the bulk of what the fire hadn't.

Only a few items had survived the impact, the aftermath and the rescue.

Those were in a plastic tub sitting in the back of Mr. Donahue's RAV4.

He was wholly apologetic. Every part of his face seemed to fall all over again as he patted the top of the container.

"One of my nephews was on the fire crew," he started, motioning with his other hand to the fallen Keller Auto. "He knew how important this place was to your and your daddy's history, so he thought quick and managed to grab a few things. Sorry it isn't more."

It had been three days and two nights since the bomb had gone off. It felt like nothing and a whole lot of everything all at once. James didn't think he was overwhelmed yet. Maybe, instead, he was still circling shocked.

He didn't feel much at all when he gave thanks to the older man.

"The fact that anything was salvaged is a good thing," he said. "I'll have to thank your nephew in person some time. And thanks for coming out to give it to me. I can't say when we'll have a place for you to come around for a chat again, though. Dad's been dealing with the insurance people, but we can't do much until the investigation is over."

Mr. Donahue was all solemn.

"It's tiring enough to be a walking miracle. You don't need to add apologizing to it too."

They stood for a moment, not saying much. James had been surprised that Mr. Donahue hadn't joined the masses trying to get gossip out of him since leaving the hospital. It had been a jarring experience. Mostly because all the people who had come asking after him had actually just been trying to get information on the woman at his side.

Wildcard Rose had made the news again.

And everyone wanted a piece of her.

Even now, it irritated James.

"What happens next, then?" Mr. Donahue asked, forgoing the questions he probably really wanted to ask. James was grateful for his restraint.

"Dad's still at my uncle's, so I told him to just stay there, and I can handle anything that pops up here." James shrugged. "As for everything else, I guess I'll take it a day at a time. There's not much else I can do."

Mr. Donahue nodded, but after James said it, he thought of the deputy.

There had been one question he had asked the sheriff, more than one time.

Keller Auto might have taken damage, but it was Rose Little who had been the target. And, if the bomb hadn't been proof of that, the men who had disappeared between the explosion and the sheriff's department showing up certainly had been.

James *did* want to know what happened next, but not for himself.

Chapter Five

Rose didn't know what to expect in life anymore, but she did guess that during her three-day stay in the hospital, a reporter or two might eventually find her. To the hospital's credit—and the sheriff's department's best attempts—no one made it past the invisible line outside of her room. At least not until the last day there.

Rose was sitting next to a vending machine, hand wrapped around a water and an empty candy wrapper on her lap, when a man sat down next to her wearing a smile. There was a cast on his arm and hand. She recognized him with a deep sigh.

"It sure is a small world, isn't it?"

The reporter from the parking lot the morning of the explosion gave her a smile and a small wave of the arm in a cast. He wasn't in a hospital gown but was instead sporting a collared shirt tucked into professional-style dark khakis. His hair was shaved close to the scalp and helped confuse her about where exactly his age fell within the thirties or forties bracket. He *looked* young but oddly felt older. The hospital's horrible fluorescents probably weren't helping that sentiment either. No one looked good beneath them, she had woefully decided after seeing her reflection in the bathroom mirror that morning.

Rose didn't feel the need to pull up a polite smile yet. It wasn't like they had met on the street again, after all.

"Living in McCoy County means always living in a small world," she said. "I could throw a rock in the lobby and probably hit one or two people I grew up with, whether we like that fact or not."

The man bit out some laughter. It didn't feel forced, but it somehow didn't feel genuine either.

Rose realized then that she had never actually learned the reporter's name. The business card he had slipped into her hand she'd placed into the pocket of her jeans. Those jeans had been stripped off and thrown away by hospital staff after the explosion.

Now, at her second meeting with this man, she had no name to anchor him.

It bothered her.

"That's true," he said. "Sometimes I forget that there are people who just stay forever in small places like Seven Roads. Just because I can't imagine wanting to, doesn't mean it isn't the plan others follow."

He was smiling. With or without his name, she found that she still wasn't a fan.

"And yet I've run into you twice in McCoy County in as many days," she pointed out. "If you're not a local then there must be something good that keeps bringing you back."

The man laughed again and Rose regretted not eating her last hospital snack in her room. At least she had already ditched her hospital gown. Thanks to Deputy Collins's wife, she was wearing an old high school T-shirt and a pair of dark sweats. It wasn't exactly her uniform, but it made her feel a lot more secure than the gown had.

Though that sense of security didn't do much as he turned to face her directly.

"And what if I said you were that good thing I'm sticking around for?" he asked.

Just as she wished she had on more professional clothes, Rose was internally berating herself for leaving her new phone back in her hospital bed. She didn't know where her conversation was about to go but she felt deeply that avoiding it would be her best play. Now she didn't have her phone to use to help her excuse herself.

So she reverted to the only other tool all Southerners wielded in the face of strangers.

Rose decided to be polite. She smiled. Before she could reply, though, he swooped back in.

"I was in an accident when I was leaving town," he explained. "I came back today to give thanks to the staff here and then saw you sitting here alone. I may not be here for you, but I can't just ignore *the* Rose Little either."

Rose was surprised at the sudden and aggressive urge to wish this man *would* ignore her. She didn't dislike reporters in general, but since her rescue at the research annex, she had become wary of them. And that had been before her adventure with the car bomb.

Rose glanced down at his hands to see they were empty. If he was wanting to record her—or already trying—whatever he was using wasn't out in the open.

"I'm not that interesting," she said, meeting his eye again. "If you're looking for a good story, I promise it's not going to be with me."

"Says the deputy who's become quite popular lately for always acting like an action hero." His smile managed to stretch even more. At this rate it would fall off his face. She was losing the polite battle.

So Rose took a breath and decided to be blunt.

"Listen, I'm sorry you were in an accident too, but if you're chatting with me now hoping for an exclusive or something you can post about what happened a few months ago or a few days ago, you're going to be disappointed. Everything I've said before, right now, or in the future is off the record. And honestly, I'm not going to say anything remotely interesting enough for any record to begin with. What happened, happened."

She balled up her candy wrapper and stood with as much authority as she could muster while looking nowhere near professional.

"Now, I have things to do, so I'll be leaving," she continued. "I hope your recovery goes smoothly and you make it back home without any problems this time."

Since there was nothing more to say Rose assumed the conversation was over. She started to turn away, relieved that her hospital room was empty at the moment.

However, the man clearly wasn't done.

He stood to his full height, a great skyscraper to her ground-level height. Then he balled his hand at his side into a fist.

Rose went on high alert.

"You know, just because you act the hero doesn't mean everyone is ready to bow at your feet and treat you like one. I was just trying for conversation, I don't need to know who you ticked off to suddenly have them going to such extremes to teach you a lesson." His smile stayed and his fist relaxed into a hand against his thigh as he spoke. However, his words had lost their shine. "You've given yourself too much credit, Deputy Little. I don't actually care about you at all."

Rose's high alert has switched to an overwhelming need to defend herself. She didn't think she *was* that interesting. She wasn't trying to give herself any kind of credit either. Hadn't he been the one who had followed her less than a week ago, praising her? Asking for her story? Had she really misunderstood his intentions?

She didn't find an answer before the man's gaze went up above and over her shoulder in a quick flit.

That smile kept. His words were absolutely sharp.

"And on that note, I think it's time to go," he said. "I have my own schedule to keep."

He was quick to leave the hallway—Rose was slow to realize what had grabbed his attention before he left so abruptly.

She turned around, looking for whatever the man had seen.

Or who, rather.

James Keller was a wall of man, wrapped in coveralls. His arms were crossed over his chest, and he was watching after the reporter's retreating back without Rose even remotely blocking his view. There was a plastic shopping bag hanging from one of his wrists, but it did nothing to take away from the sheer amount of intimidation his stance was exuding. His deep voice was just as formidable as he addressed her without looking down.

"Who was that guy?"

Rose momentarily forgot herself. She blinked up at James with an eyebrow clear to her hairline.

"Wait. Why are you here?" she returned instead.

James shook the plastic shopping bag on his wrist.

"I heard you were still in here and thought you might

want some food since the cafeteria is going through renovations. I didn't know what you liked, so I made some sandwiches. Who was that guy?"

He spoke in one, nonchalant breath until he got to the repeat question. He wasn't happy. It pulled Rose back to her senses. She turned to see the man, but he had already disappeared from view.

"He's a reporter," she said. "He tried to get an interview from me earlier this week about the—well, the other thing I went through. I turned him down. I thought he was going to ask me for another interview just now."

"What's his name?"

Rose's brow knitted together.

Once again, she hadn't learned the man's name.

If that was a note about her character or his, she didn't know.

She shrugged.

"If his business card had survived the explosion, I'd tell you."

James made a noise that sounded vaguely like disapproval. His expression convinced Rose even further of that theory.

"Don't talk to him anymore," he rumbled out.

Rose's cheeks heated at his words. She poked his chest through it.

"Hey, now. Why are you telling me—an independent, smart, and capable woman of the law, by the way—that I can't talk to someone?"

The poke did its job. His chin, and stare, tilted downward.

Green, brown and gold came together in a stare that fell the foot or so between them and right down into Rose's upturned gaze. It was only by the grace of God that she kept her expression frozen when he answered her, voice deep and brimming with certainty.

"Because I don't like him."

ROSE TOOK THE turkey and cheese sandwich. James took the peanut butter and jelly. They were eating both twenty minutes later when the doctor gave the all clear for Rose to leave. She made her sandwich disappear almost as fast as she went through the discharge process.

One minute they were eating, the next they were standing outside of the hospital.

Rose stretched her arms out wide and made a show of letting the sun hit her face.

Like James, there was some bruising across her skin. It was faded but there. Though Rose didn't seem like the kind of person to care much. She shouldered her bag and pulled out her phone with a heavy sigh of relief.

"I would very much like to *not* be back here anytime soon," she said. "I'm not knocking the service, but I'd rather not see this place for a long, long time."

James couldn't see what she was doing on her phone, but he guessed she was trying to arrange a ride. When Mr. Donahue had heard the news that she was still in the hospital, James had been sure that at least one person might be hovering around her. If only for protection's sake.

He'd thought it was more than appropriate to check. The food had been an afterthought. One he thought had been unnecessary as he'd walked off the elevator and saw Rose and a man chatting at the vending machines.

It had taken less than the walk between them to realize the man was not anyone she was friendly with. Never mind his balled fist or the smile that looked so forced.

However, Rose had been James's biggest red flag. He hadn't been able to see her face, but her body language was *off*. Considering James had seen her look more relaxed with a bomb strapped to the car they were sitting in and standing next to, her posture told him everything he needed to know.

Maybe he should have explained his bad vibes to the woman herself, instead of acting like some kind of jealous boyfriend. Instead, he'd simply given her a sandwich and been fine with not talking about the reporter again.

Now James couldn't help but wonder again if Rose actually had a boyfriend, jealous or otherwise.

"Is someone coming to pick you up?" he asked, deciding to get right to the point. "If not, I don't mind giving you a ride."

Rose shook her head, eyes still on her phone screen.

"I didn't know when I was going to be discharged, so nothing was set in stone for anyone to get me," she answered. "I'm just letting the sheriff know I'm out right now. I want to see him before he benches me completely from the investigation."

Her head turned with a swivel. Her eyebrow was raised.

"By the way, have you gotten any updates on the case? Has anyone asked you any more questions or anything?"

It was James's turn to shake his head.

"I was told I would be contacted if anyone needed anything else from me. I also got a promise that I'd be called when the investigation was over so I could follow up with the insurance company for the shop."

An expression he couldn't place flashed across Rose's features. She looked like she wanted to say one thing but decided against it in the moment.

"So you're probably not working today, then, are you?"

That conversational swerve threw James off, but he answered quickly with a no. It surprised him further when she nodded to herself and smiled.

"Then I'll take that ride," she said. "But I have one condition first."

James could have pointed out that giving her a ride was a favor, one that would help her out and not him, but the way she was staring up at him, almost excited, had his interest piqued.

He couldn't help it. He asked her what she meant.

"What one condition?"

Wildcard Rose didn't miss a beat.

"I need you to come home with me."

Chapter Six

There were a few things Rose realized that maybe she should have earlier in the day. The first was a pretty simple statement.

She was too comfortable with James. They weren't strangers anymore, but it wasn't like they were friends. Seven Roads might have been small, but it wasn't like they had been social beforehand. She knew of him, maybe even had shared a small nod or two in passing through the years, but that had been it. Even after the explosion, their status hadn't changed much.

James had been there when she had woken up in the hospital, sure, but after their talk he had gone about his way.

Then, days later, he'd given her a sandwich.

Now he was giving her a ride. To her apartment.

A place she rarely invited anyone over to visit.

Was it because of what the sheriff had told her the last time they had spoken in the hospital?

"From what I know of James, he probably won't boast about it…but I have to tell you that man went through a lot getting you out of the auto shop," Liam had told her. "Or at least what was left of it. I pulled up to the scene with Price, both of us ready to dive in until the fire department showed up, but instead we saw him carry you out of that nightmare like it was nothing."

Rose *hadn't* known that it had been James who got her out. He surely hadn't said as much during their talk. It made her feel an odd kind of guilt. She had tried to play it off.

"Well, I am pretty small," she had said. "Compared to him, especially. Carrying me should have been easy."

Liam hadn't let that sit a moment before he had humbled the comment.

"Easy or not, he cared a whole lot. I saw y'all when you came out—James was a cage around you. He wouldn't even give you up until the EMTs were pulling at him." Liam had sighed. It was anger but not at James. Still, he had some good words left for the man. "I also saw the inside of the shop. Getting you two out was a dangerous job in itself. He could have left you. He could have left you to get through the fire and the debris on your own. Instead, he managed to get you to safety and stay by your side, no questions asked."

No questions asked.

That observation was holding true.

Why wasn't James asking more questions? Could he still be in shock almost a week later? Was he waiting for privacy outside of the hospital instead? Or was he as nonchalant in his everyday life as he had been while sitting on that bomb?

Where did that calm and cool end?

And, was that the reason why Rose felt so comfortable around him in the first place?

It was like James Keller had become walking meditation.

Rose kept using her time with him to accidentally self-reflect.

It was unexpected. And annoying.

She was glad for the distraction of her cell phone ringing. It blared out the theme to *Jaws*. Rose saw her driver chuckle before she answered the only person that ringer was assigned to when they called.

"Sheriff," she said once the call connected.

Liam was quick and loud.

"Where are you? Price said you had discharged?"

Rose motioned to the truck around her though he couldn't see it.

"Yeah, the doc cleared me, so I left a few minutes ago," she answered. "I'm almost home. Why? What's up?"

Liam was somewhere noisy, but it seemed like a nice kind of noise. There were kids laughing and dishes clinking. Rose eyed the clock. It was lunch.

"I was hoping to grab you before you left. I want you to come to the department."

It wasn't a request.

"What's wrong?" she asked.

Despite the nice noise in the background, the sheriff's words were pure authority.

"Just get over here now."

THE MCCOY COUNTY Sheriff's department was small, like its staff. If someone wasn't paying attention they could almost pass it off as a large house nestled near the woods. An oddly shaped one, but a house all the same. Rose had once mentioned this comparison to Price when they were on patrol. He had laughed and told her that she only saw it as a house because her job was her whole life.

Wasn't it less depressing to think of the place you see

the most as your home instead of a small building that once had Marty Fletcher mistake the jail cell cot as a toilet in the basement?

Rose knew she should have felt bad or worried about the comparison, but she just couldn't bring herself to agree.

She let out a sigh of relief as the building in question came into full view through the windshield. The world changed every day. There was comfort in the fact that the department rarely ever did.

"Are you sure it's okay for me to come in?"

James parked the truck in the guest spot out front. He wasn't as at ease as she was, that was for sure. In fact, he was showing more stress than he had when sitting on top of an explosive.

"It's not like I have a car to drive here myself," she pointed out. "Plus, you deserve answers as much as me on what happened at the shop. That's probably why I'm being called in anyways. It's more cost-effective to just come in together."

James nodded, absently.

"Sure, I guess."

Rose gave him a questioning look but didn't pry. Not everyone was comfortable around law enforcement. That wasn't a fault to poke at.

At least, that was what Rose thought until James glued himself to her side on the walk up to the front doors and blurted out exactly what he was thinking.

"I know I'm not here to get into trouble or anything, but I have some childhood bad memories with the law and a cow can't change its spots." He put an arm around her shoulders and dropped his voice into a whisper. "Can we pretend you need my help to walk and that's why I'm here?"

Rose looked up at him with an expression she hoped showed nothing but being dumbfounded at that.

He saw the look and rolled his eyes.

"Not everyone has nerves of steel like you, Deputy Little. Let me feel needed so I can feel safe. Plus, I can't get in trouble here if I'm your plus-one. So let's have a nice cooperation." He started walking forward, his arm like a sling around her. Pulling her along with him was easy. Partly because of his height, but mostly because Rose allowed it.

Let me feel needed so I can feel safe.

James had said it so casually, in one breath, that someone else might have glossed over it entirely. Yet, Rose knew there were roots to the meaning of the phrase. Roots that went deep into the man's past.

Because Rose knew what James Keller had gone through as a child. Day two in the hospital and her curiosity about the man had seduced her to the dark side.

She had gossiped with Price, one of the few career locals she trusted to be as accurate as they were discreet.

That was how she'd found out about the time James woke up in the hospital alone.

She wasn't going to blame him now for being wary. Rose shrugged James's hand off her shoulder but kept in step with him.

"You can hold my elbow," she grumbled out. "But the second we're in front of the sheriff you better be hands-off."

"Yes ma'am," he said, voice still low. His hand closed around its designated spot. He was gentle, even if his hand was calloused and rough.

Rose only hoped no one inside made a fuss over it.

She *had* been blown up after all. A helping hand didn't seem too outrageous only a few days after.

There's that being too comfortable with James Keller thing again, she thought to herself, realizing how absurd it was of her to accept his request.

Yet, Rose didn't try to pull away either. Not even when James lowered his voice again and rumbled out another question.

"Can you limp a little or something? You know, really sell it?"

Sympathetic or not, comfortable or not, Rose narrowed her eyes at him.

"James Keller, don't push your luck."

JAMES KNEW ABOUT Sheriff Liam Weaver the way he knew about Rose—everyone in Seven Roads had done their due diligence when he had first moved to town. James had gotten most of his details from Mr. Donahue about the newcomer then.

Sheriff Liam Weaver was ex-military, a non-talker and no-nonsense law enforcement officer. He got to the point with precision and weight. Or he had, at least until he met and married his wife, Blake. The gossip about her had been more sensational than that about her husband.

She was a former sheriff, current law enforcement, and wasn't afraid to let her braids down if needed—Mr. Donahue's daughter's words. Locals often joked about which one of the two won in arguments between the powerhouse hitters. Almost everyone eventually agreed it was Blake. She had won Weaver's heart completely, and together they had a blended family that was as loving as it was exciting.

Still, when it came to his work, it was heavily rumored that when Weaver stepped into the department wearing *that look*, no one could deny he was made to be sheriff.

James straightened his back a little as the man of the hour walked into the meeting room. He believed the rumors then.

Sheriff Weaver demanded attention without ever needing to steal it.

Rose had indulged him by letting James hold her elbow earlier, but now she was tip-top, sitting up tall in the seat next to him. Tall, for her at least. James pulled his glance at her up, up and away once the sheriff had settled at the head of the table. Then both were focused on the man with the shiny badge.

"Glad to see you up and moving in person, Rose, but, again, I wish you'd called one of us first before you left." The sheriff's tone was hard but James got the impression there was affection wrapped in it too.

James felt a little tap on the arm closest to her. Rose played off both stern and concerned with a simple shrug.

"Being discharged just timed right with Mr. Keller here's lunch delivery," she said. "I was going to call once I was back home."

The sheriff's gaze swung to James.

He gave Weaver a small nod.

"That's nice of you," he noted.

James couldn't help it.

"You save me from a bomb, I'll make you a sandwich."

Neither law enforcement officer chuckled, smiled or commented on that little joke. Instead, both tensed in unison. Their eyes met and James realized he didn't like feeling left out.

He didn't have to sit with the emotion for too long.

"What's up, Liam?" Rose asked. "What happened while I was in the hospital? What did Darius find?"

James knew she was talking about Detective Darius Williams, the only detective in the McCoy County Sheriff's Department, but he hadn't seen the man yet. Instead, all questioning and statements had been handled by the sheriff and a bomb tech and specialist sent from some city unit to investigate the explosion. James had wondered if Darius was out of town or simply kept missing him.

Sheriff Weaver leaned forward. He pointed to James.

"Does him being in here with you mean you want him in here or do I need to escort him out?"

A flash of worry went through James. Then he felt a poke at his arm again.

"He's apparently my plus-one," she said. "You can just go ahead."

The sheriff nodded. That flash of worry ebbed and was replaced by focus.

Weaver domed his fingers together as he rested his hands on the tabletop and dove in.

"For once, we found out a lot," he started. "Instead of having to dig and dig to try and figure out the answer to a million mysteries all wrapped and tangled together, I think we actually have most of the facts now."

Rose's chair squeaked as she leaned forward. James knew he wasn't blocking her line of vision to the sheriff because of where Weaver was sitting, but still James instinctively rolled back a little.

"You mean you know who planted the bomb?" she asked. "And why?"

The sheriff didn't look like he wanted to nod but he did.

"Darius found one of the men who'd showed up at the

garage before the bomb went off. He was hurt and suddenly very worried about life after death and the sins that might affect him after it was all said and done. He was... very forthcoming."

The sheriff sighed.

There was no more dancing around it.

"You were targeted, Rose," he said simply. "Him, and the three other men, were told to follow you but keep their distance. They were also instructed to call a number if anyone looked like they were going to get into your car's passenger seat. Then they were supposed to record a video. They didn't know about the bomb, though, and only called the man who contracted them when they realized you were headed to the mechanic's shop and figured he might have had something planned with the car itself. He was extremely surprised when the bomb went off and the four of them fled the moment they could."

James didn't realize his hand had curled into a fist until pain bit into his palm.

He didn't dare say anything.

It was Rose's show.

"Who hired them?" she asked. "And why my passenger's seat?"

The sheriff's jaw tensed. It seemed to pain him to bite out the name.

"It was Damon Tillman."

James didn't recognize the name, but Rose sure did. Her face seemed to drain of color. It was such a drastic change from what he was becoming used to that James reached his hand out under the table toward her.

His knuckles brushed the fabric of her sweatpants.

She didn't react to it.

"Damon Tillman," she repeated.

The sheriff nodded.

James waited for a follow-up explanation. The two of them simply stared in silence for a moment.

"Does anyone know where Damon is now?" Rose said after a moment.

Her calm voice grated on James. It didn't seem appropriate for the topic, especially not when the sheriff was making no show of hiding his own anger.

"No. That's what Darius has been doing. Trying to track him down. Four men were working for him and apparently not one of them can point us in any one direction. We just know he's…around."

A knock on the door timed eerily with his last words.

A woman with long braids and a very pregnant belly walked in after he called out. Her expression softened slightly as she swung a smile to him and Rose before her gaze fell on Weaver.

"I'm sorry for the interruption, but I need to see you for a minute," she told him.

Sheriff Weaver seemed to split between alert and soft. He nodded.

"Excuse me," he told them.

James belatedly recognized the woman as Blake, the sheriff's wife, after they left.

That, in itself, was a feat considering his attention was so fully wrapped around whatever it was that Rose *wasn't* saying.

Once the door was closed and it was just the two of them, James couldn't stop himself. He fanned his hand out onto the thigh of Rose's pants and patted twice.

"What's up?" he asked. "Who is Damon Tillman?"

Rose stared straight ahead. She sighed out short.

"A consequence," she said. "Mine, actually."

James raised his eyebrow.

"Your consequence? For what?"

James kept his hand on her as the woman with a big attitude seemed to become incredibly small. He didn't understand it. He didn't like it.

If there had been more time, James might have taken a moment to wonder why he had gone from knowing *of* Wildcard Rose Little to *needing* to know her in such a short amount of time.

But, for the moment he was in, he gave all thoughts to her.

Rose shook her head. Pain contorted her face.

"For hesitating."

Chapter Seven

Five months earlier

The first tornado touched down between the county lines. It triggered one of the two sirens in Seven Roads to blare. Rose barely heard the commotion. She was with Doc Ernest in the hospital, looking at the good doctor's phone alongside Doc-Ernest-in-training, Lily.

"I knew they said the weather was going to get bad, but I didn't think we'd get tornadoes on top of flash flooding," Lily said to her mother. Doc Ernest simply shrugged.

"We had a hurricane hit us all the way here a few years back and no one predicted that would rock us like it did," she pointed out. "Like people, in the end predicting weather seems to come down to fate."

Rose, standing between them in plain clothes, didn't know about the fate part but she agreed that being caught off guard by the difference in a weather forecast and the actual weather that showed up wasn't so rare.

The severity had been slightly jarring, though. If she had known it would turn out like this, she would have spent her off time at home and not taken the drive out across the county.

Rose snaked her hand around to Doc Ernest's phone and turned the volume up. She had known the woman since they were toddlers—she'd actually babysat the college-age Lily back when the girl was small. That wasn't all that uncommon for the career locals of Seven Roads. They were born together, grew up together and aged together. They also attended all the big events together, whether they wanted to or not. Price had once called it trauma bonding. Sometimes, Rose didn't disagree.

"It sounds like this tornado is heading away from here and town. Also—given the debris tracker..." Rose tilted her head a little as the meteorologist tracked the radar live. "Yeah, I don't think that's messing up any houses or businesses. That's mostly field and trees up until County Road 72. Hopefully it winds down before it gets to the roads."

Doc Ernest and Mini Doc Ernest nodded in agreement. They had each been through a tornado or two before. There was no reason to panic until there *was* a reason to panic.

"I still bet your sheriff is getting a call or two," the older woman told Rose. "That flooding is probably washing out Mrs. Glenn's driveway and front lawn. That, plus the sirens, and I wouldn't be surprised if she hadn't already sounded her own alarms. That woman could be sitting dry and safe and she's still going to call for one of McCoy County's finest to come keep her company."

"That's only because her no-good son up and left her alone after he skipped town with his mistress," Lily pointed out. "I'd be calling for company too if I was her."

Her mother gave her the side-eye.

"Gossip doesn't become you, Miss Ernest. Not even the juicy kind."

Lily disagreed and the two devolved into a mother-daughter bickering. Rose took the opportunity to step away. She considered calling the sheriff to see if he did in fact need some help before Price's ID popped up on the phone instead.

"Hey, Wildcard, are you at home relaxing?" Price said in lieu of a greeting. He was obviously outside. The wind tore through his speakers. Rose pulled the phone away from her ear a little.

"No, I came out to eat with Doc Ernest for lunch at the—"

"Are you at the hospital?" he interrupted, volume going up a few notches.

Rose nodded to no one.

"Yeah. I got here before the weather went wonky. Why?"

"This is fate, I tell you what," Price said. "We got a call for help from those Camden people and, wouldn't you know it, they're outside of the hospital's new research annex."

There was that talk of fate again. Though the coincidence was there. The research annex was on the back end of the hospital's lot, a quick drive on a service road away from where she was now.

It was surprising to Rose that the "Camden people"—the staff running the drug trials for Camden Pharmaceuticals—were asking for help. The research annex had received all kinds of grants and funding to become a gem-in-the-wild, top-notch building. The staff inside had been rumored to have all glowing résumés too.

Price, however, was quick to explain the reason why the building's integrity didn't matter.

"Those workers are all from up North and none of

them know how to handle tornado weather," he continued. "So, instead of hunkering down, they panicked when they heard the first of the sirens start up. They tried to take their shuttle up to the hospital. Now it sounds like they got stranded on the road that runs between the annex and the county."

Rose gave a silent wave to the doc and her daughter and headed for the elevators.

"Are there any injuries?"

Rose could bring help to them if needed, but Price told her no.

"Nope, but there are eleven of them. And it sounds like they're panicking. The bus blew a tire and that put them snug in a ditch. We had a car headed that way, but the flooding is slowing us down. I called on the off chance you were wild enough to be driving around in this weather. And look at this, you're now definitely the one closest to them. Is your badge on you?"

Rose confirmed it was in her car. When she was buckled inside a minute later, she threw the lanyard it was on around her neck.

"One of us should be to y'all soon," Price said as they were ending the call. "Stay safe, Wildcard. And watch the weather. The air still feels weird."

They didn't know how ominous those words would later become. Instead, the call dropped, and Rose drove the service road attached at the back of the lot and headed toward the new, fancy, research annex.

She didn't make it far without stopping.

There were only two ways to get to the high-tech annex—the road from the hospital and the road from the county. Both converged for a three-way stop surrounded by trees. Rose understood why the bus had been stranded on the road leading to the hospital. There was a tree down, blocking the road near the three-way.

She stopped her car and jumped out to survey the damage.

The road was almost impassable, completely so for a bus. For her old car? Rose decided she could make it work. And she did. Slowly and with great caution, she maneuvered the flooded shoulder until she cleared the debris. The parking lot of the annex hadn't fared too much better. It was partially flooded and mostly covered in leaves and branches that had been stripped from the surrounding trees.

There was no bus, so she backtracked and went the only direction she could.

The road to the county was as country as they came. Dirt and gravel and underbrush creeping out. Trees lining the sides and some old fence, from the property of an owner who had long since passed on, scattered between. Not exactly a wooded area but enough oaks to shade the road even when the sun was in the sky.

Rose knew the road.

The one she stared at now was unrecognizable.

The hours of rain had seemed to collect solely in this area. She could only see patches of the dirt and gravel beneath the water. She bet that was why the bus had driven where it shouldn't have. Instead of being within the lanes, it was on the shoulder, sitting at an odd angle.

The back emergency door was open and facing her.

That was when she first saw Lloyd Harrison.

Tall, thin, and wearing an outfit that seemed to come right out of a movie—white lab coat, comically large ID badge and booties still wrapped around the bottoms of his shoes—he looked nothing but flustered as he yelled out to Rose when she stepped out onto the only part of the road that hadn't yet been submerged.

"We can't move," he cried, his voice carrying through the wind. "Our front tire blew, and we can't drive out of whatever we're stuck in!"

Rose assumed he had already spotted her badge hanging around her neck but motioned to it all the same.

"I'm a deputy with the McCoy County Sheriff's Department," she yelled out. "I'm here to help! Right now, let's sit tight and figure—"

Rose's words were strangled by a sound that made her blood run cold.

A tornado siren.

It tore through the air with an eerie echo.

Screams exploded from the bus.

"Keep calm," she instructed. "Just because it's going off doesn't mean it's near us! It just means it's in the county."

To help her point, Rose pulled her phone up and went to the local weather station's social media page. She clicked on their meteorologist's live feed, ready to prove to the panicked people on the bus that they had time to make good decisions. That this new threat was scary, but not something they had to deal with themselves.

The meteorologist's face filled her screen, focused and commanding, a map of McCoy County beneath his waving arms.

He spoke and Rose heard him, yet, months later, but she still wouldn't remember what he actually said. Instead, all her attention had stuck to the red area on the map he seemed to be so concerned about.

It turned out Rose was wrong.

It looked like they didn't have much time to make good decisions at all.

So she worked with what she had.

Rose flung herself back into the car and hit the gas. Her old car lurched into the rushing floodwaters with absolute obedience. If it had been higher, she couldn't have done it. And if she hadn't been so small herself, rolling down the driver's-side window and crawling up onto the roof of her car would have been harder. As it was, she managed both actions in rapid succession. The metal roof held sturdy as she found her balance and turned to face a wide-eyed Lloyd Harrison. Now there was only the space of her hood between her and him at the back emergency exit.

Rose kept her voice as calm as possible. She also made it as loud as possible too.

"Jump down here, climb over the car and run as soon as you hit the ground," she yelled, the siren continuing to wail in the background. "Whoever has the keys to the annex go first. We need to take shelter *now*!"

If there had been only a few people stranded on the bus, then she would have found a way to get them in her car to drive away. But true to what Price had said, there were eleven people crowded inside.

Their best bet was to use her car as a bridge and then run like there was no tomorrow back to the research annex.

She hoped.

Lloyd must have agreed. One glance at the water still going strong around the bus and he was shouting for someone behind him.

A second later a small woman appeared in the doorway.

Speed was the name of her game. She was on the hood of Rose's car with keys held high on her hands.

"I—I have the keys," she huffed out, scrambling to Rose's outstretched hand. When they connected, she pulled the woman easily up the windshield.

"The water isn't as deep behind the car," Rose said, pointing to the area just past the trunk. "Be careful and haul ass once you're down!"

The sound of wind combined with an eerie humidity in the air. The radar played on repeat in the back of Rose's mind. There was a tornado on the tracker...and that tracking hadn't been that far away from their road.

The tornado could still turn, though.

It could still dissipate.

It could—

The sound of snapping trees sounded in the distance.

Rose couldn't see past the bus but there was no ignoring the new urgency.

The people on the bus seemed to feel it too.

Up until then Rose had never met any of the Camden Pharmaceutical staff, and while their storm-panic was the reason they were all out there now, she had to admit once the crisis had a clear plan, they executed it with surprising efficiency.

Lloyd funneled people around him and down onto the car, Rose helped them over the windshield and roof, and an older woman named Claudia stood in the water just past the trunk, helping those through the transition to the non-flooded part of the road.

Once the Camden people's feet found solid ground? They ran like the devil was on their heels.

Which, maybe he was.

Rose heard the horribly familiar sound of a tornado headed their way.

They were out of time.

"We have to go," she yelled up at Lloyd. "*Now!*"

Lloyd disappeared back into the bus.

Rose was dumbstruck.

A heartbeat went by.

Then another.

It was too much.

"Hey!" she yelled, but her words were ripped up into the cacophony of sounds bearing down on them.

What happened to him?

Rose couldn't just wait around to find out.

Adrenaline coursing through her veins, she slid down the windshield and made quick work of shuffling to the edge of the car hood. She could now see into the bus.

That was when she first saw Derrick Tillman.

Unlike Lloyd, he was on the shorter side and not at all lean. He was muscular—tattoos lined the muscles visible from the short-sleeved shirt he wore with jeans. He was undeniably younger than Lloyd.

And he was also undeniably much angrier than the man.

"Hey!" Rose yelled.

Neither man seemed to listen to her as Derrick lunged down the aisle at Lloyd.

They were shouting but she couldn't hear exactly what they were saying.

She thanked years of exercise and somewhat decent balance and threw herself up and through the emergency exit. By the time she was standing inside of the bus, the men were already exchanging hits.

"Stop," she ordered, closing the space between her and the scuffle. "What are you guys doing? We have to go!"

Lloyd was closer, so Rose used every bit of her strength to pull him backward first. The move worked and he groaned as he broke from the fight and hit the floor.

The bus lurched in tandem with the power shift.

Rose yelled back to Lloyd to run.

This time, he listened.

Derrick, however, swayed.

Rose's interference in the fight had left him off-balance. He was going to fall. Rose, the only person left behind, started to reach out on reflex.

But that was when she saw it.

That was when she saw his face.

His expression.

His...rage.

And it made her pause.

It was a brief whisper of a moment. The space between two breaths.

Yet, it made all the difference.

Derrick hit the ground. Rose reached for him again. She hooked her arm around his, and pulled him up. It was a sloppy attempt made even more awkward by the disparity in their sizes. Still, they stood and started moving.

Rose was at the opening first and let go to drop down onto the hood of her car. Lloyd was still there. He reached out to steady her but she was turning around to face the bus, her hand already outstretched.

But the bus wasn't there.

And neither was Derrick Tillman.

Now

ROSE SHIFTED. JAMES SAW it in the change of her posture as she came to the ending of the story. He felt it beneath his hand too. Like her body had given in to absolute and unwavering defeat.

That defeat was punctuated by a voice he wouldn't

have recognized as belonging to the wildcard deputy, had he not been looking at her lips as she spoke them.

"The tornado barely missed us, but it was close enough that the damage was severe," she wrapped up. "The bus and the trees around it never stood a chance. Along with the floodwaters, it went from right there to—" Her gaze seemed to hollow. She let out a breath and continued the thought. "—to over a hundred yards away. Lloyd and I were lucky. He pulled us into my car and the only damage it took was a cracked window from debris. That's why everyone became so obsessed with my car. It survived a flood and tornado, but not the bus."

Rose's voice deflated to complete lifelessness.

"And not Derrick either. Once the dust had settled, we found Derrick. He was still inside the bus. He didn't make it."

James watched as the usually animated woman seemingly shut down completely. Without her saying it, he knew she was done with the story. Not only done now but maybe would never tell again.

Still, he felt the need to make some points he felt she was missing.

"Derrick's death wasn't your fault," he underlined first. "Unless Wildcard Rose has some tricks up her sleeve that I don't know about, you can't control the weather and that goes doubly for the bad parts. In fact, it seems to me that you could have left anytime. Instead, you stayed. You thought quick, acted quicker, and gave those people a chance."

James applied pressure down on her thigh. He used it and his hand to turn the rest of her body around with the chair.

Rose's eyes were dark. They also felt warm. James stared into them now, head-on.

"Your car could have stalled or been swept away. But you made it a bridge. Those fully grown adults could have figured it out from there—jump on the car, cross the worst part of the water, and run back to cover—but you stayed. You held hands so feet could move easier. You kept calm so others had more space to panic. You jumped into a worse situation and tried to make sure everyone came with you when it was time to go."

James didn't know Rose well enough to keep touching her—he knew this in the back of his mind, the same thought when he had first touched her leg—but now he wasn't sure how else to get through to her.

So he moved his hand to the side of her face.

It was so small in his palm.

"Loss always hurts. No matter if it was by your hand or not." He tilted his head a little and also smiled a little. "I saw the recording that the Camden lady took of you helping them off the bus. But I wonder if you ever watched it. All of it, I mean?"

He wasn't surprised that Rose shook her head to that. She didn't seem the type to watch something people praised as being her heroic moment. Especially when all she saw was the loss of Derrick.

"She was still recording when they made it back to the annex. It was mainly just sounds of the storm and sirens and panic *but* if you listen carefully, you can hear someone getting a call out in the background. It was to their mom. They said they were scared but that it was okay too. Because help had shown up."

He ran his thumb along her cheekbone and upped his smile.

"You risked your life to try and give eleven people a better chance at surviving a wild and awful situation, Little," he said. "One person sadly didn't make it. Ten people did. And *that* is why everyone fell in love with this story. It's incredible. Just like you."

James hadn't meant to say the last part. Or really, he hadn't known he was going to say it.

Yet, it seemed right.

So he let the words sit between them without scrambling to erase them.

He wasn't sure if Rose would let them sit for long and he didn't get a chance to see what she would do or say.

The door to the conference room opened. James dropped his hand and turned to see Sheriff Weaver looking ten kinds of angry.

He said four words.

They packed one hell of a punch.

"We have a problem."

Chapter Eight

Rose had grown up in Seven Roads. Born there, gone through childhood there, and had only left for school before coming right on back. She was as tried and true a local as Price, with roots just as deep as those of Liam's wife, Blake. And even though her parents had moved to Tennessee five years prior, and her aunt and cousin had followed them too, she wasn't short on people she could count on in a pinch.

Yet, there she was accepting help from James like she had no other options in the bag.

"I already got your shop blown up, so are you sure you want me hanging out with you?" she asked, half joking, half absolutely serious. The man had already gone through a few inches with her, now she was asking for some miles.

James shrugged the question off.

"I'm the one who offered first," he pointed out. "If you're so worried, make me sign a waiver." He cracked a smile then pointed past the windshield to a building coming into view in the distance. They had been driving for at least fifteen minutes since leaving the sheriff's department. Rose knew the area but hadn't before seen the house James had moved into since coming to Seven Roads years ago.

Not that she was sure what she was looking at was a home.

James chuckled, maybe picking up on her thoughts.

"Plus, some days I think it might be easier to just start over with this heap anyways," he said. "Having it blow up might help me more than it hurt me." He let his foot up on the gas and maneuvered them into a gravel parking spot. It cornered an open field of overgrown grass. It wasn't as wide or vast as Old Man Becker's fields on the opposite side of town, but it took some squinting to see the furthest edge near a cropping of trees off in the distance.

James put the truck in Park, puffed out his chest and made sure she was looking at him before he spoke clearly and with ample volume.

"Unless I'm in there when it blows. If that's the case, I hereby absolve you of any guilt, Rose Little." He held up three fingers like he was making a Scouts' honor sign. "I, James Keller of sound mind, invited you to my home of my own doing. Anything and everything that happens after this point was because I'm a ten-out-of-ten individual with nerves of steel and a kind, caring heart. Oh, and charming too. And funny. And a mechanic whiz."

Rose snorted.

"And apparently humble."

He gave her a thumbs-up.

"See? You understand how outstanding I am. So let's just stop this whole 'stay away' bit you've been trying to pull since Sheriff Weaver came into that room with the whole 'good news, bad news' thing." James, dare she think it, turned almost sulky. "I have to be honest though, I thought that had become our trauma-bond thing."

Rose felt her eyebrow rise at his expression, but he was already going about getting out of the truck to catch it.

James was a big, intimidating man.

He was also surprisingly childlike at times.

It was almost refreshing.

Especially after the news Liam had given them back at the department.

"The good news is we just found the bomb maker," Liam had said after stepping back into the conference room. "His name is Dave Kyler and one of the men who came to the garage at Damon's order was the one to roll on him. Darius, along with the FBI agent who came in once a bomb was in play, found Dave not too far from here. They're still talking to him, but Darius said so far it looks like he was given a pretty penny to assemble it."

Rose hadn't recognized the name but was relieved that the one with the ability to make homemade bombs might be truly out of the picture.

"And the bad news?" she had to ask.

Liam had put his hands on his hips. Another big-man gesture in contrast with his icy exterior.

"He said the original plan was to put it in your apartment, but he refused, because even though he saw you as a job, he didn't want to hurt any kids."

"Melinda and Madeline," Rose offered.

Liam had nodded, not at all happy.

James had spoken up then, to ask, "Melinda and Madeline?"

"The children of the family in the unit across the hall from my apartment."

"Which is the bad news," Liam had said.

Rose had agreed, but still she had to say it out loud.

"It means that Damon definitely knows where I live."

That one statement had led her to the beginning of a cracked concrete path that ran straight to a house that looked as frustrated and tired as she felt.

The man who owned the weathered two-story house was opposite it in cheer. Smiling once again, he waved his arm out toward the worn brick and made an exaggerated announcement.

"Wildcard Little, welcome to the purchase I'll probably never financially recover from."

James led her down the path and into the house without any more fanfare. Rose split her attention between her surroundings and the man next to her as they walked through each room. No one was hiding or ready to attack during the first-floor tour of the kitchen, dining room, living area, laundry room, or bathroom. The same held true for the upstairs. James gave a flourish when they made it to the guest bedroom she would be staying in for the near future.

It, like the bubbly personality that occasionally surfaced in its owner, was a surprising contrast to the work-in-progress look of the rest of the home. Everything was...soft. Soft on the eyes and seemingly to the touch. Even the small knickknacks and framed pictures on the walls had a feeling of warmth emanating from them.

This wasn't just a guest bedroom. It was a room that had been set up with extreme care and with a heavy feminine hand.

Was James just that good at design or had a woman helped him with this?

A question that Rose hadn't thought to ask until now blared across her mind.

Was… Was James in a relationship? His ring finger was bare but that didn't mean he wasn't taken.

How had she disrupted this man's life without knowing a thing about his life?

What if she wasn't just intruding in his life but also his—

"I know what you're thinking," James said, setting her hospital bag on top of the vanity next to the bed and interrupting her internal spiral. "Normally, I should get some kind of HGTV award for this little oasis, but I'm sad to say, this was all Mom."

Rose's worries skidded to a halt.

"Your mom?" she repeated.

He nodded.

"She said she didn't care how long it takes me to fix this place up as long as I have a nice place for company," he said. "I think she was meaning that more for her than anyone else. She wasn't exactly a fan of me buying this heap."

In a rare change, James seemed to express a feeling of doubt.

"To be honest, I hadn't really planned on it either."

He sighed and switched back to the tour in the span of a breath.

"The bathroom in the hallway is nice too and my room is on the other side of it down the hall. Feel free to roam anywhere. This place may not look the greatest but it's functional and safe. You won't go falling through any holes in the ceiling or accidentally use pipes that will spray water everywhere."

"Ah, the two movie pitfalls of renovating," she said with humor.

James shrugged.

"You laugh, but my first month here?" He pulled a blank expression. "Both happened."

That lack of emotion wiped away with a laugh. One Rose shared in.

It blocked the reality of their present predicament for a while. James excused himself to let her get settled and took a phone call somewhere else in the house. Rose used his absence to her advantage and called her parents.

Hiding what had happened with the bomb had been impossible once it hit the local news, never mind the gossip. Rose had known this impossibility would back her into a corner, so she had been preemptive and come out swinging before that happened. She had called her parents as soon as the first doctor had spoken to her once she had woken up in the hospital.

The Littles weren't totally gobsmacked that Rose had found herself in another dangerous situation. They were, however, very reactive to the fact that this time around there had been an explosion.

"Seven Roads is supposed to be a sleepy town, but I swear all you seem to be getting is nightmares!" her mom had exclaimed once she realized Rose was fine. "We can find you a better life here. One that isn't this—this dangerous!"

Her father had been less loud. And demanding.

"She's not wrong, Rosy. You have to admit your last few tumbles in Seven Roads have been pretty spectacular. Not in a good way, either."

"Which means I should be good from here on out,"

Rose had tried to assure them. "I've been through the extreme parts, now we should be at the boring, paperwork ones."

It was a lie.

But Rose had never been against telling a fib or two to ease the worries of loved ones. Loved ones who could be used against her if they came back to town to see about her. A point Rose had to underline to her father without admitting that Damon Tillman was still out there and probably would still be gunning for her.

"Hey, Dad, there's a few people still not the happiest with me and I'm worried some of that could reach up to y'all. So do me a favor and keep a good eye out there. Maybe even stay close to the house until things have cooled off around here."

Her father, ever a girl dad, seemed to be caught between talking to his baby girl and talking to the strong, independent woman he had helped raise.

"Will do," he had eventually promised. "You keep us in your loop, Rosy. Texts, if not calls, every day to let us know you're good. Put the code in it too so I know no one's messing with us."

Rose had smiled at that. She had grown up watching spy thrillers, police procedurals and action flicks with her parents. One day they had joked they needed a family code to use just in case. That joke had turned into an all-out family tradition between the three of them.

Now, sitting at a small table in the kitchen downstairs, Rose sent off a quick follow-up text telling her dad that she loved them.

She added the word *hon* at the end.

It was only by the grace of good reflexes that she kept

from jumping when James appeared by her shoulder and repeated the last word.

"*Hon?*" One syllable but it came out strong and deep.

Rose flipped her phone over onto the tabletop and crossed her arms over her chest with a scowl. One that was definitely heating.

"Well, aren't we nosy."

James held up his hands in defense as he walked over to the refrigerator.

"I wasn't meaning to be," he said. "My eyes tend to wander when my feet are." He did his Scouts' honor sign again. "No disrespect meant."

Rose believed him, so she answered his question. Though she did it with the scowl still hanging on. She might have realized she was more comfortable with the man than was normal for her, but that didn't mean *he* had to know that too.

"It's from a show me and my parents watched a few years back during Christmas. It means 'honey.' If we don't say it, it's not us."

Other people might have had an eyebrow to raise at that, but James was simple.

He nodded with total acceptance.

"That's weirdly loving, Little. I bet your boyfriend gets a kick out of it too."

If Rose had been drinking something, she would have sputtered a little into it at that.

"If I were dating someone, they sure aren't hitting the mark. Have you seen anyone around me?" She motioned to the empty room around them. "I may be wild but even I deserve someone who will show up when someone's trying to kill me."

It was an offhand comment. One that hadn't meant much to her.

Yet, it seemed to have struck some kind of a chord with James.

His smile left.

His words drove a stake into the ground.

"I'm here."

That heat from earlier expanded within Rose. She tried to play it off again, but this time, it didn't land as cleanly.

"I—I meant someone other than you. And well, the department." She forced a laugh. "Though I guess that's already more people than most get, so I shouldn't complain."

He was too far away for her to see the gold in his eyes, but the green grabbed her easy.

If he wanted to say something, he looked like he changed his mind in the middle of the thought. He shook his head a little.

Then that smile was back.

Suddenly, the small room felt much smaller with just the two of them in it.

And the heat in Rose's cheeks continued to simmer for it.

"They found Dave Kyler," the man said. "He was quick to admit you hired him to put a bomb in the deputy's apartment."

He was short but intimidating in his own right, clean-cut in his pressed, button-up and slacks, and hair styled with gel more expensive than most people's monthly paycheck. He was young too.

Not as young as Derrick had been.

Damon Tillman felt the rage in him pulse.

He didn't let it show. He had expected this news.

"Which means the deputy should have realized that I know where she lives now," Damon said. "Which means, if she's crafty, she'll find somewhere else to lay her head tonight." He felt the corners of his lips lift into sharp points. "And thankfully, she's as crafty as I hoped."

The young man opposite him, holding a clipboard and a blank expression like it was his only job in life, nodded.

"Not all of the guns for hire turned on you, but two did and that was enough," he added.

Damon nodded.

"Which already confirmed to that dear Detective Williams and sheriff that I'm still most likely in the area code."

The man agreed with his own nod. Then, despite his steely demeanor, he let some of the curiosity he'd been holding on to the last few months slip out.

"Why can't we do away with her now? We know where she is. It would be easy."

Damon felt like his smile was a knife, cutting into his own skin while it waited to cut into another's.

"Because Rose Little's being dead isn't the goal," he said. "It's the act of dying that I want to focus on."

The young man didn't ask any more questions. Instead, he gave the last of his report.

"Then I'll give Mr. Danvers the go-ahead."

Damon gave a slow nod.

"Even if she can survive this round, I doubt she will the next."

The young man left, but Damon stayed in the office. While Rose's death by Mr. Danvers would work for him, Damon couldn't help but find himself rooting for Rose just a little.

Mr. Danvers would be quick.

What came next, wouldn't be.

Chapter Nine

James made a mean everything-omelet, filled with bacon and peppers, onions and two types of cheeses. It was his go-to meal, and had been since he was a teen. Now, as a man past thirty, wearing a set of coveralls and living in a house he had bought with money he'd earned with his hands, the meal felt different somehow.

Maybe because the first person he had served it to outside of his family had not only praised it, but asked for seconds.

It was more than satisfaction for him. It was a point of pride. A pride he wore with a growing smugness as he cleared the plates and handed her the coffee she had requested.

"I could get used to this," Rose muttered, taking the coffee with a nod. "You could turn this place into a bed-and-breakfast with your kind of service."

James laughed at that. He motioned to the peeling wallpaper in the corner and then the extremely outdated countertops and appliances.

"I'm not sure many people would want to vacation here, never mind in Seven Roads. We're not exactly a tourist trap."

"Hey, don't forget the power of passers-through, especially with the motel being out of business now." She shrugged. "A little paint here and there and I could see this place working."

James started to fix his own coffee. It was more a reflex than a need. Since offering Rose a place to stay he hadn't had any trouble staying awake.

"Sadly, my plans for this place aren't as grand as all that. I just want somewhere to grow roots, house some kids, and drive me a little crazy as we both age. I don't need outsiders trying to pay me to be nice."

Rose made a noise into her coffee. James turned with an eyebrow raised.

"What, are you surprised the big ol' mechanic man bought a house specifically for future kids?" he asked.

Rose put her coffee down and shook her hands in front of her.

"Not surprised you want to, just surprised how casual you were about saying it, is all. But maybe that's because I'm so used to getting asked when I'll get married and settle down that I'm a bit quiet on the topic."

James leaned against the counter. He knew it wasn't exactly his business, but he was curious.

"*Do* you want to get married and settle down?"

He half expected a glare or a pointed barb sent in his direction at the intrusion. Instead, he was met with a shrug.

"It's not off the table," she said. "I just haven't sat down at the table it's on yet, so to speak." She let out a sigh. He wondered if her head still hurt but decided to hold that question for later. Unlike this one, he wasn't sure she would be as honest with her answer. Admitting she was in pain didn't seem to be Rose Little's strong suit.

"The last guy I dated wasn't a fan of my job and—while I get that it's not for everyone and I don't blame those who stay away—he kept waiting for me to change my mind and leave the department. Leave Seven Roads. I'm not sure if he wanted the whole white picket fence thing but I know he didn't want me wearing a badge." Her hand moved beneath his sightline under the table. Like she was reaching for her badge on memory alone.

She lifted her gaze back to his. Her smile felt watered down but nonetheless sincere.

"I know I can belong other places but it's here where I *want* to belong," she finished.

James understood her, if only for different reasons. Since Rose had given him some information, he decided to share in kind.

"I had the opposite problem with my ex," he started. "She wanted me to stay in there and I wanted to be in Seven Roads. She didn't want a house of kids, and I don't think I could live in a house without them." James ran a hand across the back of his neck. "Though I've gotten a little off-track since helping Dad with the shop. Or maybe it sounds nicer to use your 'not at the right table yet' analogy. I'm not even sure I'm in the right room as my table yet."

As he said it, he couldn't help but notice that Rose was sitting at a very real table in his very real home. On the one hand, it was surreal. On the other, it felt oddly normal.

Rose's brow drew in. She voiced her question next.

"I don't know if it's impolite for me to ask but why *did* you want to live in Seven Roads? You only lived here for a few years when you were a kid, right? Then came back a few years ago to start the shop? Why?"

This wasn't an unexpected question. James had been asked some variation of it more than a dozen times. Why had the kid with no true hometown come back to plant a flag, so to speak, in a place that he'd barely lived in before?

James pushed off the counter's edge and closed the space between them in two steps. He took her hand.

"Let me show you."

The land the old house sat on was just over one acre. It included the field and a cropping of trees just beyond it. That field of tall, wild grass looked the same as it had when he was six. Decades later and in the dying sunlight.

"When I was six, I got into a really big fight in a foster home I was staying at. It was a bad one too. I got hurt pretty good, landed myself in the hospital, and pretty much scared myself off people too. The county agency decided it would be better to shift me to a new place and, after a lot of back and forth, I landed in Seven Roads."

They were standing on the back porch, which was surprisingly not as worn as the rest of the home. James had dropped Rose's hand after they had gone through the back door, and now placed his own on the railing. The solid wood railing showed the remnants of stain long-since perfect.

He patted it once and with absolute affection.

"This was my last foster home before I went to the Kellers but that's not why I bought this place. Want to see the real reason?"

Where he expected a little resistance, he received none. Instead, Rose let him take her hand again and this time lead her out into the tall grass. The fading light almost perfectly matched his memory as they walked through the overgrown back lot at a light pace.

Not too far from the house James stopped them and turned back around.

He dropped her hand and sighed out long.

That feeling was back, just as it always was when he was here.

And that was what James wanted to explain to Rose, for whatever reason.

"I was standing about right here when my mom called out to me that it was time to leave," he said. "Dad had just packed the last of my things I'd left behind and my aunt was helping my foster family tie up loose ends. *I* was out here, running around, because I was never really big on saying bye to a place. And honestly, I think I was still nervous I'd be left behind again."

James felt Rose's gaze on him, but he kept his stare locked onto the memory. He pointed to the back porch.

"But then Mom came out there and said it was time to go home. And she didn't move until I ran all the way from here to there." James looked at the distance between him and that porch. If there was ever one stretch of land he knew better than the rest, this small run was it. "My life changed in that next house—the house I ended up growing up in—but *this* is where my little world actually changed. It's the first time I felt like I was running toward something worth running for. So when I saw it was up for sale, I came back here with Dad to check it out. And wouldn't you know it, all I had to do was stand right here and that feeling came right on back."

He gave out a self-deprecating laugh.

"So I bought the house for this one piece of land as a gift to that scared and anxious seven-year-old. We made it! It was scary and stressful sometimes, but we made it all the same."

James knew it sounded cheesy, like some kind of movie that had a lot of crying and sharing of feelings, but it was all true.

Standing in the field and looking back at the house in the distance, lights on and warm against the approaching night, was a comfort. Plain and true.

A comfort he had never shared with anyone before, he realized.

Finally, he looked over at Rose.

She was facing the house now. Her hair was cute, held up in a messy bun at the nape of her neck. James bet she might tease him for his dramatic take on the dirt and grass they were standing on. However, Rose was frowning. Even in profile, it was pronounced.

"What's wrong?" he asked.

Her voice was nothing but agitation.

"You brought me—the lady who already got your workplace blown up—to a place *this* special and irreplaceable?" She whirled around to face him. Her hands went right to her hips like she was a teacher scolding a disappointing student. "Are you kidding me? Thanks for the pressure there, Mr. Keller!"

For a second, James worried that she was seriously mad. But then she rolled her eyes at him.

"Now I'm going to be worried about protecting you, me and an entire house," she continued.

James couldn't help but smile at how exasperated she sounded, especially when she started to walk back to the house, still complaining.

"I thought it was just some silly old house you got because the housing market is horrible," she continued. "But *noooo*. It's so sentimental that it made my heart squeeze. Ugh. Now I definitely need to find Damon as soon as possible."

James's smile softened as he watched the little Little stomp her way back toward the house with fake outrage.

He waited until she was a few steps away. Like he always did, James imagined his seven-year-old self running ahead, stomach knotted up in barely suppressed excitement.

That didn't change as he started to walk now.

This time, though, there was definitely something different.

This time he had someone to follow.

THERE WAS NO news from Liam, Detective Williams, or anyone else in the next few hours. It made Rose more anxious than if there had been something to report on, bad or not. Instead, she whittled the time away by pacing James's living room, being told by James not to pace in his living room, and by going back to pacing in James's living room.

He put the TV on and managed to sidetrack her for a while but eventually Rose decided she needed something stronger than idle chatter.

So she took a bath.

The guest bathroom might have been dated but the tub was wide, deep and clean. There was even some fancy bubble bath mix beneath the sink, courtesy of James's mother, who—according to him—believed all baths should be drowning in bubbles. Rose didn't know if she agreed with it to that extent, but she poured in the lavender mix with the mindset of "when in Rome."

Thoughts about bubbles, bombs and Damon Tillman melted away as soon as Rose lowered herself into the hot water. The stress she had been carrying for days didn't go away but it had the peace of mind to pause.

Rose sighed out at the temporary relief.

Her thoughts floated around to simpler things. She wondered what she might have for breakfast the next day, what the weather might look like, about which house the couple on the TV show they had been watching ended up picking, and if James Keller took baths. Because, as she stretched her legs out and let her feet walk up the opposite end of the tub, she couldn't imagine a man as big as him fitting in one that wasn't extra-large.

She stayed with that image a little longer than she probably should have and then marveled at how ridiculous the last week or so of her life had gotten, from trying to get her car fixed to lounging in the mechanic's tub. She decided to never again judge another movie heroine who went from a normal life to a chaotic one so quickly.

Rose's thoughts doubled back to the man himself, and the image of him standing next to her in the grassy field earlier. He had been so vulnerable, so honest, with his past that Rose hadn't known what to say—what to do. Putting on an act of being annoyed at trusting her around such a precious place was a last-second effort to remain unattached to his story.

But now she let her heart ache for him.

He had been through a lot and still found the bright side. A giant wall of an optimist wrapped in coveralls and muscle.

Rose started to smile, thinking about how he was still wearing his work coveralls, when a knock sounded on the door.

Her face instantly heated.

"Yeah?" she called.

The knock sounded again.

"I'm in the bath," she added, not that he should need reminding.

Rose imagined a sheepish grin on James's face on the other side of the door. Maybe he'd come to ask her if she needed anything or warn her about the old pipes or something.

But that knock came again.

Rose shifted in the bathwater, suddenly uncomfortable.

She eyed her phone on the counter, just out of arm's reach.

Maybe James was just messing with her.

Maybe he was just trying to scare her?

Even as she thought it, Rose knew that wasn't the case. James might have acted childish on occasion, but his manners were all well-behaved man. He wouldn't interrupt her privacy without a good reason.

That was why, without thinking, Rose hadn't locked the bathroom door.

And that was how, in what felt like slow motion, Rose watched that same door open.

Her opinion of James stayed true—he wasn't the type of man to invade her privacy and that was why she had felt safe.

But the man standing in the doorway now?

Good manners or not, he was no James Keller at all.

Chapter Ten

He looked like he had simply taken a turn down the wrong aisle at the grocery store after work. Everything about him was dress-code appropriate. His blond hair was neat and cut close, his outfit was a collared shirt tucked into khakis, and his shoes might have been sneakers, but they could definitely pass if he wore them out to church.

It wasn't just his clothes and hairstyle that gave the impression of office worker winding down from a long day, it was his looks that really sold the image well.

He was around Rose's age and boy-next-door handsome. Not so much that it made those around him gawk but enough to appreciate. He had all the angles and hard lines across his face and dark eyes that ran more rich than muddy. The rest of him was just as middle-of-the-road. He looked around average-height and build. His clothes fit him comfortably, not too snug.

This man, in all respects, was the neighbor you said hi to on walks or shared pleasantries with in the concession stand line of the local high school football games.

He looked…nice.

To Rose, he was utterly terrifying.

He cocked his head to the side and slid his hands into his pockets.

"You're Deputy Little." It wasn't a question.

Rose wanted to make sure he knew it was an answer regardless.

"I am a deputy with the McCoy County Sheriff's Department, yes."

The man kept his head on that tilt and scanned her and the tub. The bubbles she had contemplated earlier had thinned but it was enough to give her a little cover. Still, she internally squirmed at the look.

That squirm went right back to terror when he snorted.

"Congratulations, Deputy with the McCoy County Sheriff's Department." He straightened his neck and pulled his hands free from his pockets. "You'll be the first person I've ever drowned in a tub."

Rose was already moving, water sloshing as she scrambled to stand.

The man was just as quick.

He cut across the bathroom and grabbed her by the throat before she could get her legs beneath her. On reflex her hands went up to try and slip beneath his grip but her body was trying to do too many things at once. She couldn't get a finger beneath his hold, and she couldn't get her balance in the tub either. Both problems together created a new one as her feet slid out beneath her.

If she hadn't been so petite she believed the fight would have gone a little differently here, but as it was, the man easily followed her fall down alongside the tub. His hand stayed around her throat as he took a knee on the tile on the other side of the tub's edge. The air against Rose's chest and stomach was replaced by the warm water rushing back over her. She threw one hand out to stop her backward descent, but he still had one hand free.

He swatted it away with little difficulty.

"Don't worry. This might be my first time, but it will be fast."

He pushed down with the hand around her neck. She tried again to swing out at him, to claw him, to do something to his arm or face or anything.

But she was too small. Her opponent was too big. The disadvantage of being in the tub was too challenging.

Still, she wasn't simply going to lie there and take it without some pushback.

Rose lifted her leg and kicked out at the man's side.

The hit landed.

It wasn't enough to end the fight, but it was enough to make his grip on her slip.

Rose didn't waste time trying to stand again. She didn't waste breath trying to threaten him or plead with him. She didn't even use the precious few seconds to take a good, decent breath.

All the air left in Rose's lungs formed one thing and one thing only.

"James!"

No sooner had his name left her mouth than the intruder's efforts followed through. The calming bath with lavender bubbles turned into a burning nightmare. Rose thrashed around with her legs but couldn't get any real traction. She blindly beat at the man's arm with one hand while trying to pry free the other from around her neck.

She was so all-consumed with trying to shift him off her that realizing she couldn't breathe seemed to come last.

But it came with a quiet wallop.

Adrenaline and panic bloomed a field of screaming flowers within her, each one yelling something different.

She was Wildcard Rose and yet she was going to die in a bathtub.

Her parents were going to be devastated.

Who was this guy?

How had he gotten in?

Was James…?

Rose's head was pounding. Her chest burned. So did her eyes. She hadn't shut them despite the soap and water above her. The blurry image of the man to the side of the tub warped and moved.

That panic turned to rage.

At this man. At his audacity.

He might kill her, but she would leave her mark.

Rose always kept her nails short for work but when it came to a last act on Earth, they could still do the job. She heard the warbled cry of pain from the man as she used both hands to clamp onto his arm and dug her nails into his skin.

If he got away, they would be able to get his DNA from under her fingernails.

It was a small, shrinking thought as Rose started to lose the will to fight.

Her vision started to tunnel as a much smaller thought bubbled to the surface.

It was guilt.

The littlest Little would scar James's forever home with her death.

It wasn't a bomb in his shop, but it was a shame all the same.

She tried to picture James standing in that field earlier. So peaceful.

The James who roared into the bathroom was not.

He didn't need any context. He didn't need any explanations or to ask any questions.

James Keller took in only one detail when he ran into the bathroom.

Some guy was hurting Rose.

That was all he needed.

James grabbed the man by the scruff of his shirt and yanked him with every bit of force he had. It was more than enough.

The man was a leaf on the wind as he flew backward and crashed onto his back on the tile. The impact pushed the air out of his lungs. More importantly, it freed Rose. Though she wasn't surfacing.

James closed the distance to the tub in two strides and plunged his arms into the water. In the next moment Rose was out and up against him.

The man behind him squelched against the tile. James spun around, Rose against his chest, and kicked the man hard. He was back against the tile and sliding toward the wall.

James would have done more, but if Rose wasn't breathing, then he—

Rose's body was wracked with coughing. She spluttered and gasped and slapped at her chest.

It was a beautiful sight.

One that spelled out his next step.

James ran out of the bathroom and dropped Rose onto the bed. She was still coughing as she looked up at him, red eyes wide.

"Phone's in my room," was all he said.

Then he went back into the bathroom and slammed the door shut behind him.

He locked it.

The man who had dared to lay a hand on Rose was getting to his feet.

His eyes widened too.

James smiled.

"I'm no unsuspecting woman in a bathtub but I sure hope you won't mind fighting me."

He didn't know if the man had a weapon hidden in his clothes but didn't give him a chance to grab for any. He was on the stranger in a few steps. He threw a hit the second he was close enough.

The man didn't dodge it, but he did block. That was the same for the next few hits James tried to land. He was hoping for a knockout punch but instead he was bruising the man's forearms and sides.

Which was fine by him.

They were still hits. He was still damaging the body, even if he wasn't hitting his target.

The man must have realized that too. He took a chance and dropped low. James's fist hit empty air. It left an opening that allowed the other man to spring up and across at him.

His shoulder connected with James's ribs.

It made him stagger back.

The other man must have thought this was a winning move. The beginning to an end he surely wanted.

But James had been through worse in his life, even before the bomb in the auto shop.

His life had built him up to one truth.

He *endured*.

James tightened the muscles in his legs and did a move he had only ever seen used once. He left his face and chest open and grabbed each of the man's biceps in his hands. James pushed the man away from him but didn't let go.

It created obvious confusion in the assailant.

James gritted his teeth.

He didn't need to land a punch to knock someone out.

Instead, he could simply use his head.

And he did.

James slammed his head against the man's without mercy. The man could no more dodge the hit than he could block it. Pain exploded behind James's eyes and his vision spotted.

But he stayed standing.

The other man did not.

His body went limp in James's hands.

James let him drop the rest of the way to the tile floor.

It wasn't a knockout punch, but it would do.

James hesitated only long enough to make sure he wasn't getting back up and then hurried to unlock the door. He flung it open just in time to see a flurry of motion enter from his right.

His fist went up, ready to rumble with whoever the intruder had brought, but the source of the motion was the woman he was ready to rumble for.

Rose was wrapped in a sheet, still dripping wet from head to toe, and a phone pressed against her cheek. Soap bubbles were still scattered across her hair. They offset the severity of the red handprint around her neck.

"Are you okay? Where is he?" Her voice was hoarse. It made the anger in him mount again.

"I'm good," he answered. He thumbed over his shoulder. "He's out. For now. Do you have your cuffs with you?"

Rose relayed the details to whoever she was on the phone with but nodded to James. She pointed to her bag in the corner. James went through it with as much respect as possible, only lightly noting her handcuffs were tangled up with a pair of underthings.

"Behind his back," she instructed.

James could hear whoever was on the other side of the phone talking quick. Rose replied in kind, but he had moved too far away to hear exactly what. Instead, his focus moved to the man as he rearranged him to cuff his wrists behind his back.

Who was he?

Where had he come from?

James had been in the kitchen when he'd heard Rose yell for him. Before that he had been in the living room. Both places gave him an easy view of the front and back doors. And even if they didn't, where he had been in each room had given him a clear sight line to the bottom of the stairs.

Had the man still managed to sneak by him?

Had he found a different way to the second floor?

Or had he already been in the house before Rose had gone upstairs?

If so, then why did he wait to attack her when she was in the bath?

James finished his task and sat back on the tile floor to face him.

His hit had busted the man's nose. Broken it, maybe. It was a mercy if that was all. James could have done a lot more.

Rose appeared at his side. Instead of sitting next to him where he had leaned back to rest on the tile, she pulled up on his elbow. Her hand was still wet. He let her lead him back out to the bedroom. She was no longer on the phone.

"The sheriff is on the way," she said. "I need to get dressed but I'm getting kind of uncomfortable at the thought of changing with him in there and someone maybe coming up the stairs."

James understood what she was asking. She'd stopped him at the one spot in the room where he could see the bathroom and into the hallway without having to turn toward each.

He nodded.

"I'll keep watch, you change."

"Thank you." Her voice was still hoarse. It grated at James.

He couldn't believe she had been attacked in *his* home.

He was supposed to protect her.

What if he hadn't heard her?

What if he'd been too late?

The what-ifs were brutal. James tried to keep his anger from boiling over while Rose went out of his sight line behind him to dress.

"That's not Damon." The sound of sliding fabric was a background to a solid-sounding Rose. "If you were wondering," she added. "I don't recognize him at all."

"Just like you didn't recognize the men at the auto shop."

"Just like I didn't recognize the men at the auto shop," she repeated.

There was strength in her voice, but that voice went quiet. So did James. Over a week of two attempts on her life, three counting the bomb, and there she was still standing. Not silent, not silenced.

James marveled at her resilience.

Even when he felt something against the middle of his back.

His mind was fast to stay his reflexes when he realized

it was Rose. She was leaning against him, her forehead warm even through the back of his shirt.

He felt her sigh out more than he heard it.

There was no denying that it shook. So did her voice when she spoke.

"Good news, we survived another round. Bad news, I—I think this round was a little too much for me. I—I might cry. C-can I stay here until they arrive?"

James knew she was already crying. He wasn't going to point it out.

Instead, he nodded.

"Do what you need to do, Wildcard. I'm not going anywhere."

Chapter Eleven

The Seven Roads Motel wasn't actually out of business. Instead, it was waiting in a limbo between the former owner and the one who was taking it over—his ex-wife. Her name was Brandy Lane, and she was the disowned granddaughter of the Lanes whom the hospital was named after.

She was also close friends with Detective Darius Williams, one of the few people in the sheriff's department who knew about what had happened at James's home.

And knew that Rose and James were now about to stay at that motel. Room 6, to be exact.

"Brandy's no-good ex is living in Texas now, so he won't barge in here asking questions or anything," Darius explained. "Not that he cares about the property. He just wanted to tie Brandy up in legal fees and paperwork before she could open it back up."

He helped them into the room and, along with James, was inspecting every inch. Rose stood in the corner, throat hurting and head throbbing. The smell of lavender was unavoidable. She suspected there was still soap in her hair.

Someone sidled into the patch of old carpet next to her. Rose could make out the braids in her peripheral. That and the very pregnant belly.

Blake might not have been a sheriff anymore, but her presence was no less intimidating. Thankfully, Rose had known Blake since they were kids, and that intimidation had never put her off the woman. She found it instead to be more of a comfort.

"Are we going to gloss over the fact that our dear Detective Williams seems to be closer to Brandy Lane than we originally thought or are we going to talk about it at length and with a lot of imagined details?"

Blake was smiling. She was trying to lighten the mood. Rose appreciated it.

"You think there's something there just because our stern, closed-off, very blunt Darius suddenly has this trust in someone we've never even known he was on speaking terms with?" She snorted. "Of course we're going to talk about this. Just let me see if I can survive this Brandy Lane's kindness first and then I'm all in for gossip."

Blake stiffened next to her. The little lightness she had tried to bring in was gone. She lowered her voice even though James and Darius were in the bathroom.

"This time, we made sure that only a handful of us know you two are staying here. In fact, only a few of us even know about what happened right now. Liam and Price are dealing with that man with a firm grip. We're keeping a lid on the whole attack as much as possible." She thumbed over her shoulder to the motel room's door. "We have different cars now, we all made sure no one followed us from James's house, and all communication between you and us have gone to personal phones and computers."

"You think someone at the department leaked that I was staying at James's instead of my apartment? Even after we tried to be careful about it?"

It had been a question dogging all of them already—how anyone could even know she was at James's house in the first place—but Rose had a hard time believing someone at the department had been the one to spill the beans. At least, not on purpose. A sentiment Blake seemed to agree with.

"Not intentionally, but we can't ignore the fact that we're all human and live in a small, usually boring, town. If even one person mentioned it to their friends or family, that would be all it took to get the town's gossip mill up and turning. So this time, we're locking the knowledge up as tightly as possible." Blake, who had switched out with her husband at James's house once it was time to leave, looked thoughtful for the first time since then. "What about James, though?" she continued. "Do we need to worry about him talking to anyone? Anyone close to him?"

"He's single."

The words popped out of Rose's mouth before she could stop them.

Blake cast her a sidelong glance. It burned Rose to see that the woman also seemed to be clamping down on a smile.

"Oh, is he, now?" Blake lowered her voice even more. It sounded suspiciously mischievous. "Did our little Little gain that knowledge naturally or did she go fishing for it?"

If Blake hadn't been pregnant—and honestly, so much taller than Rose—she would have shoulder-checked her. As it was, she gave Blake a hefty eye roll.

"It came up in a conversation about our lives while

we were hiding out. You know, from people trying to kill me."

Blake met her with an answering eye roll.

"Don't you try and guilt me just because I'm asking a reasonable personal question," she said. "Darius isn't the only one acting out of pocket."

As if on cue, James exited the bathroom in deep conversation with the detective.

Blake didn't point to him or nod his way, but Rose knew they were both all eyes on the man.

"You don't seem to mind him sticking to you."

Rose didn't know what to say to that—mostly because it was true—and was instead saved by the man himself. He walked over to them and put his hands on his hips, his brow knitted together in what felt like a subordinate giving a slightly off-putting report to a superior.

With them, though, it turned into James dropping his chin so he could stare down into the much smaller Rose.

"Despite no one using it for a bit, this place is pretty good, other than needing a bit of quick dusting," he started. "It was good on Brandy Lane to keep the power and water running too, or else this wouldn't be ideal. I'm going to start cleaning and get these sheets and blankets switched out while y'all finish up your conversation." He looked to Blake. "Unless there's something else you need from me?"

Darius and Blake answered in unison that there wasn't.

The two men went to get the supplies James had thought to bring from his house out of the car while Blake tapped the suitcase she had rolled into the room earlier.

"With the help of our FBI agent friend, we got you some more things from your apartment. Clothes, toiletries and some snacks he found in the pantry he thought you might like."

Rose's eyes widened. Blake read her thoughts.

"Don't worry. I've known the agent for a long time. He was respectful with it and even had his wife on the phone while he packed to make sure he got what you might need." Blake rubbed a hand over her stomach. "I would have done it myself, but it was decided that was a risk not worth taking."

Just in case there was another attacker lying in wait for Rose.

She didn't spell that out, though, and Blake didn't either. Instead, they said their goodbyes after James finished bringing in the rest of their things.

Then, after one last warning to be safe, it was just Rose and James alone again. It was an odd feeling to watch him. She had settled into one of the two worn wooden chairs by the air-conditioning unit and, like fireflies during a summer night, her attention seemed to flicker and float around him alone.

He hummed. She couldn't make out the tune, but it was upbeat. Slow in some parts, fast in others. He bobbed his head to match the beat sometimes, but no matter what, he focused on the chore he was currently attending to without missing a step.

He dusted every surface in the room with careful dedication. The nightstands, the table next to her, the chest of drawers opposite the bed, and even the curtains. From there he wiped them down with cleaner spray and wipes before going into the bathroom to presumably do the same. He came back and set to the flannel bundle he'd brought in earlier. True to word, it was a new set of sheets, pillowcases and quilt top.

Rose watched in absolute awe while he redid the bed as if it was the most normal situation there was.

When he was done, he took both of their bags and situated them on top of the chest of drawers.

Then he placed his hands on his hips, did a slow turn-around to survey their space, and then, seemingly pleased with himself, nodded.

"This place isn't that bad now," he said. "Honestly, the paint job here is probably better than my place."

Rose wanted to smile, she really did, but it was like sitting down had drained whatever she had left fueling her everything-is-fine guise. It was disappointing to realize that she couldn't fake it anymore, especially after getting her gusto back once she had finished crying earlier.

James filled the silence after a moment.

"I'm going to test out the shower really quick." He went to double-check the locks on the door, the clamp, and peeked out of the window. He drew back and nodded, once again to himself. Rose was starting to like the habit. As if he was constantly in a conversation with himself, and winning.

"Here, come keep me company," he added.

Rose felt her eyes widen but he merely explained by picking up the other chair. He walked it over to the bathroom and set it down just inside of the doorway.

James came back for a change of clothes, a towel he had also had the mind to pack, and then he came for her.

"I know you're strong and fearless and can handle anything thrown your way, but what we went through tonight got to me, and I'd feel a whole lot more comfortable if we could stick together for the rest of it." He outstretched his free hand. "You don't have to do anything but sit and listen to me chatter."

If it had been anyone else, she would have laughed at how ridiculous the request was. Yet, Rose took his hand. A moment later, she was sitting in another old wooden chair, facing the bed, the rest of the bathroom behind her.

True to his word, he started up the chatter quickly.

Rose listened enough to know she wasn't needed for it. He talked about Mr. Donahue and another client. Then he was talking about his trip he'd taken once to the mountains.

Rose floated in and out of the conversation long enough to catch a few points.

He liked the mountains and snow.

He liked hiking too but preferred to bike.

There was a breakfast shop he'd been to and it was nice.

He liked breakfast, especially omelets.

He'd never made an omelet for anyone other than his parents before.

He thought it might rain in the next few days.

When the shower cut off, she wasn't sure if she had missed anything else. If she did, James didn't fault her for it.

He dressed in silence behind her. When he was done with that, he reached around and patted her shoulder. She turned and looked up, up and up at him.

Gold with green and brown, all dancing around together in his eyes.

He asked a question, and she nodded in answer.

It wasn't until she was bent over, her head against the lip of the sink, and warm water running in tandem with his fingers over her hair, that she realized what he had offered.

James Keller, the giant who had broken a man's nose

like it was nothing, gently washed out the last of her earlier bath's soap from her hair. And when the job was done, he kept on going.

Without one word between them he brushed her hair out and patted it dry. A new change of clothes came next. They weren't hers but Rose couldn't find time to care. When that was done, the distance between the bathroom and the bed blurred. Warm hands led her along it and then she blinked, and that warmth had turned into a sea of flannel around her.

Somewhere, in the back of her mind, Rose knew she had finally broken down. Just as she knew that, during the entire conversation in the shower, she had been staring at the lone bed in their room.

She shouldn't be this close to James, a stranger. She shouldn't accept his help or pity. She shouldn't endanger him or the things he loved all for her mistake. She shouldn't have let him get close. She shouldn't let him get closer.

Yet, when the time finally came for the lights to go out, Rose couldn't be bothered to care when the space next to her in bed was filled with by a man she'd just met a little over a week ago.

Because there was one thing Rose knew to be true more than all the rest.

James was warm.

And, to her, that was enough.

Chapter Twelve

The window unit might have looked old, but it worked more than fine. James felt the coolness on his face and his arm that had found its way on top of the quilt. It was the first thought he had once he had woken. The second was, despite the obvious chill in the air, parts of his body beneath the sheets were unusually warm.

James opened his eyes and was met with the popcorn ceiling of the Seven Roads Motel staring back at him. The blackout curtains must have shifted during his cleaning the night before. A strip of sunlight ran from the window and into a bright line across the ceiling fan that had wobbled too much to be used.

He knew why he was waking up to this and not his room at the house.

He remembered what had happened.

And yet the surprise of what was making him so warm still got him.

James peered down at his chest and saw the reason why he had woken up warm.

Rose was on her side but also on *his* side. She had one arm thrown over his chest while the corresponding leg was intertwined with his. Her head was resting on top of the hollow of his shoulder, a position made easier to achieve thanks to his own accommodation. James realized his arm was around her, holding her securely against his side.

Had going to sleep in the same bed last night been an issue in his mind? No, simply because he had only been worried about the blank look tugging Rose's expression down.

He had wanted to make her feel safe, was all. Secure, despite the madness that had been surrounding them.

Maybe he should have worried more, offered to sleep on the floor or one of the chairs. Given her space.

But James hadn't wanted to be apart from her.

He'd wanted to be close, just within reach if she needed him.

Though he hadn't thought about it quite like this.

James didn't know what to rightly do as he stared down at Rose's sleeping face. She had already become oddly endearing to him over the last week or so—someone he wanted to help protect and get justice for—but there had also been another feeling growing alongside his protectiveness.

Appreciation.

James couldn't help but mentally applaud so many things about the wildcard. Her smarts, her tenacity, her drive for helping others. But there was another thing he had been overlooking too.

Rose Little wasn't just cute, she was beautiful.

Asleep, awake, mad or angry. Smiling or annoyed. Sitting in a hospital bed, standing calm next to a bomb, or lying fast asleep against him.

Rose was a sight and a half and James couldn't help but feel like he had slighted himself by not becoming her friend earlier.

Friend.

Was that what she was to him? Simply a friend?

James was about to try and pin down exactly what he might feel for the deputy when, among the list of things she was, he realized asleep wasn't one of them anymore.

Rose stretched her arm out over him like a cat might do after waking from a nap. Her leg followed suit before she started to nuzzle her face against his shoulder.

James was almost certain she hadn't yet realized what she was holding wasn't a pillow or blankets and decided to wait her out.

He didn't have to wait long.

Rose's body tensed comically fast.

James couldn't help it, he laughed.

"I think I might call you Little Furnace from now on," he rumbled out. "You generate a surprising amount of heat."

Maybe it wasn't the right thing to say. Maybe he should have been more considerate of the situation even though he wasn't sure what that situation was. Had Rose gotten close to him during the night on purpose or was she just the kind of person who cuddled up to whoever and whatever she was next to?

And if she had done it on purpose, had it been because she needed any sense of comfort, or had he been the specific one she needed comfort from?

James could have spiraled down a rabbit hole of questions—not even touching the subseries of the ones surrounding his own feelings on the matter—but Rose cut him off with a surprising twist of events.

She rocketed up but didn't move away from him. Instead, she whirled around and looked down at him with wide eyes and a barely contained smile.

Rose went from lying comfortably against him to tear-ing herself out of the bed like he had bitten her. She tucked and rolled off the edge so fast that James sat up quick to try and see if he needed to help her.

The sudden movement made his head throb. He winced at the pain.

Rose, managing to get to her feet, saw it.

He watched her face go from red to concerned and red. Her brows knitted together, her hands still clutching some of the quilt.

"Why are you doing that? What hurts?" she asked.

James touched his forehead.

"The part of my head I used as a battering ram yesterday." It was definitely sore. Probably bruising. "It's not a big deal, though. Just a little uncomfortable."

Rose didn't seem to believe him. She crawled back into bed and right over to him. Her eyes were locked on to the spot in question as she got almost close enough to touch it. James kept his mouth shut while she did her silent inspection.

When she was apparently okay with what she was seeing, she pulled back to sitting on her side of the bed and James saw her own set of bruising. It wasn't as pronounced as he would have thought it would be, but the once-handprint ring around her neck was still visible.

James tapped his own neck.

"How about that?" he asked. "How's that on the pain scale?"

Rose tentatively felt the area. She didn't wince.

"Fine as long as I don't touch it."

"How about your throat? You don't sound as raspy as you did last night."

Rose thought about it a moment.

"It's better," was all she came up with.

"Good."

James gave Rose some space to collect her own thoughts and stretched out wide before scooping up his phone. Rose excused herself to the bathroom. The shower turned on soon after. James couldn't help but give another little laugh.

Usually when he woke up with a woman, they would talk about what had happened or at least make a comment or two. Rose, though, wasn't like other women, he was finding.

No one had called or texted James since his last communication with his dad the night before. Still, he decided to send a few quick texts to his parents. They were simple messages, just saying good morning and to have a good day, but it was small interactions like those that meant a lot to James. Especially when his mother replied with a little picture of a kitten half-asleep next to an oversize mug.

That was why he was smiling when Rose reappeared, wrapped in a towel and hair dripping wet. Adrenaline shot through James as he was sure something was wrong, but this time her expression halted any action.

"I think I get it," she said in a flurry of barely contained excitement.

"Get what?"

"Why Damon has been attacking me like he has, instead of just outright killing me easy."

James didn't like the way she phrased it but he was also invested.

A smirk pulled up the corner of her lips.

James was once again bowled over by how beautiful the woman was.

"I think it's time we paid our friend from last night a visit."

An hour later, Rose was standing between the bed she had slept in, the man she had slept with in it, and the sheriff of Seven Roads. It was a triangle she hadn't thought she'd ever be a part of but there she was, not only in it but excited to be there.

Simply because she had finally found a piece to the bizarre puzzle to finally make the last week less bizarre.

Price, settled in the corner, looking half-dead as he clung to his coffee cup, was the opposite of enthused. According to a quick chat with Liam he was ending a shift of helping Darius. When he had heard Rose wanted to talk about a possible lead, he had decided to end his night with the news.

Looking at him now, she wondered how bad *she* must have looked the night before. Just thinking about it was nothing compared to how she had woken up. She had been more attached to James than a koala to a tree.

What was worse?

James hadn't at all seemed fazed.

In fact, he had joked.

The situation would have been more mortifying if her shower hadn't dislodged a memory. One that she was more than excited to share now.

"The big thing that has been bothering me so much about everything that has happened in the last week is how absolutely unnecessary Damon's attacks have been," she started, once all their attention was back on her. "A bomb in and of itself is a big, big thing and usually fits a particular pattern or has some kind of reason behind it. With Damon, though? He has no history of being remotely involved in explosions or using them to act out his anger. And you said that the bomb maker even confirmed he was hired for this one bomb?"

She asked the question to Price, but the sheriff answered for him.

"Yeah, the maker said he accepts small jobs and the FBI agent working the case had a file full of two jobs he'd done before for clients. All he had on Damon was a one-time meeting and two messages found from a burner phone."

Rose nodded.

"Then there's the gunmen who showed up at the garage," she went on. "Four of them hired completely separate from the bomb maker but with the job to follow my car."

"And, according to their snitch, they were supposed to watch you and only act if something happened to your car," Liam added. "Then, when they did act, they were told to shoot to kill."

Rose snapped her fingers.

"Which makes no sense," she jumped in. "It's like Damon wants to kill me but make it unnecessarily difficult for himself. Then there was the man last night."

A shiver tried to run itself down Rose's back. She suppressed it but knew James was watching her do it. As she spoke he moved to her side to lean against the chest of drawers she was standing in front of.

"Darius said you found out who he is, right?"

It was Price who nodded now.

"Duncan Danvers," he said. "Last known to live an hour from here and on probation for assault and battery. He's not...the brightest of the bunch but he also refused to say a word until a lawyer got to him."

"And as far as we know, none of the gunmen, the bomb maker, or Danvers are connected," Liam said. "Other than the gunmen and the bomb maker being contacted by Damon at one point."

Rose hadn't recognized the attacker in James's house or his name. Which helped make her point even more.

"So, let's just say for argument's sake that this Duncan guy was also hired by Damon to take me out... He could have done it several times over if he'd simply brought a weapon." Out of her peripheral vision Rose saw James tense. She knew he still felt guilty for her being attacked in his home, but it wasn't his fault. None of this was. "Instead, this Duncan guy specifically said he had never drowned someone before, like he had waited patiently for me to get into the bathroom before coming in. Doesn't all of this sound ridiculous?"

The men around her agreed.

"Some people *are* ridiculous," Price offered. "Maybe Damon likes being flashy in his supposed acts of revenge. It's not like we haven't run into other dramatic perps who did a whole lot when doing a little would have gotten the job done."

"And normally I would agree but this morning I remembered a conversation I had about the video of me going viral after the bus situation." Rose pictured the reporter at the hospital, cast on his arm and anger in his gaze. "He said I was acting like some kind of action hero...because that's what some people called me. An action hero."

Rose handed her phone over to Liam. She had an article already up on the screen.

"More specifically this one article that went viral along with the video of me."

Liam started to read the article without being asked

to. When he got to the part she wanted him to see, his eyes widened.

"Okay, stop leaving me in suspense," Price said from the corner. "Don't leave me hanging. What does it say?"

Rose opened her mouth to respond but Liam was faster. His tone had a new, undeniable hint of excitement.

Not happiness at what was happening but at the idea of having a new lead.

"The article talks about her bravery and breaks down what it means to be an action hero. He goes over his favorite stereotypical problems that the heroes go through during their time in the spotlight. There's... There's a list."

Price was done with sitting. He hurried over and shared in reading.

Rose didn't need to see it again. After remembering hearing about the article, she'd pulled it up with a quick Google search. She and James had read it several times while waiting for Liam and Price to show up.

James proved how well he had been paying attention too, as he recalled the three situations that had more than caught their eye when reading it earlier.

"The classic group of lackeys that eventually turn on each other. The bomb strapped to someone the hero loves. And then—"

"'—the drowning scene, bonus points for the hero being trapped in some kind of vehicle while it's happening,'" Price finished, reading directly from the post.

Whether the coffee had finally hit his system, or the article had, his eyes were wide-open now.

"We don't have a body of water near here large enough for that, but I imagine a bathtub will do in a pinch," Rose said.

Liam shook his head. Price mimicked it.

"So, what are we guessing here?" he asked. "That Damon is pretending you're in some kind of movie where you're the lead?"

Rose didn't have any solid proof—she didn't even know much about the man himself—but as soon as she had read the article, she felt it to be true.

It was a theory but a theory that made sense.

"Because of that viral video, for one moment in time I was praised around the world for being a hero," Rose said, finally getting to the bottom line. "And I think, now the brother of the one person I didn't save wants me to die like one too."

Chapter Thirteen

Liam and Price took off with promises that they, along with Darius, would figure everything out. Rose stood by the window, peeking around the curtain like a little kid watching her parents run off to have fun without her.

She turned around, clearly dejected.

It was another endearing moment for the woman.

James doubted she was in the mood for the compliment.

"You said you trust them, and they do good work," he reminded her without preamble. "So we should let them go and do that good work."

Rose heaved out a long sigh.

"I did say that, and I do trust them, but I want to *help* them too," she wallowed. "This whole thing is about me, after all. Just sitting around here with you isn't doing anything but wasting time."

James made a pained sound and clutched at his chest.

"Wow, Wildcard. Way to hit me where it hurts."

Rose openly scanned his expression. She must have judged his words as the joke he intended. She waved through the air between them with slight annoyance.

"You know I don't mean being with you is a waste,"

she corrected. "I mean us sitting here with nothing to do is a waste."

Another moment of endearment.

He smiled into it.

Rose was too distracted to note it. Her brow was crinkled, and her gaze seemed to hollow. Those gears that never seemed to stop turning were going faster again.

"There's got to be something we can do… Let's talk it out one more time? It just all feels so ridiculous that I'm having a hard time processing alone in my head."

James waved his hand.

"Then join me out here and I'll help the best I can."

Rose nodded and started to pace across the seen-better-days carpet. Her hair was cinched up tight in a slick bun that contrasted with the casual cut of her clothes. The boots she had put on gave her an inch of height but she still looked impossibly small making a groove in the carpet as she went back and forth. If he had seen her without context, he couldn't have imagined anyone would go to such lengths to hurt her.

Though, maybe he was projecting his own surprising yet steady feelings of protectiveness for the woman.

"The author of that article is, according to the website, based in Mississippi," she started. "If Darius doesn't find anything that links him to Damon, I'm going to assume Damon found the article and is just using it as his own plan."

"It *was* one of the most viewed press pieces during that time," James said. "Even the comments on it had a lot of interaction."

She nodded. Then she paused.

"So let's say that's his outline as a middle finger up to everyone calling me an action hero. But why wait five months to do any of it? Was it a funding thing? Was it a planning thing? Why wait that long?"

James hadn't thought about that yet.

The timing of it was a little odd.

"Maybe it was a grief thing?" he offered. "Or, you know, he might not have instantly wanted his revenge against you. Something could have triggered him sometime after." He didn't know how true that was, though. Darius had confirmed with the bomb maker that he had been hired by Damon less than a month after the bus incident. "Or the gap could be because he was getting Derrick's affairs in order. Didn't you say their parents were much older and lived up North?"

"Yeah, but I'm not sure how hands-on Damon might or might not have been." Rose's voice went soft. "To be honest, I don't really know much about Damon. I only spoke to him once. At the hospital. After he identified Derrick's body. It wasn't a very pleasant conversation on any front."

James had wanted to ask about this before, because, aside from him doing an internet search, he also didn't know much about the man behind the attacks. Only what Rose had told him at the sheriff's department, a conversation that felt like it had happened years ago and not a day. Now, though, any and all details could be important, so he didn't hold back with his questions anymore.

"How *did* that conversation go? Between you and Damon, I mean."

Rose slowed her pacing.

"I shouldn't have talked to him but I—I was upset. Guilt and anger and being so dang tired from all that adrenaline finally leaving my system. I *shouldn't* have talked to him, but I did." She sighed. "I apologized for hesitating and that opened a can of really angry worms. He had me detail out everything that happened and I told him everything I told you."

"The fight between that Lloyd guy and Derrick on the bus, you mean?"

She nodded.

"Poor Lloyd too, he just happened to walk by when I was done. Derrick went over to him and, even though I couldn't hear what they were saying, they were definitely heated. Price eventually had to break their fight up and send—"

Rose came to a halt.

"Lloyd," she said, interrupting herself.

"Lloyd?" James repeated.

Her dark eyes were like saucers when they swung to his.

"I understand targeting me after the viral video and press, but don't you think some of that anger might have gone to the man who actually fought Derrick?"

James didn't know why he hadn't given another thought to Lloyd before. Now a rising sense of urgency pulled at his gut.

"When is the last time you saw Lloyd? At the hospital after the storm?"

Rose took her phone off the small table. Her thumbs were lightning-fast across the screen. Still, she answered.

"I actually ran into him at the hospital about a month ago when I was visiting Doc Ernest… The Camden Pharmaceuticals people eat lunch in the hospital's cafeteria since the research annex doesn't have a big kitchen…" Her focus narrowed in on her phone.

James left her to her silence.

He hadn't known Rose all that long, but he thought he

now had a handle on how she operated. At all times, Rose Little was charging forward, eager to protect someone. It made her brave and reckless and earned her the nickname Wildcard. She disregarded herself for the sake of others. It was mostly a commendable trait.

It was also a terrifying one for the people who cared about her.

And James cared.

He had since she had pulled him into the service pit, when she had agreed to pretend to be hurt at the sheriff's department to make him feel better, after he stood with her in the field behind his house, every second he had spent saving her from the tub the night before, and hours after he had shared a bed with her.

James cared about Rose to the point of distraction.

Something he hadn't felt in a very long time.

It was and wasn't surprising.

Rose Little may have been small, but she had more than proven she was absolutely mighty.

And he simply wanted more.

It was a quick epiphany. One that had James nod to himself to confirm he felt the change. Now wasn't the time to talk about it, though. Instead he kept to his chair and waited for the woman of the hour to plan her next move. Because no matter what it was, James knew he would follow.

She could protect everyone else, because James would protect Rose.

He just didn't realize then how quickly he was going to have to do so.

"BETRAYED BY SOMEONE you trust, a close-corridors fight in a precarious place, something to do with heights, and a high-speed car chase through a bustling city."

Rose was paraphrasing the last of Payton Abbot's favorite action hero encounters with as little enthusiasm as possible. She looked up at the giant wall of a man standing pressed up against an actual wall and narrowed her eyes.

"Unless you and the department have other plans, I don't think I'm going to get betrayed by someone I trust," she continued. "As for the close combat fight in a 'precarious' place—I'm not even sure what that means—and something to do with me being on the edge of a cliff or something, I feel like those could be difficult to mastermind even if Damon outsourced. I'm not even sure we can count the car chase one since we're not exactly a bustling city. But maybe the city part doesn't count. Damon seemed okay with changing the whole drowning thing to some random man ruining my bath."

James had had his eye on the doors to the hospital cafeteria for almost fifteen minutes. Even as he spoke now, he kept his gaze fixed.

"I'm not sure if you're talking about all of this like it's nothing as a way to cope or not, but let it be known, I'm not a fan of how casual you're making this sound."

Rose had already picked up on that fact. The man might have a calm poker face but his body always gave him away. He had been tense ever since they had come to the hospital, doubly so when Rose was recognized by one of her friends on the staff. Now she could see the tension clearly in the line of his shoulders and the tightness of his jaw.

That tightness managed to stay there when he added another thought, just as grumbly as the previous one.

"And let it also be known, that no, I will not be the one who betrays you. So you can throw that idea right on out."

Rose didn't say it, but she hadn't even entertained the idea of James betraying her in any sense of the word. An odd thing, considering she hadn't even known the sound of his voice until a week ago. Now that sound was a comfort. A promise of being there. A calm place in an extremely unorthodox storm.

Also a voice of reason.

Because James was right.

Joking about everything—being so casual talking about how determined someone was to take her life, money and prison time be damned—was the only thing keeping the panic in her down. She had already been stressed with the bomb and the gunmen at the garage but after the man in the bathroom?

Everything had changed.

Church clothes or not, that man had truly scared her by invading a space she'd never imagined would be dangerous. He had overpowered her quickly and had nearly taken her life. All while she had been naked.

That small detail might not have seemed like a big deal in the grand scheme of things, but to Rose, it might have been the worst part.

She had been utterly vulnerable, not a stitch on or no weapon in sight.

If it hadn't been for James…

Rose peeked up at the man again.

She didn't want to even think about it.

As if she had voiced her thoughts out loud, the man in question swung his golden-rimmed gaze her way. He thumbed back over his shoulder.

"Isn't that our guy?"

Adrenaline shot through her, breaking up thoughts of panic and of James and the comfort he brought. Rose swung her head around James's shoulder so fast that if she had been wearing her hair in a ponytail it would have smacked him good.

"That's definitely Lloyd," she confirmed, staring at the group of people who had just left the cafeteria. "Doc Ernest said the Camden people always take lunch at the same time during the week. He's the one in the back on his phone. The good-looking guy with the blond hair."

James snorted but was already moving. She heard him mutter beneath his breath.

"I didn't need that last part."

Rose didn't respond to his cheekiness. Instead, she let James take the lead and approach the group by himself. She held back out of sight. Only a few of the people who had been there during the storm still worked at Camden now. That didn't mean she wanted to chance falling into a catch-up by running into them. Her current plan was simple: see if Lloyd had had any contact with Damon since the storm or had any dangerous run-ins recently.

Rose didn't need to chat past that.

Lloyd seemed just as uninterested in the usual pleasantries when he rounded the corner with James in tow. His eyes widened at the sight of her, but he didn't smile.

"Deputy Little, what a coincidence, I was just about to try and find you."

Rose shared a look with James.

Unlike the last time she had seen him, Lloyd Harrison looked somehow worse for the wear. Which was saying a lot, given their last danger-filled interaction had been in the middle of a flood and a tornado. There were dark circles beneath eyes that were tinged red. He also seemed to have lost some weight.

Maybe Rose wasn't the only one Damon had been targeting after all.

"You were looking for me?" she asked.

Lloyd nodded. His tired gaze shifted between her and James before he lowered his voice.

"I think it's time we had a talk." He nodded to James but kept his eyes on her. "A very private one."

Chapter Fourteen

James had no idea what was going on, but he did know everything had gone wrong.

"Rose!" he yelled, not for the first time.

The woman might have been small in size but what she lacked in height she more than gained in speed. She ran full tilt down the hospital hallway like she was running for her life. The problem with that?

James was the only one behind her.

"Sto-stop!" he yelled out, nearly tripping over a patient coming out of a room. He sidestepped the confused woman and focused back on running after the woman confusing him.

Rose started to slow but only so she could take a turn in the hallway. He could hear her shoes squeak across the floor. James wanted to use her slower pace to his advantage, but it just wasn't in the cards, with his physique. He took the turn a lot less gracefully than her, losing him even more distance between them.

What had happened?

Why was she running?

James chanced the quickest of looks back down the hallway he was leaving.

There was no one chasing them. Absolutely no one.

But it had to have something to do with that Lloyd guy. If he had time, James would have cursed the man. He never should have stepped aside to give Lloyd the privacy to talk to Rose.

"Listen, he obviously looks scared," Rose had argued when it was clear James didn't want her to be alone with the man. "He could have some answers. Some answers we need. And he could also need *us*. If Damon blames me for not saving Derrick because of a hesitation and he's been going through all of this? Maybe he's been doing much worse to someone else."

Rose had reached out and put her hand right into James's. It was small and warm and soft. Her expression was none of those. Her expression was hard, sharp. Determined, angry. Excited for something. Ready for anything.

Wildcard Rose.

She wasn't asking permission.

Not that he would have been in the right to give it.

So he had relented, but only so much.

"I'll go stand over there so I can keep you in my sight," he had warned. "No going into off-limits rooms or secret passageways to make Damon's job easier for him."

She had nodded and pointed out a spot at the intersection of the hallway he had been standing in.

"Out in the open but not in a crowded place *and* you can see me."

That had been fine. That had been good.

That still hadn't worked.

Rose and Lloyd had started talking without any issue. Lloyd seemed tired, Rose open to listening to whatever he was saying. No one passed through their hallway or

James's. No gunmen or Damon or creep in a collared shirt showed.

And then everything had changed.

Rose hadn't even looked his way before she turned on her heel and ran out of sight. Lloyd did the same.

But in the opposite direction.

By the time James had made it to their hallway, the choice of whom to follow had been a no-brainer.

Now that no-brainer had him thoroughly confused.

Rose wasn't stopping for him.

Why?

The hallway they turned into wasn't as long as the one they had come from. If he was tracking right, it turned into the back section of the hospital before hitting a bank of elevators. There was a doctor's clinic somewhere near here that he had taken Mr. Donahue to once. A clinic in the hospital that had its own small parking lot.

Where they had parked earlier before walking around the other side of the hospital to avoid as many eyes as possible.

That Rose, he realized, was heading straight for.

He heard the impact of her throwing open the Exit doors to the parking lot before he saw daylight streaming through them.

"Rose! Stop!"

She didn't.

The doors shut before James could reach them. When it was his turn to open them, it sounded like an explosion as he rammed right on through.

Heat hit him in the face and made the sweat already starting to bead down him gain more traction. James didn't care. He wasn't going to stop running until he caught her. Even if that meant running every inch of the hospital or—

James felt his stomach sink.

He had driven to the hospital in the truck they had borrowed from a deputy at the department...but Rose had the keys. She had taken them after he had complained that the key ring was too bulky for his jeans.

Now he wished more than anything he hadn't been such a baby about it.

Just then he saw what Rose's speed had won her.

Halfway across the lot, she was already getting inside the truck. James didn't bother calling for her again. Whatever was happening, she didn't want him to be a part of it.

But that didn't stop him from trying.

James pushed his big muscles as far as they would go at the truck with all he had.

Wildcard Rose?

Not even a man like him could catch her if she didn't want him to.

She slammed on the gas as soon as the truck started.

James missed her by mere seconds.

Rose not once looked his way.

Wherever she was going, she was going to face it alone.

Rose wasn't used to the truck. She didn't know how much speed it could handle and how much grace she needed to give it without letting her foot off the gas pedal. Instead of playing it completely safe, but also not putting her entire life on the line by slinging it around at ninety miles an hour, she split the difference.

When she came to the metal gate that separated the Reynolds Farm and the Seven Roads Cemetery right off

County Road 72's start, she hit it at a cool forty miles an hour.

The truck whined at the hit, bumped her around a little, metal twisted a little more, but it took out the gate without taking her out. And it didn't pop a tire as far as she could tell.

Small blessings, she thought, as she started to haul tail again.

The Seven Roads Cemetery had changed names three times in its one-hundred-year existence. No one really got buried there anymore and not many people in town had people already there, so the through traffic had become less and less over the last few years. Five months ago, the entire place had been shut down after the storm dislodged some graves and nearly destroyed the main office.

Damage or not, though, Rose knew her way around.

Knuckles white against the steering wheel, she bypassed the decapitated office and took the main road that ran around the entire two-acre plot of land. Gravestones, old and weathered, dotted the land to her right. Big oaks, some damaged from the same storm, were lined up at her left. Her target, though, would be right up ahead in a few seconds.

Rose's stomach tightened as the phone in her pocket vibrated.

She knew who it would be.

She knew what he would say if she answered.

She knew what he would say when she told him why she was out here.

James would tell her to turn around. To stop. To wait.

To not listen to Lloyd's warning.

To not willingly go into danger.

To not make it easier for Damon…

But what James didn't realize was that she was doing this for him.

"While you've been dodging his attacks, I've been playing his games," Lloyd had said, exhaustion in his every word.

"Damon's?" she had parroted.

Lloyd had sighed.

"He sure started it," he'd said. "I thought I found a way out but then you finally showed up."

"I don't understand. What game? What's going on?"

There had been no hesitation in Lloyd's answer, no emotion either. Just that exhaustion. How had his co-workers not seen it? How had no one stopped him to check on him?

"I've been playing hide-and-seek," he'd said, not at all showing signs that he was kidding. "But only one person can find me and you just did." He'd glanced down at his phone. "And he knew you were here before I did. He sure is everywhere."

Lloyd had sighed again, an all-consuming weight seemingly dragging him down. Rose had almost turned to James then, red flags springing up to make a sea around them, but Lloyd had been quick.

"Don't let him know what I'm about to tell you or we're both going to lose."

Lloyd had just finished a phone call when they had first seen him, and he let her in on the conversation.

"We have ten minutes to get to the groundskeeper's house at the Seven Roads Cemetery. If we're not there by then and if we're not alone, bad things will happen to whoever they took."

Rose hadn't for the life of her expected that.

"Whoever they took?"

Lloyd had flinched.

"That's all he said."

The sea of red flags took over the land too.

Lloyd, however, hadn't tried to reassure her or persuade her after that. But she wasn't sure any words could convince her faster than his utter look of resignation.

Rose had believed Lloyd then.

Still, she wasn't a fool.

"We could still call for help," she'd said.

Lloyd had shaken his head.

"I'm not taking that chance again. I've already learned my lesson." He had flinched again before putting his phone in his pocket. "The time starts when we leave the hospital. What do you want to do about the big guy over there? He looks like he'll stop us and get himself killed for it."

Every word Lloyd had said lacked inflection, lacked emotion. Just matter-of-fact.

It sealed the deal for Rose right then and there to take this seriously.

There had been too many unknowns.

What she *had* known was she wasn't going to lead James into a situation that would put him and someone else in danger.

"My car is in the side lot," she had said.

Lloyd, despite his obviously deteriorated emotional state, had understood.

"We'll split up," he'd said. "Whatever happens, I suggest you get there in ten minutes."

Rose had wanted to turn to James, to call his name, to take him with her, but she put her trust into fear.

Now she had two minutes left as the side road that branched off to the house behind the cemetery came into view.

Everyone local to Seven Roads knew about Groundskeeper Demetri's old house. Demetri was the last person to live there and die there, and since his time it had become the famed haunted house of the town. Teens went there on haunt nights and spoke to Old Demetri like he was a ghost lying in wait just for them. It was an easy way to kill boredom on a Friday night and an easier excuse to snuggle up with a special someone when things got too spooky.

Rose couldn't fault anyone for it because she had been part of some of the first groups of teens to start the tradition of haunt nights and fake ghost-whispering. Blake and Price had even shown up a time or two with her, because when you grew up in a place as boring as Seven Roads, you had to get creative.

Now, seeing the old two-story, Rose felt true fear grip at her heart.

Not only because of the unknown but because there had been a detail about the property she had forgotten.

There was a small pond behind the abandoned house.

Was that why she had been told to come there? For another attempt at a drowning scene?

Or was this just part of Damon's revenge for Lloyd?

Rose shook her head to herself and slammed on brakes, skidding to a stop on the overgrown grass next to the house. Her phone started to vibrate again.

She ignored it.

If she was wrong, it was only her life in danger.

If she was right and coming could save someone? Could keep James safe?

Those odds she could make peace with.

Rose didn't waste any more time. She ran up to the porch and took the steps two at a time. She went for the door handle, but the door was already cracked open. She pushed it open with her foot and on reflex went for her gun.

It wasn't there.

Neither was anyone in the foyer.

Rose listened but heard nothing but her heartbeat thundering in her chest.

Was this part of the movie scene? Was this part of a game? *Had* Lloyd told this bizarre lie simply to separate her from James?

No sooner did she start to doubt everything than she finally heard something in the distance. She walked in its direction, going from the old foyer to the kitchen that was at the back of the house. In its prime, it was probably the most beautiful of rooms with big, open windows running along almost every wall, facing out toward the dock and pond. Great for watching sunrises and sunsets and making the job of groundskeeper all the more relaxing.

Now some of the windows had long since been broken. Others had molded. Some had vines that had come through. One had plastic poorly taped across it.

Yet, despite the dilapidated state of them, Rose could see what she realized was just for her.

She also understood the noise she was hearing.

A man was standing on the dock, clapping. There was something next to him but she couldn't make it out completely.

Not that it mattered much.

Something had been set in motion, and it was time for her to find out what and why.

So she took a quick breath and pushed open the back door. Once upon a time it had led to a patio that had housed many a party back in her day. House bands and wannabe DJs, kegs and constant chatter. She'd had fun here then. Dancing, talking, playing around. A teenager without too much to worry about, thinking only about how to kill boredom.

Twenty or so years later, Rose walked across the same concrete with a heaviness that only grew with each new step.

Because the man clapping was none other than Damon Tillman.

And now she could clearly see what he was standing next to.

It was two cinder blocks. If that wasn't terrifying enough, the rope hanging around his arm sure did the trick.

Chapter Fifteen

No one had yet asked *why* Rose hesitated to reach out to Derrick Tillman. She suspected that the few who knew she felt responsible for his death thought she did so because the situation had been chaotic. There was a tornado coming, a flood already raging, and eleven ducks she had been tasked with single-handedly getting in a row.

It had been a lot, so hesitating might have just been a problem with the environment.

But that wasn't true.

Rose had hesitated for the same reason her feet faltered as she walked out onto the dock now.

When she had reached out to Derrick on that bus, she had seen something so intense that her body had reacted by simply stopping.

She had seen his expression.

More aptly, his rage.

It hadn't fit his face, contorting the youthful handsomeness into an awful mask of anger, making every angle across it a startling addition to the already nerve-wracking situation. In that moment, that anger had felt dangerous. Too dangerous, like a hammer racing toward a window that already had several cracks spiderwebbing across it.

So Rose had hesitated in caution.

Because every part of her at that time had believed that Derrick Tillman was ready to unleash that rage. And bringing him closer to the ten other ducks she needed to get to the pond?

Her body had acted before she could stop it.

We can't afford that anger, it had said.

She had squashed that thought a few seconds later, reminding herself that, anger or not, rage or not, he was still one of her ducks, but it had been too late.

Now, coming to a stop a few feet from Damon, she could see the same rage that his little brother had been wearing, written clearly across his face.

It didn't occur to her until that very moment to wonder where Derrick's anger had come from.

The origin of Damon's anger, however, was no secret.

"You know, I had no doubt you'd come here, Deputy."

His head was shaved close, dark hair matching an outfit that had been picked with stealth in mind. He wore black clothing and work boots. There was a cell phone in his left hand, a gun in his right.

He held the cell phone up to his sight line, but the gun was down at his side.

Rose glanced around the rest of the dock. There was more rope behind him, also another set of cinder blocks.

"The way I see it, I didn't have a choice," Rose said.

Damon laughed, though it was wholly unkind.

"Normally, I would have said you just like the attention, but now, I guess I understand it." His fake laughter melted. He was seething next. "This is why I've never liked them."

His phone vibrated and his gaze switched to its screen.

Whatever he saw must have been something he was waiting for. He nodded to himself.

Then he threw his phone into the water.

"Action heroes," he continued. His laughter came back. Again, there was no humor in it. "Did you know that Derrick was obsessed with them growing up? You couldn't walk into our house without seeing some kind of action movie on the TV. New ones, old ones, popular ones, ones that barely anyone had heard of…they were always there, filling the rooms of childhood." He smiled, briefly. "I asked Derrick once if he wanted to be one of the heroes he loved so much but he said no. He just liked the idea of them."

He sighed.

Rose looked at his finger next to the trigger.

"Someone, who by all accounts could have left the story at the beginning, decided to stay. To go against the insurmountable odds and try to make everything better."

The anger in him was still there but Rose didn't understand where he wanted it to go. Instead of being aimed at her, it seemed like it was burning him.

"Who did you take, Damon?" she ventured. "Where are they?"

Damon seemed surprised by the question. It smoothed into another smile that sent a shiver through her.

"Does it matter?" he asked. "It could be your parents or that boyfriend of yours or eleven strangers on a bus, you would always come, right? Because that's what heroes do."

A creeping cold started to move through Rose.

It was a lie.

Damon had no one.

No one but her.
And she had given herself over willingly.
Damon searched her expression. He nodded as if hearing her realization, but continued with his speech.

"But me? I never liked action movies. Those heroes Derrick loved so much? They were all the same. No matter the planning, the cause, the circumstances, they always found a way to fix everything. To come out on top. But we never saw all the choices that had to be made, all the consequences that had to happen. We never got to see everyone's problems and worries. Their burdens to bear. We didn't see the hospital bills, the cost of living, the price of milk."

He shook his head.

"We saw heroes escaping quicksand and badly trained men with guns. We saw car chases and fights in the subway. Bombs attached to toilets and bodies floating at the bottom of lakes."

Another shiver went down Rose's spine.

Damon didn't catch it.

He did, however, regard her with another pointed stare.

"You know, I think it was fate that they compared you to something Derrick—the man you didn't save—loved. I just wanted to show the world that you weren't a hero, after all. Not to Derrick, not to me."

Damon seemed more tired now than mad. His shoulders sagged a little.

Rose didn't understand the attitude.

He had her where he wanted, right?

No weapon, no backup. Just herself and good intentions.

"What do you want now, Damon? Why am I here?"

She eyed those cinder blocks.

Damon seemed unperturbed.

"Because the reason I dislike heroes the most is they're foolish," he said. "And I'm no fool."

He lowered his gun just as the sound of footfalls on the wooden dock behind her sounded.

Whoever the newcomer was, he didn't glance their way.

"Betrayal by someone you love was going to be my masterpiece at the end of all of this," he said. "But it looks like that's my scene now."

Damon threw his gun into the water like he had his phone.

Rose had no idea what was happening but, for some reason, she simply couldn't look away.

Because Damon Tillman was smiling again.

This time, there was no anger in it. No hate or rage.

This time, it seemed genuine.

His gaze moved over her shoulder.

He said one last thing before all hell broke loose.

It was simple.

"And I'm okay with it."

JAMES KNEW HE had only a short amount of time before the sheriff's department was on his tail. He didn't blame them or the man he had basically carjacked in the parking lot. Desperate times called for desperate measures and there was no way in hell he was going to just sit around while Rose had jetted off to who knew what. Much like during the chase through the hospital, Rose had a considerable lead ahead of him. It was only by sheer luck that he'd seen another car booking it out of the main lot by the time he reached the main road.

It was Lloyd Harrison.

Two cars managed to get between them before James could ride his tail and, because of those two cars, he was slowed down enough that he lost Lloyd on a turn onto County. James cussed up a storm as he raced down the new road without a car in sight.

There was no way Lloyd had been that fast. He had to have turned off somewhere.

No sooner had he had the thought than James spotted tire marks streaking through the dirt and grass off the shoulder ahead. He slowed.

Then he saw the metal gate of the Seven Roads Cemetery, on the ground, bent and broken.

Rose.

As soon as he was past the gate, he was more confident in his choice. Two sets of very distinct tire marks had kicked up dirt and grass along the road leading to the left. James followed that for what felt like an hour but must have really only been a minute or two. When the road started to curve to the right, though, he saw the trail of tire marks veer in the opposite direction. That road led in between trees, away from the open land of the cemetery plots.

James reduced his speed as he went left. If he had been a tried and true local, he would have probably known exactly where he was headed. Instead, he was caught off guard when a large house came into view in the distance.

It had seen better days, that was for sure.

It also had seen Rose.

Their borrowed truck was parked off to the side, alongside the vehicle Lloyd had been driving. James didn't even bother turning the car off. He barely put it in Park before he was leaping out and running.

The smell of mold and dust filled his nostrils. Humidity tightened its grip. James knew he wasn't, but it felt like he had been holding his breath since the hospital. There was no one and nothing that jumped out of him.

"Rose!" he yelled, caution now be damned.

Silence.

Was she somewhere in the house? Where and who else was here?

He ran to his left and into what must have been the old living area. She wasn't there. James ran in the other direction. His steps echoed.

"Rose!" he yelled again.

This time, the silence was gone.

"James!"

It was her. Faint, but he heard her.

He skidded to a stop before pivoting to go back to the entryway.

"Rose! Where are you?"

He heard her call him again. It was coming from outside.

James ran through a kitchen and through a door that was already wide-open. Two steps across the patio and he saw the dock. It was long, notably withered, and stood over a pond he'd never known existed.

If it had been a different situation, he might have appreciated the peaceful scenery.

But what he saw frightened him as much as it relieved him.

"Rose!"

At the end of the dock the most beautiful woman he had ever seen turned to her name.

He didn't know what he expected but when she yelled for him, he listened.

"Hurry!"

James ran so fast, at one point he wasn't even sure he was touching the ground. It was just pure propulsion from where Rose wasn't to the spot by her side. The closer James got, the more confusing the details became. No one was with Rose but there was blood on the wood next to her. The clothes she was wearing, however, were clean. The only thing that had changed since he had last seen her at the hospital was the rope she was currently untying from around her ankles.

Rope that was attached to a cinder block near the dock's edge. Two more cinder blocks were next to her.

She didn't seem like she was hurt. Yet her expression was panicked.

He didn't know why.

Rose pointed to the water.

"Save him," she yelled.

James didn't need to know more. He didn't need the details to make sense. Context wasn't the key to getting him to act.

It was Rose.

She needed him to do something.

So something was what he did.

Without a single question, James dove into the water.

The house might have been warm and the outdoor air humid, but the pond was absolutely cold. It hit James's body like a ton of bricks as he immediately started swimming downward. He opened his eyes once he adjusted and the cold was less jarring, and scanned the area.

He didn't know who this *he* was, and he didn't know why he needed saving, but the second James saw the body sinking toward the bottom, he readjusted his aim.

The man looked like he was standing straight up in the water, his arms suspended above his head, his shirt loose and floating in the same direction. James made it to his waist and realized how the cinder block fit into everything.

The man was tied to it.

Just like Rose was tied to one on the dock.

James didn't have time to be angry. The man wasn't moving.

He dove deeper down to try and see if the rope was tied around his ankles too. The water was murky, but James was able to find where the rope connected. Luckily it was around one ankle, not both.

Water displaced above him as James set to undoing the knot. He didn't turn to see who had jumped in. He knew it was Rose.

She attached to the other side of the man, using him to reorient herself so her feet were touching the ground. James's chest started to burn with the effort. He was running out of time.

Rose must have realized it too.

She reached out and touched him before pointing to the surface.

But James wasn't leaving her again.

Instead of dealing with untying the knot completely, James did the next best thing.

He ripped it apart.

Whether the knot was bad to start with or the rope was already frayed, it came undone fast. The man shifted and Rose's positioning finally made sense. She pushed off the ground with her arm wrapped around the man's waist.

Together with James, the three of them sprung up to the surface.

James hit it first, gulping up the air. Rose came second. She was already yelling for him.

"Help me! Help me get him to bank!"

It was a struggle at first but soon they found a system between them that worked. The man didn't fight back at all, which made sense considering he wasn't breathing when James hefted him up the bank and pulled him to a flat area of grass.

"He's—he's been in the water for—for over a minute," Rose huffed out. She shoved her hair off her face. She didn't meet his eye. "He's been—been shot too. I need—I need to call this in but my phone—"

James yanked his phone out of his pocket but felt instant relief.

"It's waterproof." He started a call to 9-1-1 while Rose put pressure on the bullet wound in question. It was near his shoulder and the sudden force didn't stir him either.

"Who is this?" he asked.

James was utterly shocked at her answer.

"It's Damon. I—I need you start CPR while I go—"

She tried to stand, James kept her down. He might not have known what had led to Damon being the one tied to a cinder block and shot, but he doubted it was Rose's doing, considering he had found her tied up too.

So there was a third person.

Someone he hadn't seen yet.

"Who shot him? Who tied you two up? Was it Lloyd?"

Her eyes widened. A dispatcher answered the call, her voice floating up toward them. Rose simply nodded.

"Where did he go?" James's muscles were tensing, his adrenaline surging one more time.

"The house. He's—he's armed."

James didn't give two licks.

He ran back to that house, clothes soaked through, and yelled Lloyd's name like an angry sermon.

What he hadn't counted on was the man calling him right on back.

Lloyd Harrison was standing by a window on the second floor. The window treatments were still there, framing the dirty glass with stubborn dignity. It was the only thing in that room that seemed to belong.

Lloyd didn't. In fact, he didn't look like he belonged anywhere. His clothes were baggy, his hair limp, his expression dull. He looked like he had already been written out of the world, but his body just hadn't caught up yet. He rested one hand on the window frame; the other was wrapped around a gun.

His gaze was slow as syrup as it moved between the outside world and James in the doorway.

James was dripping on the hardwood. His chest was heavy from anger and effort. His fists were empty but balled.

He had never met or seen Lloyd Harrison before that morning and now the man was squarely in his sights.

"You tied her to that block," he breathed out, his voice as low as he'd ever heard it himself.

Lloyd hardly reacted.

"Damon did," he said, voice just floating along. "Then I tied Damon up. Then I shot him and came here. I saw you two jump in to get him. I can see Rose is trying to save him now too. Because that's what heroes do."

James was taken aback at the honesty.

"You know, I don't much care for the whole hero thing or games, but I get now why Damon was so angry." A small, watery smile swirled over Lloyd's lips. "His brother used to call him a hero too, and then, the day he died was the day he stopped. I never really got how much that must have hurt until now."

He let out a breath. It was short and didn't drag him down. Instead, it seemed to be just another motion he was going through. Then he smiled again. James couldn't tell what emotion it was coming from, but it didn't feel fake.

"I don't think he ever really blamed Rose, though," he continued. "I know I don't. It wasn't her fault. It was… it was that storm. That damned generator." He let out a small laugh. "It's funny how one single point of failure can wreck so many things."

James took a tentative step forward. Why this man was waxing poetic, he didn't know, but that gun needed to be gone.

"I don't know what's going on, but it sounds like you shot a man who was aiming to hurt you and Rose. We can be calm and talk about the rest of it."

Lloyd didn't seem to mind him creeping closer.

James got the impression that Lloyd had stopped minding anything at all.

He let out one last little sigh.

"If you want this to end here, I suggest you don't repeat what I'm about to say, but, well, I think it should be said." He glanced out of the window. James was about to spring at him, but he raised the gun and placed it against his temple.

When Lloyd looked back at him, his smile was the only thing left that seemed alive.

"Damon is really good at tying knots, but Rose sure got out of it easy, didn't she? I could have pushed her in the water too, tied to that thing, but I didn't. I guess we're not all that bad, in the end." Lloyd turned back to the window. His last words haunted the empty room.

"Close your eyes now, Mr. Keller. This won't be pretty."

James ran forward, yelling.
He didn't make it.
The window treatments kept on hanging but Lloyd Harrison was gone.

Chapter Sixteen

Rose was screaming but she didn't move from her spot on that patch of grass.

"Shots fired!" she yelled down at the phone. "James? James!"

No one responded. The house was too far back, and she couldn't see which room the sound had come from.

She also couldn't stop.

She continued heart compressions on Damon Tillman while her own heart shattered around them both.

James had gone into the groundskeeper's house after Lloyd and now Lloyd had shot him, and Rose felt as helpless as a person could.

She could go see. She could leave Damon on the wet ground, covered in blood and not breathing, and no one would fault her for it. The man who had masterminded the attacks meant to kill her over the last week… The man who had told all his hired helpers that he was out for revenge. That for him to be happy, Rose had to die.

She could leave him right there.

And no one, *no one*, could say she did wrong.

Except…her.

Tears hot and heavy blurred her vision and streamed down her face. Her head hurt. Her heart hurt. The world hurt.

But she kept on with her compressions.

She wouldn't leave Damon Tillman any more than she would leave James had he been beneath her hands. Not when she could still help. Not when there was still hope.

But James could be the one who needs you now, up there, Rose couldn't help but think. *And you're here with someone who hated you so much.*

Rose didn't hesitate, despite herself.

In fact, a part of her believed that James would tell her to do the same.

Still, it hurt.

Rose screamed out in anger and fear and anguish and exhaustion.

She called James's name again, absolutely certain that Lloyd had used one shot to end him. A shot that he never would have taken had Rose stayed with him at the hospital.

Rose's body was wracked by sobs.

She didn't feel Damon move at first because of it.

Then she realized her hands were moving without her.

Rose held her breath and looked down.

Damon was coughing, water spewing from his mouth.

Then his eyes opened.

Rose let out a breath that absolutely shook.

Then she was scrambling to her feet.

"Don't move, help is on the way," she yelled down at him.

Rose stumbled her way up and away from the pond and ran to the patio with everything she had.

Then everything she had quickly met a wall.

She blinked into the impact before realizing it was her wall.

James said something—she was sure of it—but she didn't hear a word.

Rose collapsed against him.

His arms were warm and strong as they held her up.

In the last week—in the last day—the world had gotten loud, messy and complicated.

But right then, Rose felt only him.

Night finally fell.

The Seven Roads Motel was empty again. James's house was not.

Sheriff Weaver's badge was on his hip, but his hands were around a beer. It had been offered to him once his shift had officially ended. He hadn't had any sip of it, but then again, James also hadn't had a drink of his either. Instead, they were on the back porch looking out at the field of tall grass.

They had been sitting in silence a bit while they waited for the sheriff's wife to finish seeing about Rose. Both women were upstairs in the guest bedroom. Without being asked the men had given them space.

That morning had been a lot.

Now they were all trying to wind down.

Though there were still concerns. Weaver seemed to guess at James's main ones. He spoke into the night air with a tiredness that James couldn't deny he felt a bit too.

"The doctors say Damon might not wake up at all, but if he does, he has a detail on him until we get a better sense of what's what," he said. "But Darius and I agree, we think there's nothing else out there waiting for Rose. Whatever conflict went on between Damon and Lloyd, it seemed to put a stop to whatever might have come next. Still, it might not be a bad idea to let her stay with you a few more days."

No one could make Rose do what she didn't want.

That said, James had already decided he wasn't going to let the deputy be alone. Whether that meant her staying at his house or him camping outside of her apartment, he was more than prepared to follow her lead.

But he wasn't about to say that to her boss. Not without her okaying it.

Instead, James nodded.

"I'll look after her," he promised.

Weaver was pleased. He scratched at the label on his bottle. James felt his eyes on him but kept his gaze ahead. James bet the sheriff was wondering about the two of them—Rose and James. Weaver had been the first to arrive at the groundskeeper's house and the first to see Rose, completely folded into his arms.

She hadn't moved from that position until the EMTs had arrived and insisted on checking both of them. That was when she had finally seen the blood on his sleeves.

"Is that blood?" she had asked, strength zipping through her tears. "Are you hurt?"

He had smiled down at her but felt no joy in it.

"It's not mine."

He'd told them about Lloyd then, upstairs in that room. There was no saving him, and when Rose had finally left his side to talk to a newly arrived Price, James had told the sheriff everything Lloyd had said.

Almost everything.

"If you want this to end here, I suggest you don't repeat what I'm about to say…"

If Lloyd had acted any differently, if he hadn't seemed so sincere, James wouldn't have omitted anything from the sheriff or Detective Williams. Yet, he couldn't find anything to doubt in the man's warning.

So James kept Lloyd's last words to himself. If there was any chance it could keep Rose safe, he was going to take it for now.

Maybe that was what Sheriff Weaver suspected now. Maybe he knew James was withholding something. Or maybe he was just tired.

He let out a long breath and turned back toward the field.

"I think it might rain this week," he said after a moment.

James turned his bottle around in his hand, the condensation wetting his fingers.

"We could use just a little of it," he said.

"That we could," Weaver agreed.

They sat in silence, not a bad one, until Blake appeared at the back door. She had one hand on her belly and the other reaching for her husband.

"It's time for us to go to sleep," she told him. Then to James, "You too, Mr. Keller."

Both men stood.

"How's Rose doing?" the sheriff asked.

Blake looked caught between sad and okay.

"She'll be okay. She just needs some time to process, is all." A smile lit her face. She spoke softly to her husband, but James was reassured by it too. "Don't worry. Wildcard Rose will be back after a good, well-deserved rest."

That cheering outlook led the three of them back through the house to the front porch. The sheriff said he would check in on them the next day while Blake encouraged James to focus on keeping Rose at home for a bit.

"That girl can roll with a lot of punches but staying put to heal from them has never been her strong suit," Blake added. "Not to step out of line here, but I don't think she'd mind healing if you were staying put right there with her."

James told her not to worry. He'd make sure she got the rest she needed. Then the Weavers locked hands and walked slowly to their car. He couldn't hear everything they said but he spied them looking up at the stars together.

He turned off the porch light to give them some privacy.

James had only spent one night away from his house, but it felt like a lifetime ago. He went through each room, checking every inch to make sure everything was like it had been.

Then he came to a stop at the guest bedroom door.

It was open enough that James could make out Rose, lying in the bed.

She was facing away from him, wrapped up in a quilt.

James had already told her good-night, knowing she was exhausted, and she had returned the sentiment, eyes swollen and heavy. So there was no reason for him to go in to see her now. No reason to talk to her. No reason to be near her.

He could go to his own room across the hall and probably fall asleep in a wink.

Yet, James couldn't move from his spot at the door.

She was safe now.

His house was safe.

There was no reason to worry. There was no reason to hover. There was no—

James pushed open the door and walked around the side of the bed. Rose opened her eyes to the sound. She didn't say a word as she watched him.

She didn't say a thing as he took the covers off her.

She didn't make a sound as he scooped her up into his arms, her side against his chest and bare legs dangling freely while he walked her out of the guest bedroom and across the hall.

Instead, she let him place her directly into his bed, watched him get in beside her, and accepted the covers he pulled up over them both. He reached up and clicked the light off and kept that silence going until a few minutes passed.

Then, he told her something he had never told another soul.

"When I was a kid, I got into a really bad fight with a teenager in the same foster home as me. He was pushing around a girl in the home with us and I tried to protect her. I did some damage to him but I was just a little thing and I had to have two surgeries on my arm. I had nightmares after that, recurring bad ones that carried on for years. I'd wake up screaming and crying, and sometimes when it got really bad, I'd just completely shut down until morning. When that happened, no one could get me talking. It was like I was dead to the world. Everyone thought the nightmares were from the fight and the surgeries and getting moved around from foster home to foster home, but it wasn't any of that."

He couldn't see her but knew Rose was looking up at him from her pillow. He took a breath and told her the secret he had kept since he was six.

"The thing that scared me the most was when I woke up in the hospital after my surgery. It was night, the room was dark, and I was alone. And I stayed that way for maybe twenty minutes before a nurse came in to do her rounds. But that twenty minutes? It felt like a lifetime times two. Small, hurt, and in the dark without any idea of what my future looked like. I didn't know if I was okay, I didn't know if I was in trouble, and the worst part, I didn't know if anyone cared about me either." James could still feel that terror, those fears that had him frozen in that hospital bed until a nurse came in. "Since then, I have spent every day working on making a life that never puts me in that situation again. Making sure I can one day help other kids never feel that too. And I think I've done a good job of it so far. I can sleep by myself in a dark room and not worry about a thing. But I'm here to tell you something right now, Rose Little."

He rolled onto his side to face her.

He imagined her dark eyes searching him but could only make out her silhouette now.

Even that brought him comfort.

"For the first time in my life, the idea of falling asleep alone bothered me more than waking up by myself. So, if you don't mind, I'd like you to stay with me tonight. At least until I fall asleep, just so I can know you're here. So I can know that you're safe. If that's okay with you."

In the dark Rose Little said four words.

"It's okay with me."

Her hand went beneath the covers and found his. She

interlocked their fingers together and, a few minutes later, she was asleep.

James listened to her even breathing, felt the warmth of her hand in his, and smiled into the darkness.

Finally, he let out that breath he had felt like he'd been holding all day.

Then, he slept.

Chapter Seventeen

Rose had never had a problem falling asleep. She had never felt fear at waking up either. For all her life, she had been fortunate enough to not worry about the before and after of something she had clearly taken for granted.

When she opened her eyes the next morning, Rose felt appreciation for the warmth in her. Because of the warmth next to her.

James Keller was a big, scary man at first glance. Tall and wide and muscled, eyes sharp and clear, words low and often concise. He wore coveralls coated in oil and grime, lived in an isolated old house, and when he wasn't smiling, he looked like he was forever uninterested.

But boy, how different he was to Rose now.

She looked up at the sleeping face resting next to her. She had fallen asleep facing him, hand in his, and now she woke up in the same position. James was on his side, facing her, his arm outstretched and resting softly on her hip while the other was tucked beneath his cheek.

Despite his intimidating appearance, Rose saw the softness in him.

He cared and he was loud with it. He was quiet with it.

He held her, carried her and stayed by her side.

This man whom she had known less than two weeks. This man whom she had continuously endangered.

But had he ever complained?

Had he ever blamed her?

Not even when his family's shop had burned down.

Not when he'd been hurt getting her out of the debris.

And definitely not when he had waited at her side in the hospital to wake up after.

Rose felt her cheeks heat at the memory.

"I have a thing about hospitals," he had told her then. "When I was a kid, I woke up in one alone and it really did a number on me. Now I try to make sure that it doesn't happen to others if I can."

Rose had heard about James's backstory enough to know about the fight that had landed him in the hospital, but that had been it. She hadn't known that he had woken up alone, in the dark, feeling unloved. And that was why he had stayed with her then, a stranger.

He didn't want her to wake up alone.

The warmth in Rose's cheeks spread to her chest. She became less aware of how intimate they were in their closeness and instead focused on how she felt.

A few minutes later, she finally understood.

But when James started to stir, she decided to keep it to herself for a while.

As much as she appreciated the soft and warm, the last twenty-four hours—and honestly, the past several days—were still sitting heavy.

Especially now that she had a safe space to think on it all.

"You know, we could sleep in, and no one would care." James's eyes were still closed but his lips twitched like he wanted to smile.

Rose rolled her eyes on reflex. She eyed the window on the other side of the room.

"Tell that to your lack of blackout curtains," she said. "I may be able to do a lot of things but sleeping in the sun only works for cat naps."

James let out a little laugh and, in sync, the two of them stretched. His arm lifted from her hip, then they both rolled onto their backs like it was a daily routine.

"I've been meaning to get some, but I'm usually up and at the shop by six," he said. "Once I took over the shop's day-to-day I realized it was easier to get some stuff done before it actually opened and before Mr. Donahue showed and got to chatting." He folded his pillow to prop himself up. "Also, to be fair, no one's complained about the lack of curtains, so I keep putting it off."

Rose's eyebrow went up. She was about to ask how many people he had had in his room when the man cleared his throat.

"Which would definitely be because no one has ever stayed in my room before," he clarified before she could ask. "Just in case you were wondering."

Rose held in her smile but didn't comment past that.

"There's nothing to be shy about, Mr. Keller," she teased. "We've all lived a life before now."

What they were doing now felt normal.

What had happened the day before didn't.

Rose doubled back.

"It's Damon and Lloyd's lives now that I don't understand." The tone shifted, and so did they. Rose sat up and James mimicked the move. Whatever warmth they had shared just being in one another's company the night before chilled into calculations.

"Yesterday there was…a lot going on and I don't think

I really talked about how much of it bothered me. I mean the reasoning behind what had happened."

Rose had given Liam, and by extension James since he hadn't left her side once until they had gotten to his house, a play-by-play of everything that had been said and happened once Lloyd appeared on the dock. She had been matter-of-fact with the retelling. Now she was looking at the overall story.

"So, Lloyd came down the dock, Damon threw his gun into the water, and then tied me to the cinder block, all without talking. Lloyd tied Damon to the other one after that. Then Lloyd shot him and walked off. Just like that." It had felt like watching a bizarre movie. One left on mute until the gun went off and the force had pushed Damon's body back into the water. "And, while I have a lot of questions from all of that, Damon allowing himself to be shot is what gets me.

"He talked about being betrayed by someone he loves, but how was he betrayed?" she continued. "He had a gun, he had time, he had drive, and yet, he just gave in. Threw his weapon away, let his feet be tied to concrete, and even let Lloyd help him to the edge of the dock before he was shot. And James, he *smiled* while it happened." She shook her head, unable to shake the image. "With me, Damon was angry. Full of rage. Then, at what he thought would be his death, he accepted it with what felt like happiness?"

She held up another finger, deciding she had enough questions to tick off points.

"Which leads me to the Lloyd of it all. You said he talked about heroes and how he understood now why Damon had been so angry. Then he killed himself? Why? Did he betray Damon? And what exactly *was* the betrayal? Getting me to the dock to try and kill me only for Lloyd to come out and take on Damon instead? If that's true, then why didn't he fight back? Why did Lloyd just leave and do himself in like that? Why—"

Rose had been ticking off her points haphazardly. She had nine fingers up and was going for ten. James interrupted the move.

He took both of her hands in only one of his and pushed all three to the space on the bed between them.

She turned to meet his gaze. Green, brown and her new favorite, gold, took her in as quickly as his hand had.

"Sometimes, we just don't get all of the answers." His voice was deep velvet. Smooth, soft. "And the answers we do get, we might not get all at once."

He squeezed the top of her hands.

"Whatever went down yesterday, it was the end of something so why don't we honor that with starting something new today?"

Despite herself, Rose felt her eyebrow go sky-high.

"Something new?" she asked, mind pausing the merry-go-round of questions she had. "Like what?"

Belatedly, Rose realized just how close they were.

James's lips turned up at the corners.

"Come downstairs and you'll see."

A few minutes later Rose met James in the kitchen. There was coffee made and breakfast in progress. She sat dutifully at the eat-in kitchen table, waiting for their something new to start. James, however, didn't explain and started to talk about a TV show Mr. Donahue had told him about while he finished cooking.

Rose tried to stay on task but found the conversation distracting. When he added his famous stuffed omelets? She forgot to ask again. Later, after they had moved to the couch to watch the show, she thought again about what he'd meant. That question was replaced again by idle chatter between them.

A few hours later, they were walking through the field behind the house, Rose following him as James talked about his goals for fixing up the house. He had some landscaping ideas too for the front of the lot, but he didn't seem keen on ever changing the back. At least not the tall grass they were moving through. He reached down on occasion to touch the grass, like a parent affectionately patting the head of their child.

Around then Rose thought about what he had meant by starting something new.

She ran her hand across the top of the grass and followed him instead.

She didn't ask again.

THREE DAYS WENT by like that.

Simple days that were neither eventful nor boring.

They ate together, watched TV together, went on walks around the property together, and when it was time to sleep, they did that together too.

The first night this happened, they both used excuses of still being wary of everything that had been going on. The second night, those excuses were given with much less enthusiasm. The third night, it felt like habit.

James moved the covers for Rose to get in first—while she talked about whatever throwaway topic they had landed on for that moment—and then got into bed himself once she was settled. He nodded and mmm-hmmed at all the right places while plugging his phone in to charge and Rose put on her hand lotion before handing it over to him. They kept their conversations going until the lights were off, but even after, they carried on for a few more minutes.

They fell asleep without touching, but that never held true for the mornings.

James always had an arm around or on her. Rose always had her face resting on him or against him while wrapped around his arm or leg. Or both, just as she had in the motel room.

And they never talked about it. Even as they detangled in the morning, neither one of them stated the obvious.

Or questioned why they weren't questioning it.

Those three days and nights became routine. Comfortable and safe.

So when Doc Ernest's daughter Lily called her the morning of the fourth day, Rose couldn't help but feel a sense of loss.

"You told me to let you know if Damon Tillman had any visitors, and one finally showed up," Lily said. "She's talking to the doctor right now."

"She?" Rose lowered her voice so James couldn't overhear her from the kitchen. It was his turn to do the dishes.

Lily also lowered her voice.

"Yeah," she said. "And she seems really upset."

Damon had been moved out of the ICU the day before, but as far as Rose knew, he hadn't woken up yet. And he might not. She hadn't gotten any more updates about him or the case since Liam and Blake had left the night they had brought Rose and James back. Rose, however, had reached out to Lily before James had swayed her into taking a break from everything.

Lily's answer had put her right back onto all her questions, all her concerns.

Rose came back to herself with guilt riding shotgun.

That guilt carried her to look into the kitchen.

James looked no less mighty rinsing dishes.

She could stand there, stand in that house, and be with him, and while the rest of the world went about its own business, she could be happy. Be content.

But she wouldn't be Deputy Rose Little.

"If she starts to leave, try and stall her," she told Lily. "I'm on the way."

Chapter Eighteen

The woman was young. She was also very, very sad.

"That's Wynonna Harrison, Lloyd Harrison's little sister," Price whispered at her side. "She came in yesterday to handle everything for Lloyd but is here for Damon today."

Rose and Price were inside Lane Medical lurking in a hallway, watching the young woman fiddle with the vending machine down the hall from Damon's room. An even younger deputy named Cameron was sitting in plain clothes on the bench next to his door. The department was on rotation to keep an eye on the suspect until the case could be officially closed.

"Hospital security is nice but Damon took on one of our own, so the sheriff wanted the department to handle it," Price had told her earlier in the car as they drove from the house to the hospital.

Price had agreed to give her the ride to and from as a favor to their friendship since she wasn't allowed back to work until the next day. Even though she had been resting—something Rose Little never did—he understood better than most that sometimes you had to see something all the way through before you could stop looking at it. That friendship and understanding, though, apparently had limits.

"I have a feeling James wouldn't be too happy about you sneaking away to go see the man who's been trying to kill you," he had said, flatly.

Rose had rolled her eyes.

"I'm not sneaking and I'm not going to see Damon either," she had responded. "I'm going to see the *person* who is seeing Damon. Plus, last I heard Damon hasn't woken up yet."

Price hadn't seemed all that convinced.

"All I'm saying is that I'm not lying to James about where we're going, so I'll stay in the car while you figure it out."

Rose had taken offense to that.

"Who said I have to lie to him? I'm a grown woman. I can go where I want."

She had stayed true to that word. She hadn't lied to James about where she was going. She had simply decided to leave him a note instead.

It wasn't like she *was* doing anything wrong. And she *was* a grown woman after all, but somehow she felt a whole lot of guilt for going. Doubly so that she hadn't asked him to come too.

She had tried to reason with herself that it was because James had already been through so much because of her. He didn't need to do the technical parts like tying up loose ends too.

Was this even a loose end, though?

Rose watched as the young Wynonna bought a drink. After she took the can, she stayed standing right there.

"Hey, why don't you take Cameron to the cafeteria?"

Rose said to Price. "They finished fixing it up already. I'll even give you some cash to throw around."

Price snorted.

"Spot me a ten and we're in business, Little."

She did but Rose knew he wouldn't actually spend it. In all of the years of their friendship, he'd never taken her money. Just her barbs and stubbornness. Rose decided one day she should thank him for being such a good friend. Until then she waited for him to lead Cameron away and then walked over to meet Wynonna before she could go back inside.

Rose could see the red-rimmed eyes, the tiredness. She also saw recognition.

"You're Deputy Little," she said.

Rose gave her a polite smile.

"I am. And you're Wynonna Harrison? Lloyd's sister?"

If there was any resentment or anger or worry about Rose, someone who had been a strange part—but a part nonetheless—in her brother's death, she didn't show in. On the contrary, she also seemed polite.

"I am," she said with a nod. "And I was really hoping to find you. Could we talk?"

They sat in the bench seats next to Damon's door. The room next to it and across the hall were empty and the staff had just finished their rounds. The two women were alone for now.

And they both made quick use of that privacy, starting with Wynonna.

"I've already heard what the sheriff had to say and the detective too, but I'd really like to hear from you what happened the day my brother—" she stopped herself and took a breath before continuing "—the other day. If you don't mind."

Rose didn't.

She told the woman everything that had happened, leaving no details out. There was no way to soften the impact of Lloyd's death, but Rose had seen enough in her career to know that having the whole story could help the loved ones left behind move on.

And Rose wanted that for Wynonna because she obviously had been very close to her brother.

When Rose was done with her retelling of the events she had gone through, the younger Harrison was drying her eyes with a tissue she had pulled from her pocket.

Rose was going to give her some time before starting in with some of the questions she had and was thinking of offering to go get the younger woman something to drink or eat, when Wynonna shook her head.

"This doesn't make sense. None of this makes sense."

Rose's attention snapped back to her like a rubber band.

"What do you mean?" she asked.

Wynonna put her tissue down and angled her body to face Rose more directly. Her brow knitted together as she spoke.

"They said that they think Lloyd killed himself because Damon was threatening him with something but then Lloyd was able to get the upper hand last minute. But Damon would never do that. Not to Lloyd. Just like Lloyd would never do that. Not to Damon."

Rose's confusion must have shown on her expression. Wynonna stopped.

"I'm sorry but why wouldn't Damon hurt Lloyd?" Rose asked. "You make it sound like they were close."

The other woman responded with no space between.

"They were."

Wynonna looked as bewildered by the question as Rose felt about the answer.

"Damon and Lloyd were close?" Rose had to clarify.

Wynonna nodded.

"Since they were kids, or teenagers, really. You didn't know?"

Rose didn't. After Derrick had passed, she had only ever seen Damon and once Damon had started to attack her, the only information they had found about him had been basic. He lived alone, not married, no kids. He was a consultant for a business that Rose had never really paid attention to.

Why would she have?

It had been so cut-and-dried.

Damon blamed her for Derrick's death, and he wanted revenge.

Lloyd had seemed like a simple addition to that plan.

"I had no idea."

Wynonna looked down at her phone. She let out a breath.

"There's actually a pretty big age gap between me and Lloyd," she started. "We weren't actually that close because of it until our mom died. Our dad was a truck driver and never really home, so Lloyd kind of took over as my parent. Then one day our dad just never came home. If that wasn't enough kicks to the teeth, I got really sick when I was twelve. That's the first time I met Damon."

Wynonna ran her thumb over her phone screen. She kept staring down at it, but Rose suspected she was seeing a memory instead.

"They had just graduated high school and instead of going off to college and doing normal things eighteen-year-olds would do, they got jobs at a local restaurant and paid for my treatment. One would work day shift and the other nights and the same went for staying with me." A smile briefly passed over her lips. "A nurse complained once that it always smelled like fried chicken and alcohol in my room."

Wynonna looked up as a couple walked across the end of their hallway. The reality of where they were must have sobered her.

Her head lowered again.

"That's how I grew up, though. From twelve until eighteen I had two brothers, two best friends, two parents. Whatever you want to call them, they were always there. Day in and day out. The big stuff and the little stuff. For seven years I saw Lloyd and Damon every day, and after that, I saw them during breaks from school. Holidays, special events. My college graduation. And if one of them couldn't make it because of work, the other always showed. I was *never* alone because of them. Never. Not once. Their love for me? For each other? For our little family? Has been the best part of my life. And now? Now I'm being told that Damon was betrayed by Lloyd? That Lloyd tried to kill Damon? Then himself because of some unknown reason?"

Tears had started to fall down the woman's cheeks.

They were full of frustration.

"I'll never ever believe that," she said. "And if you had seen them together, you wouldn't either."

Her frustration devolved into sorrow. She pulled more tissues out of her pocket and sobbed into them with palpable feeling.

Rose didn't ask any more questions after that.

For one, no matter what Lloyd had done, his sister mourning him was a separate matter altogether. She deserved peace. Rose wasn't going to beat through that to answer her curiosity.

And secondly, Rose believed she had the answer she had wanted most.

Why had Damon and Lloyd been so gentle with such violent acts? Why had Damon let himself be tied up and then shot without an ounce of fight in him? Why had Lloyd, the one who had seemingly beaten the bad guy, walked away only to end his own life?

The answer was something Rose had never even considered as a possibility.

Love.

That was why Damon had smiled like that, even at what he believed would be his end.

Which meant that their last stands made no sense... unless someone else was forcing their hands.

Normally, Rose would have wondered what could force two men to abandon their plans of revenge and their love for one another so quickly and in complete agreement.

But after hearing Wynonna praise Damon, Lloyd and their little family, and Rose was absolutely certain of the answer now.

It was her.

Someone had threatened Wynonna, their sister, their best friend, their child.

And so they had gladly gone to death.

Rose watched the young woman cry.

She had come to the hospital with questions in hopes of getting answers to help her move on. To put closure between her and Damon Tillman's violent attempts to take her life.

When Rose left later, she left with a new purpose burning a hole through her chest.

She was going to find the third man.

And she was going to make him pay for what he had done.

THE WEATHER WAS done being fickle. The heat and humidity gave way to rain just a half hour before Rose came back. It wasn't a big downpour, but it wasn't a misting either. It would have watered the flowers, had James bought and planted them.

He sat on the front porch, looking out at spots he had been thinking about starting a garden. Never a man with a green thumb, but he thought he'd do fine enough with the simple flowers.

He was sitting there on the front porch, arms crossed over his chest, when Price's cruiser drove down the driveway.

James stood and grabbed the umbrella he had leaned up against the wall next to him. He opened it with purpose; he walked to the passenger's door with frustration.

Rose's gaze was downcast when the door came open. Price called across the seat to him.

"I wanted to get her home before the rain, but it snuck up on us. Looks like it might keep up until tomorrow afternoon. Nothing too bad, though."

James felt his jaw clench but didn't direct his ire at the deputy, especially since he had been the one to give a follow-up call to him once they had gotten to the hospital.

"The more I think about the way she was acting, I'm not so sure Rose told you where we were going," Price had said. "With everything that's been going on, I figured you might be a little more worried than the rest, so I wanted to make sure you knew she was okay."

James had thanked him and they had ended the call. The keys James had had in his hand stayed there until he finally put them back on the hook.

The note James had found on his bed had indeed said she was going to take care of a few things with Price. But that had been it. No other details and, when he had called her, her phone had kept ringing until getting to voicemail.

Price had timed his own call well.

James had been ready to drive out and search for the woman before it had come in.

He had been relieved.

Now he was grumpy.

Rose must have sensed the mood.

"Thanks for the ride, Price," she said, a little louder than what felt like normal. Instead of waiting for a reply she was out of the car and hurrying to the house.

James nodded to Price before easily catching up.

He thought he heard laughing behind him, but James's focus had only one aim now.

When they got to the porch, James lowered the umbrella and shook it out.

Rose was smart. She used the time to escape inside.

Four of her quick steps, though, was a lazy two steps for him.

Rose made it to the living room and only had enough time to turn around and face him, hands up in defense.

"Listen, before you say anything, I know I should have talked to you before I just up and left but—"

She might have been a whole lot smaller than him, but in that moment, her lips were an easy reach.

James felt Rose stiffen against his kiss but he wasn't intending to prolong it.

Not without saying exactly what was on his mind first.

James pulled away but only enough to give space to his words.

"Rose Little, I'm mad at you."

Chapter Nineteen

He held her chin, tilting it up to catch those hazel eyes she had grown so familiar with. That didn't mean they couldn't confuse her from time to time, like now.

Rose blinked up at the giant man who had just interrupted her with a kiss.

"Excuse me?"

James didn't retract his words. Instead, he doubled down.

"I'm mad at you, Rose Little. I'm mad that you left without saying anything and I'm mad that you didn't answer my call. I mean, even Deputy Collins felt like I deserve some kind of check-in to know you're okay after everything you've been through. That we've been through. I know you're Wildcard Rose but sometimes I think you use that as a pass to run headlong into danger and it's okay." He shook his head, truly looking the part of a man angry at having been left in the dark.

Rose started to say something—she wasn't sure what—when he continued.

"And that's what I thought I was mad about before you got here. You, being you, running into the unknown swinging. But then I saw you and I realized I'm really just mad at me. I'm mad I didn't give you a good reason for you to take me with you. So I'm going to make sure I give it now."

That frown didn't lessen but his words seemed to soften.

"I like you, Rose Little," he said. "I want to be with you whether we're eating breakfast, talking about TV, or surviving explosions in service pits. I don't need you to stop being Wildcard Rose. I just want to be by your side when you're doing it. I want to help you, I want to fight for you and with you. I want to do the hard stuff and the boring stuff. I want to finally tell Mr. Donahue I officially can't date his daughter because some loud woman one day pulled up into my garage without an appointment and then told me she couldn't just leave me alone."

He finally smiled.

"I want your good news and your bad news, Rose Little. I want your chaos and your calm. I want—"

The man sure was talkative. That was what Rose was thinking when the last vestige of her self-control finally snapped.

It was her turn to do the interrupting and interrupting she sure did.

Rose threw her arms around James's neck and fastened the two of them together. She started with their lips and then folded against him with every curve and surface of her body that she could.

If James was mad at the cutoff, he certainly didn't stay that way.

His tongue was hungry, and it parted her lips in unison with his hands running down her sides. It was light work after that.

James cupped her backside in his hands and had her airborne in a second flat. Like they had rehearsed the move, Rose wrapped her legs around his waist, all without breaking their kiss.

If anything, the new position made the pace even more frenzied.

James made surprisingly quick work of getting them from the living room to the second-floor bedroom in one heavy-breathing journey. And he did so in a way that only stoked the fire within Rose higher.

He had her horizontal two steps inside of the bedroom, careful to cushion her body from the drop down.

Sadly, the move ended their kiss.

Luckily, it gave him the space to do something even more riveting.

James Keller was already a handsome, good-looking man, but the second he rid himself of his clothes, Rose knew something else to be just as true.

His height wasn't the only big thing about him.

Rose couldn't help but stare a little longer than she originally meant to. James noticed and let out a laugh.

"I've got good news and I've got bad news," he said, his fingers working the last of her clothes down her legs.

Rose struggled to keep her composure as cold air started to hit all the right spots.

"What—what is it?"

James didn't smile. He smirked.

"Good news is, I'm about to spend a good amount of time with you in this bed, Deputy." To emphasize his plans, he brought his naked body flush with hers and moved his fingers down between her legs.

Rose gasped in surprise and felt her breathing quicken from a new kind of pleasure.

James's gaze went from hers and then down to her lips.

He pushed deep inside of her and watched as her mouth opened in appreciation.

Then he laughed again.

"Do you want to know the bad news?"

He picked up the pace and all Rose could do was manage a nod.

Still, he didn't answer right away. At least not with words.

He hit the right spot and worked it until Rose's body bucked up against him in a dazzling twist of release. It wasn't until he captured her mouth in his and devoured her a little longer there, that he moved himself to the part of Rose that wanted him most.

His words weren't warm or soft. They weren't gentle or quiet.

They were hot and they were ready.

"The bad news is, I do believe you might be sore in the morning."

Without any more teasing or talking, he thrust inside of her with a nearly overwhelming force.

Nearly.

Rose took him in with a moan that would have made her grateful that house was empty.

That moan was one of many that afternoon as his good news really did pan out. They stayed tangled in his sheets until the sun started to set. Once they had exhausted themselves and Rose lay there trying to catch her breath back, she already knew he would be right about the bad news.

Though, to her, what she had just done with James could never be counted as bad.

A belief she took into that night when round two started up in the shower.

By the time they had found themselves truly, truly exhausted and back in bed, Rose didn't have the stamina or focus to remember what it was she wanted to talk about with James before this all had started.

Maybe if she had, what happened next might have gone a whole lot differently.

JAMES ADDED A set of blackout curtains to his online shopping cart the second after he woke up the next morning. The sun wasn't completely out—the rain was being lazy in its walk across Seven Roads—but there was enough of it to make Rose start stirring from her own sleep.

James hovered his hands over her eyes, cutting off a beam that was particularly precise, but it wasn't enough to keep her in her dreams.

Rose's eyes fluttered opened a minute or two into his attempt. When she saw his hand, though, she only laughed.

"Not even the mighty James Keller can compete with the morning sun."

James felt the vibration of her stretching out her legs before that vibration ran up to her arms. She didn't go for the normal starfish pose since she, as per her usual habits over the last several days, was already wrapped tightly around his bicep.

She shook him lightly, then became nosy about his phone.

"Don't tell me you're the kind of man who shops online all of the time, even in bed."

James snorted.

"Only when I'm buying the necessities," he countered. He held his phone closer so she could see it more clearly.

"I *am* the kind of man to be generous, though. Need me to get anything for you? Say the word."

Rose rubbed her forehead against his arm as she shook her head.

"I'm pretty happy with what I have already, thanks."

James wasn't sure if that was a nod to him, but he felt the warmth of it anyways. Confessing his feelings to the deputy the day before had been a spur-of-the-moment decision made from a spur-of-the-moment realization. But he didn't regret it. He certainly didn't regret what had come after either.

Now, however, he was realizing that Rose hadn't returned those feelings. At least not in words.

But who was he to nitpick?

Surely she felt enough of something for him to do what they had done multiple times the day before. He didn't need the words.

At least not now.

"I'm starting to think you're a pretty relaxed woman. At least, when not on the clock. Then again, I still have never seen someone as calm as you when you were staring down at a seat covering a bomb."

James regretted the mention as soon as he said it. He didn't want to remind Rose of the close calls they had encountered, not when the last week had been so kind to them, but he felt her tense and knew it was already too late. The damage was done, and the damage was Rose pulling away from him.

"I'm sorry," he hurried. "I didn't mean to bring any of that stuff up. It's just one of those once-in-a-lifetime things I can't believe happened."

She shook her head.

"It's not that. I just realized I haven't told you what I found out yesterday."

And that was when James learned about Wynonna Harrison and her brother's past with Damon.

"Before I left, Wynonna told me that even though Damon helped raise her with Lloyd, Derrick only visited on occasion," she added at the end of the retelling. "Derrick and Lloyd were friendly but not at all like Damon and Lloyd. They *were* close enough, though, that when there was a position open after Lloyd was hired into Camden Pharmaceuticals, he reached out to Derrick, who was looking for a job. That's how the two of them came to be on that bus five months ago while Damon wasn't around."

"And no one knew about Lloyd's relationship with Derrick's brother?"

Rose said no.

"I'm guessing they probably wanted to avoid any conflicts at work or about how Derrick got the job. Though I guess I don't know for sure. Just like I'm still not sure why the two of them were fighting on the bus, especially during a tornado." Rose's face scrunched up. "Or why Derrick would look so hateful at a man that his brother obviously loved very much."

She fell into a silence while she probably was thinking about the possibilities.

James, on the other hand, realized he had reason to apologize now.

"At the time I thought keeping it quiet was the right play but I'm not sure that's the case anymore." Rose's eyes widened. "I'm sorry I should have told you this sooner."

It was James's turn to recount a conversation. His was all about Lloyd, up in that second-story room before he had taken his own life.

Rose wasn't angry at his omission. She seemed to be enthused by it.

"The day Derrick died he stopped calling Damon a hero," she paraphrased. "It wasn't my fault that Derrick died. It was the storm… The generator."

Rose rocketed upright.

It was so sudden James sat up next.

She turned to him and spoke fast and with her hands too.

"The generator. The damned generator. It was supposed to be the top-of-the-line and kick on no matter what. But it didn't that day. That's why they got on the shuttle in the first place. 'One single point of failure' that messed up everything."

James started to pick up what she was putting down.

"Lloyd was doing something and the power going out messed it up. That means he was probably doing something he shouldn't have at the research annex? And Derrick found out?"

"Something that must have included Damon and *that's* why he was so mad at Lloyd," Rose jumped in. "That's why he stopped calling Damon a hero."

Rose didn't wait to finish the conversation. She was scurrying out of bed in her underthings, quickly searching out a fresh pair of clothes.

James followed suit, though he didn't know exactly what they were going to do next.

Rose continued once she had a pair of jeans in hand.

"If Damon and Lloyd were working together to do something illegal at the drug trial, then them turning on one another like that would make sense, if they *both* hadn't been ready to die." She pointed at him, jeans waving through the air in the process. "*But* what if there was a third person in on it? Someone who knew enough to know where to hurt them."

James found a shirt and tugged it on, heart starting to beat a little bit faster. Her excitement at a possible breakthrough was oddly contagious.

"But why get you there for the end of it?" he asked. "Or do you think Damon just got interrupted during his revenge plot against you?"

Rose did a combo between a headshake and a shrug.

"I'm not sure but maybe Wynonna has more information about Lloyd's time at Camden," she said. "Maybe she can remember something that we can—"

Rose stopped herself as her phone started to vibrate on the nightstand.

She hurried over and made a little noise after she scanned the new alert.

"It's a text from Cameron… Oh my God."

"What?"

James was at her side in a flash, as if he could somehow fight the phone if needed.

It wasn't good news and it wasn't bad news.

But it was shocking news.

"Damon Tillman is awake."

Chapter Twenty

There was still one thing that was bothering Rose, and for the life of her, she couldn't catch the thought. It bothered her like a small pebble caught in her shoe. No matter how many times she tried to shake it out, it stayed.

It rubbed.

It annoyed.

She felt James's gaze fall on her. After the elevator doors closed behind them, he finally asked if she was okay.

Rose couldn't decide, so she did a half shrug and head tilt.

"I'm not sure," she admitted. "There's…something I'm forgetting? But I'm not even sure where there's space to have forgotten something. We've gone over every question with an answer now or at least a confirmation that we still need an answer. Nothing has been left undone, right?"

She faced him full-on and took a tiny step forward. It put her close enough that she had to crane her head back to look up at him while he tilted his forward to look down at her.

If she hadn't been so focused on trying to solve her

problem, she thought she might blush at the closeness. Especially since James had been right—she *was* sore from their previous trysts between the sheets.

As it was, she gave him the most serious of expressions to know she meant business.

"Or *do* we have any other outlying questions? Things we were trying to answer before what happened out at the cemetery?"

James turned thoughtful.

"The only other thing I was wondering about was how much trouble was I going to get into for basically stealing a car from someone at this very same hospital last week." He shrugged. "But the car wasn't damaged and the sheriff sweet-talked that guy into forgiving me since he knew him. So that's that for me."

Rose stifled a smile, despite herself.

The man whose car James had taken was bingo buddies with Liam's newest father-in-law. Rose still was waiting for the time to ask him about how *that* conversation had gone. She bet Blake had also gotten a good kick out of it.

But Rose was still feeling *bothered*.

The elevator arrived at its destination. The doors slid open but Rose didn't move from her spot yet.

"There's *something*," she reiterated. "And it's really bugging me."

James reached down and put a thumb between her eyebrows. He pressed the crinkled skin there, gently.

"Don't worry, Little," he said. "I believe in you. You'll get there."

It was a simple pep talk but it did the trick. Rose decided to try and shake off the feeling and come back to it later when she had the mental space for it. In her experience not every detail always shook out. Sometimes you had to eventually just walk away.

Or sometimes the thing that's bothering you walks into your elevator.

No sooner had the doors slid open than a man nearly bowled her over.

Her reflexes were normally spitfire-fast, but James beat her this time. His large hand wrapped easily around her hip before tugging her back. She thudded softly against his chest, a wall of muscle she now knew in the most intimate of senses.

"Excuse me," the newcomer offered. He kept his face on the control panel but offered a lackluster nod in their direction. Rose narrowed her eyes at him while James told him it was no problem.

That was when she saw the cast on his arm.

The rest of the details synced up.

Rose knew this person. At least enough to recognize him.

It was the reporter.

The man she had met the day of the explosion. Why had she never learned his name?

He didn't make eye contact. Rose was grateful for it. The last thing she needed was to have to deal with the media at the moment. A member of the media who obviously had a distaste for her based on their last interaction.

James pushed her forward before the doors could close. Rose allowed it, eyes still narrowed. That bothered feeling stayed as they walked away and down the hallway toward Damon's room.

She had bigger fish to fry, after all. With Damon being awake they could hopefully get some answers and find a new direction to go in to find who had actually been pulling the strings.

But nothing had been that simple so far and that theme continued on.

Deputy Cameron wasn't sitting outside.

No one from the department was.

Wynonna also wasn't there. Not at the bench and not in front of the vending machines.

"The vending machines."

Rose stopped. That piece that had been missing. That pebble in her shoe.

The dang vending machines.

James's eyebrow rose.

"The day that man came in and attacked me in the bathroom… We couldn't figure out how anyone even knew I was with you. We figured if anyone from our trusted circle told, it was an accident. Or maybe someone from the hospital saw us leaving together or someone saw us in the car. But there *was* one person I know for sure who saw us together that day."

She looked over her shoulder in the direction of the elevators.

"The reporter who was talking to me next to the vending machines," she clarified. "The one you told me not to talk to again because you didn't like him."

Adrenaline surged within her. Along with a feeling of stupidity.

"The first time I met him was the morning before the explosion on the way to my car, then the next day here… He even called me an action hero. What if *he's* the third person?" Rose's eyes widened as she turned back to James. A more sobering worry hit her. "And if he is, then where did he just come from?"

Rose didn't wait for an answer. Instead, she threw open Damon's hospital room door.

The scene inside only confirmed her new theory.

"Oh my God, James, call for help!"

The missing Deputy Cameron was lying on the ground, blood pooling around him. The hospital bed next to him was empty. Rose, having learned her lesson over the last few attacks, did something she hadn't yet done around James.

She pulled out her service weapon.

Then she was running back down the hallway.

"Sheriff's deputy down in Room 214," she yelled out to the nurses' desk as they came up to it. Someone screamed at the sight of her gun but Rose yelled off the rest of her instructions. "Suspect just left. Shut the hospital down, now!"

Then Rose really kicked it into gear.

She slammed open the door to the stairs and hoped the elevators were as slow as usual.

James didn't complain and instead ran down the two flights of stairs ahead of her. He hit the exit for the first-floor door before Rose even saw it. Which meant when she made it out to see the front of the elevators, she was already late to the fight.

The reporter pulled a gun up just as James swung around to grab her waist.

Rose could have flinched, ducked, dropped her weight and let James do the rest, but there was more than one reason that she wore the nickname Wildcard so well.

She actually had some skill to back it up.

James put his arm around her and pulled her along with him to the corner of the hallway. Rose let it happen but she didn't turn around. Instead, she had her gun up and aimed.

Rose might have been known for running into danger without a plan but people often left out the part where, once she was in a situation, she didn't back down. If her boots made any noise as they slid across the floor, she didn't hear it.

The gunshot she let off was just too loud.

The reporter bellowed out in pain as her hit landed. The force and surprise must have offset his trigger finger to fire late. James was able to pull her the rest of the way around the corner before he could get a shot off.

The glass windows over the side parking lot exit shattered in response to the miss. Screams sounded in the distance. Someone cut in on the overhead announcement system, but Rose wasn't paying attention to anything else.

She stepped out of James's hold and yelled out to the reporter.

"Sheriff's department, throw your weapon away or—"

He apparently wasn't having it.

James cut her off.

"Listen! He's running!"

Rose quieted in time to hear a heavy bang. It wasn't a gunshot this time.

"He ran back into the stairwell!"

Rose led the charge to the door they had just come from and kicked it open. No shots or attack came their way.

There was blood, however. A trail ran up the stairs, dotting the concrete and giving them the direction they needed.

Rose peeked out between the floors and looked up.

There was a small space between the railings. She could see all the way to the top floor.

The reporter wasn't waiting to catch sight of her and shoot. He was climbing up without stopping.

Rose didn't have a clear shot of him.

Which meant they chase was still on.

"Be careful," James ground out, but Rose was already running.

THE RAIN HAD slacked off, but the roof was still freshly wet.

Rose burst out from the stairwell and nearly fell because of it.

James was at her elbow and caught her quickly by the back of her shirt. Like in the hallway downstairs, the change in gravity didn't stop her. The instant her momentum swung back, she was on the man's heels, yelling again for him to drop his weapon.

This time he didn't turn and shoot. He also didn't stop.

The roof that they were on was one of three different heights along the hospital's main building. Right now they were on the middle height. It led to another roof that was a floor lower.

For a second, James thought the man would jump off their roof for the one below. It wouldn't be a fatal fall but there was no way it wouldn't hurt. It would also be hard for them to reach him without finding a ladder or going back inside to get to the stairwell that serviced the middle building.

He could try the escape, but it would cost him. And judging by the drops of blood they had been passing on the way there, he was already paying the price from Rose's earlier hit.

The man must have run the risk himself. He stopped near the edge of the roof.

Rose yelled out again for him to drop his weapon.

He didn't, but he did lower it to his side.

"Be careful," James urged again.

Rose kept her aim on the man and stalked forward, slowly walking at an angle as she went, as if making a half circle behind him. If he turned around to shoot, he would waste time adjusting his aim because of it. James followed her, trying to stay as quiet as possible while also staying close enough to Rose in case he needed to act.

Rose continued to watch the man. James eyed his gun.

"You're hurt," Rose said, voice carrying with authority across the shrinking distance. "Put the gun down and we can take you back inside for medical treatment."

The man barked out a laugh.

His words carried with just as much ease.

"You know, I called him an idiot."

James and Rose had made an arc around the man so now they stopped at the edge of the roof as well, just with several feet between them. The man stayed facing the edge, his profile showed his gun at his side and blood dripping down the same arm. Even though he had laughed, there was no smile there now.

"Who?" Rose asked.

"Damon Tillman. The man who was supposed to kill you but apparently didn't." The man laughed again. "I understood why he wanted to kill you, even if I thought it was a waste of time, but the way he *wanted* to kill you? Making a fool of *you* by showing everyone that the little action star could die as fantastically as the way you saved everyone else. I *laughed* at him for that. I really did. It was such a waste of time, such a waste of resources and money. And yet..." He sighed. "Now I wouldn't mind something grand to take you out too."

James balled his fist.

He didn't move, though.

He was acutely aware of Rose's body language.

James hadn't lied to her the night before. He didn't want her to stop being Wildcard Rose. He didn't need that from her or for her. She was who she was.

James didn't need her to give up anything to make space for him.

He was already at her side, ready.

And he wanted it to always be like that.

Especially in the tough spots.

So James stayed his steps and waited for her move. The second she did was the second before he did too.

"You're talking like you didn't have any part in the attacks against me," she called out. "I find that hard to believe."

The man didn't bother even looking their way.

"Why would I take revenge on you?" he asked. "Revenge costs money, patience. Emotional torment. It's a waste. I don't even get out of bed unless I'm getting paid to do it and you think I'm going to budget men with guns and car bombs?"

He shook his head.

"Love is nice but money? Money is life."

He lowered his head.

A breeze swept through. Rose's hair moved with it. The woman, however, was as still as a statue.

"Then why did you get involved with Damon and Lloyd and Camden Pharmaceuticals?" Rose tried. "If you thought what Damon was doing was ridiculous, why do you need to come here and deal with him at all?"

She was giving out details they hadn't yet confirmed. And the man didn't hesitate to answer.

"Because I thought they understood that money is always the goal. That love doesn't pay the bills. It doesn't fix the broken air conditioner or pay for college. They understood how expensive the world is… But that didn't stop Damon from letting his love for his brother fester into guilt and anger. That didn't stop Lloyd from letting his love for his sister become some self-imposed sacrifice. And that didn't stop them from deciding to keep you alive when their death and yours would have kept me from killing Miss Harrison as a consequence."

He lifted his head again but still didn't look their way. He coughed before continuing. James saw blood come out. Rose had done more damage than James had thought.

"I don't understand any of you," he continued. "Damon spends a fortune trying to kill you, but in the end, he spares you. And now you're here, trying to get me, someone who never hated you, in some—what?—kind of sympathy for him? For Lloyd?"

Rose didn't answer. Instead she asked an important question, belatedly.

"Who are you?"

The man laughed one more time.

Rose shifted just a little at the noise.

"Someone who has a question."

Rose slid one foot back ever so slightly.

James realized she was shoring up her stance.

He waited, tense.

The man didn't wait for her reply.

He sighed out long. James could see blood from his mouth even in profile.

"Would you let me go if I offered you two money?

More than you'll probably ever make in this lifetime? Would you walk away then?"

James watched as Rose moved her finger from next to the trigger to on top of it.

He reached out and placed a hand on her hip.

"No," she answered. "I won't let you get away with what you did to them. To Damon and Lloyd. To their family. Not for any price."

The man turned, gaze finally landing on hers.

He looked genuinely confused.

"Damon wants you dead and you're still trying to help him," he said. "Why?"

Rose answered him coolly. James realized later that she must have known already that it would be the last words she'd say to the man.

Her words were soft yet strong.

"Because it's what heroes do."

The man raised his gun, aiming right at them.

James didn't move a muscle.

Rose did.

The man never got a shot off.

Wildcard Rose had already pulled her trigger.

Chapter Twenty-One

Everyone thought Damon had fled the hospital, but to their utter surprise, he had only gone as far as the next room. Wynonna apologized profusely on his behalf.

"I saw that man in the lobby when I was downstairs," she told Rose, describing the reporter to a tee. "I recognized him. I never knew his name but he visited the house around the time Derrick passed away. Him and Lloyd got into a big yelling match. I never heard what they said but I remembered Damon left with him. It was actually the last time I saw Damon until now."

After seeing him, Wynonna had pieced together the same conclusion Rose had. Someone else had to have been pressuring her brother and Damon. She hadn't known all of the facts but that feeling, coupled with impressive speed, had gotten her to take Damon to the only safety she could reach. Deputy Cameron had come in during the brief moment between her coming in and the reporter showing up. He too had gotten a bad feeling from the man, and when Cameron had asked to see his hands, the reporter had attacked. Cameron hadn't been shot but knocked around good enough that he'd gotten a broken nose and a concussion.

Not too bad considering the man who had attacked him had died on the roof no more than ten minutes later.

That man remained nameless for one more week until finally Damon was able to talk.

And talk he did. To Rose first, of all people.

"His name was Paul Martinez. He hired me and Lloyd to copy and then disrupt the Camden Pharmaceuticals drug trial data. Paul was getting paid by Camden's competitors and was paying us a lot to help. We needed the money to clear some debt and, since the drug only treats insomnia, we decided it was the lesser of evils if we botched it instead of some of the other Camden drugs that help treat sicknesses." Damon had quieted. Rose had given him the space to get to the hard part of his confession. "The day of the storm, the generator didn't work, and the backup power cycled wrong. Instead of everything being shut down, they actually got some of the power back for the computers before they left on the bus. Lloyd said that's how Derrick saw the encrypted message he had been trying to send out before. It was highly incriminating for Lloyd. And me."

His eyes had grown red at that.

"Derrick was always smart, but I don't know why he chose to confront Lloyd on the bus. Not when it was already dangerous. Maybe…maybe he was really upset and afraid and it just came out. But no matter the reason why, he confronted Lloyd on the bus. And well, you were the only person who saw what happened next."

Damon had said that was when their faux reporter Paul had stepped in.

"Lloyd said that there was no way you heard what they were fighting about, but Paul was never one to let his money be in danger. He thought you might know something and when he saw how angry I was at you… he played on that anger to try and get you out of the way. Just like us, who had made too much trouble in his book. He wanted all three of us to go out at once. And what better way to have that happen without anyone looking too deep into it?"

"Your revenge against me," Rose had guessed.

Damon had nodded.

"When he realized I couldn't get you myself, he told us how to stage our deaths and, if we didn't listen, he threatened Wynonna."

Paul had given Damon and Lloyd proof that men were watching the young woman. Men they couldn't protect her from.

It had scared them enough to accept their final scene together.

The betrayal Damon had told Rose about referred to Paul's betrayal of them, not Lloyd's betrayal of him.

"No matter what we went through in this life, we never turned on each other," Damon had said, choking up a bit as he did so. "Lloyd was my person and Wynonna was *our* person. Even when we didn't agree with each other's decisions, we never lost sight of each other."

That was why they had accepted what they believed to be their only option left.

Their lives for Wynonna's.

But to Damon's surprise, when it came to killing Rose in the end, both men had decided, without even speaking, to give her a fighting chance.

Damon was good at tying knots but had left hers loose in case Lloyd had thrown her in. Lloyd had watched Damon go over the edge of the dock but had left Rose alone.

"I think Paul would have left you alone had we both died, especially if you didn't go after him or bring up anything about Camden. But you saved me."

Damon had looked at her then with an expression that she couldn't decipher.

Unlike Paul, he didn't ask her why.

Rose had been glad for that. She decided she was over talking about heroes.

Everyone involved had simply made choices.

Some hadn't worked out, some had.

MONTHS LATER AT Damon's trial, Rose would speak on his behalf for a lighter prison sentence. Wynonna would thank her after.

"I know it's not the same as Lloyd being there, but no matter what happens, I'm going to make sure Damon is never alone. Just like he did for me and my brother."

Rose didn't know Lloyd well, but she imagined he would have been proud of Wynonna's decision.

During all the trial and its aftermath, the drug trial at the research annex would be shut down for an extensive investigation that would reach into Camden Pharmaceuticals and its competitors, finding two more cases of attempted tampering with other trials elsewhere. Rose would keep up with the public updates but eventually would decide to stop after a while. Paul was gone, Damon and Wynonna were trying to heal, and Rose had finally shaken the press's fascination with her.

They had all done their parts and it was time to move on.

And move on they did.

Once the investigation closed, the insurance people finally got everything they needed for James and his father. Keller Auto was rebuilt and had a grand opening party that nearly the entire town of Seven Roads attended. The sheriff's department was the most vocal about their excitement. Mainly because, like Rose, most of the staff had fallen for the only mechanic in town.

James had been a sight and a half, standing next to the old service pit they had jumped into, with a smile on his face and a baby in his arms.

"And *this* is where Rose Little fell for me," he joked.

"Didn't you technically fall after *her*?" Price teased, his daughter Winnie punching him in the arm as a warning to behave himself. He kept on with a laugh. "You know, *after* she pulled you off a bomb?"

James waved his free hand through the air, careful to not jostle the newest member of the McCoy County Sheriff's Department family. Her father, the sheriff, was standing near them holding the hand of his other daughter while Blake held on to their son. They laughed along with Rose's parents as they had come in.

While they had wished Rose would have had a less dangerous experience while meeting a man she liked, they couldn't argue with the results. Her father had also taken a liking to Mr. Keller, both men prone to walking around the shop when they were in town and chatting about who-knew-what. Mr. Donahue, one of James's favorite people she realized quickly despite James pretending that he didn't like the man's constant chatting, was also there and more than ready to mingle.

And when Rose and James were married, he even cried.

But before all of that moving on happened, James had taken Rose home from the hospital that night and then to bed.

They were tired, through and through, but somewhere and sometime between the sheets, James held her close and sighed out long.

"I have another good news, bad news thing but I think it might make me sound a little needy," he said, all soft and warm.

The lights were off but Rose still glanced up at him from her spot resting against his chest. She had already gotten used to this position, it making her fall asleep faster than anything else. But now she made sure to fight that urge.

"Bad news first this time," she decided. "I'd like to end today on a good note if we can."

She felt him nod.

"Bad news, I realized today that you didn't actually say if you liked me too," James said. "I mean I said it and then we had a great time and all after, but who knows, that might be Rose Little speak for I like you all right but not *that* much."

Rose struggled to keep a laugh in her chest and out of her next words.

"Ah, and the good news?"

"The good news is, even if you don't like me, I have all of this free time until the new shop is up and operating, so getting you to fall for me should be a piece of cake."

Rose lost it at that. She laughed against him until he was laughing with her too.

He started to stroke her back when they finished. Knowing him, that could have been the end of the conversation, at least that night.

But Rose decided to tease him because there was just something about James Keller that made her feel comfortable, safe, and loved enough to do so, even with such an important topic.

"How about I make you a deal?" she said. "You buy me some blackout curtains so I can sleep in on my off days, and I'll like, love, and stay with you for as long as you want?"

Rose's head bounced up and down a little as James let out a hoot of laughter.

"What?" she asked, worried the joke had been too much.

James kept going. Only after a moment did he get his words out.

"If that's all it takes, then I can't wait for you to see what's supposed to be delivered tomorrow."

Sure enough, the next day just after lunch a package came in.

It was the set of blackout curtains James had already bought two days prior.

A month later, Rose officially moved in. Five months after that they were married in the field behind the house.

James would go on to confuse everyone in attendance when he credited their entire love to a set of curtains.

Rose, however, would absolutely smile.

* * * * *

COLTON'S BLIZZARD GUARDIAN

KATHERINE GARBERA

For Sandy Harding, agent extraordinaire who goes above and beyond for me and always has my back!

Chapter One

It was blustery and cold when Ava Colton got out of her car and hurried toward the Baldwin Memorial Hospital. The white stone-and-concrete building was large and housed multiple wings. It was one of the top teaching hospitals in the state. Didn't matter that she'd been listening to beach music and dreaming of a getaway to anywhere sunny and warm. Winter always hit her extra hard in February.

She liked it in January, when the first snowfalls of winter meant she could spend time snowshoeing and cross-country skiing. But come February…things got tougher. Which really wasn't all that bad considering her latest patient's recent experiences. Fern Hensley had been rescued from a makeshift cabin after being roughed up and drugged, and now the woman was struggling to deal with the trauma of being kidnapped and left in that cabin for dead.

As a psychologist, Ava was working with Fern trying to help the other woman process everything that had happened to her. Not that it was ever easy to move on from trauma. Something Ava was intimately familiar with. She'd been stalked by an ex-boyfriend in college, and while she'd never been kidnapped or beaten, she knew what it was like to lose her sense of safety.

Walking in through the main atrium, Ava always found herself admiring the large rock formations that were designed as seating for hospital visitors and the abundance of Native American sculptures and art decorating the space. Her cousin Sassy probably knew most of the artists by name.

She smiled her hellos to the staff on duty as she walked into the hospital and down the corridor that led to her office. The doctor who'd been seeing Fern usually left some notes on her current condition. The woman had been in the hospital for four days. Her recovery was no doubt hampered by fear and uncertainty.

It was hard not to let rage build if she thought too long about what had been done to Fern, her protective instincts flaring. Instead of giving into her rage she focused all of her energy on helping Fern heal. That was her mission—to give Fern the tools she needed to heal mentally from everything that had happened to her.

"Morning, Ava," Darla said. The other woman was in her mid-thirties, with short blond hair. She had a rounded face and easy smile.

Darla was her rock. She ran the psychiatric department and had been here for almost fifteen years. She was very organized but also a good listener. Currently they were both binge-watching a current reality television show where ordinary people are taken out of their everyday lives to compete with each other. As a psychologist she loved watching the way people reacted to everything and how the slightest change in behavior often made everyone suspicious of them in the castle.

"Did you watch our show last night?" Darla asked.

"No. Went to my parents' for dinner. I'll catch up at lunch so we can dish later," Ava said. She planned to keep her office door firmly closed when she was in it, which meant she'd stream the episode on her phone. Chay Benally a tall Navajo man with dark brown eyes and black hair kept stopping by her office trying to get her to give him information from Fern. She had nothing to tell him that wasn't in the police report. Her patient either didn't remember or simply didn't want to talk about what had happened to her.

"Looking forward to it," Darla said as her phone rang.

Ava went into her office, closing the door behind her. Shrugging out of her coat, she hung it on the hook on the back of the door and then walked around to her desk to turn on her laptop. She saw the photo of her and her cousins that had been taken last summer and smiled as she always did. Their family was large and the faces were all smiling a mix of Caucasian and Navajo. Thanks to her Aunt Bly.

Fern didn't smile, exactly, when Ava walked into her room, but the other woman did nod at her. She was starting her recovery, but it was going to be a long trip. Ava always let her patients set the tone for the sessions. It helped to build rapport.

"How are you doing today?" Ava asked.

Fern was twenty-five and had long brown hair, which she'd braided and left to lie against the hospital bedsheets. Her hazel eyes were direct, but her smile never reached her eyes. From her records Ava knew she was a medical coder, so she had to have some knowledge of what was going on with her situation.

She never discussed it. In fact, she really hadn't discussed much yet. She answered questions in short answers—mainly yes or no. But Ava was determined to get her talking…she might not be chatty, but the other woman had been found near the edge of the Navajo Nation. After a fire broke out in the makeshift cabin where she'd been held by two men who'd kidnapped her while she'd been walking to her car in downtown Oso a few blocks from the doctor's office where she'd worked.

Oso was a town more than one hundred miles from Dark Canyon. Fern had been given injections of a drug that kept her knocked out while she was held captive. The men had been coming daily to feed her and take care of the generator but then suddenly stopped coming.

"Feeling a bit better," she admitted. But her leg had been severely broken—her physical recovery was going to be just as serious as her mental one.

"Being somewhere safe will do that for you," Ava said. Remembering when she'd been stalked by a guy she'd been casually dating. There was nothing like that feeling of insecurity to really wreak havoc on every detail of daily life.

"Yeah."

"So, we left off on when you woke up alone in the cabin…"

"Yup."

"Do you want to talk about it?"

"Not really," she said.

"What would you like to discuss?" Ava asked her.

Fern shrugged.

"The cops were in here with a baby… I think they thought she was mine," Fern offered. She looked fragile and like her spirit had been broken.

"Do you have a child?" Ava asked.

"No," Fern said, shaking her head. "Definitely not. I can't take care of me…"

"I get that," Ava said. "Do you want to talk about the baby?"

"Not really. I mean, I probably should say yes then we could talk about that…but no."

"It's okay. You're in control here—we can talk about anything."

"Anything?" Fern asked.

"Sure. Like, how do you feel about cowboys? I like a man who knows how to wear a pair of jeans."

Fern relaxed against the pillows of her hospital bed. Moving to cross her arms over her body before realizing that she was connected to the IV. "I do too. Can't help that."

Ave stayed with Fern for another twenty minutes until she faked falling asleep. Ava sighed quietly and left. Having struggled with grief after the death of her fiancé, she was very aware of the different techniques that could be used to get people to leave you alone. So, she didn't press Fern. Her patient needed time, and Ava understood that better than anyone.

As Ava was heading back to her office, Marg Lesser stopped her. "Hey, Ava, are you available to foster for a few days? We have a baby girl—still trying to figure out who she is exactly."

"Yes. I can take her," Ava said. She'd been fostering for the last year or so. At twenty-nine, she was settled in a way that she hadn't anticipated. But her life was good. She liked her house and her job and her family. Her community needed her, and her work was fulfilling. But she had always dreamed of being a mom, something that she wasn't too sure was still in the cards for her after Greg's death. Fostering satisfied that need in her, and the children and babies she fostered needed to be loved. And Ava had a lot of love to give.

"I'll stop by your office after my shift," Ava said.

"Thanks."

CHAYTON BENALLY DIDN'T really love coming into Dark Canyon. He had enough work to keep him busy on the Navajo Nation as a Tribal Police officer. He'd been an officer for almost five years. He'd gone to Salt Lake when he was eighteen just to get away and joined the police department there. But he'd missed home, and his grandmother wanted him to move back. So he'd applied at the tribal police…and he found he was more content.

His usual routine of patrolling and filing reports had been interrupted by the discovery of a woman near the border of the Navajo Nation. Ava Colton's younger brother Ryan had been on duty and was the firefighter who rescued Fern.

The fact that she was so close to the Nation raised a few questions for Chay. However, he hadn't wanted to add to the trauma the woman had already experienced, so when he came to the hospital, he'd tried to speak to the psychologist who was working with her. *Ava Colton.*

Damn if she wasn't one of the stubbornest women he'd ever crossed paths with. Stonewalling every question he asked and now dodging him while he waited outside her office for her return.

He caught a glimpse of the tall, athletic woman at the same moment that she spotted him. Ava did a one-eighty—heading back into a corridor of the hospital he wasn't allowed to enter. Her assistant, frustratingly, hadn't been cooperative, either. Sighing, Chay asked Darla to inform Ava he'd stopped by—*again*—and headed out to the parking lot to figure out his next move.

He'd already spoken to Ryan Colton, the firefighter who'd rescued Fern, but he had no leads on the men who'd taken Fern or any idea if either of them were Navajo.

Spotting a familiar tall redhead leaving the hospital, he had an idea. Granted, not a great one, but it was an idea. And he wanted to put to rest that niggling thought that this might be connected to someone on the Navajo Nation.

So he followed Ava as she drove to the grocery store, where she quickly spotted him. He smiled and waved at her, getting out of his Chevy Tahoe.

"Hiya."

"Hi. What are you doing?"

"Trying to talk to you," he said. "I left a message with Darla. Did you get it?"

A flash of annoyance passed over her face quickly. "I did. As I told you yesterday, there's nothing new to report. Fern is still recovering and hasn't shared any new information with anyone."

"Do you think I could question her?"

Ava crossed her arms under her breasts and stared down her nose at him. She had to be close to five-nine, and with the hiking boots she was even taller. A lesser man might have been intimated.

"Is that supposed to be an answer?" he asked when it was apparent she wasn't going to say anything else.

"I was hoping you'd back down," she said. "I'm not sure if she'd answer your questions. At our next session I can mention you want to talk to her. Or you could try going through her attending physician."

"I'd appreciate that if you think it will work?" he

asked, glad for the information she'd provided but more interested in the barrier she'd clearly tried to wedge between them.

"Yeah, I can ask," she said with a shrug. "If that's all, I need to get moving. I'm on my lunch break."

"Thanks for asking Fern. I'll stop by tomorrow to find out what she said."

"No need. You left your number with Darla, no doubt. I'll just send you a text." Ava turned, walking into the grocery store.

He watched her for longer than he wanted to admit. He was intrigued by her on a personal level, which he wanted to ignore,

Chay's peace of mind and the safety of the women on the Navajo Nation and surrounding Dark Canyon depended on it. That area was too wild and untamed. A place where it was too easy to snatch and hide women.

While it had happened before, Chay wanted to make sure it didn't happen again. Too many missing and murdered relations in the Navajo Nation weighed on him. It was a constant worry for his people, his friends and neighbors.

It was a crisis that was affecting many reservations and the number of missing indigenous women had been ignored for too long. There was a movement where a red hand was painted over the mouth to bring attention to the fact that so few of the missing received large scale media attention. Chay couldn't change what the rest of the country did, but he was damned sure going to protect and find those missing here.

And he needed to know that none of his people were involved in criminal activity.

His phone pinged with a text from his grandmother

reminding him he was coming to dinner that evening and informing him that she expected him to be on time. Chay smiled to himself. Two sassy women in one day.

In a way Ava reminded him of his grandmother. She didn't take any crap, either.

SHE FELT LIKE someone was watching her as she got out of her Chevy Trax, heading back into the hospital. A light snow was falling, and she slipped on a patch of ice as she looked around to see if anyone was in the parking lot with her. She noticed a Chevy Tahoe leaving. *Chay.*

That man was determined to get his questions answered. Actually, everyone was. Poor Fern needed time to recover, but Ava knew that the trail could grow cold unless police moved quickly on following up any leads.

But that was tomorrow's problem. Right now she was going to collect the baby who had been named Gracie at the fire station where she was found and take the nine-month-old home. She hadn't had a baby to foster before. She'd had two brothers, one six and one four, last summer. They'd been a lot of fun, and they still video chatted with her once a month.

Dr. Meadows waited for Ava in her office. Though they both worked at the hospital, their paths didn't cross that often. She'd been the attending physician for the boys and now Gracie.

"Hi, Hannah," Ava said as she entered the other woman's office.

"Good to see you. Did you have any trouble with the items I suggested?" Hannah asked.

"None. Pretty easy to find. My parents still had a crib and high chair, so Dad brought those over this afternoon."

"Must be nice being related to half the town," Hannah said with a smile.

"It is," Ava admitted. She sort of took it for granted that she could pick up the phone and call her parents. They always were there for her. Sometimes they could be a bit much—whose parents weren't? But they were there when she needed them. "Mom sent some blankets as well."

"The baby was wrapped in one. It's a Diné design," Hannah said.

"Good. Is she Native American?"

"We're not sure. I'm running a DNA test, and we'll know more soon. Want to come and meet her?"

"Yes." Ava followed the other woman down to the nursery, where Gracie was cooing softly in her crib. The little girl looked up at Ava, their eyes meeting, and she made another gurgling sound.

The little baby was being treated with antibiotics, and Ava would have to administer other meds. But she had no signs of abuse or broken bones, which was a good thing.

She glanced at Hannah. "Okay to pick her up?"

"Yes, of course. You've signed all the paperwork and she's yours to take home," Hannah said.

Ava carefully lifted the little girl out of the crib, supporting her back and head the way she'd been taught in the infant first aid course she'd taken. Gracie reached out her pudgy hand and grabbed a chunk of Ava's hair, tugging with a lot of strength.

Ava laughed and untangled the baby's hand, cradling her to her chest as she turned to face Hannah.

"Looks like she's taken with you," Hannah said. "I'll get her discharge papers signed and be back in a few minutes so you two can leave. Her bag is packed over there. I'll bring her prescriptions back with me, too."

"Thanks. Where's her blanket?"

"It's in the bag over there."

Hannah left, and Ava was alone with Gracie.

"Hi there. I'm Ava. I'm going to be taking care of you," she said.

The little girl didn't seem fussed about that. She continued cooing, her eyes wide as she watched Ava. There were times when she rethought her decision to stay single and not have kids of her own...this was one of them. Overpowering emotions flooded her as she rocked the baby back and forth.

It was something she craved. But she also guarded her heart when it came to relationships. Losing her fiancé had taken her a long time to recover from. It was only through her biweekly therapy sessions that she'd been able to start moving on. But he had been the love of her life...there wasn't going to be another one.

Growing up with parents who adored each other, Ava wouldn't marry someone she didn't love or who she was just really good friends with. She had friends—she could hook up if she wanted to, her life was good as it was. There was no missing spot to be filled by a partner or husband.

Greg was still alive in her heart. He'd been a kind and caring man. The perfect boyfriend after the controlling and abusive man she'd dated before him.

Shaking her head, she went to get the baby bag. Inside was a snowsuit, which would keep the baby toasty and warm when they stepped outside. Ava laughed to herself as she struggled to get Gracie into it.

The little scamp liked to kick her legs when she was on her back, but eventually Ava got her zipped in just as Hannah returned with the discharge papers. Ava zipped up her own coat, picked up Gracie and shouldered the bag to leave.

"If you need anything, call me. My cell is on the discharge papers," Hannah said.

"Thanks," Ava said. She didn't anticipate calling anyone. Mainly because she really liked to figure things out on her own. She and Gracie would be good.

"We're a team now," she said to the little girl. "You've got me in your corner."

She knew the baby didn't really understand her but wanted the girl to know she had someone. Ava meant for life, which Gracie would learn as she grew up.

It had gotten darker while she was in the hospital, and she was careful as she made her way to her Trax and opened the door. The car seat had been set up in the back seat. She tucked Gracie in and then double-checked she was secured before putting the baby's bag under the seat and getting in. Firing up the engine, she cranked the heat and leaning over to check the baby one more time before heading home.

Her house was on a residential street with lots of families. She drove carefully toward it, happy to have Gracie with her. In the middle of all of the incidents going on around Dark Canyon, this was a bright light.

Chapter Two

Three days later, she was no closer to getting Fern to open up than she had been the first time they spoke. It made sense to her. The other woman was dealing with a lot, her body, mind and spirit broken and trying to heal. She also was afraid to go home. It seemed to Ava that the woman was in no hurry to leave the hospital.

Luckily Chay hadn't stopped by with more questions. Maybe he was respecting her when she'd told him she'd let him know if she heard anything. That would be a nice change from his normal bulldozing.

She was off today, and Gracie had been fussy all day long. She'd called her mom, who had suggested she put the baby in her car seat and take her for a drive, which Ava had done. The baby fell asleep in the car, but when she got back home and carried her into the house, Gracie started crying again.

She'd paged Hannah, and the pediatrician had advised her to check Gracie's temperature and asked her several questions to rule out infection or any other ailment. "Sorry, Ava, sounds like she's just having a bad day," Hannah said.

"Both of us are," Ava said jokingly. "Well, I'll just keep holding her. Hope that helps."

Walking the baby around seemed to help a little bit. Her doorbell rang just as Gracie started to nod off, and Ava went to see who it was…hoping it was her mom. She could use someone else to hold the baby so she could go pee.

It wasn't her mom but Chay Benally. Standing on her threshold, he put his hands up near his shoulders in a gesture of surrender. "Sorry to drop in on you, but I was hoping to follow up on our conversation from the other day."

She glared at him. "I can't even begin to think while she's crying."

"I'm sort of a baby whisperer," Chay said. "If I get her to stop crying, can we talk?"

Ava doubted he'd be able to achieve that, but nodded and handed the baby to him as he stepped into her hallway. She closed the door behind him as he was talking to the baby in a soft tone.

"I have to run to the bathroom. Be right back. The living room is that way," she said with a gesture.

After doing her business, she checked her hair, realizing she had a bit of spit-up on her shoulder and she looked as frazzled as she felt. Taking an extra moment to braid her hair so that it fell over one shoulder, she splashed some water on her face and then took her shirt off, turning it inside out so the spit-up stain was hidden. She looked…well, *better* was a relative term, but there it was.

Going back into the living room, she heard nothing but the ticking of her grandfather clock. Her living room was decorated with overstuffed chairs and a long couch that her mom had helped her pick out when she'd moved in. Chay sat in the large armchair nearest the fire. Baby

Gracie lay in his big arms sleeping. *That little traitor*, Ava thought, but she smiled at Chay.

"Not sure how you managed that," she half whispered in a very low tone.

"Told ya—baby whisperer. Where's her bed?" he asked.

Ava led him down the hall to the room where the crib was set up. He placed her in it and then covered her with the Navajo blanket. His hands lingered on it for a moment.

The blanket looked so familiar. In the past, Diné woven blankets had been given to family and friends. This one was old and well-used as if it had been a cherished possession passed along to this tiny baby. The motifs and designs looked familiar; in fact he saw some that he knew his grandmother used especially the tiny moon on the edge of the blanket.

The moon was considered sacred and female for the Diné people. His grandmother and aunties all used it in their designs.

He turned and she followed him out of the room after she turned on the monitor.

"So I guess you owe me," he said.

It wasn't fair that he looked so good when he was so irritating. But he did. That thick black hair, eyebrows that framed his dark brown eyes with laugh lines and that mouth… Lord, she had a hard time not wondering what it would be like to kiss him. Which wasn't appropriate at all.

"Yeah, I'm not going to back out of answering your questions. Want a coffee?"

"Yes, please," he said.

She led him into her kitchen and gestured for him to

take a seat at the table while she made a pot of coffee. There hadn't been time today to do anything but take care of Gracie.

"Is Gracie part Navajo?" he asked.

"We're not sure. I'm fostering her," she added when he looked confused. "She was found at the fire station. They named her Gracie. Dr. Meadows is doing a DNA test. Do you think she might be?"

He shrugged as if he didn't want to say more. "That blanket…looks familiar."

"In what way?" Ava asked as she poured two cups of coffee. "Milk or sugar?"

"Neither," he said.

She added both to hers before bringing both mugs to the table and sitting down across from Chay. He smelled good, too. Darn him.

He was a good-looking man, which she was just now noticing. Maybe her gaze had been softened by his magic with Gracie. She'd really started to believe she had some natural mothering instinct, but Gracie was challenging that belief. It was a lot harder to mother a baby than Ava had realized.

"The blanket?" she asked.

"It just is similar to one that I had as a boy. I don't know why that is. My grandmother and aunties all weave so maybe that's why it seems that way. I noticed the motifs used are the ones my grandmother uses. I'll have to ask her about it."

"Does she sell them?" Ava knew authentic Navajo rugs were worth a lot of money and the weavers could name their own prices. They were generally sold at festivals around the state.

"Blankets aren't sold. Rugs are and she does sell hers, but the blankets are just for family," he said.

"Could she be yours?"

"Definitely not," he said.

"Celibate?" she teased.

"Careful," he retorted.

They both watched each other as they took a sip of their coffees. Both of them waiting for the other to make the first move. He had nerve. She liked it.

"So, about Fern Hensley."

"What do you want to know? Most of what I have heard is from the sheriff's report," Ava warned him.

"Has she been able to describe either of the men who were holding her?" Chay asked.

"Not really. The descriptions are vague. Tall, dark hair, big... I mean, it would be half the men in Dark Canyon."

"Or on the Navajo Nation," he said.

Ava agreed.

"Did she go into more detail of what she remembered before the men stopped showing up?" Chay asked. He had a notepad where he was taking notes. The ballpoint pen looked small in his hand, and his handwriting was bold, with slashing strokes. She watched him for a moment before realizing that she was.

"No. Just that they kept her drugged. She'd wake up and they'd give her food, make sure the heat was working, drug her again and leave. She woke up one day and they didn't come back. She panicked and knocked over the heater trying to free herself and the fire started."

HE COULD TELL Ava was upset for Fern. She kept turning the mug in her hands as she spoke. Not looking up at him. If he were one hundred percent honest, he'd have to admit he hadn't just stopped by today to learn more about Fern. Something about Ava had stuck with him when he'd gone back home.

To prove to himself that he wasn't at all into her, he'd stayed away. But today had been slow and he'd figured the drive to Dark Canyon would fill up a chunk of it. Seeing her and the baby she was fostering.

That blanket was right at the front of his mind. His mom had dumped him on his paternal grandmother when he was six years old. Sometimes he dreamed of that day. Saw himself from outside his body, holding his grandmother's hand as his mom got in that junker of a Ford she used to drive and drove away with a plume of dirt spraying up from her tires as she did.

She'd never come back. She'd called twice and had sent a Christmas card one time. She'd died when he was fifteen—they'd gotten a call from Atlanta. His grandmother and he had driven out to see her buried. It was cheaper than bringing her body back. The blanket that Grandmother had made for his dad at birth had been gone, and he hadn't thought about that blanket until he'd tucked little Gracie in.

"Thanks for sharing that. You're right, it's not news, but just hearing the details again gives me a chance to process it in a different way," he said after a minute or so. When he'd first joined the police department in Salt Lake, he'd been paired up with an older cop, Butch Lawrence. He'd been injured recently and was on desk duty and light patrol work.

Butch had told him to check his prejudices at the door. Wait until he got all the facts before making a decision. It had served Chay well. There were many times when his first impression of a crime or crime scene was to attribute it to an addict…and too many times that was the case, but there were always other options. Butch was a bit different on the force because he saw each person for who they were first, not as a perp.

He figured if the men who'd held Fern were Navajo she would have mentioned it, but he wasn't ruling it out until he had another suspect.

"You're welcome. I think the cops want to question her again. She's asked that either I or my brother are present."

"Why your brother?"

"He's the firefighter who found her," Ava said. "He keeps checking on her."

"You Coltons are caretakers?"

"Yeah, especially if someone seems to have no one," she admitted.

"Like Gracie… Would you mind keeping me posted on her?" he asked, knowing it was time to finish his coffee and get back to his office.

"I don't mind. Do you think she might be Navajo?"

"I do think there's a chance—in fact if you want to run the sample through our reservation database, it might help find a match," he said.

"That's great news. Let me message Dr. Meadows. Should I give her your contact details?"

"Yes. That would be great."

Ava took out her phone and sent a message to both him and the doctor. He just watched her typing on her phone. Her hair had been braided but she'd missed a strand that was sticking up a little toward the back of her head. She'd turned her shirt around and well, hell, she looked so damned cute.

Putting her phone down, she caught him staring at her. Raised both eyebrows at him, meeting his stare squarely.

"I could hang around for an hour if you want to grab a nap," he offered. He knew she was tired, and a baby took a lot of energy.

"Do I look that tired?"

"You look great," he said, keeping it real. "But I know how it is with babies. You know I'm an upstanding guy. I'll sit in my truck with the monitor if it makes you feel safer."

"I feel very safe with you," she admitted. "I'm not a good napper, but I could use a shower. Would you mind if I grabbed a quick one?"

Still buzzing from hearing her say she felt safe with him, he nodded. He hadn't dated in a while, and really, with his job and his grandmother he had a full life...well, sort of full life...okay, not full at all, but he was content with what he had. Being interested in a woman who lived almost an hour from him wasn't a smart idea.

But there it was.

"Take your time. I'll have another cup of coffee and wait here for you," he said.

"Thank you!"

She left the room quickly after he poured himself another mug and sat back down, looking down at his notes. The investigation wasn't moving forward for him, and he'd hoped to be able to rule out Diné involvement in it, but so far nothing.

Dr. Meadows messaged back her contact where he could share the database, too. That baby...was she related to him? His mom had been a troubled woman. Grandmother had reiterated that more times than Chay had needed her to, but as he'd gotten older, he realized she'd done it so he'd know it wasn't him. He hadn't been what had made her leave.

Which was a nice message for a child, but for a man

who made his living watching people and looking for the truth, it was uncomfortable. His mom had left because being on the reservation wasn't the life she wanted. Having a kid wasn't for her, either.

He hoped she'd found what she'd been looking for in Atlanta, but given that she'd died of an overdose, he was pretty sure she hadn't.

AVA COULDN'T GET Chay out of her mind all afternoon. Gracie had a good nap, and then when the baby woke up she was in a better mood. Ava put the Navajo blanket on the floor and let the baby roll around on it and play with the soft toys that Ava hadn't been able to resist buying.

Watching Gracie, she had the local country music station playing in the background. The baby was trying to roll over but seemed to do it accidentally, which always surprised her and made Ava laugh.

The next few days were similar. While she was at work, they had a day-care center in the hospital where she left Gracie. Fern was starting to get stronger and was willing to talk more, but not about what had happened. Ava knew that each of her patients took their own time to talk about their trauma, so she just kept showing up so that Fern knew she wasn't alone.

Dr. Meadows asked her to come by her office. Ava was a bit surprised when she got there and Chay was in the office.

"The DNA results are in. Gracie is one-quarter Diné and shares DNA markers with people in the region."

"That's wonderful. Officer Benally also thought her blanket was familiar. Could he be related?"

"It's hard to tell from the just the DNA. Do you have any siblings?" Hannah asked Chay.

"None that I know of. If she's Diné, I think she should be raised with her people," Chay said.

"I agree. It's probably a good idea to get Marg in here so she can start working with tribal authorities."

"I'm happy to facilitate that. Thank you for calling me in with the results. Did she share markers with anyone else?"

"Just you and your grandmother," Dr. Meadows said.

"Oh, wow," Ava said. Chay had said no siblings that he knew of. So, there was a possibility he had relatives he didn't know about...

Chay just nodded. His face told her it was a closed subject, and she was happy to leave it be for now. Marg would work with the tribal authorities to find a home for Gracie. Which was a good thing. The little girl deserved a happy, solid home life.

"Any more information on Annie Ross?" Ava asked.

"Not much. The sheriff has an open investigation. Now that we know Gracie was Annie's daughter, we can maybe help piece together more of Annie's story."

Everyone agreed that would be good.

"I'm done for the day if you want to come and hang out with Gracie," Ava offered as she and Chay left the office.

"I'm...not sure she's related to me," he said haltingly.

"Well, I guess the DNA isn't conclusive and that blanket might be tied to your family."

"Maybe," he said.

"You're pretty good with her. I think she's been missing you," Ava said. Sort of making that up, but there had been times when Gracie had seemed to look around the house as if expecting to spot Chay.

"Sure she has. I have to get back to the office, but I'll stop by tomorrow if that's an open invite," he said.

"It is." Ava wanted Gracie to know her relatives, even if she was placed in another home—knowing Chay going to be a good familial bond for the baby as she grew up.

"It's a date," he said.

"A date?"

"Yup."

"Okay, bring some coffee cake or doughnuts to go with the coffee then," she said.

"Not doughnuts…that's a cliché for a cop. But I'll bring something for you," he said, putting on his hat as he walked away.

She just watched him leave, smiling to herself. She liked him, which totally surprised her, because it had been a while since she'd really felt anything for a man.

Going to pick up Gracie from the day care, she bundled the baby up and headed home. Once again she thought she felt someone watching her but put it down to paranoia. After reading the police report with the details of how Fern was abducted earlier that day, Ava knew she was processing some leftover anxiety from when her college boyfriend had stalked her.

Just that sense of not being safe. The same thing had happened after she watched a psychologic thriller. It had been so creepy and chilling she had to sleep with her light on for weeks after that. Her mom had pointed out that thirteen was too young, but a boy that Ava had liked had invited her to go see it.

Woman, take warning.

But Chay wasn't asking her to see a movie or really to do anything except help in his investigation. It was all on her.

That moment she'd held Gracie, something had shifted inside of her. A longing she hadn't been aware of had sprung to life, and each time she rocked the little girl to sleep or went to watch her playing in her crib first thing in the morning, the longing grew.

She wasn't going to struggle to give the baby to her forever home. Which Ava thought was a good thing. It reminded her she was alive. She'd been settling into just existence before she'd started fostering kids. It wasn't all hearts and flowers or easy at all, but it was what she needed.

Getting home, she made dinner for herself then fed Gracie. "Ready to watch some reality tv?" she asked the little baby, whose eyes were getting heavy with sleep. Tucking Gracie close to her, she held her as she tuned into that castle in the Scottish Highlands and Alan Cumming with his outrageous outfits. This was exactly what she needed to clear her mind and get ready for tomorrow.

Chay was coming over again. He'd said "date," but she knew it wasn't a *date* date. Still, she was looking forward to seeing him again.

More than she'd expected, too.

Chapter Three

Ava's mom liked to call her first thing in the morning for a chat when she had something on her mind. The rest of the time they both sort of did their own things. She'd just put Gracie down for a nap, knowing that Chay was going to drop by for their date sometime today.

She should have been more specific about the time instead of just inviting him to stop by...

"Ava...you there?"

"Yeah. Sorry, was watching the baby monitor," she lied. "What did you say?"

"Aw, I remember those days," her mom said. "I asked if you'd heard that the Annie Ross's murder might be related to the men who took Fern Hensley."

Ava curled her legs up underneath her and shifted the phone to her other hand. "No, I hadn't. How did you hear that? You know you shouldn't listen to gossip, Mom." Using the phrase her mom had used so many times when Ava and Ryan had been growing up.

"Ha-ha. Ryan was here for dinner. He mentioned it because of the connection to Fern. Seems that Annie had filed a missing-person report on her friend and roommate

Camille Lancaster. Some of the details of her friend's abduction match how Fern was taken."

"When did they find all of this out?"

"Yesterday, I suppose. I'm not really sure. But it's scary to think of all these women being taken and brought to our town," Mom said. "You be extra careful."

"It is scary," Ava agreed. "But most of the women were taken elsewhere, right? I should be fine. You, too."

Her mom huffed. "Of course I will. They're going after young women."

"You're still young, honey," she heard her dad say. The phone was muffled, and she suspected her parents were kissing before her mom came back on the line. "Still, I want you to stay vigilant."

"I always do," she said.

"Good. So when are you going to bring that cute baby over so I can cuddle her?"

She agreed to a day next week when Ava was off again and then hung up with her mom. The information her mom had given her would help Chay's investigation, she thought. It would also give her some background to start questioning Fern on.

The other woman didn't want to talk her abduction. Given that she tried to let Fern guide their sessions, she imagined the other woman didn't want to talk about it.

Her street was quiet, as it usually was on a Thursday morning. Most people had gone to school or work, and there weren't a lot of stay-at-home parents on her street. In fact, if it wasn't for Gracie, Ava would be volunteering at the homeless shelter today.

She checked on Gracie, who was still sleeping. Standing over the baby, Ava had so many questions. Why had Annie Ross abandoned her at the fire station? Had she realized that her questions were leading men who were kidnapping women to her?

It must have been difficult for Annie to leave her baby. A part of Ava felt strongly that Annie would have come back for her. Maybe that was just because she wanted that for Gracie.

She tucked the Diné blanket closer around the baby and went to the changing table where she had left some clothes to be folded. It felt like someone was watching her, and she pushed the sheer curtains aside to look up and down the street.

Nothing.

That conversation with her mom must have spooked her more than she'd guessed. She was a woman, so she always took extra precautions. She called her friends when she was walking home alone. She texted them when she went on a first date with a stranger. She walked with her keys out to use as a weapon late at night when she left the hospital and the parking lot was almost empty.

But sometimes all the precautions weren't enough. Women who did everything right were still taken and hurt. Like Fern and Annie Ross.

Feeling safe in her house wasn't even enough. She had double locks on her front door because of that one incident in college. She'd never known for sure how Daniel Wayne had gotten into her apartment or why he'd been waiting for her there. Luckily she'd been with Greg, and that had been enough to frighten Daniel off.

Rubbing her hands up and down her arms, she left the baby's room. Daniel was still in prison. He'd stalked and attacked another young woman after she'd reported him and gotten a restraining order. There were times when she realized just how lucky she was to be alive.

For some reason Daniel Wayne hadn't killed her… maybe Greg's presence.

But Greg was gone. God, she was getting sucked into a negative thought spiral. She dropped down on the floor and sat in the lotus position. Centering herself, she started to some box breathing. Counting and concentration on her breath pulled her mind away from the past and her fears and straight into just breathing.

It took her fifteen minutes before she felt calm enough to get up. She heard a truck in her driveway and went to put the coffee maker on. Getting to her front door just as the doorbell rang.

Opening it, she took a deep breath.

Chay.

He wore a thick sheepskin jacket and a pair of jeans and boots. He took off his aviator-style sunglasses, putting them in his breast pocket. He had a Tupperware container in one hand and held his hat in the other.

"Hope I'm not too early. We never set a time," he said.

"You're just right," she said, stepping back so he could enter. He put his hat on the hook near the door and looked down at his boots, handing her the Tupperware.

"Shoes off? I didn't ask the other day."

"I don't mind if you want to keep them on unless they're slushy."

He toed his boots off, and she watched as he bent down to stand them neatly side by side. When he straightened, he noticed her watching him.

She flushed slightly. He had a nice butt. It wasn't illegal to look at it.

HIS GRANDMOTHER HAD made a batch of blue corn cookies for him to bring over. She was intrigued by Gracie and had seconded his desire to have the baby raised on the Navajo Nation. He'd invited her to come along but she already had plans with her best friend, Fiona. They liked to get together and weave and talk.

Which was fine with him; he'd sort of wanted to be alone with Ava again. She had her hair down today and wore a henley top and a pair of faded jeans. She had socks on her feet that were patterned with hearts. It wasn't just that she might add something to his investigation—actually, he'd pretty much given up on that front. He liked her. She was sassy and funny and caring. He'd seen how much she loved Gracie and cared for Fern. She was very protective of the injured woman.

Seemed she might like him, too.

"Like what you see?"

"Yes. Also I have some news for you…that you'll need to verify. Let's go into the kitchen so we can chat and enjoy what you brought."

He followed her, this time taking in the photos on the wall. Most of her house was decorated with photos of family rather than art. There were two cross-stitched scenes that had been framed and hung as well. One was of a German shepherd named Brandy and the other was of a house and had the title "Home."

She had poured two mugs of coffee and had one sitting in front of the seat he'd used last time when he entered. She'd set out some cloth napkins as well. The baby monitor was near her side as she sat cross-legged on the chair across from him again.

"What'd you bring to eat?"

"My grandmother's blue corn cookies. She made some fancy ones for you," he said, opening the box to reveal the heart-shaped cookies. "She's getting ready for Valentine's Day."

"They look really nice. Can't wait to try one," she said.

He held the box out to her and she took one, taking a bite and closing her eyes as she chewed. He couldn't take his eyes off her, watching the enjoyment spread over her face. She opened her eyes to find him watching, and he didn't look away.

She licked her lips. "Delicious."

He simply nodded and popped a cookie into his mouth. After he'd washed it down with the coffee, he said, "What about the investigation?"

"I'm not sure how, because I heard this via my mom, but it seems that Fern's abductors might have be responsible for taking Annie Ross as well. There are details that match between Fern's abduction and the abduction of a friend of Annie's. She heard this from my brother, who is a firefighter and was the one to rescue Fern."

That was a solid lead. He'd had plans to stop by the Dark Canyon police office while he was in town, but maybe he should speak to Ryan Colton as well. "That is interesting. Any more details on Annie Ross? Was she found near a cabin as well?"

"No. Not at all. She was just dumped in the wilderness and left to die from exposure. When she was found she had extreme hypothermia and died as a result."

"Had she been drugged like Fern?"

"I really don't know," Ava said, taking another cookie. "I think my cousin Jacob Colton with the National Parks ISB is conducting the investigation because of where Annie was discovered."

"I'll get in touch with him. Thanks for this," he said.

"No problem. Mom called to warn me to be extra safe."

"Why?"

"Three women have been taken."

"I get that. I wondered if there was something particular that made her concerned for you?" he asked.

She took a deep breath, looking down at her coffee mug. It was a while before she shrugged. "I had a stalker back in college... I think all these young women being taken reminded her of that."

Her words were even, almost nonchalant, but her hands were white where she gripped the coffee mug, giving away her unease. Reaching over, he put his hand on hers and squeezed. Of course he wanted to tell her she'd be fine, but he couldn't guarantee that. No one could. He hoped she would be. Chances were a woman as connected to Dark Canyon and a Colton to boot wasn't going to be taken, but there was no promise of that.

Gracie let out a loud yell. Ava pulled her hand from his and dashed down the hallway, calling over her shoulder that she'd be right back.

She'd left the monitor so he watched her talking softly to the baby as she got her out of bed and changed her diaper. They both came back into the room a few minutes later. Gracie saw him and threw her entire body forward he reached up to take her from Ava.

"Told ya she missed you."

He laughed as the baby girl's hand wrapped around his finger. Her eyes were big and brown, and as he looked down on her rounded face, he felt something tug deep inside of him. She looked like his people. The DNA had already proved that she was one-quarter Diné and shared genetic markers with him.

Could she be the child of a half brother he'd never met? As always when it came to his mom he had more question than he'd ever get answers for. It would be easy to just write it off because she was dead, but the truth was even when his mom had been alive she'd been elusive. He had never known her, not really. And he'd wanted that. Wanted to know the only parent that had been alive when he'd been a kid.

That strengthened his resolve to find a good family for Gracie on the Navajo reservation. To ensure that she grew up close to her relatives so she'd know where she came from. His grandmother had been a strong figure and raised him to know his past and directed him to find his own path to the future. Something he truly respected and appreciated. There was no one he loved as much as he loved her.

But that didn't mean he hadn't still missed out on having his mom.

WATCHING CHAY HOLD Gracie made Ava feel warm all over. She took another of the blue corn cookies to distract herself from the domestic scene. It wasn't like she wanted to date a guy who wanted kids. The world they lived in made her think twice about wanting to bring children into it. But there was something about Chay that was changing her mind.

He'd be such a good father. She doubted he even saw that in himself. Though she was still getting to know him, it was easy to see that he projected himself as a loner. Yet he'd brought her cookies his grandmother had made. He was determined to find out who had kidnapped Fern and keep the Navajo Nation safe as well as the town of Dark Canyon.

He cared. Way more than she suspected he wanted the world to know. Maybe it was the fact that she was a psychiatrist that gave her insight. But she didn't believe that. Chay was gruff at times, but there was also that way that he smiled, joked and looked after others.

When he'd put her hand over hers, not saying words that she would struggle to believe, like promising her safety, she'd known that the like that had been slowly blooming within her was starting to grow. She'd struggled to explain to her parents and younger brother that nothing anyone could say or do would ever make her feel safe again.

Something that she might need to share with Fern to help in the other woman's recovery. Ava really liked to keep her past in the past. But her mom's call had stirred up those old feelings, and there was no shaking it.

The deep breathing had helped, and having Chay here was going a long way to reminding her of all the good men there were in the world. Watching him hold and play with Gracie made her smile.

She shoved aside her own feelings. "Has Marg reached out to you yet?"

"Marg?"

"From Family and Child Services?" Ava asked, getting up to refill both of their coffee cups. She'd been talking to the other woman about Gracie's DNA results and trying to find her biological father.

"She did. I referred her to the Tribal Children Services so they can work together to find the right family for Gracie," he said, then looked down at the baby. "Yes I did."

He tickled Gracie's neck, and the baby laughed when he did it. The sound was so sweet and happy that Ava couldn't help but smile.

She appreciated that he must be using proper channels to ensure Gracie ended up with a relative. Ava was a big believer in finding the best families for her foster kids…well, that one other time. "Do you have cousins or siblings?"

"None that I know of, as I mentioned the other day. Why?" he asked. It was odd for her to think of him having such a small family when she was related to half of Dark Canyon.

"Just wondering who Gracie will end up," Ava said. "I really love this little girl and want the best placement for her."

"I think everyone does," Chay said, taking a sip of his coffee while still holding Gracie.

"Was your grandmother excited to have a new grandchild?" she asked him. Her mom was itching for grandchildren but didn't really pressure her or Ryan.

"No. Gracie isn't ours," Chay said softly.

"But she could be, right?"

He stood up and handed the baby to her as he paced away from her to the kitchen sink looking out the window on her backyard.

"No. She's not going to be living with me. I'm a workaholic who lives in a very remote cabin. I'm not going to be her permanent family. I'll check in on her and make sure she's okay, but she needs a real family."

Ava rocked the little girl, who caught a strand of her hair and tugged on it. "Families come in all shapes and sizes."

"I appreciate that."

He put his hands on his hips, his head falling forward.

"Sorry if I'm pushing, but I just want her to be with the right people," Ava said.

"She has no family that we know of—yet. I'm not the right person to raise her," Chay said.

"Why do you believe that?"

"I just do. Thanks for the coffee and the information. I'm heading out now," Chay said.

She followed him into the entryway, where she had a bench that he sat on to put his boots on. Holding Gracie on her hip, she just watched him. A part of her wanted to push further, but she knew he wasn't going to give her any more information. He was defensive and running away.

Which surprised her. He had seemed more tenacious than that. She guessed she'd hit a nerve and would have to tread more carefully. But she knew she wasn't going to drop this. Seeing Chay and Gracie together convinced her they'd make a good family.

"I'm sorry if pushed too hard, but I have to follow my heart. Family is one of my greatest strengths."

Chay stood up with his boots on, walking toward her so that he towered over her. "Family... I don't have what you do. It's just my grandmother and me."

"And Gracie."

His eyes closed, and he shook his head. His frustration with her was plain to read and she knew she should stop. But at the same time, there was a bond between Gracie and Chay that she wanted to nurture.

"It could be. You're really good with her."

"That's because she's not mine," he said. "My grandmother is the caretaker in our relationship."

There was more to that than she could unpack in this moment. Chay was leaving angry, which she didn't want. "Will you come by again?"

"Maybe."

"Don't be a brat," she said.

"Don't try to boss me," he returned.

"I do have a habit of that," she said, offering him a half smile.

He smiled back. "I can see that."

"It's just hard not to boss when I'm usually right."

"Being right is important?"

"Not always, but about family it is."

"What makes you so sure? You barely know me."

Reaching up with her free hand, she touched his face. A tingle went up her arm. "I know you, Chay Benally. I see you."

He leaned down almost as if he was going to kiss her. Her eyes drifted closed, she leaned in and she felt the brush of his thick hair against her cheek as he kissed the top of Gracie's head, then winked at Ava and left.

Chapter Four

The National Parks SBI department had a good working relationship with the tribal police department. Chay had been in touch with lead investigator Jacob Colton since the beginning. The information he'd gotten from Ava meant there it was time to check in again. Since he was already in Dark Canyon, he reached out to Jacob and asked to stop by.

Jacob was broad shouldered and over six feet tall. He had blue eyes and medium brown hair and his face was similar to Ava's. The special agent was in the office, working more leads in the investigation with his team. Chay hadn't met many of them in person.

"Chay Benally, good to see you. I see my aunt has been busy," Jacob said with a laugh. Chay had caught him up on what he'd heard via Ava.

"Yeah. Thought I'd stop by and get the official rundown," Chay said, taking a cup of coffee from Jacob.

"Sure, have a seat. It's hard to get much out of Fern. We do know that she was taken in Oso by two men in a dark van, but she has been hazy on her descriptions. I'm hoping to get in to speak with her again, but she'll only talk to me if Ava or Ryan is with her."

"Fair enough. She's scared and only trusts the two of them. He rescued her and Ava's the only one she can talk to," Chay said.

He remembered how he'd been after his mom had left and he had to go to school. Seemed like he hadn't spoken to anyone for the first three months unless his grandmother was in the room. The fear that had silenced him had been strong. There was nothing stronger than the fear of being abandoned. Something he knew. Feeling like you had no one in the world to rely on was harrowing.

"Yeah, I get it. We were curious if Gracie was Fern's, but she ruled that out. The DNA brought back a match for Annie Ross…she was in the system for a few arrests."

"Was she from Oso?" Chay asked.

"No. She was from Wilson. She shared an apartment with Lori Stevens and Camille Lancaster. Camille disappeared and the other women filed a missing-persons report, but nothing came of it until Annie started digging around.

"She learned that Camille was taken by two men in a dark van. I read the report. I have a call into the Wilson Police Department, but haven't heard back from them."

"That doesn't really mean much, does it?" Chay asked. It was hard to link the two women unless they had a match on the van.

"Well, I did a little more digging, and both Camille Lancaster and Fern Hensley have no family. They were in the foster care system and aged out. I just think…it's a connection," Jacob said.

"Interesting," Chay agreed. He pulled out his notepad and jotted down the information. The foster care system was overworked, he knew that. It was easy to think that everyone was an adult at eighteen years of age, but those kids had no backup network. For himself he had his grandmother. He'd left home, sure, and ended up in Salt Lake, but she talked to him once a week.

"I'll look further into the women and see if I can find out more," Chay said. They spoke a little more about the investigation before Chay left the station. With Ava pushing him hard to think of adopting Gracie, he was reluctant to try to speak to Fern via Ava again, but he'd never been a man to back down.

He knew in his heart that he didn't have it in him to be a father. Little Gracie deserved two reliable parents. He'd done okay with his grandmother, but as a kid he'd been very aware that it was just the two of them. He had friends and cousins, but it wasn't the same as having two parents.

Pulling into the hospital parking lot, he texted Ava to see if she'd come with him to talk to Fern.

Ava: I'm on my way to see her for our session. I'll ask her if she'll speak to you after. It would be an hour. Okay?

Chay: Sure. I'll grab a coffee and wait.

Ava sent back a thumbs-up.

He thought about how sassy she'd been pushing him to adopt Gracie. Her passion was something he admired about her. Instead of going into the hospital he called his grandmother.

"Grandson."

He smiled. She always called him that when she was with her friends and couldn't really talk.

"Grandmother. You going to be free later?"

"Sure am. Want to come by for dinner?"

"Yes."

"See you then," she said, hanging up the phone.

Sitting in his truck, the afternoon sunlight was brighter in winter than summer. He watched the people coming and going. Some of them easier to read than others. They all had their stories and worries. Things that drove them to be here for whomever they were visiting.

He added his. Fern had given her hazy memories, but now that he had learned of the connection he wanted to see if she had more details on the dark van. The men... he felt pushing her for a more concise description wasn't going to work. He could only guess, but he thought those men would be a source of fear for her.

His phone pinged, and he looked down to see that Fern had agreed to talk to him after her session as long as Ava was in the room. He sent back a thumbs-up and then went into the hospital to the cafeteria and got some lunch.

Using his smartphone he remotely logged into the database that held all missing persons. Camille had been twenty-two and Fern was twenty-five. Using their age range, he narrowed down the list. It was larger than he wished it was.

There was more than a handful of Navajo women on there as well. He downloaded the list to his desktop remotely. He would go through it when he got back to his office. There had to be more of a connection than just age. His neck tingled and he looked around the cafeteria.

Since it was after lunch, it wasn't that busy. He didn't notice anyone looking at him. Shrugging, he finished his lunch and went to meet Ava and Fern.

AVA WAS TRYING cognitive behavioral therapy today with Fern. It was clear to her that Fern wasn't ready to delve into the past, but she'd expressed the fact that she'd been keeping her mind foggy so she wouldn't have to.

She was on pretty intense pain meds, which helped her to disassociate. Once Fern had come out of the coma, she had refused to take any further pain meds. She'd been unconscious when Ryan found her, possibly from smoke inhalation. Ava understood that Fern was a recovering alcoholic and feared being drugged again. But Ava knew that wouldn't last for long.

"How are you feeling today?"

"Truth?"

"Always."

"Better. My leg will heal. Not sure it will ever be one hundred percent. I was worried about having to do a lot of physical therapy and maybe never walking properly again," Fern said.

"That would mean a big lifestyle change, wouldn't it?" Ava asked her.

Fern shrugged.

"Do you miss your daily life?" Ava asked.

Fern looked down at her bed and started to make little triangles out of the blanket, pulling it up until she had a neat row of them. The fidgeting was concise and the other woman was using the pattern to soothe herself.

"So, no." Ava said.

"I mean, I don't know really. It was just the same thing day in and day out…then everything changed and now I feel… I'm back here and everyone keeps telling me I'm safe. But I don't feel it. I'm a solitary woman.

"Then I had a new routine, wake up, have those thugs who kidnapped me would come in and try to feed me and drug me again. That was the cycle of my life. I was just dazed and confused and the days blended together.

When I woke up and they were there... I was scared, Ava. Why wouldn't I be scared? They were my captors and I hated them. Even if I still can't remember their faces."

Ava wanted to hug the other woman, but as a professional she couldn't. "Because they were keeping you alive. You knew that for you to survive, they had to come and feed you. You were bound and left alone in a dangerous situation. Your fear was perfectly natural. It's okay that you hoped they'd come back."

Fern chewed her lower lip and looked away. "I didn't exactly want that, either."

"Makes sense. You wanted to be back home."

"I did. But now that I'm here... I feel odd. Like I've changed but the rest of the world hasn't. I don't want to tell anyone because then...well, you're nice and everything, but I really don't want to have to do this for the rest of my life."

Ava smiled gently at the younger woman. "I get that. We all have trauma, and our brains and body deal with it in different ways. Right now, your strongest routine and 'life' memory is the cabin. Given how traumatic your rescue was, that is going to take time to fade in your mind."

Fern nodded. "So what do I do?"

Ava wasn't sure what would work for Fern; they'd only had a handful of sessions, so it was going to take time to get to know her better. Plus she was still recovering from everything that happened to her.

"Tell me about your day here," Ava invited. Wanting the other woman to have something to focus on.

"Well, Nurse Cassidy comes in really early," Fern said.

"What does she look like and do when she comes in?" Ava asked, leading her through her day.

"She has blue eyes and reddish-blond hair. It's really

pretty. She doesn't wear makeup or anything, but I can tell she takes time with her hair. There is always the smell of strawberries around her, and she smiles when she says good morning. She takes my vitals and then checks my IV."

"Does she chat with you?"

"Yes. Tells me how good I'm doing. Asks what I had for dinner the night before and how Andy treated me overnight."

"Who's Andy?"

"He's my night nurse. He's totally by the book. He's really quiet at night when he comes in. I freaked out the first night."

"That's to be expected. You woke up and there was a stranger in your room," Ava reassured her.

"Andy felt really bad and started to bring one of the junior nurses with him. She came in first, checked on me. It was nice. I mean, he didn't have to do that."

"But he did," Fern said.

"Yes. He has a Superman tattoo on his forearm that he got when he was sixteen to remind himself that he could do anything."

Ava nodded. "Do you use the tattoo to signal safety?"

"I guess. I hadn't thought of that way, but you're right. I know that Andy's not going to harm me in anyway. So he feels comforting, so does Cassidy, and I can tell you're wearing Daisy by Marc Jacobs… I like that."

"Good, you're building a new normal for yourself," Ava said. "When you feel the memories of the cabin creeping in, remember the routine and people and the smiles here. Go through your day here in the hospital. That will ground you here. Make this start to feel like your new normal."

Fern nodded. They spoke some more about other things she could do when she felt herself slipping into the past. "Are you sure you're up to talking to Officer Benally?"

"As long as you are here with me," Fern said.

She left Ava to go and get Chay. He waited for her in the floor waiting area. Her first thought was of that almost kiss they'd shared in her foyer. It took her a minute to realize she was staring at his mouth. Finally she tore her eyes away, but not before he lifted one eyebrow at her.

She just shook her head at him.

"She's...go gently. I'm not sure how much information you'll get from her. If I see that it's causing her any kind of agitation, I will ask you to stop and leave."

"Of course. I don't want to make anything worse. I just need to hear from her what she remembers."

THE HOSPITAL ROOM had two guest chairs, and Fern invited him to sit down in the one that was farthest from the bed. Ava pulled a chair up between him and Fern. Fern looked so small on the bed.

It reminded Chay of how he'd felt when his mom left. He pulled out his notebook to distract himself from that unpleasant memory.

"Thank you for meeting with me," he said.

"You're welcome. I really don't want to talk about what happened, but I also don't want anyone else to go through what I did," Fern said.

"That's what we are all hoping to avoid. In the report—" he glanced down at his phone, where he had her statement up "—you mentioned you were walking out of your office..."

"Yes. I'd finished working."

"What do you do, or did you do?"

"I'm a medical coder," she said.

"Did you notice anything odd in any of the transcribing you had done? Make a report to anyone?" Chay asked.

Ava watched him work, which made him want to impress her. He'd had time to gather his thoughts while he'd waited for the appointment. One of the things he'd learned from his mentor was to be methodical. Slowly work through every detail. It had led to a record number of arrests and convictions for the perpetrators that Chay arrested.

"No. Nothing like that. I don't believe it was work related…them taking me," she said.

"Probably not, but better to cover all bases. Who is your boss at work?"

Fern gave him the name; he jotted it down.

"Had you been out and maybe rubbed anyone the wrong way?"

"Uh, I didn't really ever go out. I had lunch with some work colleagues at Chili's at Christmas, and that's about it. I'd made two runs to the library to pick up books and DVDs I'd put a hold in for."

Chay jotted that down.

"Okay, so, the men who took you. Did you notice them at all before the day they abducted you, perhaps turning up in places you frequent?" he asked.

She shook her head and wrapped her arms around her body. For a minute she closed her eyes, breathing deeply, and Ava leaned closer to the other woman. The tension left Fern's body and she opened her eyes. "No. I didn't see them when they took me, either. I heard a van pull up behind me. I was grabbed…it was terrifying… I tried to get free."

Chay felt compassion for the ordeal that Fern had survived. She went on to tell him that she couldn't see anything when they dumped her in the van. She kicked and hit out at them but felt the prick of a needle and got drowsy as her hands and feet were bound.

"What's your next memory?"

"The guys coming in to feed me," she said.

"Would you be able to describe them to me?"

"I really can't recall what they looked like. They weren't visibly Native American, if that's what you're asking," she said. "They sounded like they were from Utah, like the guys I know. One of them was taller than the other."

"My height?"

"A bit shorter, I think. I wasn't really clearheaded. Whatever they were giving me was pretty strong. I really hated being drugged. I had no control over anything, and it stirred up memories from when I was a teenager. I sort of focused on the granola bar they kept trying to feed me. I threw it at them once, but they only came once a day, so I was hungry. They let me use the bathroom and then I'd pass out again. It's all just so hazy."

That fit with what she'd reported. "Then one day you woke up and they weren't there?"

She shook a little bit, wrapping her arms around herself again. "It took me a while, maybe an hour or so, to realize that I was awake and they weren't coming. It was the first time in days that I was aware. Cold and scared, I tried to figure out how to escape."

She looked at Ava and spoke directly to her.

"I wasn't sure if they were coming back but was afraid they'd get back before I could get out of the cabin. I was panicking. I just wanted to get away from them."

"That makes sense," Ava said softly. "You did really well. Got away, and even though you hadn't meant to knock over the heater, that fire saved your life."

Fern nodded. "Funny how an accident did that."

"Maybe your subconscious knew it would be a signal and help would arrive."

"Maybe it was just dumb luck," Fern said wryly.

It was the first glimpse of personality he'd seen from her, and he hid his smile. He asked her a few more questions, but after the fire there had been others involved, so he had multiple accounts of what had happened.

"Did you see any signs that anyone else had been held in the cabin?" he asked her as he was wrapping up.

"I didn't think to look," Fern said. "I'm sorry."

"Don't be. You've been very helpful," Chay said. "Thank you again for talking to me today," he said, standing. He tipped his head to Ava, who smiled at him, and then he left.

There wasn't much new information from Fern, but hearing the woman's story gave him more insight. Her life was pretty solitary. A thought circled in the back of his mind that he wanted to dismiss, but it was hard to. No one had filed a missing-person report for Fern until she had missed four days of work.

Fern didn't have any close ties. She worked in a doctor's office, with a few friends from work, but that was it. She lived alone. He knew she had been in the foster care system, as had Camille Lancaster from Wilson. Was that the connection? Maybe someplace in the foster care system where their paths had crossed?

He waited in the hall for Ava, who looked surprised to see him when she came out. She led the way down the hall, and he followed her. When they were at the elevator, she propped her shoulder against the wall.

"Get what you needed?"

"I think so. Thank you for arranging it," he said.

It was really hard to stop thinking about that moment when he'd almost kissed her at her house, but his mind was distracted by the case. He said goodbye to her when they both got to the bottom floor, and he watched as she went to her office.

Chapter Five

Focusing just on young women from twenty-one to twenty-five who were missing was a lesson in heartache. There were too many of them, too many families who didn't have answers. He couldn't help remembering when his mom had left and all the sleepless nights he'd had wondering where she was and if she was ever coming back.

Wes, who had started two days after him, was at the desk next to his, filling in paperwork for a break-in the night before. There was almost always something happening around the reservation. This thing with kidnapping and keeping a woman near the edge of it—Chay didn't like it.

Rubbing the back of his neck, he reached for his coffee cup, but the bit in the bottom had gone cold. He swallowed it anyway and then went to refill it before opting for water instead. He drank too much coffee. Walking around the almost empty office just to stretch and clear his head, he thought of Fern. She'd looked so small in the hospital bed when she'd been talking about being taken.

Starting with the missing-persons report that Annie Ross had filed on Camille Lancaster, he went over the details matching them to what Fern had revealed. But because Annie had only secondhand knowledge and the officer who'd taken the report hadn't included much other information, Chay suspected that Annie's drug offenses and the fact that her friend may have had the same influenced the slim report.

But Camille Lancaster...he ran a check on the woman and found out she'd been in the foster care system in Wilson. Nowhere near where Fern had been raised. Was there a connection there he was missing?

Cross-referencing the missing young women with the foster care system, he got several hits. Like sixty percent of the woman on the list had been in the foster care system. Of that number, many of them had been reported because they missed work. There were a handful that had been reported by a partner or a roommate.

Carefully, he started to compile a list. There was no obvious connection to these women other than they all seemed to have no one in their life. No close family or friends to miss them when they disappeared.

He sent the information he'd gathered to Jacob and then leaned back in his chair to stretch his back. Tomorrow he'd start following up with the local police departments and get the missing-persons reports together.

His phone rang, and he glanced down to see it was his grandmother. A quick glance at his watch confirmed he was late for dinner. Uh-oh. She wasn't one who liked it when he missed their time together.

"Sorry. I'm leaving the office now," he said as he answered her call. Getting to his feet, he grabbed his jacket and headed out of the office, waving goodbye to the night officer on duty at the front desk.

"I figured you would be. You've got fifteen minutes to

stop and pick up some flowers for me," she said wryly. He could picture her standing in her kitchen, talking to him from her landline because she refused to rely on her cell phone.

"I already have them," he retorted. When he had turned sixteen, he had started bringing home flowers for her. It was a simple way of saying thank you when he'd been too confused inside to express his emotions for her. She'd saved his life. He knew it. There was no way he'd have become the man he was today without her influence.

"See you soon."

He hung up, unable to stop thinking about those missing women. The foster care system did the best it could, but when young people turned eighteen they were adults. There was no safe place for them to move to. There was some housing, but it was rough and in some places riddled with gangs, drugs and violence.

Fern had moved beyond that living situation and had had a good job and her own place. But being abandoned took a toll. Moving from place to place made it hard to form connections. All of those missing women were in the same boat.

Someone was taking advantage of that. Someone who had access to the foster care system and would know when a kid aged out?

He dialed Ava's number to ask her.

"Hey, it's Chay," he said when she answered.

"Hey."

"As a foster carer, what kind of information are you given?" he asked.

"About what? Gracie's family? I have access to knowing who her parents were if they are known. I fostered two brothers in that situation but with Gracie I only know what you do. What is going on with the criminal investigation into how Annie died. Is that what you are asking?"

"Sort of. Would you be able to find out who is aging out of foster care?"

"I don't know. I can ask around, but that doesn't seem like information that would be shared," Ava said.

"Thanks. No need to ask anyone else," he said.

"Sure."

"I have to run—I'm late to dinner with my grandmother," he said.

"Oh, you better get going. 'Bye."

Tomorrow the top of his list would be finding out if there was a list of kids who aged out and who had access to it. He needed to see if there was any crossover in skills. Some reason why all of these women were taken. As a medical coder, Fern might have read some sensitive information that she wasn't aware of. He hadn't thought to check what job Camille Lancaster had.

Pulling into his grandmother's driveway, he smiled as he always did. It was hard not to remember his first glimpse of the house and how scared he'd been when he saw her in the doorway. His mom hadn't told him much other than that he was going to stay with his grandmother for a little while.

It wasn't the first time she'd left him with someone, but it was the first time the person had been a relative.

He walked to the front door, the Gerber daisies he'd picked up at the grocery store in one hand. There was some light snow falling, but it was February, so that was to be expected.

He knocked, then let himself in.

"In the kitchen," she called.

Hanging his coat on a peg near the door and taking

off his boots, he went to find her. He gave her a hug and a kiss on the top of her head.

"Good to see you."

They ate dinner before she asked why he'd called earlier. "There's a baby in Dark Canyon that was left at the fire station. She's part Diné. She was wrapped in a blanket that had a little moon in the corner. Just like all of our weavers have done for generations."

Grandmother sat in her thoughts for a few minutes, and Chay let her. That was a lot of information to digest.

"I would like a great-grandchild."

"Whose baby could she be? Did Mom have another kid? I know Dad didn't." His father had died when he'd been a baby.

Grandmother pursed her lips. "Not that she told me. But I can't rule it out. Are you involved with the child?"

His mom hadn't exactly kept in touch with them. But he hadn't been sure if his grandmother had had any contact that she hadn't shared with him. There was one year when he'd been twelve that he'd really wanted his mom to come to his birthday. Which she hadn't.

"No. I'm not made to be a father. But I want the baby to be raised with The People. Also I wanted to get your opinion."

"Smart. I think she should be raised here. I'm not sure why you believe you wouldn't be a good father, though."

"Grandmother," he said with a sigh.

She just tutted at him. "You're so much more than you give yourself credit for."

AVA'S CALENDAR WAS free until the afternoon, and she made an appointment with Marg at Family Services. Gracie was in a chatty mood on the way to the meeting and kept up her babble as they were seated at Marg's desk.

Marg's office was smaller than Ava's and had three big filing cabinets lining one of the walls. There was a poster of the Dark Canyon National Park on the other wall. Marg was about Ava's age but always looked tired. Her brown hair was always up in a messy bun and she wore a pair of horn-rimmed glasses.

"What's up?" Marg asked.

"With the DNA results in and matching Officer Benally, I thought it would be nice to have Gracie spend more time with him."

"Oh, thank God. I was afraid you were going to say you couldn't keep her," Marg said.

"No. I'm keeping her for as long as I'm needed. I've spoken to Officer Benally—"

"Does he want to adopt her? What's his connection to the child?" Marg asked, riffling around on her desk for some papers.

"He's got about a twenty-five percent genetic match with her, which would make him her uncle or maybe cousin," Ava said. Chay had been adamant that he didn't want to raise the child, but Ava was convinced if he spent more time with Gracie that would change his mind.

She knew from growing up with a close-knit group of cousins that bond was strong. Chay would feel the same way, she just knew it. Also he was magic with Gracie—it was as if she knew that he was related to her somehow.

"Okay, that's a good connection. I'll have to talk to the court. You were cleared to foster her, but because of the investigation around the mother's death… I'm not sure they'd allow a switch."

"That's fine," she said. Especially since Chay didn't

want to take Gracie. "I was hoping we could spend some time on the Navajo Nation and with Chay and his grandmother."

"I don't see that as a problem. But let me run it by the court first. I should have an answer for you in a few days."

"Great," Ava said.

"Do you need anything else?"

"No. She's such a little sweetie. She's a bit colicky at times but her doctor said that's normal for her age. She's finished her course of medicine and seems to be bouncing back from the infection."

"All good. Thanks again for taking her on short notice."

"You know I didn't mind," Ava said.

She left Marg's office, and since she had more time off and it was one of those clear, cold winter days, she drove to the park to go for a walk. She hadn't been outside much with the snow and slushy weather. Using the baby carrier that strapped around her chest, she nestled Gracie close to her body, making sure they were both bundled for the cold.

Fern's story had really stuck with Ava. It was odd how a person could go through life making their plans and routine and have it all taken away in one moment. Fern's life really didn't sound much different to Ava's own. Except she had her family that she saw once a week or more, depending on what everyone had going on.

Thinking about it made her feel a bit paranoid. There were other people in the park, and she didn't notice anyone staring at her. Mostly it was moms and preschool-aged kids and a few adults sitting on the benches.

Nothing to really cause concern, but she'd always felt safe in Dark Canyon. Something she'd brought with her to college, and that had been a mistake. Having grown up where everyone knew her or her family had insulated her to what it was like to truly be around strangers. Here in Dark Canyon, even people she didn't know she had a connection to.

Not so in college. She went to the swing and sat down on it, pushing herself and looking down at Gracie as they swung. The baby's eyes went wide and she laughed as they came back down, which made Ava smile.

She kept swinging for about ten minutes until the cold started to settle into her jeans and she needed to get them both back someplace warm. Walking back to her truck, she stopped for a moment, tipping her head back toward the sun. Thanking God for the beautiful day and this tiny person to share it with.

Once they were back in the car, she headed to the hospital to get ready for her shift. The day-care workers were happy to see Gracie, and Ava kissed the little girl goodbye, realizing that it was going to be very hard for her to see Gracie move on to her permanent family.

She really needed to remind herself that this was temporary. Just temporary. Gracie wasn't her baby, and she wasn't going to be her mom.

She had a few outpatients scheduled for the afternoon, conducting those sessions in her office. The day went slowly, giving her too much time to think. Mostly about Gracie and, of course, Chay.

That man had a well of caring in him that he probably wasn't aware was very visible whenever he held Gracie. She was sure if she just put Gracie in his arms more often, he'd start to realize it. Of course, he'd also told her to butt out. But in this case she was sure she knew what was good for both Chay and Gracie.

Before she could talk herself out of it, she picked up the phone and dialed his number.

"Benally."

His voice was so formal, she couldn't help smiling. He was so serious at work. "Colton."

"Ava? Good to hear from you. What's up?"

His voice warmed, which made her smile. It wasn't smart to start catching feels for Chay. He was working on a case, which she was sideline involved in, and she wanted him to adopt Gracie. "I was wondering if I could bring Gracie to the Navajo Nation to visit with you. Give her a chance to see where she's from."

There was a short pause. "I'm off tomorrow."

"I am, too. I'll drive out around ten or so, and maybe we could have lunch together. You can show me around."

"I'd like that," he said.

"Me, too." She hung up the phone feeling very pleased with herself. She'd be subtle, but she wanted to nurture the bond between Gracie and Chay until he could no longer stomach the thought of the baby being raised by anyone but him.

Singing to herself as she carried Gracie to the car at the end of the day, she realized that she still felt that sensation of being watched. Turning quickly, she didn't see anyone close behind her…she scanned the entrance to the hospital but the doors were closed. Probably just her imagination.

THE BEAUTY OF Dark Canyon and the surrounding land between the city and the Navajo Nation consumed her as she drove. Gracie had fallen asleep when she'd left her neighborhood. Ava had her road trip playlist on. The trip between the Navajo Nation and Dark Canyon was about an hour. It had snowed overnight, and the land glistened as the sun reflected off the pristine white blanketing the landscape.

It was nice to have a full day off. She loved her job, but there were times when a patient's story was hard to disassociate from. Her mom always said that was what made her a good therapist, and her mom could be right, but that didn't make sleeping any easier.

Chay was chopping wood outside his home when she pulled up. He lived a bit remotely, but she liked it. The rustic cabin felt like it was part of the landscape. Smoke was coming from the chimney, and the scent of a fresh pine fire was in the air. He put his ax down and came over to greet her as she hopped down from the driver's side.

"You made good time," he said.

"Got a bit of a lead foot when I'm on the highway. Know better than to speed in town."

He smiled at that and opened the back door to lift Gracie's carrier out of the car seat. "How you doing today, yazhi?"

"Yazhi?"

"Little one."

"I like it," Ava said, following him up the natural stone steps into his cabin. She sat on the bench near the door to take off her boots as she took in the open-plan space. She could see a breakfast bar with the kitchen behind it. The living and dining rooms flowed into each other. One wall was dominated by bookcases and a stone fireplace. Another one was floor-to-ceiling glass doors that let the landscape serve as all the art the room needed.

There was a large leather couch, some side chairs and a big recliner next to a side table that had a coffee mug and some books on it. She suspected that was where he sat.

The Navajo blanket over the back of the couch looked very similar to the one that Gracie had been wrapped in.

"I know you wanted me to show you around, but I thought we'd start with my place. Give you a chance to stretch your legs before we do more driving. Also, Gracie might need to get out of the car seat."

"She does," Ava agreed, taking the carrier from him and getting the baby out of it. Waking up, she was always sort of all mushy and sweet. Her eyes blinked a few times as she yawned and stretched. "I'll need to change her diaper."

"There's a bathroom down that hall." He pointed to it.

Taking a diaper and wipes out of the bag she'd brought in with her, she went to change Gracie. The bathroom had a natural wood countertop that had been treated to be water resistant, and there were double sinks. The floor was the same stone that was in the rest of the house, and the rug under her feet had the repeated motifs she'd seen on the blanket.

Talking to Gracie as she changed the baby. "We're at your uncle Chay's house. I think you're going to like it here. We'll find out more about the motifs that were on your blanket. He has a bunch in this house."

The baby made a cooing, questioning sound, which Ava responded to before tickling her little feet and getting her back into her clothes. Today Ava had her dressed in a pair of overalls with a long-sleeved onesie underneath. She wore socks that matched.

"There you go."

Hurrying back out, she noticed Chay had set the blanket on the floor in the living area and poured two cups of coffee. "Figured she'd want to play...is that the right word for a baby her age?"

"It works. She is currently a big fan of trying to eat her toes. I have some toys in the diaper bag as well," Ava said. He was already halfway to being a good carer for Gracie. But she knew she was drawing connections that might not be there. He'd also gotten her coffee and had just made the living room ready for both of them.

Ava cautioned herself so she didn't push too hard, but it was difficult as she observed Chay with Gracie. When she saw something that she knew was right, there was no stopping her.

Chay got the bag and brought it over as she set Gracie in the middle of the blanket. They placed a soft book and a giraffe that jingled when it shook next to her, along with some teething keys.

Chay went back to his recliner, and Ava took a seat on the couch close to Gracie.

"So what did you have in mind?" he asked as she got comfortable on the couch.

"I've never been out here before. I would like to see the community where she'll be raised. Have you thought any more about raising her yourself?" Ava tried to be nonchalant about it. Like she hadn't broached this subject with him more than once before.

He tilted his head to the side, giving her a narrow look. "I don't need to. I've already told you I'm not doing that."

She tried to look serious as she nodded at him. "I respect that. But can I point out that you are doing a lot of things that a dad would do?"

"You can point out whatever you want to. Doesn't mean you're right."

"Agree to disagree," she said lightly. She'd given it her best shot and his answer was still no.

"Are you going to be like this all day?" he asked, and she could tell she'd pushed his last button.

"Maybe."

He almost smiled.

"Well then, we will leave as soon as you finish your coffee. I think you'll like meeting my grandmother," he said.

"Why?"

"She's sassy like you. Also likes to boss everyone around. I'm interested to see what she makes of you."

Ava wasn't sure how to take that at first but decided it must be a compliment. They chatted about the weather. It had been a pretty erratic winter so far. But mostly she found herself watching Chay as he watched Gracie… and being aware of his eyes on her when she turned to gaze at the baby…

Chapter Six

He'd never had a woman at the cabin other than his grandmother. He was a solitary man and liked his peace, but there was something about Ava and Gracie that felt right. Something he was adamant he wasn't going to delve too deeply into.

Ava had something on her mind. It wasn't what she was saying, it was just that he'd started pick up on her little tells. Like the way she looked intensely at him and then just sort of glanced away without mentioning a thing. What was that about?

He wanted to talk to her as well…well, ask her out. See if she'd be open to exploring that moment when they'd almost kissed. He was particular about the women he slept with. Guess it all came down to him not being a casual person. His mom…she had been too casual. Making connections with everyone, expecting it to last, and then when it hadn't, crashing hard and losing herself in drugs. The truth was he was careful. He didn't need a therapist like Ava to explain his behavior to him.

He finished his coffee, aware that these two women were stirring feelings he wasn't ready to unpack. It was time to show her around the Navajo Nation here in Dark Canyon and then send her on her way.

Except he'd just been toying with asking her for a date. Those dual desires warred inside of him. He wanted to be safe. Wanted to protect himself from being hurt. Wanted to stay ignorant as to whether he was just like his mom or not.

Ava gave him a sweet smile as she got to her feet and took her mug into the kitchen. She moved with a fluid grace that he'd have to be dead not to notice. All long limbs and swinging hair.

Turning, she caught him watching her and tipped her head to the side, studying him again. But it was different this time. More female speculation. Interest and curiosity.

The same as his?

Was she wondering what he tasted like? If he had coffee breath at this moment? He was willing to risk it to find out what *she* tasted like. She'd probably be willing to risk it as well.

"Chay…"

"Ava…" he teased back.

"You're watching me."

"I am. You're watching me back."

"I definitely am…"

She trailed off. There was a *but* or an *except* implicit at the end of that phrase. "What's stopping you?"

"You."

"Me? Ava, I'm not saying no." He held his arms out to his side. Glancing back at Gracie to make sure the baby was safe, he noticed her eyes were closed and she was sleeping with the giraffe in her hands.

"It's not that."

"Then what?" He took a step closer to her.

She chewed her lower lip and then shook her head. "Promise you won't get mad."

That didn't sound very promising. He put his arms down, crossing them over his chest. "I'll have to hear it first."

"Oh...it's not... I was just going to say that I like you and I wouldn't mind kissing you, but I'm not sure what you have in mind."

"Well, let's kiss and see where it goes," he said. "Not sure why I'd be mad at that."

Her mouth quirked in a half grin. "That's not the thing...before we start anything I have to tell you that I really think you should be Gracie's adopted father."

Well, fudge. That wasn't what he'd expected at all. And she was right to caution him not to get mad, because it did piss him off. "What the hell? I told you I'm not father material. Gracie is a sweet little one, but that's it. You and me? We don't truly have anything to do with her."

She took a step closer to him. The scent of her floral perfume teased him and he turned his face away. He didn't want to like her or be turned on by her right now. She'd ticked him off bringing this up.

"But we do. I think you avoid caring about people and keep everyone at arm's length. I'd want more than that if I got involved with you."

He got his back up. Putting his hands on his hips, he glared at her, but she just raised her eyebrows at him. "I'm not even sure we'll like kissing each other. This is a bit much, don't you think?"

She came closer to him, not stopping until there was barely an inch of space between them. Then she reached up and cupped his jaw. "No. I really like you, Chay. There is a spark between us. I think about you when you're not around. I miss you. So if I kiss you, I know myself well enough to realize I'm going to want more. I'm not sure you can deliver."

Well, hell.

That rocked him back on his ass. He could barely think with her hand on his face, her breath teasing his neck and her gazing into his eyes. God damn, she was so sincere as she looked up at him. He'd have to be a stronger man than he was to resist her.

"I'm good with you and me. I can give you what you want. I'm not going to agree to anything with Gracie to get you."

"I'm not asking that," she said. "I'm just trying to figure out if you are cautious or completely closed off. That's my dilemma."

He took a deep breath. She wasn't the first woman to ask him that. Usually it was after a few dates and they'd slept together. But Ava was cautious. He didn't know why…maybe he should be asking a few questions.

But who wanted to delve into baggage when there were sparks between them? "I'm cautious."

She nodded and then went up on her tiptoes. Her hand on his face slid to his shoulder to balance herself as she brushed her lips against his. He almost groaned at how good she tasted as he put his hands on her hips and pulled her closer to him. Opening his mouth, her tongue tangled with his and he knew that this woman was going to change him.

The way she talked and tasted. The way she felt in his arms, setting fire to his blood. The way her honesty made him want to be a different man than he'd been before.

Chay. He was stirring her in a way no one had in a very long time. That feminine part of herself she'd thought had died with Greg. Shoving that thought away, she concentrated on his kiss. It was bold and strong, like the man himself, but tempered, also like him.

He let her set the pace, which suited her. He tasted of coffee and man. He smelled of the outdoors and the smoke from the fire he had going in the fireplace. His hands on her hips were strong, but he made no move to pull her closer. Just kissing her and exploring this spark between them.

She'd overtalked it, so in a way she felt very lucky that he'd still kissed her. But that was the way she was. No two ways about it. She overthought everything and needed to sort stuff out in her head before she acted.

His tongue rubbed over hers, and a shiver raced down her spine, making her lean forward slightly until her breasts were nestled against his chest. He groaned, lifting her off her feet. She wrapped her arms around his shoulders, deepening the kiss.

The doorbell rang, startling her. Chay lifted his head, his skin flushed and his expression tense as he set her on her feet, turning away. He took a moment, breathing deeply before he walked to the door. She hurried back to the sofa where she'd been sitting to check on Gracie.

The baby was sleeping, and Ava got her blanket from the diaper bag and covered her with it. A cold draft seeped into the room as Chay opened the door.

"Grandmother."

"Grandson. Didn't realize you had company," she said as she kissed his cheek and then walked into the house.

His grandmother was shorter than Chay and had gray

hair that she wore in two braids. Her smile was friendly as she noticed Ava and she nodded at her.

Ava waved back and then felt totally lame. "Hi there."

"Hello. I'm Aponi Benally. But you can call me Grandmother."

"I'm Ava Colton," she said, going over to shake the older woman's hand. "Nice to meet you."

"Ava...you're the one fostering the baby?"

So Chay must have told her about Gracie. "I am. She's sleeping over there, if you want to see her."

"I definitely do," Grandmother said. "Chay, take this to the kitchen."

She handed Chay a Tupperware not unlike the one he'd brought to her house. "Are those more blue corn cookies?"

"Yes, and some winterberry muffins," Grandmother said.

"Yum. I'd love it if you'd share the recipe with me so I can try to make them. They were so good."

"I'm happy to. Are you a baker?"

"Not unless slice and bake counts. But I am trying to learn one new thing each month."

"Any baking counts. Why don't you stop by my house one day soon and I'll show you how to make them?"

"I'd love to," Ava said. "This is Gracie."

Grandmother got down on the floor next to Gracie, touching the blanket that covered her with one hand.

"Chay mentioned this blanket is similar to ones you make."

She nodded. "I send them to friends and family so I could have made this one for her."

That would be sweet and a universe type of connection between the two of them. If Gracie was Chay's cousin, then that would possibly make her Grandmother's great-grandchild. Ava wanted to ask more but felt like she'd pushed Chay far enough today with bringing up that she thought he should raise Gracie.

"I wondered that, too," Chay said as he came back to join them, bringing a hot drink for his grandmother. "I was going to show Ava around the town."

"I can watch this little sweetie if you two want to go," Grandmother offered.

Well, this could be awkward. Ava couldn't leave Gracie in the care of a stranger. The day care at the hospital was approved, but that was it. She looked at Chay, and he smiled and nodded.

"Thank you. That's a very generous offer. I'm working with the case worker to allow Chay to have more time with Gracie, but as of right now I can't leave her."

Grandmother nodded. "Of course. I should have realized. How long have you been fostering her?"

Ava told her it had only been a few days and recapped the story of how the baby had been found. "The DNA test revealed she was Annie Ross's baby. Though the birth wasn't registered."

Grandmother chanted something Navajo and Chay closed his eyes, so Ava did the same. It felt like a prayer, so she offered her own to God about Annie Ross. She hoped that woman was resting in peace. Hoped having Gracie in a good home and with a good family eventually would somehow be communicated to the dead woman.

Ava's heart hurt a little bit thinking of how Annie must have felt out in the wilderness all alone, knowing she had Gracie back home. Her last moments, given that she'd died of exposure and hypothermia, must have been filled with pain and delusions.

"What brings you out here, Grandmother?"

"I started digging around and trying to figure out if your mother had any more children."

"Did you find anyone?" Chay asked.

Ava wasn't sure if she should stay for this conversation. "Should I go and leave you two to talk?"

"Not necessary," Chay said.

"There's not much to tell. I didn't find anything. I started in Georgia, where she died. Maybe you can pick up the trail," she said to Chay. Then turned to Ava and smiled. "He's a very good investigator. He was decorated when he was on the Salt Lake City force."

"Really?"

"Yes."

"I want to know more about it," she said, turning to Chay.

But he just shook his head. "Another time."

AVA AND HIS grandmother got along very well. Not really a surprise. He'd guessed they would. Gracie woke up and he realized they weren't going to take a tour of the town, so he threw together a soup while the women played with the baby.

In the kitchen he watched Ava as much as he wanted to, since she was involved with her conversation with his grandmother. Ava was totally focused on the conversation she was having, which he admired. She hadn't pulled out her phone one time or tried to steer the conversation. Instead she seemed genuinely interested in his grandmother as she talked about weaving and the motifs she liked to use.

"The crosses are the Spider Woman."

"I'm not familiar with her. But I'm pretty sure you don't mean the Marvel superhero."

Grandmother laughed. "No, I don't. Though she is a superwoman. She is a protector and helper of all humanity. I always start with that motif in a weaving because that's one we can all use."

"This diamond pattern is so pretty. Does it have meaning, too?"

"It represents the mountains. The Four Sacred Mountains formed the boundaries of the Navajo and provide essentials to The People." Chay listened to his grandmother sharing the supernatural power that each of the four mountains held.

The Four Sacred Mountains were Sisnaajiní in the East, Dibé Nitsaa in the North, Dook'o'oosłííd in the West and lastly Tsoodził in the south. They formed the ancient boundaries of his people. Chay hadn't grown up on the Navajo Nation until he'd been dumped there by his mom, so he didn't always feel the strong spiritual connection to all things, but the mountains spoke to him.

Maybe because, like him, they'd been used. They looked strong on the outside, but they were littered with mines and erosion underneath. God, there was a metaphor. There were good, strong parts of his emotional being thanks to his grandmother, but those early years traveling around with his mother, never sure if he was staying in a town or a school, had left their mark.

Ava had been right to point out that he did keep everyone at arm's length. It was just easier when you never knew what was coming next.

Though he'd been here for the last five years. And if you counted his time with his grandmother, then he'd been on the Navajo Nation for the longest. This was the place he felt safest.

Might seem silly for a man as big and strong as he was admit, but Chay didn't lie to himself. It didn't lessen him or his masculinity to admit that he had fears. They weren't easy to dismiss. At the end of the day, everyone needed someone to love and feel like they were loved in return.

And Ava hadn't been asking him for that. Not really. She'd just wanted to ensure she wasn't getting into a relationship with someone who couldn't emote or admit they had feelings. He got that. His mom... Today was just stirring it all up.

The way she'd look at him, almost as if she resented him, at times, then other times hug him so tightly he couldn't breathe and tell him he was the only good thing she'd done with her life.

He made sure the heat under the pot was low enough to create a simmer and then walked toward the foyer. "Watch the soup."

He didn't say anything else or even wait for a confirmation, just put on his coat and went outside. He walked until he was in the tree line, throwing his head back and looking up into the winter sky. All gray and thick with clouds. Snow still falling but not heavily.

The flakes fell on his face, making his cheeks wet. He felt the warmth and knew there were tears mixed in with them as well.

He felt a hand on his back and looked down to see Ava standing there. She had her coat on and concern written all over her face. He rubbed both hands over his face and looked down at her.

"What?"

"You looked like you needed a friend," she said.

God, when hadn't he? Butch had said something similar to him when he'd taken him on as a partner. "Yeah, you, too. All you do is work and volunteer."

Turning it back on her was deflection, but it was also the truth. They were similar but also so very different.

"So true. It makes me... I was going to say feel like I have someone. Which is silly, because I have my parents and brother and cousins. But I haven't had a one-to-one connection in a long time."

"Me, either," he said. But he knew that he had that connection with Grandmother. She was solid and strong. She gave him space when he needed it and pushed her way in when she decided he'd had enough. Probably why she'd shown up here today.

"Not you. You and your grandmother are close. I can see it. I had that with my aunt Kate."

"What happened?"

"Cancer. She died almost three years ago. I still miss her. I guess it's different with a grandmother or aunt than with parents. They just love you."

"Yeah," he said. His mom... Anyone was going to be more stable. He often wondered if she'd loved him at all. He was sure she did—she'd told him that one time before she left him here that she did. And his mom wasn't one to sugarcoat things so he'd believed her. "We should get back inside."

She slipped her hand in his. "I like your grandmother."

"I have a feeling she likes you, too," Chay said.

"Why'd you say it like that?"

"I don't need two bossy women in my life," he said, unable to keep the smile from his face. Just having her hand in his made him feel lighter.

"Oh, you definitely do," Ava said.

The rest of the afternoon was spent quietly talking and eating soup. He held Gracie and admitted to himself that if he were a different man, he would have tried to adopt her. But as he waved goodbye to Ava and Gracie and then his grandmother, he knew he wasn't a different man.

As fun as today had been, he needed to get back to work, figuring out the connection between the two women found in Dark Canyon.

Chapter Seven

That kiss. Really, she'd put it from her mind as much as she could, and Gracie had kept her busy as she always did while Ava fed her dinner, played with her, got her bathed and then into bed. But now that she was curled up on the end of the couch a book in her hands, she realized she wasn't thinking about the epic romantasy she was reading, but instead about Chay.

God, that man was messing with her mind. She had a plan for her life. It was straightforward and easy to follow. All she had to do was stick to it. After Greg had died, her life had shifted. The one she'd envisioned for herself was gone and she'd had to adjust. After Daniel Wayne had been arrested, she'd realized that she'd been stifling her own desires, living in a sort of stasis filled with fear. Fear of Daniel but also fear of trying things. Fear of actually putting her heart at risk again. She'd started volunteering.

Her aunt Kate had been the one to suggest fostering. And after her aunt's death, when the numbness of grief had subsided, she'd applied. It hadn't been a hard decision. Aunt Kate had said during one of their many talks that the only regrets she had were the love she'd kept.

It hadn't made much sense at the time; Ava had almost thought it was the medicine talking, but now she understood it. Every day Ava made the choice on who to engage with and who to actually show she cared for. A part of her had thought that being kind to strangers had been what had drawn Daniel to her, so she'd stifled that part of herself until she'd slowly been strangling.

The little boys she'd first fostered had been a baby step back into the world she'd once taken for granted. And she'd been rewarded in ways she'd never expected from that. Gracie was easy to love. So sweet and innocent.

But Chay was more complicated. Liking him had her nerves buzzing and her head filled with…images of what she'd like to do the next time they were alone. But he wasn't a baby who hadn't had time to build up a tough outer shell.

He was a complicated man who had his own baggage. Her pointing it out probably hadn't been the smartest choice, but she was back to the fact that she really liked him. So she'd had no options.

Letting herself like him wasn't something she could control. She liked the way he smiled, the way he just got things done and his determination not to let the crimes committed against Fern go unpunished.

Her heart melted every time he held Gracie. No matter what Chay thought, he had the makings of a man who could be a really good dad. But his mind and his past told him otherwise.

A part of her wanted to come at Chay like a therapist. Break down what he had told her and shown her and figure out how to help him to change his behavior. But the feminine part of her wanted Chay just for herself. Wanted to uncover the man he was as they got to know each other.

He'd asked her on a date.

She'd hedged. Hadn't answered because his grandmother had arrived.

Grabbing her phone, she opened the message app and stared down at his name. Was she going to do this?

Or was she going to continue staying safe in her cozy little home, not taking any risks with her emotions and protecting her battered heart?

The answer wasn't simple.

As she'd told her clients more than once, it wasn't easy to risk getting hurt again. The mind made her cautious to protect her from experiencing that kind of loss again. Except... Chay made her want to take a chance.

Before she could second-guess it, she tapped his name and started typing.

Ava: Hey. It's me. Ava. I think you were asking me out on a date earlier. Where did we leave that?

She hit send and then put the phone facedown next to her on the couch. She wanted to check it to see if he was responding. Though it was after eleven, so he might be sleeping. She went to the kitchen to keep from obsessively watching her screen to make a cup of tea.

The kettle was on the burner when her phone pinged. She raced back over to the couch and picked it up.

"Be cool," she warned herself but she totally wasn't as she saw Chay had responded.

Chay: I'm not sure. You were hesitating.

Ugh. He was so right to call her on her own shit. I'm not now.

Chay: So I'm guessing it's a package deal with you and Gracie, right?

It is. She couldn't leave Gracie with anyone. Maybe she could get permission but as Marg had stated the courts were being careful while Annie Ross's murder was being investigated.

Chay: Dinner at your place? I'll cook. You two provide the entertainment.

Dinner at her place. She glanced around, realizing she needed to get a new tablecloth and maybe some nicer dinnerware. She tended to use the same plate for everything. She never hosted anyone at her place.

Ava: Friday works. Any food allergies?

Two nights away. Bubbles of excitement filled her stomach.

Chay: None.

Ava: Games, movies or karaoke?

He used the double exclamation marks on her comment.

Chay: Not a singer.

Ava: Really? With that deep voice I bet you sound pretty good.

Chay: You like my voice?

Ava: Yeah. So game or movie?

Chay: You choose.

Hmm…she had few days to decide. The kettle whistled, and she walked back over to it with her phone.

Ava: Gotta go. Good night. See you Friday.

Chay: Night.

Her heart was racing as she poured the water over a bag of Sleepy Time tea. It was silly to be so smiley and happy after texting with a guy. But this was Chay and he was funny. She couldn't wait to see him on Friday.

PULLING TOGETHER AN investigation was a lot of grunt work. Sitting at his desk, reading reports and making calls. Trying to piece together if there was a connection between Annie Ross and Fern Hensley wasn't that easy. There was a part of him that worried he and Jacob were making one just to explain what had happened. He'd worked a lot of cases. And no matter how many he'd closed, he still always wanted to understand the why.

The missing women on his list had one thing in common. But other than all having been through the foster care system, that was it. Their paths hadn't really crossed in or out of foster care.

Some were known to the police before they'd gone missing and had dabbled in drugs and sex work. Others were just regular women with stories similar to Fern's—just doing their thing trying to get by.

His alarm went off, reminding him he had to get to the grocery store before they closed. The date with Ava wasn't until tomorrow night, but he had in mind to make a stew that tasted better the second day. He needed to get it started tonight so that tomorrow night it would be perfect.

Which reminded him. He called his grandmother.

"How's it going?" she asked when she answered.

"Busy. Long day trying to figure out these missing women," he told her.

"You'll figure it out. You always do. What's up?"

"I have a date with Ava tomorrow night and I'm bringing my stew over. How do you feel about making some bread dough for me that I could bake at her place?"

"I can do that. I'll even make a winter berry cake for you as well. She loved those muffins I made," Grandmother said.

"Thanks," he said. He hoped she knew how grateful he was to have her. "Did you have any doubts about keeping me? When Mom left?"

"None. Even though I didn't know anything about raising a boy and your grandfather had died not long after your mom left," she said. His grandfather was already dead when Chay was brought to live with his grandmother.

"So you were settled into living your single woman life, huh?" She'd still been young when he'd been dropped on her door. She'd raised her daughter, and having him might not have been what she'd wanted.

"Oh you. Not really. I have Fiona and my weaving. But I was content. I don't have a problem with silence."

Something he was aware of. He'd had a problem with it when he'd first moved in with her, but she'd taught him how to use the silence to find peace and balance in himself. Not that he'd been an easy or eager student. "I'm not sure I could do what you did."

It was odd, because he'd told Ava he wasn't considering adopting Gracie, but these questions had been in the back of his mind. The thought that maybe he could do it, but his fear that he wasn't going to be good enough to raise a little girl.

"It's not about ability. You have the skills. It's about... the life you want for yourself. When I saw you with your mom, something shifted inside of me. I hadn't been aware that I had a grandson until that moment. I knew I wanted to know you and have a relationship with you."

His rubbed the back of his neck. They never really talked about this. "I hadn't realized."

"Why would you? You were a kid and you had a lot going on. For me, the moment I crouched down in front of you, I was hooked. I knew I would do whatever it took to keep you in my life."

His heart flooded with love for this woman. She'd given him a life. As a child he'd been scared of being left by his mom, but his grandmother had raised him and given him strength.

"I love you."

"I love you, too," she said, letting the silence buzz on the open line. "You didn't ask but I think you'd be a good father. And I'd love to have some great-grandchildren."

He knew she did. Their family was small—just the two of them, with a few distant cousins who lived down in Arizona. But mostly it was just them. "I know you do. Might not happen."

"No pressure. You have to make the life that is your own. Not one that's for me," she said. "Make sure that they are your choices and not a reaction to your mother's."

"Yes, ma'am," he said.

They said their goodbyes and he looked at his desk. Did she think he was still reacting to the way his mom had left him? It was true that given his upbringing, his mom's struggles and never knowing his father, it did make him think twice about having a family of his own.

He knew how fragile they were. Look at little Gracie. She reinforced that. The baby had had a mother who no doubt loved her, but now she was on her own. He might not be sure about adopting her, but he could find out who her mother was and why she was murdered. Having answers about her was going to matter to Gracie one day.

He sent a brief email to Jacob updating him on the information he'd gathered that day and then got ready to leave the tribal police office. He said good-night to the officer on duty and then walked out to his truck. The night was cold and dark, as if it were midnight instead of only 6:00 p.m.

That was winter. The season seemed to drive you inside. So what was Annie Ross doing wandering around in the wilderness? And why would she have left her baby behind? What had been important to her?

Camille's disappearance? He'd really like to talk to the officer who took that missing-person report, but he'd missed him all day. He would try again tomorrow.

He needed to know more about the woman so he could follow the trail and find out what linked her and Fern.

Ava hurried down the corridor to Fern's room. When she got closer, she noticed the door was partially closed and heard voices and some laughter. Hesitating, she glanced at her watch. She was about five minutes early for their session, so she had time.

It was nice to hear Fern talking. Ava hadn't realized that she had friends or family. From the story that Fern had told, she'd thought the other woman was alone in the world.

But then she recognized the voice.

"Ryan?"

"Oh, hey, Ava. How's it going?" her brother asked, standing up from the guest chair.

"Pretty good. What are you doing here? Everything okay?" she asked him.

"Yeah. Just checking on Fern," he said.

"I keep telling him I'm fine," Fern said, a slight blush to her cheeks.

"I need to see it with my own eyes," he said gently. "I guess I'll let you get down to business."

"To defeat the Huns?" Ava and Fern said at the same time.

They all started laughing.

"Sorry, it's just when someone says that I'm back to being a kid and watching *Mulan*," Fern said.

"Same with us," Ryan said. "'Bye, big sister. Later, Fern."

Ryan left the room, and Ava watched Fern as she smiled to herself. It was nice to see the other woman relaxed. That was it. She hadn't been relaxed one time since the fire, but Ryan had done that for her.

"So, let me close the door and we can get started."

Making sure the door was closed, Ava sat in the chair her brother had left, noticing that it was still warm and sort of indented. She wasn't Junie B. Jones, but she was pretty sure her brother had been there for a while.

"How are you feeling today?"

"Better. I've been using the techniques you mentioned last time. Whenever that feeling of dread takes place in my stomach, I go through my day. It's really helping me."

"I'm glad to hear that. Is there anything on your mind?" Ava asked.

Fern talked a little bit about her leg, which was healing up nicely. She thought that she might be moved out of the hospital.

"How do you feel about that?"

She shrugged and did that thing, making pyramids with the blanket on over her legs and then flattening them out. "Not sure. I feel safe here."

"That makes sense. The hospital is the first place you haven't had to worry, so transition from here is going to take you some time. Did the doctors give you a date?" Ava asked, making a note to speak to the hospital staff and find out when the move was going to happen.

"No. Just that I was healing up nicely…which just made me think they are going to want me to leave. Also I don't have good insurance—I'm not even sure who's paying for this," Fern said.

"It's okay. It's all being taken care of, you don't have to worry about that," Ava said, knowing that Fern's bills were being covered until the investigation was finished.

"One less thing to worry about," she said.

"Do you want to talk about another one?"

She shook her head. "It's nothing concrete. Just fear that those guys will somehow come back. I mean, am I being ridiculous? Why would they risk coming to the hospital?"

But those men hadn't seemed impervious to risk. "You're right. The nursing staff, doctors and myself are all stopping by to check on you."

"And Ryan," Fern said.

"Does he visit you a lot?"

"Pretty much every day," she said. "He's nice."

"He can be," Ava said. "As a little brother, he can also be a bit of a pain."

"I guess," she said.

Ava realized Fern was forming an attachment to her brother, which was fine and would probably go a long way to speeding up Fern's recovery. But how did Ryan feel about her?

It had always been her policy to never meddle in his life. Was she going to change that now?

Maybe. Fern was vulnerable, and her brother, who had a big heart, might not realize how attached the other woman was becoming.

"Have you been working on that list I asked you to make?" Ava had suggested Fern make a list of things she was looking forward to once she left the hospital.

"Some. I'm not ready to share it," Fern said.

"You don't have to. It's for you. I'm glad you're doing it."

They spent the rest of the hour discussing other techniques that Fern could use to get ready to leave the hospital. "Try to picture something that would make the new place feel like home. It could be a view out the window or something on your dresser or nightstand. Just an item that makes it feel like it's your place."

Fern glanced toward the closet where a balloon had been tied to one of the handles. The slogan on it read You Are Essentially Awesome!

"The balloon?"

"Is that silly?"

"No, it's perfect. You have it here with you and can bring it to your new place. What else would make it homey? Anything I can bring for you?"

"No, that's okay."

"Not even a cat with a motivational quote poster?" Ava teased.

Fern laughed and shook her head. "I think that balloon will be enough. I'm not a collector of things."

"What do you collect?"

"Memories," she said.

"Do you want to share any of them?" Ava asked her. She hadn't delved into anything in Fern's past—she knew the other woman had been in the foster care system, but Fern hadn't brought it up. Ava was here to discuss whatever Fern had on her mind.

"Just one. When I graduated from high school, my foster mom gave me a balloon that said 'The Future Is Yours.' I think…this balloon is giving all the same feels."

That was a nice connection. They talked for a few more minutes before Ava left. Fern was making progress and healing nicely, but there was a part of Ava that feared the other woman was putting on a show. At some point the memories of what happened to her were going to become bigger, harder to contain. Ava hoped that the techniques and conversations they'd had together would be enough to help her when that time came.

Chapter Eight

Work was stressful and Gracie was cranky, probably because of the new tooth that Ava could see trying to poke through her gums. Chay was meant to be at her place at six, and Ava still was in her work clothes and now had dried baby food on the front of her sweater.

It took all of her willpower not to join Gracie and start crying. Fern was making nice progress, but Ava had other patients, and her Friday group was starting to be the toughest.

It didn't help that it was winter. One of her patients, Alice, struggled with anxiety and depression and long walks were really the only thing that helped her, but the weather lately had been so inclement she hadn't been able to get out, so she'd been walking almost six hours a day on her treadmill, which wasn't working. Her nails were bitten to the quick and she hadn't been able to sit still the entire session until Ava had decided they would go and walk around the park she'd taken Gracie to the other day.

That had worked, but Ava was worried about Alice, even as she knew she had to give her the space to figure out how to help herself. She hadn't thought of making laps around the park, which of course felt obvious to Ava, but she wasn't struggling the way Alice was.

There were days like today when she wondered if she was making any difference. She'd volunteered maybe too quickly to take on Gracie to foster. She had no experience with babies, just had somehow figured she could do it.

God, she was wrong.

It wasn't easy. Those pictures she'd had in her head of rocking a sleeping baby or playing with her as she learned to roll over and start crawling felt like they were mocking her.

The doorbell rang, interrupting her negative thought spiral. She glanced at the clock and then down at herself. There was no time to change. That had to be Chay.

Gracie seemed to cry louder as Ava scooped her out of the high chair and walked to the door.

Opening it to see Chay standing there with a large cooler near his feet.

"Oh no."

"Exactly. I'm sorry I'm not ready for our date."

"No problem," he said, catching Gracie as she threw herself toward him. He turned his head down to the baby, kissing the top of her head. "What's the matter, little one?"

"I think she's teething," Ava answered, picking up his cooler as he walked into her house.

She followed him into the kitchen, slightly reassured to see that Gracie was still crying, even for the baby whisperer.

"What are you supposed to do?"

"I've put some topical numbing stuff on her gums, but it's not working. My mom can't remember what worked for me and Ryan. Do you think your grandmother has any ideas? If not I'm going to call the pediatrician."

Chay handed Gracie back to Ava, and the little girl burrowed her head into Ava's neck, holding tightly onto Ava's hair with one of her little hands. "Let me ask."

Ava made a few circuits around the living room as Chay called his grandmother. She heard him talking but couldn't really hear what was being said over Gracie's crying. But it seemed she was wearing herself out. As Ava turned to make her fourth trip around the room, Gracie let out a big sigh and quieted down.

She glanced at Chay. His eyes were wide and he cupped his hand over his mouth to whisper to his grandmother. Neither of them wanting to do anything that might startle her awake again.

Ava made another loop around the room as Chay came over to her. "Want to try laying her down?" he whispered.

Ava nodded. "Pray she doesn't wake up."

Walking at the same rocking pace she'd used in the living room, she took Gracie to her crib, and Chay helped her get the baby settled. She made a little moan and then shoved her fist in her mouth, sucking on it as she continued to sleep.

They both backed out of the room as quietly as possible. Neither speaking until they were in the kitchen.

"I can heat dinner up on the stovetop, which should be quiet. I have some fresh bread and a cake that my grandmother made," Chay said.

"Sounds lovely. Would you mind if I went and got a little more date-ready?" she asked him. She didn't want to admit it, but she needed a cry to relieve the stress of the afternoon and evening.

"You look lovely, but go on. I'll get her if she wakes," Chay said.

"Thanks. Did your grandmother have any advice?"

"To let her cry it out," he said wryly. "Guess Gracie already had that idea."

She smiled at him and then closed her eyes. "Thank you."

"For what?"

"Just being you," she said, realizing how true those words were. He'd been calm, hadn't minded she wasn't ready for their date or focused on him. Probably why she'd agreed to the date. There was something about Chay that she just plain liked.

"Can't be anyone else," he admitted. "Go on."

She left him in the kitchen. She wanted a shower and needed it to mask the sounds of her own crying, so she hopped in, but as she washed herself she realized that having Chay at her side was more helpful than those tears normally were. Just by showing her that he'd been unsure as well made her feel better. How the heck did first-time parents cope?

It was harder than she'd imagined having a baby. Poor Annie Ross, who'd been alone—how had she handled it? Was that why she'd been out in the wilderness? Ava would give anything to have a chat with Gracie's mom. Anything to have her still alive so that maybe she could help Annie and little Gracie. So that their family would still be together.

CHAY DIDN'T GO on a lot of dates, so he didn't have a standard to judge this one by, but if he had to rate it he'd say it was one of his best. To keep the noise down in the house, Ava had mentioned she had a fire pit, and they'd gone out to her patio to eat the stew in front of the fire, bundled under blankets.

She was pressed next to his side, which was doing all kinds of things for his libido, making him very aware of the shape and feel of her. But he didn't need her close to be in this state where she was concerned. There was something about Ava that just got to him.

"When I was growing up, my dad used to do this on the weekends."

"Make a fire?"

"Yeah, he said it was devices down and time to get our butts outside. I have to say your stew would give his chili a run for the money," Ava said.

"Nice to know. What devices? Did you have a cell phone?"

"Yeah, but that was just for texting…remember the old days when you had to use a numeric keypad to text?"

He laughed. "You really had to work to send a text."

"Yeah. Looking back I'm not sure it was worth it to ask Sydney or Frankie if they wanted to twin on Friday."

"Twin?"

"Yeah, that was big in middle school. We'd match outfits for the day and do our hair the same. Like high pony, braids or straight with the straightener, with the Mary-Kate and Ashley Olsen products we'd all begged our moms to get for us from Walmart."

"Wow, that sounds like something. Are there pictures?"

"Unfortunately, but luckily they are all at my parents' house, probably in a box somewhere. What about you?"

He shrugged. "Not really. I didn't get a phone until I left for Salt Lake."

"To be fair, I never really needed one," Ava admitted. "Did you have a Nintendo DS?"

"Nope. None of that. I had my grandmother, books and a big chip on my shoulder and a grudge to nurse."

She tucked her leg underneath her body as she turned toward him. "Want to talk about that?"

Never had she sounded more like a therapist than that moment.

"I'm not your patient."

"I wasn't thinking you were. It's just you brought it up, so it makes me think you might want to talk…or you could be like me and just want to share stuff without diving too deeply into it."

"What don't you want to talk about?" he asked, turning the conversation back to her, because no, he didn't want to discuss the sullen teenager he'd been.

"The fact that most of the time I needed to be the same as my friends to feel like I fit in," she admitted. "Ridiculous, right? I mean, I'm a Colton, so I already have that and everyone knew who I was. But I'm not like everyone else. What about you?"

"Same. Not like anyone else, but really hearing you now, I realize we were probably just like everyone else. There is something about being a teenager that makes you feel so isolated. Like you're the only one who's not fitting in."

She put her hand on the back of his neck; her fingers were cold, but then she leaned up and kissed him. Just the side of his cheek. "You're smart."

"Maybe. Not as smart as I'd like to be," he admitted. Realizing he was minutes away from taking the kiss he really wanted but she'd tucked her arm back under her blanket. "I'm still not sure there's a real connection between the women who've been taken all over the state."

Safe topic. Sort of.

"What is the link?" she asked.

"It's loose. They were all in foster care. But not the same family services or any other connection."

"Except that they have no family, right? I mean, that's a connection," Ava said.

"Yeah. But it tenuous. Why would someone target women like that?" he asked her.

She tilted her head to the side. "I'm not sure. But they'd be able to do whatever they wanted without anyone causing an uproar over their disappearances. I mean, in most cases it was only after they didn't show up to work for a few days which is how Fern was listed as missing."

Chay took another bite of his stew. "And then she went into the system. People do leave and move on. The fire and the circumstances that Fern outlined are the only reason I'm pursuing this line of investigation. That and Annie Ross."

Ava put her bowl on the ground. "I'm curious about her as well. What was she doing all the way out here?"

"Something we might never know. The only thing, and it's a weak link that connects her to Fern, is that Annie had filed a missing-persons report on a friend of hers. And both Annie and her friend had aged out of the foster care system, like Fern."

She tipped her head to the side, studying him. "Back to your theory. It does seem worth pursuing."

"Maybe. I mean, right now we know two men drugged and kept Fern in a makeshift cabin. Annie was found just wandering in the wilderness. Unless someone had a grudge against those two women…there's not much there."

A grudge had been his first thought, but neither woman moved in the same circles or had anything really in common. So he was back to someone—a gang, maybe—targeting woman who aged out of foster care.

"I bet you'll figure it out," Ava said.

"Why's that?"

"You seem like a very thorough man, Chay. Someone who doesn't give up until they get answers."

He put his own bowl on the ground next to hers, stretching his arm on the bench behind them and drawing her closer to him.

"I am a very thorough man," he confirmed, bringing his head closer to hers. "Right now I need to confirm that one kiss we shared wasn't a fluke."

"Fluke?"

"Yeah, did I imagine you tasted better than anything I've ever tasted before or am I making that up?"

"We better find out."

HE TASTED LIKE STEW, Chay and the wildness of being outside. She burrowed closer to him, pulling her blanket with her as she shifted so she could deepen their kiss. He felt so right, tasted so good, and for the first time that day, she really felt like she wasn't on edge.

A lot of that was down to their conversation. The way he'd just let her talk about whatever and shared his investigation with her. It felt normal. Something she hadn't had since Greg had been killed. This quiet sharing was what had made her love Greg as much as she had.

They hadn't been twins sharing all the same likes, but they had both just appreciated and listened to each other. She felt those tears that had refused to fall earlier burning her eyes, and she blinked, pulling back from Chay.

"I guess it wasn't a fluke," she said, but she could hear the thickness in her voice and knew that this kiss had stirred some emotions she hadn't really ever processed fully.

"Guess not. You sure you're okay?" he asked, looking at her with that gaze that seemed to see all the way to her soul.

"Yes and no. The kiss was great and I haven't... I haven't felt this way about someone in a really long time, so it's making me emotional."

"Ah," he said.

"Ah?"

"I'm not sure how to respond to that. I mean, I can tell the guy must have meant something to you, and I'm not so much of a masochist that I want to ask about him."

"He did. We were engaged," she admitted anyway.

"He broke it off?"

Why had she started this? Why? But given the day she'd had, maybe she should have expected this. "He died in a car accident."

"Whoa. Okay. Now I feel like a dick."

"No. Please don't. It's just you make me feel safe and comfortable and happy the way that Greg did. I wasn't expecting that on our first date," she admitted.

Chay looked at her for a long minute before pulling her to him and wrapping her in a big hug. He just held her tucked up against him, their blankets between them but the heat of his breath against the top of her head. He didn't say anything, and she understood that.

This was their first date. Too much was happening between them too quickly. Or maybe at just the right pace, she thought, snaking her arms under his blanket to wrap them around his middle and hug him back.

They stayed like that for a few more minutes before

he let her go and stood up. "Think we can make some coffee and eat the cake inside?"

"If we're quiet. I think Gracie is really sleeping well. She's been getting a solid six to seven hours a night in a stretch recently." Very aware that she was talking about Gracie instead of discussing what she wanted.

But really, was there a way to ask a guy if he felt the same way about her without making it even more awkward than bringing up her dead fiancé? Probably not. Coffee and cake were safer.

Except after thinking about Fern and Annie and even her patient Alice, she realized that she didn't always want to play things safe. There was no guarantee that she and Chay would have more dates or as much time as Ava wanted for this relationship to unfold.

Take risks.

It was funny, but her aunt Kate and her mom had both said those words to her, but for different reasons. Her mom always wanted her take chances with her job, to look outside of the box, to follow her gut. Well, she guessed Aunt Kate was the same, but she had thought that Ava needed to take risks in her personal life. Kiss the guy she wasn't sure was a forever man and go on dates with the ones that didn't seem like a perfect fit.

"Did I make you uncomfortable?" she asked once she put the coffee on and he was getting the cake out.

"When?"

For a minute she almost said *never mind* and let it drop. Almost pulled back into herself but then remembered how challenging the day had been. How challenging her life had been...wasn't it time to stop hiding from what she truly wanted?

Every instinct she had told her that Chay was worth

the risk. So she took a deep breath. "When I said you made me feel good?"

Chay rubbed the back of his neck and turned the cake around on the plate she'd provided for him trying to do something but she couldn't guess what.

"Chay?"

"Yes."

"Because you don't feel like that about me?" she asked. Even as a child she'd always been one to keep probing until she got to the heart of whatever the issue was. Right now she needed to know if he felt like she did about him or if he'd come just to see the baby again—maybe a motive. Or if he'd just been curious, as he'd stated on the porch.

"No, Ava."

Okay, well, that didn't really answer her query. "What then?"

He shook his head. "Remember that kid with the grudge I mentioned?"

She nodded. His teenage self. "What about him?"

"He's still a big part of who I am today. I think you should know processing emotions isn't one of my strong suits. I can't talk about my feelings, and I'm not really good at identifying them. If that's not enough for you, I can respect that. But I'd miss you, Ava. I really like you."

He sort of stalked over to her. Putting his hands on her shoulders so she had to tip her head back to look up at him. "Making you happy made me happy, too."

Chapter Nine

The boy with the grudge. All she saw was a man who had a lot of caring inside of him and no way to let it out. When he was this close to her she couldn't really think about anything other than kissing him. It was that mouth of his. Full lips, stubborn set to his jaw, just made her want to ruffle his hair and pull him closer…

So she did.

Put her hands on either side of his face, went up on tiptoe and brushed her lips against his. His parted and she felt the warm rush of his breath as his tongue swept into her mouth. Closing her eyes as Chay's arms went around her, pulling her closer until she stopped thinking.

God, the warmth of his body enfolded her, and his hands slid down her back, cupping her butt as he drew her more firmly against him. The nudge of his growing erection against her belly made her squirm and try to get closer as she deepened the kiss.

He pulled his mouth from hers, his mouth on her neck. Holding on to his shoulders, she tipped her head to the side to give him more access to her skin. One of his hands slid up under her sweater, warm against her back. His finger stroking the small of her back in just these small sweeps that sent shivers through her.

She wanted to touch him. Maneuvered herself until she could get her hand under his shirt. He'd worn a button-down with the tail left hanging out, and as she snaked her hand up under it, she groaned when she encountered the soft cotton of a T-shirt.

He laughed against her neck, which made her smile and her nipples get perky.

"What's the matter?" he teased.

"I want to touch you," she said.

"You are," he pointed out.

"Touché." There was a lightness in Chay at this moment that she didn't normally encounter with him. She undid the buttons of his shirt and then looked up at him, their gazes meeting as she tugged his T-shirt from his jeans and pushed her hand under it.

He was hot and hard. Her fingers moved across his abdomen and around his waist.

His breath caught in his throat as he waited to see what she would do next. She drew her fingernail up his back, lightly, and watched as his pupils dilated and his breathing got the smallest bit quicker.

His touch on her back changed. His fingers no longer just randomly stroking her but instead moving more deliberately, stroking her with intent as his hand moved down her back to her butt and dragged her even closer.

His mouth was on hers again, his tongue in her mouth as she felt the ridge of his erection against her center. She moaned again, felt it echo in their joined mouths as he thrust his hips against hers.

He felt so good.

She heard some noises, knew that Gracie was waking but tried to ignore it. She didn't want this moment with Chay to end. Not yet.

Just another few moments, Gracie, she thought.

But the baby was awake and crying for Ava.

Chay set her away from him and nodded toward the hall. "Go on."

She hurried to the baby's room. Her heart was racing and her entire body was throbbing. If only Gracie had slept longer, but it wasn't the little sweetheart's fault she was awake.

"Hello, honey. Ava's here," she said. In her heart she almost wanted to say *Mommy's here*, but didn't give in to that impulse. She wasn't going to be Gracie's mom; she was her foster mom, sure, but it was important for Ava to remember this was temporary.

Gracie looked over at her, stopping her crying as she did so. Her hand was still in her mouth, and Ava lifted her out of the crib, cuddling her close.

She changed Gracie's diaper and then carried her down the hall. Chay wasn't in the hallway; instead he'd moved to the living room. He had the TV on with the volume down low.

"There you are," she said.

"Yeah. Didn't know if I should stay or go but didn't want to ghost while you were taking care of Gracie."

"Thanks for that. I don't mind if you stay," she said. Actually, she wanted him to stay. There was something so homey about this moment. She wanted it to last.

"I can stay until midnight," he said. "I've got the early shift tomorrow."

"Great. Um…did you pick a movie?" she asked him.

"Nah, this was on."

She glanced at the screen. It was one of the Marvel movies with the superheroes. "I haven't seen this one."

"I might have. It's hard to remember them all."

"Yeah. I think this is my favorite superhero movie." Ava sat down next to him, and Gracie, who had her pacifier in her mouth, reached for Chay. He took the baby, holding her against his chest, and then reached for Ava and pulled her up against him.

"So I what I remember is that Bucky killed Tony's parents and Cap knows but hasn't told him. And then the general wants them all to sign some kind of accord, which basically limits what they can do."

"And they don't want to?" she asked.

"Well, half of them don't," he said. "Setting up an epic battle."

"Good, I like to see my superheroes battling," she said, curling her legs under her and putting her hand on his stomach as they watched the movie.

Chay was so warm and comfy next to her, and as she watched Gracie, the little girl started to get sleepy again. Maybe she'd just been lonely. Ava felt her own eyes getting heavy as the movie played on. She put her hand next to Gracie on Chay's chest, and Gracie wrapped her fist around Ava's finger.

Closing her eyes for just a second, Chay's hand rubbing her shoulder and the soft sound of the television lulled her to sleep.

CAREFULLY, CHAY ADJUSTING the sleeping Gracie higher on his shoulder and moved Ava off his shoulder so he could stand. But he didn't want to move from the couch. It felt like home in a way that he'd rarely experienced. There were only a few moments in his life he could remember feeling like this. Always they had been with his grandmother.

Ava Colton was weaving some kind of magic around him, and he was helpless to stop her. The rational part of him knew that this wouldn't last. The baby was only temporarily in Ava's care. She was only in his life because of a case and the baby she wanted him to adopt. Something he knew he wasn't going to do.

So letting himself feel anything toward these two women had stupid written all over it.

While he wasn't the smartest man on the planet, he'd always been wise enough to steer clear of emotional entanglements. Had promised himself when his mom walked out of his life that he wouldn't give anyone the power to hurt him like that again.

He was self-sufficient, took pride in the fact that he didn't need anyone, but damn. He hugged both of them closer to him. He wanted them to be his.

Want was so different. So dangerous. It made him believe that if he took a risk then he'd…what? His mind wasn't going to let him form that thought.

The movie was over. He'd muted it so the noise didn't wake either of them. He knew he had to leave to drive home and get some rest before his shift tomorrow. But the couch felt so comfy and these two sleeping ladies held him in a net that he wasn't even trying to break free from.

Ava stirred, her eyes opening sleepily. "Hi."

"Hey, there. Enjoy your rest?" he asked.

"Yeah. Your shoulder is comfy."

He wriggled his eyebrows at her, tempted to tell her she should try the rest of him. But he felt vulnerable. Something he really hated. So kept his mouth shut.

"Oh, look at the time. You said you had to leave at

midnight," she said, getting up and then reaching down to take Gracie. A strand of her hair brushed against his forearm, sending a tingle of awareness through him.

"I've got her," he said, getting to his feet. "Also, it's okay. I didn't mind."

Oh, he a thousand percent hadn't minded holding her while she slept. The only thing better would have been in if they'd been in his big king-size bed and he'd made love to her before she drifted off.

"Well, thank you," she said, wiping her hands on her jeans. "What do you say I return the favor and cook you dinner at your place tomorrow night?"

"Yes," he said. "Why don't you come early and we can go for a hike before dinner?"

He had the early shift at work so should be home by two. He was off on Sunday as well, so maybe...what? Was he really going to keep seeing her? She made him long for things that he'd given up wishing for a long time ago. He didn't want to be hurt again. Didn't want to risk his heart.

There was a part of his subconscious that didn't see Ava as a risk. But his mind did.

She was too...tempting. It wasn't just her curvy body or thinking about having sex with her that had him losing sleep. It was her smile, the way she sassed him and tried to boss him around. Even though he'd made it clear he wasn't going to adopt Gracie, she kept showing him... that he could. That there was a world where he might be a father to this sweet baby.

He started to sweat at the thought. Turning away from Ava, he took Gracie to her bed and nestled the baby in her crib. He traced the Navajo designs that were as natural to him as breathing. Seeing the spider woman, knowing she'd protect little Gracie, he leaned down to kiss the baby's forehead before turning to walk to the hallway.

Ava waited for him there. "You're so natural with her."

"I'd have to be a monster not to be," he said. He wasn't about to let her continue to build something in his own mind where he'd risk being a parent to Gracie. His biological mother had walked away from him. More than once. And when she'd left him the last time, he'd never heard from her again.

Sure, he wanted to be all whatever, but he'd waited for a call or a letter from her. A DM or something on socials, but she hadn't been on there and she'd never reached out. The next time he'd seen her, she'd been in her coffin.

"I've got to go."

"Yeah. You okay?"

No. But it wasn't manly to admit. His grandmother would scoff at that. Since when did being manly mean not having emotions? *The world demands it, Grandmother.*

Without a word, she hugged him. Wrapped her arms around his center and held him, her head over his heart, her hair hanging down over his arm.

He resisted but knew that it was a losing battle. Hugging her back, he closed his eyes and rested his head on top of hers. This woman.

Breathing in the floral scent of her body spray, the other essence that was baby powder and the combined fragrance of Ava and Gracie. His heart beat slowly, steadily. Almost as if he could hear a word repeating with each beat of his heart.

He ignored it as long as he could. As he gave her a gentle kiss and said goodbye. Walking to his truck, he didn't allow himself to acknowledge the word until he had left her neighborhood and was on the highway.

Home.

There it was. Repeating with each steady beat of his heart. The farther he was from Ava and Gracie, the louder his heartbeat and that word seemed to get.

AVA WAS RESTLESS after Chay left. Her nap made it harder for her to fall asleep, so she curled up to read in the corner of the couch where he'd sat. The scent of his aftershave was faint on the pillows.

This night...she hadn't experienced anything like this since Greg. She'd sort of thought that she wouldn't connect with a guy again. Not like that. It seemed to her that real connections with other people weren't that common. It took a lot to find someone she really understood.

Not that she understood Chay. He was so complex, but there was a part of him that she totally understood. Maybe it was her being a therapist that helped her to see it, which she knew was dangerous.

She needed to see him as the man he was and not as a patient, which she totally did. But at the same time, she saw him clearly. Or she thought she did. He pushed so hard against being a father to Gracie, yet he instinctively *was.*

He loved that little girl, and Ava couldn't blame him. Her heart was full of Gracie. Ava was trying to tell herself that being Gracie's foster mom was enough, but combined with Chay's presence in her life, she was starting to want more.

Things that she believed had died along with Greg in his car accident. Of course she was young and there was the possibility that she could adopt a baby on her own, but she knew that wasn't her dream.

Gracie and Chay were just there in her mind's eye

when she looked to the future. Their faces growing older alongside her own. It wasn't something that she was sure would happen, but she craved it.

Like nothing else she'd wanted since Greg had been in the hospital and she'd been praying he'd recover. It hurt to want something that badly. She knew better than to let her guard down, but it almost seemed as if it were too late.

Her guard had dropped the minute that Chay had taken Gracie into his arms and gotten her to stop crying. He'd said baby whisperer, but it was more like he was an Ava whisperer.

Just doing and saying the right things. And it wasn't forced. He wasn't playing a part, he was just being himself.

Not perfect in any way. He was gruff. That was obvious. He wasn't overly chatty, but then, she didn't need that. He was funny. And when he laughed, his eyes crinkled, and God help her, it was hard to breathe when she looked at him and he was laughing.

He wasn't made for her, but it felt as if he had been. All those secret parts of herself she kept hidden felt okay around him. Like she didn't have to pretend to be the best version of herself.

Given that he'd seen her twice with baby food and other mess on her clothes and hair, he knew she wasn't perfect. It wasn't like everyone was demanding she be someone she wasn't, but it had always just been easier to act normal…whatever that was. Watch the same shows and listen to the same music. Be that person that everyone felt comfortable around.

But she'd been short with Chay. She'd fallen asleep on Chay. She'd kissed the socks off Chay. He hadn't run away. He kept asking her to do things with him, and her heart that had been sleeping so long, not really sure that it could love again, awoke.

It was beating steadily and making her feel emotions that she'd shut away. There was no denying it. She liked him.

Thinking about seeing him again in fourteen hours made her stomach feel like it had butterflies. Curling her legs underneath her, she reached for her phone. Looking through the recipes she'd saved, she wanted to make this dinner the best one. She wanted to impress him.

Wanted to show him all the best qualities she had. But she wasn't a master chef—in fact, she barely got by. Also, what if he thought she could cook and expected her to keep cooking for him?

Ugh.

Laying her head on the back of the cushions, she realized that as much as she thought he liked her for her, it was hard to keep herself from trying to morph into someone she thought he'd fall for. *Not healthy, Ava.*

Forcing herself off the couch, she sat cross-legged in front of the fireplace. The last embers of the fire that she'd had going when Chay had been there were dying.

She put her hands on her knees and let herself fall into a meditative state. Took deep breaths and called out the things she loved about herself. Reminded herself that if Chay didn't like those parts, then he wasn't for her.

Were her feelings just a natural extension of her love for Gracie?

That would make things both complicated and easier. If it was an extension, then she could pull back. Stop letting Chay's smile make her warm and gooey inside. But if it was natural…that was scarier. She had no idea how she was going to keep from falling in love with him. She knew better than anyone that love didn't mean you got happily-ever-after.

At the same time, could she deny herself the chance to see what was blooming between her and Chay?

No. Of course she wasn't going to deny it. She might not be a huge risk taker, but how often did love like this come along? Not that what she felt for him was love… but the potential was there.

Her back started to hurt from sitting for too long, so she trudged off to bed, no closer to an answer than she'd been before.

Chapter Ten

Marg sent a text letting Ava know that she was cleared to start having unsupervised visitation with Chay and his family for Gracie. Sweet. This was going to work out, she felt it in her bones. Of course, she was going to have convince Chay that he wanted it as well.

Something she'd bring up when they were at his place. It wasn't going to be easy for him to hear, but Chay had the bones of a man who craved family. Of course, that was her therapist training helping her to see that he needed it. But the woman who was starting to fall for him…well, Ava knew in a way she was pushing her own agenda. Trying to get herself to a place where…she could feel safe enough to start dreaming of a future again, where she wasn't alone.

Her phone rang, and she glanced down, seeing it was her mom. Chay had been called in to work and pushed their date to just dinner.

"Hey, what's up?"

"Just checking in on you and baby Gracie. Also I could use your help with the charity event I'm planning," Mom said.

Her schedule wasn't too hectic for the next few weeks.

Though she had been spending most of her free time with Chay. "I can probably come over on Thursday. Will that work? Have you started a Pinterest board?"

"Sent you a invite this morning. I want to make sure this one stands out. I've already got a few photos of the vibe I want to create." Mom ran the Colton Foundation as a nonprofit, because she always said wealth was vulgar. They held an annual spring event. She always ran the committee.

Her mom always delivered ideas, which took the events to the next level, which was probably why no one else volunteered when she asked if anyone else wanted to plan it. Her mom's creativity came naturally to her. Ava struggled to see outside the box. She tended to be more *this is how it's always been*.

"So with Gracie…"

"Yes. Do you need me to come over and hold that little sweetie?"

"When we visit. I can't leave her alone with anyone who's not court approved because of the investigation," Ava warned her mother, not wanting her to be offended that she couldn't really babysit. Her mom was cool but sometimes mentioned that she hoped to be a grandmother someday. Which Ava always warned her would be down to Ryan.

Though she was starting to have think seriously about having a family of her own again.

"Makes sense," Mom said. "It's so sad what happened to the mother. Do they know any more about her?"

"I don't really think so," she said; her mom was so easily distracted, and maybe that was a good thing. She wasn't sure she wanted to tell her mom she was pushing

Chay toward adopting Gracie. Yet she needed another perspective.

"Um... I've been seeing a guy who shares DNA markers with Gracie. He's not really ready to be a father, but he's great with the baby and I think..." Trailing off so maybe Mom would pick up what she was putting down without making her say it. She'd always been bossy around people she cared about. It was her fatal flaw.

Her mom sighed heavily. "Honey, that's a tough one. Not everyone wants to be a parent or is actually capable of doing it. I can tell from your tone that you want this guy to be Gracie's adopted father, but that has to be his decision."

"Of course. I meant more giving him opportunities to be around the baby and get to know her. I mean, until I started fostering, I never would have thought I was capable of taking care of a child."

"Trial by fire. That's what I said to your dad when we had you. Never had a clue what we were doing. You were a testing grounds," her mom said with a laugh.

Ava laughed, too. She'd heard that story before and knew her folks had figured it all out as they were raising her. Sort of the way Ava was doing with Gracie.

"Thanks, Mom. Glad you got it right for Ryan."

"Oh, I still was fumbling along. The main bit of advice I can give you and your friend is that there is no one way to parent. Kids are different and constantly changing. Once you figure out something that works...it no longer does. Kept me on my toes."

Her mom had an interesting way of looking at parenting, and it did make sense. Pushing Chay hard wasn't going to work—he'd just get his back up. She'd adapt her plan so that he was just with Gracie more. And since they were sort of dating, that made sense.

"I'll see you on Thursday. Gotta run, I have a client in fifteen minutes and need time to prep."

"Perfect. Love you."

"Love you, too."

Hanging up the phone, she knew she had to be very careful how she moved forward with Chay. Marg had gone to the courts to get permission for Chay and Aponi to have visitation at Ava's suggestion. But in her mind it was a first step. Something she wasn't sure how Chay would react.

No one liked to be told that someone had done something in their own best interest. Sounded like Ava was butting into his life. Which she one hundred percent was.

She wasn't sure how she'd feel if Chay did that to her.

But she wanted to try. For the first time since Greg's car accident, she felt like she was ready to risk her heart.

Dating him had made her feel so much happiness. Taking out her phone, she glanced down at a photo she'd taken of him and Gracie when he'd been cuddling the baby. Her heart felt full and her pulse sped up.

Her gut told her that pushing him to be Gracie's father was the right thing to do. Not just for Gracie, but for him as well. Chay needed someone to give all that love to. While she hoped that they'd continue to fall for each other, there were no guarantees. A child of his own, though…that could be the answer.

FOLLOWING HIS LEADS on the different women who'd gone missing, Chay built a pattern. A lot of times his old sergeant used to say that the truth reveals itself in circles or squares—there's always a line connecting everything.

That resonated with Chay. There had been a line connecting him and his mom to the Navajo Nation here in Utah, one that she'd tried to sever so many times, but even in death she couldn't.

Same with baby Gracie. Her mom had brought her here...maybe looking for the father. Though there was no DNA connection to the father, and Chay's gut told him it would be hard to find. But there had to be a line somewhere.

He'd have to go back and trace his mom's path after she'd left him. It was entirely possibly she could have had another son. She'd spent a lot of her time high or drunk and hooking up in different places they'd stayed in. But he wasn't entirely sure how to find a child that she'd never mentioned.

She'd left him in Utah and died in Atlanta. She'd hated to fly so would have driven or hitched her way across the country. Too much territory to cover? For a lazy man, Chay thought. He wasn't going to make it a priority, because he had a case he was working on. But he knew he couldn't let this go. If he had a sibling...were they still alive? Did they want their kid?

Hell, that was the main reason why he was reluctant to have a child of his own. Children were vulnerable in ways that affected them as adults. He'd never asked his grandmother what it was his mom was running from. She'd never volunteered it, but Chay could guess it had to be here.

Mom had never wanted to live on the Navajo Nation again. She wanted to be a part of the bigger world. Had sought a path that would keep her out of here. Until him.

She'd never said she regretted him, but she hadn't had to. He'd guessed.

His phone rang. Happily shoving away those thoughts, he answered it.

"Officer Benally."

"Chay, it's Jacob Colton. Are you getting anywhere with the database?"

"You were on my list to call this morning. I am. There's a pattern, but it's loose to say the least." He gave Jacob a rundown of all he'd found. There were fifteen women in total whose missing-persons circumstances matched Fern Hensley and Camille Lancaster. "But the locations are all over the state of Utah. So motive… I've got nothing."

"I have a call in to the town where Fern lived to speak to the officer who took the report there. I'm also hoping to hear back from Victor Olson at the Wilson Police Department. The reports I've gotten online are pretty standard. Not much detail. It's always better to have a chat."

"Definitely is. I will give him a call as well, see if I can rattle his cage. I'm still trying to get more details from Fern but won't push."

"Yeah, I talked with her. That part of the job—talking to victims—is the hardest part."

"I've got no love for it, either."

Jacob hung up a few minutes later, both of them agreeing to touch base in a few days. Chay spent the rest of the morning reaching out to the different police stations trying to speak to the officers who'd written the reports.

He spoke to two, and both times their statements were similar. They victim was a solitary woman with few connections other than jobs or maybe a neighbor. He already knew they'd all come out of the foster care system and asked each officer if they'd spoken to the care homes.

They hadn't, because as far as they had been concerned, it was an isolated incident in their town.

Chay added that to his list of to-dos. Maybe these women had something that the police reports were missing. Were they all extremely beautiful or had blond hair or a skill set that no one else knew about?

Where was the line?

Taking out a yellow notepad, he wrote down, *foster care—that's the first line. Where had the girls come from? Could that be the second line?*

They'd all been taken, which was a line at the bottom. He drew one. Making it a curve and adding in the cities they'd been taken in. Plotting out the distance between them all.

Pulling the map toward him, he tried to see if there was a pattern there. But they were all equal distance apart.

Transporting the women would be an issue if they were connecting. Fern had been held near tribal lands, but she'd been alone. He hadn't thought to ask her if she'd seen signs that someone had been there before her.

He called Ava, but her phone went to voicemail.

"Hey, it's me. When you are with Fern again, would you ask her if she saw evidence that anyone had been held in the cabin before her? Looking forward to dinner later."

He called back one of the officers he'd spoken to earlier. "Do you have any abandoned places on the outskirts of town?"

"A few. Mostly they turn into squats for homeless or addicts. Why?"

"We found a woman at an abandoned cabin. I'm searching for a connection to her abduction," Chay said.

"I'll take a drive out there. What am I looking for?"

"Well, the woman here was held alone, bound and kept drugged. They came by once a day to feed her and then drug her again. So... I'm not entirely sure what you'll find. Maybe signs that someone's been there."

"No promises," the officer said.

"Thanks for checking."

It was almost time to go home, so he typed up his notes and sent an email to Jacob updating him on what he'd found.

AVA SAW SHE missed a call from Chay when she came out of the pediatrician's office. Gracie was in for her nine-month check-up. The office had limited hours on Saturdays which Ava had to take advantage of because of her work schedule. The baby was doing well but a little weepy since she'd had a shot. Ava planned to take her back to the park where they'd walked the other day.

The weather was clear and crisp. Having the sun on her face felt so good. She listened to Chay's voicemail, the sound of him talking sending a sweet thrill through her. Parking, she took her time gathering her stuff and getting Gracie out of her car seat.

The baby was sucking her thumb, which the doctor said wasn't an issue right now. Out of the corner of her eye, Ava thought she saw a dark-haired man watching her. Pushing her sunglasses up on her head, she turned toward him, but no one was there.

God, was she getting paranoid?

Was it just that she was afraid to let herself be happy with Gracie and Chay?

Getting Gracie into the front baby carrier, she put her hat and gloves on as she double-checked she had her keys and that the truck was locked before she headed toward the path.

"This is nice, isn't it? Sorry you had to get a shot today.

You know that's just to keep you healthy," she said to Gracie, rubbing her hands on the little baby's feet. Gracie murmured back a response around her thumb.

"What's that? You need a treat if you're going to forgive me?"

"Uh-huuh huuuh."

Ava took that as a yes. "The sun feels good, doesn't it."

More of that some response. "Are you trying to talk?"

"Uh-huuuh," she said again.

"I can't wait for that. It will be nice to chat about things, won't it?"

"Uh-huuuh."

She kept making that sound as she shoved her entire fist in her mouth and Ava acknowledged she was probably just talking to herself. But she knew that babies socialized by having conversations, so talking to Gracie was what was needed.

For herself, she was pretty sure she needed to talk to her therapist. Seeing someone watching her…that was an old fear. She knew that Daniel Wayne was still in prison.

Ava had gotten a restraining order and had moved apartments to avoid Daniel, but his next victim hadn't been so lucky. He'd attacked and beaten her and was currently serving a fifteen-year sentence.

Tipping her face up to the sun, she let the heat of it warm her from the inside out. Reminding herself it was okay for her to be happy. It was okay for her to have a baby and to be dating Chay.

Chay. She'd already made a note to bring up the cabin when she spoke to Fern the next time. Of course she wanted to get answers for them both. Ava suspected that Fern's recovery was hampered by her fear of those men who'd taken her, but knew part of it also stemmed from her previous drug addiction. The other woman was in such a fragile state right now.

That and her insistence on not taking any pain medication. Though all the medication did was dull the pain, it would make it easier for Fern to sleep. But Ava totally understood and supported Fern's decision. The recovering addict wasn't about to take anything that could start her down that path again.

Ava rubbed her hand on Gracie's back as her watch pinged. It was time to head back home and take the lasagna she'd prepped earlier over to Chay's. Tonight was going to be fun. Ava had spent the day no closer to deciding how she was going to broach visitation with Chay; hopefully it would simply come up naturally during the conversation.

But if not…she'd bring it up.

Bossy didn't mean that she wasn't right. Tempering her need to urge him to do this with what her mom had said wasn't easy. But she was determined to do it.

Getting home, she changed Gracie and put the baby down to play while she finished getting everything ready to go to Chay's, loading the food into a cooler and getting that into the vehicle before she got the baby bundled up and settled into her car seat.

Gracie looked a bit sleepy, and Ava was hopeful she'd nap on the way out to the Navajo Nation so she'd be rested for the evening.

Again she felt someone watching her. Peering up and down the street, she only noticed a car parked on the street at the Petersons' home. But they'd mentioned their daughter and her boyfriend were coming up for a visit. And as she looked more closely, the car seemed empty.

Stop it.

Rubbing her hands on her thighs, she got into the truck and closed the door firmly. Unable to stop herself from hitting the lock button twice, she confirmed that no one was hiding in the back seat.

Her heart was racing and no matter how many times she verified she was alone in the truck with Gracie, she didn't feel safe.

Her hands were shaking. Talking deep breaths until she felt calmer, she repeated her mantras.

I am safe in my hometown.
My parents and brother are nearby.
Chay is looking forward to seeing me.
I have a mission with Chay.
Show that man he's meant to have a family.

Calmer now, she turned on the vehicle and deliberately didn't drive toward the Petersons' so she didn't give in to her paranoia. Daniel Wayne was still in jail. Feeding her fears was just going to send her into a spiral.

She turned on her upbeat music playlist because hearing "Mr. Blue Sky" always cheered her up.

Singing along as she drove out of her neighborhood, she lied to herself that she felt safe. But it wasn't until she pulled onto Chay's property and saw him standing in the doorway of his house that she truly relaxed.

He waved at her and came to help her with Gracie, but before he opened the back door, she threw herself into his arms. He hugged her hard back.

"Okay?"

"Just missed seeing you." No way was she going to tell him about her feelings. He didn't need to know that she was manifesting her worst nightmare just because she wasn't sure she deserved a happy future.

Chapter Eleven

She hugged him so hard he felt it all the way to his soul. Taking a deep breath that he felt against the side of his neck, she stepped back. She'd missed him. No one had said those words to him before.

Grandmother might have experienced that, but she'd never said those words explicitly. Ava…she messed with him on so many levels. The case was the reason he came into her life and while he didn't wish harm on anyone, he didn't regret it bringing them together.

He grabbed Gracie's car seat, the little one happy to see him. He hauled her into the house behind Ava, who clicked the lock on her truck several times before following him.

"You sure everything is good?" he asked.

"It's just something from my past. Let me get the lasagna on and check on Gracie's diaper then we can talk."

He took Gracie from the car seat. "I've got the yazh."

Tucking the baby up against his chest, she babbled as he walked her to the couch, where he made quick work of changing her diaper. She kept grabbing her feet as he tried to put the onesie back on her. So he tickled her stomach, which made her laugh. The joyous sound filled the living room.

He finally got her back into her onesie and then settled her on the floor on the Navajo blanket.

He placed the toys that Ava had packed in the bag around her. She rocked back and forth, almost rolling over. He waited to see if she would...

"Can I nudge her onto her belly?"

"You can place her on her belly. Why?"

"I think she wants to crawl."

"I've been wondering about that, too." Ava perched on the couch next to him, and they both waited to see if she'd do it on her own.

She did.

Ava grabbed his hand, a big smile on her face. "Yes, Gracie. Go, queen."

She moved both her arms and legs, her head held up but couldn't get her knees under her.

"Soon she'll be moving, and then look out," Ava said.

"You'll have to look out," Chay reminded her. "You were going to tell me about what had you spooked."

"I will. But first, I wanted to let you know I spoke to Marg at child services, and she's agreed that you and your grandmother can have visitation with Gracie," Ava said, sinking back onto the couch next to him.

She was being casual, but more than once she'd mentioned she thought he'd make a good dad. "Why would she do that?"

"You're her closest DNA relatives," Ava pointed out.

Of course. "One of us is nearly eighty, and the other is a tribal officer who is on call a lot. I'm not sure—"

"I'm aware you don't want to be her new family. But

do you really not want to know her at all? Regardless of the future, you're still her uncle and great-grandmother."

Which his grandmother would love. He was being stubborn because...he was starting to accept the way things were. Him dating Ava and Gracie being there, but him not having to commit to taking care of either of them.

He liked Ava more than any woman he'd dated before, but he was still the man his past had made him. Liking her hadn't given him a magic elixir to fix his abandonment issues or the fact that caring for another person made him feel weak.

"Of course. If I jumped to the wrong conclusion, I'm sorry."

Chewing her lower lip, she shook her head. "Only partially. I really believe you and Gracie need each other. But I'm not going to push. Spend some time with her and see how it goes."

"What if it doesn't go well? If I'm not this guy you're hoping I'll be when it comes to parenting a baby," he asked her. Because at the heart of this matter was the fact that he cared for Ava. He wanted to be the man she needed him to be. But forcing himself into a role wasn't going to work.

He wouldn't do that.

"I'll still like you, Chay. What's happening between you and me...it's not about Gracie," she said, shifting up to her knees and kissing him.

There was no time to think; the moment her lips brushed his, his mouth opened. Tugging her even more off balance and into his arms. He leaned backward, taking her with him until she straddled his lap. Hands on his shoulders, she lifted her head.

Their eyes met. Affection and desire passed between

them. He felt little hands on his feet. Lifting Ava carefully off his lap, they both peered down at Gracie.

"We should video this," Ava said, carefully moving off the couch and grabbing her phone from her bag.

"Impressive," Chay said. "She's really smart."

"She is," Ava said, both of them noticing that she continued babbling the entire time as she shifted herself around, trying to turn but not really understanding how to do it.

Chay watched these two females who were so important to him. Gracie rolled over so she wasn't near the couch and started crawling again. Ava was behind her like a documentary filmmaker, trying to capture every moment.

He wanted this for himself. Badly. There were no guarantees with life; hell, he knew that better than most. But reaching out and engulfing both of these two in his arms, keeping them in life…that was something that frightened him more than…well, fuck him…more than being left behind by his mom.

He wasn't ready to admit that either of them could mean that much to him. That wasn't what a second freaking date was about. Also, he'd just told Ava in plain terms he wasn't going to be a father to Gracie. But in his soul it felt like he already was Ava's man and Gracie's father.

"Get down here—I'm going to try to take a video with us and Gracie crawling," she said.

Probably it would have been safer to take the video for her, but he found himself lying on the floor next to Ava as Gracie crawled in front of them. Ava's arms weren't long enough, so he took her phone and got the video and then the photo she wanted.

It felt natural to kiss Ava, so he did.

SOMEHOW THEY ENDED up eating on the floor with Gracie crawling all around them. Chay had taken the cushions off the couch and made a boundary for Gracie so she'd stay in the living room with them.

"I think this dinner is nicer than mine," he admitted.

"Because Gracie crawled?"

He shrugged, not wanting to admit that, but yeah. The baby totally made the difference. "So what was it you were dealing with when you arrived?"

Her soft laugh told him she knew he was changing the subject. She took another bite of her lasagna, chewing very carefully, before she cleared her throat.

"I dated this guy in college…not for long, just a couple of dates. He was really controlling and always telling me what I felt and thought. So I broke up with him."

"Good. No one should do that. Sounds manipulative."

"It was. Anyway, he wouldn't take no for an answer and started just showing up at the coffeehouse where I used to study with my friends, but that was a public place, so I didn't think much of it until I noticed he was always following me. Like, to my classes, my job, and I saw him in the hallway of my apartment building.

"I clearly told him to stop doing it. But he wouldn't and he got really angry. He hit me…"

Chay didn't like where this was going. Ava seemed to be getting smaller, shrinking into herself, wrapping her arms around her waist. He shifted around until he could drape his arm over her shoulder, but slowly to make sure she'd welcome it. She did. Nestling closer to him, so they both faced the fire.

He took her plate from her when she handed it to him, putting them out of Gracie's reach.

"What happened then?"

"It got ugly, but a neighbor came out and told him she'd called the cops. Daniel left. I filled out a statement and got a restraining order."

"Did it work?"

"At first, not really. He just stayed farther back, and he could enter the coffee shop because it was on campus and he was a student. I just… I just never felt safe. So I think with what happened to Fern and Annie and Annie's friend, it's all stirring up those emotions again."

Chay rubbed his hand up and down her arm. "Perfectly reasonable. What happened to Daniel?"

"He found someone else to obsess over, but she wasn't so lucky. He sexually assaulted her and beat her up worse than me. He's in jail now."

"I'm sorry for her, but it's good he's in jail. I'm glad to hear that," he said. He wanted to probe further and get more details, but it was clear Ava was spent from sharing her story. "Want to stay here tonight?"

She tipped her head back on his chest, looking up at him. "Maybe…"

"I'll have to up my charm factor," he said dryly.

"You're plenty charming. I don't have a crib for Gracie and don't know how she'd do sleeping without it."

"Want me to come home with you?"

"Yes, but not because I'm scared of my past," she admitted. "I don't know why I'm doing letting fear control me, but a part of me… I'm afraid I'm doing it to keep from falling for you."

All he heard was *falling for you*.

"I'm falling for you, too."

She turned more fully into him, burying her face in his chest. Her words were muffled when she spoke, but he could still hear her. "I'm scared."

Me, too.

But right now, one of them had to be strong. So he kept that quiet. "There's no rush. We already decided this takes as long as it takes."

"This?"

"Our relationship."

"Yeah, we did. You're pretty great, you know."

"I do."

She mock punched his shoulder as she sat back up. "Good kisser, too."

She got to her feet and then bent to pick up Gracie. He couldn't help noticing her butt as she did so. "Thanks."

"Sure. If you need to talk more, I'm here," he said. And meant it. Ava couldn't know that for him this was what made them feel more like a couple. Quick hookups and short-term relationships had been his norm. And in those no details of the past were shared. In fact he was pretty sure more than one woman had been making up the story of her life, which was cool because they were never going to be anything but strangers.

But with Ava that wasn't the case.

Already they were more than strangers. They were almost friends. Yeah, friends. That was new to him, too. A loner all his life, and now he had a woman who he wanted to call his girlfriend and who was definitely a friend.

And Gracie.

He had a little niece that a part of him wanted to be a father to. Wanted to step up the way he saw in Ava's eyes she was expecting him to.

Except that didn't feel as comfortable as Ava. Probably because she was grown and could handle herself if things went south. Gracie couldn't.

That little one had been through more in her short life

than many had. Losing her mother, being left at a fire station...not the way anyone wanted their story to start. She needed a father who could shower her with love and ensure that she never felt like she hadn't been worthy.

A man who knew his own worth.

Chay wasn't there yet. He could admit he had value at the station and to his grandmother. But anywhere else he struggled. He wanted to be Ava's man, but at the same time, did she deserve someone without his baggage? Maybe. But he wasn't stepping aside. He wanted her and was going to do everything in his power to try to keep them together.

GRACIE FELL ASLEEP after Ava fed her, and she knew it was time to leave. Past time to get her stuff together and go home. But the fire was cozy and Chay... Chay was incredible. There was nothing she wanted more than to stay right next him for the rest of the night.

But she had work tomorrow. Also, it hadn't been bullshit when she'd said Gracie had never slept away from her crib. Of course she might have before she'd come into Ava's care, but Ava was following some child development tips from a book she'd read. Routine was key to socializing and raising someone to function as an adult.

A lot of those behaviors started in the early stages.

"So...am I coming home with you?"

A little thrill went through her. "Don't you have work tomorrow?"

"I need to catch up with Jacob about the investigation, so I can start my day there. It's up to you."

"Yes. I'd like that," she admitted. Her body had been in a low-level hum all evening. There had been lots of kissing and touching while they'd eaten, talked and played with Gracie.

"I'll grab my work clothes and stuff and be ready to go," he said.

"Chay?"

"Huh?"

"Adult sleepover," she said just because she wanted to be clear she wanted him in her bed.

"My thoughts exactly."

She gathered up all of Gracie's things and carefully put the sleeping baby into her car seat carrier before tucking her blanket in around her. Gracie gave a little coo in her sleep, and Ava brushed her lips on the baby's head.

Chay might have been unsure about being in Gracie's life, but she could tell he wanted to be. It was so clear the way he played with her and encouraged her to crawl. Her heart almost ached for how clear it was that Chay needed more than his grandmother as family.

Aponi was the best and had done a wonderful job raising Chay, but it was clear to Ava that they both craved a larger family. She saw it in the way that Chay watched Gracie.

"Ready?"

"Yeah. Let's go," she said. She'd put the leftover lasagna in Chay's fridge so he could have it for dinner tomorrow. She was working a later shift at the hospital. She rotated being on call with two other therapists at the hospital to cover anyone brought in overnight.

Chay carried his duffel and Gracie's car seat. After getting the baby settled, he lifted Ava into the driver's seat, kissing her hard and deep. "Just to give you something to think about."

As he walked to his truck, she watched him until she realized he was waiting for her to go. The drive back to her house was a million times better than the drive to his. The stress she'd put herself under earlier had dissipated.

It seemed like something she should have remembered. The power of the mind was immense, and a real or imagined threat could be just as strong. She pulled into the left side of her double-car driveway, leaving room for Chay's vehicle. They both got out and hurried inside, as the temperature had dropped below freezing.

They got Gracie into bed. She didn't feel unsure or awkward as she led Chay down the hall to her bedroom. She showed him where to put his clothes, and they both washed up and brushed their teeth.

Which was a bit awkward. "I don't like to spit in front of other people." Her toothbrush was in her mouth.

"I won't look," he promised, turning away as he continued brushing his own teeth. She spat and rinsed and then moved aside so Chay could and then he pulled her into his arms, his breath against her cheek a moment before she felt his lips on hers.

"Minty fresh," she said.

"You still smell like strawberries," he muttered, his mouth moving down her neck.

"They make me feel sunny." Her words might sound like gibberish, because all she could feel was the heat coursing through her body.

He lifted her off her feet, carrying her into the bedroom and falling onto the bed, keeping her on top of him. "You make me feel that way."

Framing his face with her hands, she was glad she'd changed into her nightshirt while he'd been putting his clothes away, feeling his big, warm hands on the back of her thighs as she straddled him.

"Same."

He'd taken off his shirt and wore only a pair of boxer briefs. She'd spent most of the time in the bathroom trying not to ogle him, but now that he was in her bed it was a different story. The bedside lamp was on, casting them in its warm glow.

She leaned back on his thighs, and he stacked his hands behind his head, watching her. Taking her time, she drew her hand down his chest and back up again. Pushing down on his muscly chest.

"What are you doing?"

"You have no give. I like it. You're a strong man," she muttered. Chay was so masculine in so many ways…so physical and gruff. Ava found she really liked that.

His hands moved to the front of her thighs and then slowly upward until the nightshirt was pushed up to reveal that she didn't sleep in her undies.

The back of his fingers brushed against her. She moaned, parting her thighs to give him access as she pulled the nightshirt over her head and tossed it aside.

Her hands were on his body again, pushing his boxer briefs lower until his cock was in her hand. Hard, warm, thrusting up toward her. She stroked him and then reached for the box of condoms he'd put on the nightstand, tossing one to him.

He put the condom on, and she straddled him as he sat up, wrapping his arms around her so that as she took him all the way inside her, she felt as if she were enfolded into his body.

His mouth was on her neck and shoulder, biting, kissing that made her hotter and drove her higher. He thrust up into her, one hand on her waist, the other on her butt, urging her faster and faster until she felt her orgasm wash over her. She threw her head back and cried out his name.

He continued thrusting and, a moment later, sucked hard on her neck as he came, too.

His hands roamed up and down her back as they both clung to each other. Neither wanting to move until he rolled them gently to their sides, drawing the cover up over her, leaving her only for a moment before he came back and held her through the night.

It was the best night of sleep she'd had in a long time. Confirming that she wasn't falling for Chay. She already had.

Chapter Twelve

Chay's alarm went off way too early. He pulled Ava closer to him as she sleepily opened her eyes. "What is that?"

"Sorry, I've got get going. I'll text you later. Maybe we can make plans again?"

"What do you mean, maybe? We're dating, right?"

"Yeah," he said, trying to play it cool, but the truth was he was new to this, which he'd been honest about with her.

"What is this? Cold feet?"

He didn't answer, swinging his legs off the bed and sitting with his back to her. "Not at all."

Her arms came around his waist as she rested her head on his shoulder. "What is going on?"

"This is the furthest any relationship as ever gone for me." Somehow it was easier to admit it when he wasn't looking at her.

Kissing his neck, her hands rubbed up and down his chest. "Well, this one's not ending."

For now?

He didn't ask that out loud, but the fear was there in the back of his mind and in his heart. He liked Ava so much that he felt like he was going to explode from the emotion. It was overwhelming and not at all the way he liked to operate. There had to be some way to get himself back in check.

"Good to know. So text later? I've got to shower," he said. As much as he knew it would probably be healthier to talk to her, he needed to get moving. Start his day and pretend that absolutely nothing had changed.

"Yes. Go. Want coffee?"

He nodded, and she climbed out of bed, hair tousled around her shoulders. He couldn't tear his eyes from her. Raising both eyebrows, she gave him a secret smile. "I thought you were in a hurry."

"I think I can spare a few minutes," he said as he tumbled her back to bed and made love to her. When they had both come and were exhausted, she lay next to him. "I really have to go," he said.

"I know. Come back tonight?"

"I can't. Come to mine? I think we can find a portable crib for Gracie," he said.

"Okay. I'll do that. My last session is done at six, so I'll be late."

"That works. It's my night to have dinner with my grandmother. So she'll be there. I was thinking…well, about Gracie. Grandmother does want a great-grandchild."

"Wonderful! So you'll try to adopt her?" Ava asked.

"No. I wasn't saying that at all. Just that visitation would be nice for my grandmother."

He read the disappointment on her face. But she just took a deep breath and nodded. "Sounds good."

Guessing how hard it was for her not push him, he kissed her again before heading to the bathroom for his shower. When he came out, there was a coffee mug on the dresser, and he heard the sounds of Ava singing to Gracie.

For a moment he just stood in the domesticity. He could have this. All of this could be his. Just reach out and take what Ava was offering him.

He suspected she wanted a family as much as he did. But she came from a solid home life and had loving parents and a brother. What was holding her back?

His watch pinged, reminding him that he was running late. He had a meeting at the tribal police headquarters at ten, so he needed to speak to Jacob early and get back to the Navajo Nation.

Ava had made him two breakfast burritos, which she'd wrapped in foil and handed to him with a to-go coffee mug. "Figured you wouldn't have time for food. Don't expect this all the time." She said that last with a smile.

His heart was ready to burst—a feeling of happiness coursing through him so deep and strong that he had to look away. This was too much. The world would never let him keep this.

He swallowed his fear for now. He kissed Gracie's head and tickled her under the chin before hugging Ava and grabbing the food she prepared.

"Thanks."

"No problem. 'Bye."

"Byebyebyebye," Gracie said.

Ava's eyes flew to his. "Did you hear that?"

"I did."

"'Bye," he said directly to Gracie.

"Huuuuhhh."

Ava laughed. "So, not totally sure yet. I'm going to keep working on it with her."

"Me, too. 'Bye."

Driving to the National Parks ISB offices, eating one of his burritos, he didn't want to think about Ava and Gracie. But they were in his head. The smell of strawberries and baby powder probably clung to him, and he didn't mind.

He'd never wanted to claim a family as his own, or make one. Taking nothing from his grandmother who'd raised him and loved him. He'd always felt like a burden to her. She had raised her daughter's kid when he had shown up. Her life had been, and still was, full of friends and activities, but she'd taken him on.

Never really complaining. That wasn't her way. She didn't regret him being her life, she'd told him once. That he'd given her a gift she'd never expected to have.

But Ava and Gracie were different. There was no blood bond or sympathy because he'd been left on the doorstep...something he shared with Gracie—maybe that was why he cared so deeply for her.

He couldn't analyze it. Affection didn't work that way. Those two were in his heart, maybe as deeply as his grandmother was. Something the hadn't anticipated and wasn't entirely sure he knew how to handle.

But he would.

Wherever Gracie ended up, he'd make sure it was a kind, loving family. He'd be the best damned uncle she could ever have. It was almost easier with Gracie than with Ava.

Being the best man he could be for Ava, that was something he had no idea how to achieve. But he was determined to try. There was something about her that made him want to forget that hurt boy he still was and reach out again.

The only thing in his way was him. And he was stubborn and scared and hated both of those traits, but there they were. Making the burrito he'd been enjoying a moment ago taste almost sour in his mouth.

MAKING BREAKFAST? STILL SECOND-GUESSING that move, she drove to the hospital. The sun was bright this morning and traffic a little heavier than usual. Gracie was still chattering but hadn't made any other sounds like saying 'bye to Chay.

After she dropped Gracie at day care, she hurried to her office, not stopping to chat with anyone before she had to be in Fern's room for their session.

Probably a good thing she had a busy day, or she'd spend most of it mooning over Chay. Last night had been one of the best of her life. He and Gracie were weaving their way into her heart.

"Hello, Fern," she said, walking into the room, noticing the scent of her brother's cologne as she did so.

"Was Ryan here?"

"He stopped by at the end of his shift before heading home."

"That's nice," Ava said, but she was concerned for Ryan. Fern was recovering from a lot of trauma. Connections she formed now were going to be strong and deep. Something she wasn't too sure her brother was aware of.

Making a mental note to do the big sister thing and call him later, she smiled at Fern.

"How are we today?"

Fern played with the comforter as had become her habit when she was avoiding talking.

"Fine."

"Hey, it's okay to have an off day," Ava reminded her. "What's up?"

"My leg really hurts. I can't sleep. It's been so sunny I wish I was outside, but the PT said I can't until I make more progress."

"You can't walk outside but…what if we bundle you up and sit in the quiet reflection area?" Ava suggested. "We can do your session there."

"Really?"

"Yes. And the nurses will take you outside if you want to go out."

Fern nodded to herself. Smooshing down the blanket pyramids she'd made.

"Don't want to go out?" Ava asked. Suspecting that it was due to the fact that she'd been kidnapped. In this hospital room she was safe. But she wanted Fern to figure that out. Telling her what was holding her back wasn't going to help her move past this trauma.

"Lame, right? I'm in the hospital and there are tons of people around, but I'm still scared to leave this room. Even when they come to take me to PT, I freak out a little bit."

"That's natural—not lame at all. I was afraid to leave my apartment in college for a while," Ava admitted. "Everyone has dealt with fear similar to yours at some time or another. Maybe not for the reasons you have, but our minds are capable of fear to protect us."

"Well… I wish mine would get the message I'm safe," she said with a mirthless laugh.

"You're making a lot of progress. You have nurses in your room at night—how's that going?"

"Much better," Fern admitted. "Actually really good. Two nights ago I was annoyed they woke me up."

"Nice. That's more like it. How did you feel?"

"Normal. For a few minutes, I felt like my old self," she said.

"Good. So about going outside...."

"I don't think I can do it today," Fern said after a moment.

"How do you feel about trying an exercise that might help you get ready to go out?" Ava asked.

"Sure. What is it?"

"Let's make a list of all the evidence for you being kidnapped again and then disprove it. We'll work on it together...how does that feel for you?" Ava asked, not wanting to push Fern into anything the other woman wasn't ready for. But knowing that Fern needed to retrain her mind to accept that there wasn't a kidnapper around every corner.

"I'm not sure. But it will be a distraction, so I'll do it," Fern said with a lot of determination. The woman had grit, which Ava admired.

They worked on the list for a while. Fern putting down her fears. There was no rationale for why the men kidnapped her. She hadn't heard them talking about what they were going to do with her. They hadn't sexually assaulted her. Just kept her drugged.

"Give me one reason why they wouldn't come back," Ava said.

"They'd be arrested or questioned. There are cops in the building and I'm being guarded," Fern said.

"That's a good one. Do you have another reason?"

"It would be easier to get another woman who's on her own," Fern admitted.

"True." Ava added it to the list.

"They grabbed me in Oso. That's probably a town

they know well... I don't think anyone's been taken from Dark Canyon."

There was a question in her voice. "To my knowledge, no one has been taken here. How do you feel about the list?"

"It's a good one. But I'm not sure that's enough. I mean, I want to be outside and feel the sun but...for Pete's sake—my hands are shaking thinking about it." She held her hand out toward Ava.

Ava took her hand and squeezed it. "Last night I was so paranoid I was being watched I locked my car three times to make sure it was extra locked while I was driving. I get the fear you are experiencing. Finally I got to my destination and there was no one following me. My mind could relax only when I felt I was safe."

Maybe she'd overshared, but she wanted Fern to realize that she wasn't alone. "Thanks for that. Makes me feel a little less isolated knowing that this kind of thing happens to you, too. This is going to be with me for a while, isn't it?"

Ava squeezed her hand before letting it go. "For the rest of your life...but with the right tools, like the evidence list, the intensity and frequency will slow. It's just allowing yourself to do what you need to in order to feel safe. There is no wrong reaction. Okay?"

Fern nodded slowly. "Thanks, Ava."

"No problem." They chatted a bit more before she remembered Chay's question. "Officer Benally asked if you remember seeing any signs that anyone else had been held in the cabin?"

Fern leaned back against the pillow, closing her eyes as she made those pyramids out of the blanket and then opened them. "No, but I was so groggy and then when I was awake frantic to get out. There could have been."

"Thanks for that. I'll let him know. Next session we'll see how you feel about going to the bench outside."

Fern gave her a quick smile and a determined nod. Ava left a few minutes later.

BY THE TIME Ava arrived at his house that evening, Chay was tired and very cranky. His grandmother was in a good mood and shooed him out to chop more wood for her, which he'd deliver when he took her home. Chopping wood was the perfect thing for him at this moment.

One of the worst parts of himself was the way he sunk deep inside. Even as a grown-ass man, he still had the sulky teenager longing to come out. The investigation was stalled until the men who took Fern screwed up. He'd asked an officer to go check out areas in around Wilson, but the officer's wife had slipped on ice and broken her ankle, so he'd been out sick.

No. Big. Deal.

The axe fell in time with each of the words to underscore that he needed to let it go. But he wasn't.

He felt like there was a ticking clock and if they didn't make a break in the case soon, someone else was going to be taken. Maybe this time they wouldn't be so lucky to get her back the way they had with Fern.

Though that was all down to Fern. That woman was a strong one, and Chay admired her.

"Want some company?"

Not really.

Part of his crankiness was also down to Ava being so great. He hadn't found a flaw yet. She'd been pushy about Gracie but backed off when he'd asked her to. Just another great thing about this woman.

"Sure."

Because he wasn't an asshole and knew she'd be hurt if he sent her away. But he kept chopping wood, bring up another hunk to be splintered. Focusing solely on his work and not on the fact that she stood next to him in her heavy winter coat, with her knitted hat on...a new one.

"Want to talk about it?"

"Nope."

She gave an exaggerated sigh.

"Sorry. I'm not fit for company. That's why Grandmother sent me out here."

She moved to sit on a stump facing him. "Why is that?"

Shrugging as if he had no clue. Knowing it was because his relationship with her felt like it was going too well. Also, this was date three. No one had made it to date three before. What if three was his new limit?

Which he totally wasn't going to admit to her.

"Last night...when I drove out here, it wasn't just the past I was running from," she said.

He glanced over at her. Ava had a way of intuiting what he was feeling. He both liked and hated that.

"I get it. I'm definitely one foot in my past and one foot right here in the present. I'm totally aware that I could be fucking you and me up. But I can't seem to get around it."

She stood up, putting one hand on her hip. "That's what I'm talking about."

"So you're feeling stalked..." He got it. A bit slower than he normally was, because all these emotions swirling around him like a heavy fog made it hard for him to really see clearly.

"Do you think if you let me and Gracie in, someone will come and take it away?" he asked.

"I don't think it, but I've been fine for years, and then as soon as I start dating you and fostering Gracie, my mind is all on high alert. Looking for someone watching me, waiting to take my security and happiness away again," she said, rubbing her hands on her arms.

He put the axe down on the stump, went over to her and hauled her up against him. "They'll have to go through me."

Her arms went around his waist. "Thanks."

"Only Grandmother has stayed. And part of that had to be obligation, you know?"

She pulled back and shook her head at him. "You're entitled to your feelings, but never say that to your grandmother. She'll be hurt. She loves you. She raised you because she wanted to. We both know there were other options for her. You matter to her. You matter to me, too."

She had a point, but it was easier to say it was obligation than to have to face the fact that if his grandmother loved him for who he was…than his mother must have never loved him. It was complex and hard to unravel. So much of those feelings were tied to who he'd been at six. Not the man he was today.

"Thanks for that. I've never been on more than three dates with a woman. You matter to me. I don't want to let you down."

"You haven't."

"Come on in, you two. Gracie just said Mama," Grandmother called from the door of his house.

Taking Ava's hand in his, they hurried to the house. Even though he promised himself he'd only be Gracie's uncle, he was prouder than any father could be at her words. That girl had a lot to say…not unlike her foster mother.

In his heart, though, he already saw Ava as her mother. How were either of them going to move on once Gracie was placed in her forever home?

For the first time, he actually admitted to himself that he might want more than just being Ava's boyfriend and Gracie's uncle. He might want it all.

Chapter Thirteen

Dropping by the firehouse wasn't a great idea, but Ryan was dodging her calls. Probably because she'd sent a text saying let's talk. What had she been thinking? She'd thought about using their daily Snapchat streak to do it, but that wasn't right. Snapchat was for fun.

She'd left Gracie at day care and run over on her lunch break. His truck was in the parking lot, so she knew he was there. She was tempted to text him they needed to talk about their parents because that would get him to text back, but that just felt mean.

Grabbing the strawberry muffins she'd picked up before coming over, she hopped out of her truck.

She clocked the moment he noticed her. His back stiffened and he said something to the guys before coming to meet her outside the station.

"What are you doing here?"

"You're ignoring me," she said.

She handed him the box of muffins.

"'We need to talk'…you're not Mom, Ava."

"Duh. I had a session with Fern yesterday, and she mentioned you'd been stopping by to visit her."

"Is that a crime now?"

"Okay, if you're going to be like this—"

"You should just go. I'm not doing anything other than checking up on her. She's alone here. Stuck in the hospital. She needs a friend."

Ava hugged her brother with one arm, but he held himself stiff, probably because of her interference. "She does. You really do care about people in our community. I love that about you."

"Yes, I do. So what's the big deal?"

"As you said, she doesn't have a lot of friends, and she's come out of a scary situation... I don't want to see either of you get hurt."

Ryan shook his head at her. "Give it a rest."

She never knew the right tack to take with Ryan. "Listen, I'm your big sister. I can't say I remember the day Mom and Dad brought you home, but I've known you all your life, and if I can keep you safe..."

"Safety is a construct, Ava. You know that better than most."

"I do. I just... Be careful. Both of you are—"

"Adults. Thanks for the muffins," he said, turning away.

Ugh. She'd screwed this up big-time. "Want to play a video game this weekend?"

He stopped walking, glancing over his shoulder. "Maybe. Want to stop butting into my life?"

"Maybe. Love you."

"Me, too."

Feeling like she'd sort of salvaged things after she one hundred percent made them worse, she went back to her truck. It wasn't like she was coming out of left field. Her parents worried about Ryan as well after the hiker he'd lost last year. It had taken a toll on her brother, who hadn't had a big loss like that in his life.

Ryan was the much-loved youngest child of a close-knit family. Ava felt like she'd looked out for him, but the truth was Ryan had always been golden. He genuinely cared about everyone. He'd been friends with the kid who sat by themselves in school. Helped in the community and generally tried to save everyone.

Even when she'd come home from college scared to be alone, paranoid that someone was always following her. She wanted to do the same for him. Let him know he wasn't alone. But she'd never been able to find the words to tell him that.

For all her training and knowledge in helping others, getting through to Ryan or her parents had always been a struggle. Now Chay was starting to fall into that area.

The more she cared for a person, the closer their relationship was, the harder she found it to be objective and to separate the help they needed from her affection for them.

She wanted to wrap Ryan in a big hug, tell him that he couldn't save everyone, but there was a reason her brother was a firefighter…he needed to try.

Putting on her sunglasses, she started the truck and headed back to work. As she drove, she noticed a late-model sedan…the same one that had been parked in front of the Petersons' house a few days ago. That day when she'd almost let panic get the better of her.

Ignoring the car, she pulled into the hospital parking lot. Breathing a sigh of relief as the other vehicle kept driving. Evidence like she'd told Fern to find, that no one in that car was following her.

She stopped by the day-care center for the last ten minutes of her lunch break. Gracie clapped her hands when she saw Ava and said, "Mamamamaa," which of course made Ava's heart melt.

"Gracie, you're such a smart girl," Ava said.

"Mamamamamaaa."

She took her phone out and took a video to send to Chay.

"Gracie, say hi."

"Huhh, mamamama," Gracie said.

"Can you believe how smart our girl is?!"

She stopped the video and texted it to Chay. Kissing Gracie on the head and hugging her close. When she set her down, the little girl crawled back to the toy she'd been playing with.

"She's really starting to thrive," said Misty, one of the workers in the day care.

"Yeah. She feels safe," Ava said. But it was a reminder to herself that safety and routine were the keys to healing when it came to trauma. Her warning to Ryan may have been misjudged. Fern might be helping him to heal as well. Seeing the woman he'd rescued thrive was the best prescription for reminding him that he was good at his job.

Getting back to her office, she noticed her door was open and normally she kept it closed. Not open a lot, just slightly ajar. Maybe she'd left it that way. She had been in a rush to see Ryan.

Going inside, she checked her computer hadn't been accessed and that no files had been taken. But her desk looked fine. Chay didn't text back…which of course he didn't have to, but she kept checking her phone.

Which wasn't healthy. She put her phone on her desk and focused on work. Chay had been clear that three dates was the most he'd ever been on with one person. Was she painting him the way she wanted him to be or as he truly was?

The video that Ava sent was sweet, and he saw what she was doing. Or was it manipulative? It was hard to separate well-meaning from manipulative. He'd seen a therapist twice. Once right after his mom left him to make sure he was okay to go to school. Those sessions had been difficult, but he'd done what he had to in order to stop going.

It hadn't taken him that long to realize what the therapist wanted to hear him say. So he'd done it. Told her what she wanted. Grandmother didn't buy it for a second, but she understood why. She just loved him and gave him space.

Space.

It was the one thing he hadn't had with Ava. He liked her, and if it was just Ava, maybe he'd be handling the relationship better. But there was Gracie.

A baby girl that he was growing closer to. He'd mentioned to his grandmother about the visitation, and she was so excited. Already she was prepping for the baby's visit.

Chay knew the more time he spent with her, the harder it was going to be to keep her out of his heart. He had the job to concentrate on. Reminding himself that work had been his savior as an adult.

Jacob sent an email with an update on some of the police stations that Chay hadn't had time to talk to. They'd decided to split the list. There had to be something more they could find.

The officer he'd been talking to go back to him. "The house showed signs of people having been there, but other than smelling of urine, some used needles and discarded clothes, I couldn't find anything to link it to our missing woman. Sorry, man."

"It was a long shot." Chay wasn't ready to give up on this thread of the investigation. "Thanks for your help. Hope the wife is better."

"Yeah, she's getting there."

After hanging up, he wondered if there were more abandoned cabins on the edge of the Navajo Nation. Grabbing his hat and coat, he let his team know he was going to be out for a while.

Driving back to where Fern had been found, he inspected the charred remains of the cabin. There had to be something they were missing; Chay just wasn't sure he'd find it before another woman was taken.

But women went missing every day. He knew he was reaching a little...trying to tie the reasons together. Some women disappeared because of abusive relationships or even unwanted kids...

Chay realized that he was trying to give each of these women a motivation. Including Annie Ross. She'd been found dead, but her child could have been with her at some point, and maybe that meant that Annie hadn't wanted to abandon Gracie.

Chay scratched his chin, walking around the charred cabin. Fern and Annie didn't seem to be connected. He knew there had to be a line connecting them. But what was it?

Foster care was a nice start.

Both women, actually all three of Annie's friends as well, had been shuffled around and hadn't found a forever home. Had Annie been on her way to making one when she'd stumbled into something else? Or was she just a woman with bad judgment who'd died in the wilderness?

Please God, let there be more to it than that. Let Gracie have meant something more to Annie than something she'd left behind.

His phone pinged. Ava again.

In this mood, he didn't want to talk to her. That feeling of being not worthy was so heavy that he could barely even read her message. Going back to his truck, he called his grandmother.

"Hello."

"Ava says we can have visitation with Gracie. Do you want to see her tonight?"

"We've already discussed this. Are you okay?"

"Yes."

"So, no," she said gently. "Where are you? I know you put that tracker on my phone, but I can never find it."

"I'm at that cabin where the woman was found. Just looking for anything that might give us a clue as to why she was held out here."

"Did you find anything?"

Nothing but his past. And he hadn't been left in the wilderness. Except it had felt like that. He'd been raised in cities throughout the Pacific Northwest before his mom had brought him back to the Navajo Nation. The reservation was small compared to the cities he'd lived in. Too much open space and vistas that he'd never seen before. He'd felt like a foreigner.

"Chay, yazhi talk to me."

"I'm lost in the past, and it ticks me off because I can see a future where…"

No way was he saying *I could be happy*. But that was

what he felt. Yet there was a thick iron chain around him, keeping him stuck where he was. Isolated and alone.

"The past is the foundation of who you are. You've grown out of the broken foundation that you were born into. You are strong today. Part of this community and a protector of our people. And of all people. That's who you are."

All things he knew, but when he was in a spiral it was hard to believe it. "Thanks, Masani."

"You're welcome. Why is that charred house affecting you?"

"I don't know. Part of it isn't going to make sense to anyone but me. But Gracie's mom was also found out here wandering, and it is making me remember how lost Mom was. How I couldn't help her."

"You were a child."

He wasn't anymore. It should be a case like any other, but this one, probably because he'd invited Ava and Gracie into his life, felt very different.

The stakes were higher and though he never wanted to fail, this time he knew that he couldn't. He needed answers.

CHAY FINALLY RESPONDED to say he was busy with work but his grandmother would love to see Gracie. It took her about a minute to get over being hurt. He'd told her he was in new territory. She should give him some grace. But it felt like her heart was on the line, so she struggled.

She texted Chay back asking for his grandmother's address and then headed toward the Navajo Nation. She'd spent a lot of time hiking and snowshoeing in the Dark Canyon National Park but hadn't visited the Navajo Nation until recently. She was starting to like it.

Gracie fell asleep on the drive, leaving Ava alone with her thoughts. One positive to Chay semi-ghosting her was that she was no longer feeling like she was being watched. Her mom always said the Lord gives and the Lord takes away. Everything had balance in life.

Her clients, like Fern, found it as they slowly recovered from the anxiety and trauma that held them prisoner. Slowly they replaced one thought pattern with a new one. She had been doing that for a while now. Finding her place in the world as a single woman.

She liked it. Though her parents were happily in love, they'd never pressured her to only view herself as someone's wife, and she never had. She had loved Greg, and being his wife would have been deeply fulfilling, but after his death, she hadn't thought she had to find another man.

Not until Chay.

It was more that he fit her than that she needed a man. She felt like it was Chay she wanted. But he wasn't sure.

So she needed to give him some space. She'd keep up contact with him for Gracie's sake, but otherwise she'd be cautious.

Except, how was she going to do that? Now that she'd started liking him and had slept with him.

Sex had never been casual for her, and if she hadn't felt like there was a future with Chay, she wouldn't have invited him into her bed and her life.

Ugh. She was in a spiral. Luckily, she was almost to the reservation. Glancing down at her map for a second to check the directions, her truck must have swerved, because she almost hit a car overtaking her. The other vehicle honked, driving her off the road, scraping by her as it kept on going.

Her heart was racing and her hands were shaking as

she slowed her truck to a stop. The other vehicle kept going.

Ava couldn't. That had scared her so much her hands were shaking.

She checked on Gracie. The baby was fine and hadn't noticed anything. Reaching back, Ava tucked her blanket closer to her.

Doing some box breathing helped to slow her racing heart, and as she saw the headlights of another vehicle coming in the other direction, she got herself back on the road. She was surprised the other vehicle that had brushed her hadn't stopped. People in these parts tended to.

Putting on her upbeat music playlist and blasting "All Over the World." Forcing herself to sing along although a couple of times she almost lost control and started crying. Finally she made it to Aponi's house. Pulling into the driveway, she felt like she could breathe a little more easily.

Aponi stood in the doorway as Ava got Gracie out of her car seat. "Welcome to my home."

"Thank you. I'm so happy to be here," Ava said. When they were all inside, she looked around, trying to be subtle to see if Chay had come over.

"He's not here," Aponi said.

"Of course. He's busy with work." Ava didn't believe for a second that he needed to work this case 24-7.

"There's more to life than work," Aponi said. "But Chay is very good at his job."

"He is. I know that he won't stop until he finds the men who took Fern." She saw a photo of Chay on the wall in his tribal officer uniform. "You should be very proud of him."

"I am," Aponi said. "I'll make us some tea, and then can I hold Gracie?"

"You can. Actually, I can put the tea on if you want to hold her."

Aponi agreed. "It's been so long since I've held a little one."

"Since Chay?"

"No, his father."

Aponi sang a little song in Navajo to the baby as they waited for the kettle to boil. Ava knew she shouldn't pry into Chay's past, but she wanted to understand him. To figure out if she was being dumb by feeling hurt and still wanting him to be a part of her life.

"Where is Chay's dad? He's only mentioned his mom," Ava said. "Don't answer that. I'm just trying to figure stuff out, and I shouldn't go behind his back."

Aponi looked at her with wise eyes. "You like my grandson."

"A lot. But he's not making it easy."

"He wouldn't. Easy isn't Chay's way."

Which made perfect sense. But really wasn't helping her much. The kettle boiled and they had their tea, moving to the living room so Aponi could watch Gracie crawl around on the floor.

Ava started to relax and, instead of keeping her thoughts on Chay, saw how much Gracie enjoyed being with the older woman. "Did your people find out any more about her DNA relatives?"

"Just the connection to Diné. Chay has run a search to find out if you have any other DNA matches that weren't known to you, but I think that was a dead end as well."

"It's always been just us. His father died when Chay was a baby and his mother died when he was a teen. I'm not sure if she had other kids. I think the strongest possibility is that she did. That this child would have been his half brother's."

Ava didn't want to think what that would mean to Chay. Having a sibling he didn't know about. Was that other man alive? No one knew.

Aponi shared fun stories from Chay's childhood, and Ava stayed until nine before she left to drive home. As much as she wanted to go by Chay's place, she resisted. When he was ready, he'd reach out to her.

Chapter Fourteen

Pulling into her driveway just after ten, Ava was glad to see her home. It had been a long, emotional day and really all she wanted was to get Gracie changed and to bed so she could get some sleep. Put this day behind her.

The porch light was out, because *of course* the bulb would die on this already crappy day. She got Gracie out of the car, holding the baby with one hand as she fumbled with her keys. As soon as she got to the front door and put her key in the lock, the door swung open without her turning the key.

Freaking out a little but keeping calm because of Gracie, she removed her key and double-timed it back to the truck, getting in the driver's side and hitting the lock button as soon as they were both inside.

Her pulse was going so fast that she was sure the neighbors could hear her heart. Gracie was watching her with those sweet, innocent eyes. She stroked the baby's back as she hit the speed dial for her mom.

"Ava—"

"Someone broke into my house, Mom."

"Where are you? Are you safe?"

"I'm in my truck in the driveway. The door was open and the front porch light was off."

"Dad's on his way. I'm calling 911."

"I should have done that."

"You did the right thing. Stay in the truck. Doors locked."

"They are."

Her mom talked to her until her dad arrived. He had his gun but waited until the cops arrived, along with her cousin, Jacob, who worked with the National Parks ISB. They checked her house and found that it was empty.

"We need you to come in and make sure nothing was taken," Jacob said.

Her dad hugged her tight and then offered to hold Gracie while she went with Jacob to inspect the house.

Her hands were sweating even though it was below freezing. Now the one place that she'd always been comfortable felt scary. They went room by room through the house and when she got into the kitchen, her blood ran cold.

Someone had rearranged her canisters in size order. She'd had them scattered around, but they'd been moved to the center of the counter underneath the cabinets.

"See something?" Jacob asked.

She pointed at the canisters, wrapping her arm around her waist. "Daniel did that at my apartment."

"Daniel Wayne? Isn't he still in jail?" Jacob asked.

"Last I heard," Ava confirmed.

"I'll check on that. This is more than likely tied to Annie Ross and her baby. Even though she died of natural causes, there's a lot of suspicion around the circumstances. Your dad's insisting you go home with him tonight. The house is safe if you want to go pack a bag for yourself and Gracie."

Her dad was sitting in the rocking chair in Gracie's room, the baby sleeping against his chest.

"Everything here?"

"Yeah...but the canisters in the kitchen were moved around," she said, catching him up as she shoved a bunch of diapers and clothes into a bag for Gracie.

"I hope this doesn't affect Gracie," she said to her dad as she finished gathering her stuff. "She's just started to feel like this is home."

"It's just a few nights. Mom called a friend and found a portable crib, so she'll be sleeping with you in a safe place."

"Thanks. I should have just called the cops, but you guys were my first thought," she said.

"As we should be."

"Ava, you okay?" Ryan's voice echoed through the house.

"In here," Dad said.

Ryan came over and gave her a hard hug. "Sorry I was a brat earlier."

"You were justified." Her voice was muffled against his winter coat. Now that her family was here with her, she didn't feel as panicked as she had before. But still... could Daniel be out of jail?

Those canisters...her gut told her it had to be him. Or someone who knew him? She wasn't entirely sure. She felt scared and unsafe.

"Want to ride with me back to Mom and Dad's?" Ryan asked.

"I'll drive your vehicle over," Dad said. "Take this little angel with me."

"I can drive, you know."

"We know," Ryan and Dad said at the same time.

That feeling of being loved and taken care of washed over her. She could take care of herself, but for tonight she was glad she didn't have to. Her family was always there for her, the way that Ava knew she'd be for Gracie.

It made her wonder if Chay felt the same way about his grandmother. He thought he was safe by not allowing her and Gracie into his life. He had never experienced life as a Colton, where everyone knew you and had your back.

Maybe that was part of what had him pumping the brakes with her. She knew she was focusing on him, trying with all her might to keep her focus on figuring out Chay instead of the fear that had taken root in her stomach as soon as she realized her house had been broken into.

It was one thing to suspect it was Daniel, but the truth was women were being abducted. Fern had been. What was to say that she hadn't been targeted as well?

Or were they after Gracie?

Had Annie Ross been involved with someone who was part of Fern's kidnaping? So many questions and too few answers.

When they got to her parents' house, Ryan stayed for a cup of decaf before heading home. Dad went to bed because he had to be up early, but Mom just sat next to her on the couch.

Not saying a word, just letting Ava have the time she needed.

"I'm scared."

"You'd be silly not to be. But no one is going to hurt you or Gracie. We'll make sure of it."

"Thanks, Mom." Her mom might run a charitable foundation and be a rather slight woman, but the fierceness in her tone reassured Ava. She understood her mom a little better now that she had Gracie. There was nothing that Ava wouldn't do to keep that baby safe.

Ava knew sleep wasn't happening for her, and since her mom was sometimes a bit of a night owl, she didn't feel guilty about staying where she was.

"How's the silent auction fundraiser coming along?"

"Well, as you know, I have the Pinterest board started and I've just spoken to Sassy and we're going to use the Zephyr Gallery for the event."

Her cousin Sassy owned the gallery and was an artists' agent. The event being held there would be profitable for the Colton Foundation but also help to spotlight Native artisans and crafters. Aponi had mentioned Sassy had already been in touch to invite her to display some of her rugs and offer one for sale in the silent auction.

"That's great. Do you have a menu yet? Aponi has these blue corn cookies that are delicious and would pair well with this type of event," Ava said.

"Aponi?"

"Chay Benally's grandmother. I was at her place earlier tonight. She's excited to have a great-grandchild, even though it's through Chay's mother and not her son," Ava said.

"How does Chay feel about that?" Mom asked. "Did you push?"

Ava wanted to deny it. "You know me. I tried to be chill about it, but it's hard, Mom, when I know what's best for everyone but they won't listen to me."

Her mom laughed. "It's a burden we Colton women must bear."

"I also was ham-handed with Ryan. He's visiting with Fern a lot, and I didn't realize how close they were becoming."

Her mom's brow furrowed with worry. "He hasn't been the same since the hiker last year."

"Precisely why I wanted to just warn him to take it slowly," Ava said. Her brother would be furious if he heard them discussing him. "I think he will. Just know I wasn't as cool as I wanted to be. Tell me about the artists you have lined up for the silent auction."

Her mom did. Ava felt slightly better about turning her attention away from Ryan and back to the auction. "Want to play with me?"

Her father wore noise-canceling headphones to bed to help him sleep, so the music wouldn't disturb them.

"I haven't practiced in a long time."

"When were you ever regular about it?" Mom teased.

"True. Let me check on Gracie." Ava darted down the hall to find the little girl sleeping soundly. She'd had an exciting day with her new words. And of course crawling all over the place.

"Good night, angel. You're safe," Ava whispered before kissing her and leaving the room with the door ajar.

Mom was at the piano bench, her fingers moving fluidly over the keys, warming up by playing scales. Ava sat next to her and took the octave above, seamlessly picking up where her mom was.

They did scales for a good five minutes, Ava making a few mistakes before the muscle memory kicked in. She found when she stopped thinking about playing, she was better. Letting her subconscious and her fingers do the heavy lifting.

"What shall we play? Classical or pop?"

Pachelbel was challenging and would draw her out of her head. But the song that was on replay in her mind was "A Thousand Miles" by Vanessa Carlton. Her mom had sent her that song when she'd dropped Ava off at college. "'A Thousand Miles.'"

"Perfect. I was thinking that, too. Want to start?"

"Yes."

They switched around on the bench. Taking a deep breath, closing her eyes, she heard the song in her head. The musical notes on the staff appeared in her mind, and her fingers started moving.

As she played, she was aware of Mom joining in, but her mind was floating free, thinking about the people who mattered to her. The ones she'd make a journey for no matter the distance or time it took.

Her family, of course, but then Chay's face. Aponi's face. Gracie's. They were the new family she'd created with indelible threads whether she wanted to admit it or not. Whether Chay wanted to admit it or not. The connection was there.

She knew she was being a little bit selfish not messaging him that her home had broken into. He'd want to know, and she was doing it to hurt him back because he'd avoided seeing her tonight.

When the song was over, she hugged her mom and told her good-night, going to bunk down in the room where they'd set up the crib for Gracie.

Playing the piano had made it clear that she needed to contact Chay.

Ava: Hey. Sorry for the late text. Didn't want you to hear it from Jacob or someone else. My home was broken into tonight. Gracie and I are fine. We're staying with my parents.

Hitting send, she went to wash her face and brush her teeth. When she got back into the room, she avoided her phone, doing her nighttime mediation routine to try to find some semblance of normalcy. But it escaped her.
Finally she picked up her phone.
Chay was responding. The dots showing up and then disappearing for what felt like an eternity.

Chay: Glad you're okay.

No way was that all he typed for that long.

Ava: Me too.

Chay: I should have been with you. I'm sorry for today.

Ava: You needed space and I was crowding you.

Chay: Don't take that on. You needed me.

Ava: I still do. But when you're ready. We don't have to barrel into anything.

Chay: What if I want to?

Her breathing got a little heavier at the thought. She liked him and she'd missed him. She'd even told herself that she would give him the space he needed, but the truth was she wanted to be with him tonight. As safe as she felt in her parents' house, she knew she wouldn't truly feel secure until he was next to her.

That was dangerous thinking for a woman who'd learned to be independent. A woman who promised herself she'd never depend on anyone again. A woman who settled into her blankets happy to text with her boyfriend.

IT TOOK ALL of his willpower not to get in his truck and go get Ava and Gracie and bring them to his house. Anger, fear and guilt were a potent cocktail running through his system. He'd fucked up. He knew that.

Fear had led him to push her away and now…well nothing had happened to her, she was safe enough, but fate had given him a reminder that he was going to miss her whatever happened.

Chay: Still there?

He wanted to talk to her but doubted video chatting at this time of night in her parents' house was a good idea. Hell, if he hadn't chickened out, she might be sleeping in his bed right now, neither of them aware her house had been broken into.

Ava: Yeah. Wasn't sure how to respond.

Chay: I get that. I said let's go slow and then hit pause. But it was just pause. Not stop.

Ava: Good. Wasn't sure.

Chay: Be sure. Can I see you in the morning?

Ava: Yes. At the hospital around ten.

CHAY GOT TO the hospital at nine because he was anxious to see Ava. He would have gone to her parents' house but thought that might not go over well. He'd spoken to Jacob, who felt strongly that the break-in was tied to Annie Ross and her child.

"Ava was worried about Daniel Wayne, but I'm checking to make sure he's still in jail. It makes more sense that this is connected to Annie and the baby. I'm going to keep looking into it," Jacob had said when they talked on the phone.

Chay had reassured him that he'd keep a close watch on Ava and Gracie. As soon as he saw her truck pull into the parking lot, he was out of his. Ava stepped out of the vehicle, and Chay drew her into a tight hug.

She looked tired and small. Funny, because she always seemed so big and fierce, and he'd never expected her to be anything else.

Her arms wrapped around him, holding him tightly. The affection he had for her threatened to overwhelm him, so he looked up at the sky to distract himself. He saw signs of a snowstorm in the clouds.

"Are you working today?"

"I am. Just one session and then…"

"Stay with me? Just for a few days until Jacob and his team have a chance to figure out if this is tied to Annie Ross."

"Are you sure?"

"Positive," he said, opening the back door and getting

Gracie out of her car seat. The little one smiled when she saw him and called him "mama."

"Nice." Putting his arm around Ava, he drew both of them close to him. "You two had me worried."

"We're okay. Luckily I wasn't home," Ava said.

"That is a good thing. Remember the other night when you thought it was PTSD that had you feeling you were being watched…"

"I am trying not to think of the possibility that I really have someone watching me, but it's hard to shake."

He shouldered Gracie's diaper bag and then watched as Ava locked her truck. Taking her hand in his, he walked with her to the hospital's side entrance. "Another reason for you to stay with me. Kidnappers might think twice when there's a man involved."

"Or they could shoot you," Ava pointed out. "I don't want to put you in danger."

"I'm not arguing about this. I want you to come stay with me. I'll be fine," he told her. He wanted to order her to come with him, but he was smart enough to know better than to say that out loud. But whatever she decided, he was going to be with her. If she wanted to stay at her place or at his.

"Don't get cocky," she warned him. "We'll stay with you. I need a crib for Gracie."

"I already got one. If I hadn't gotten cold feet yesterday, you would have seen it."

She looked up at him, her eyes clear with worry and fear and affection. "I can stay with my—"

"Enough. It's time for me to man up. Stop running from every person I might feel something for. Don't make me repeat that again."

She hugged him and then took Gracie from his arms. "Oh, I might. Seems to me that you said you like me."

Like her? Hell, yes. It was more than like, but he wasn't ready to delve into that yet. "I might."

"Ha."

He followed her into the day-care facility where she normally left Gracie. Ava stopped and looked back at him. "Do you think she'll be safe here? Will the staff be?"

He wasn't entirely sure. He'd taken the day off to come and check on Ava and Gracie. "I'll keep her while you work. Give me a chance to spend some time alone with her."

A little bit he was baiting her to see if she'd tell him what a good dad he'd make. He could tell she knew what he was doing, because her eyes sparkled, and despite the faint circles under her eyes from lack of sleep, she looked a bit like her normal self again.

"Okay."

"Okay...really, that's all you have to say to me?" he teased as they went into her office.

"Yup. I mean, I don't have to point out how good you are with Gracie—you already know that. You're just in denial."

Throwing his head back and laughing long and hard. He was in denial about a lot of things surrounding his two girls. Maybe as far as admitting to it out loud, but in his heart, there was truth. And while he didn't know how he'd be as a parent long-term, he already cared deeply for Gracie, and watching over her while Ava worked felt right to him.

Chapter Fifteen

Cassidy Garner was in Fern's room when Ava arrived for their session. The other woman had pretty blue eyes and strawberry blond hair pulled back in a ponytail. She waved at Ava as she walked in.

"Heard you had a scare last night," Cassidy said.

"Yeah. We're fine now. My parents went all overprotective. I spent the night with them."

"Be glad you have them," Fern said from the bed.

"I am every day," Ava said. "How are you feeling today?"

"Not too bad. The pain is at a manageable level," Fern said.

"Let's keep it that way. It's totally okay if you want some medication for the pain. No one is going to call you weak for taking it," Cassidy said.

"I know."

Cassidy said goodbye, and Ava took a seat near the bed were she normally sat during their sessions.

It was cloudy today, so little chance that Fern wanted to be outside. To be honest, there was little chance she wanted to be. It was bitterly cold, with an artic blast coming down on them.

"What happened to you?" Fern asked.

"Someone broke into my house. They think it might be related to the baby I'm caring for," Ava said. Not sure how much Fern would remember about Ava's personal life. Ava really didn't like to talk about it too much.

"Annie Ross's baby, right? Ryan mentioned the baby had been left at the fire station," Fern said.

"Yes. Her mom was found in the wilderness not really dressed for the weather. She died from hypothermia."

Fern's hand clenched into a fist. "I'm sorry to hear that."

"Does that stir up memories?" Ava asked. Certain it would.

"Some. I mean, I was lucky that I started that fire I guess. I could have been like Annie Ross."

"Possibly. But your situation is different. Do you want to try to unpack some more of what happened? I know you said they kept you drugged and that you hated it."

"Yeah, sorry. It's just as a recovering addict, I really hate feeling strung out. And there's always that chance I relapsed."

Ava sympathized. "Is that why you're refusing the pain meds?"

"Some. Mostly I want to be aware of what's happening around me," she said.

"I don't blame you for that. So for today…are we ready to talk about the cabin?"

Fern took a ragged breath, fingers working those pyramids on the blanket. Her gaze firmly averted from Ava.

"No, but I really am not sure putting it off is helpful, either," Fern said. "I have to start getting better."

"You are doing wonderfully. No pressure. It's just as you recover and start to regain your strength, your mind will relive a lot of what happened. I want to give you a chance to talk about it. It's always better to get things out."

Fern toyed with a strand of her hair and then closed her eyes. "I didn't eat the food at first. They offered me a granola bar, and I threw it at them."

"Bet they weren't expecting that."

"No. One of them hit me. I remember that. Then there was the needle, which sort of sent me into a spiral."

"They injected you with drugs?"

"Yes."

Ava sat forward. "Oh that's a lot. What about this tattoo?"

Fern touched the side of her neck. "I can't remember getting it, but I probably always had it."

"When did you discover it?" Ava asked, taking careful notes. She had a feeling Chay would want to know about this.

"I had a nightmare two days ago. Things are getting tangled in my head. I was a heavy drinker as a teenager, and a lot of my memories of that time are fuzzy…like it might be a dream and not real," Fern said.

Ava jotted that down. She kept her gaze on her notebook, because at this moment she was so angry on Fern's behalf. These men had reintroduced something that Fern had taken steps to move past. She'd had so much trauma already. None of it seemed fair.

But then, when had life ever been fair?

Ava went over and squeezed the other woman's shoulder gently. She wanted to hug her but didn't want to cross the patient/doctor boundaries. The tattoo was a rose with a dollar sign. It wasn't the typical teenage one as far as Ava could tell. It might not mean anything, but she thought she'd mention it to Chay.

Why had Fern been taken? It was hard to understand it exactly, but she knew that Chay would figure it out.

"Is it okay if I mention this to Officer Benally? This might help in his investigation," Ava said.

"That's fine. I don't want to show it to anyone," Fern said.

"You won't have to," Ava promised. No one was going to make this woman do that. Not while Ava was around. "I promise you. If they want to ask you more questions—"

"I don't have answers for him."

Ava did hug her that time. "You don't have to."

Ava turned the conversation from the past to the present. "So, no sun today...how do you feel about that?"

"Good. I wasn't going to be able to go outside, and now I don't have to disappoint you."

"I would never be disappointed. You are so brave. We only need to go outside when you are ready."

"Maybe never," Fern said.

"You'll get there. You've come a long way. Don't doubt yourself, lady—you are the bravest woman I know."

CHAY FOUND A quiet corner of the cafeteria and got Gracie sitting in a high chair playing with one of her toys while he reviewed some information that had come in overnight from one of the other police stations he'd contacted.

Not much there, Chay thought disappointingly. He heard someone walking toward them. Ava.

She took a seat across from him after kissing Gracie on the head. "Hey, you two. Got a minute?"

"I think she has all the time in the world, and I always have time for you," Chay said. Still feeling a little uneasy at how much he liked her but knowing that he wasn't going to back down from it. Guilt gnawed at him for last night.

She'd needed him, and he hadn't been there. If there was one thing that Chay was really in tune with, it was that. He'd needed his mom a million times, and filling the void left had made him into the tough ass he'd thought he was until Ava.

"What's up?"

"Um…were you aware that Fern has a tattoo that she doesn't remember getting?" Ava asked.

"No. I wasn't. I don't think Jacob was, either," he said. "Where and what does it look like?"

"On her neck, and this is a rough sketch. She doesn't remember all the details and she has a cast on her leg so this is what you'll have to go on." Ava handed him a piece of paper that had been torn from a notebook.

Chay looked down at it. "This almost looks like a brand, maybe?"

More talking to himself than to Ava.

"What does that mean?"

"Human traffickers mark their property."

That sent chills down Ava's spine. "Do you think that's what happened to Fern?"

"I'm not sure yet. I have some paperwork to do but should be done here in an hour or so."

He was being so calm, as if he hadn't just said *human trafficking* to her. But maybe that was the way he had to be in order to get the job done. "You good with me taking Gracie to the National Parks ISB offices?" he asked.

Ava beamed at him, and he realized he was playing straight into her fantasies of him as a dad. As much as he was reluctant to talk about adopting Gracie, Chay did spend a lot of time with the little girl.

"Yeah, that's fine. Text when you're back and I'll meet you out front."

"We'll come in."

Chay wasn't taking any chances. The tattoo on Fern could link her to a trafficking gang. Prove that she was taken for a purpose. Human trafficking seemed to be the main motive. Still, he would be happier if he could tie those other disappearances to the same gang. He wanted to talk to Jacob about the case.

"I don't need a bodyguard."

"Too bad," he said. Meaning it as well. The break-in last night now seemed more important than ever. Had Annie Ross or her friend Camille Lancaster been taken for the same reasons as Fern? He needed to call the medical examiner and see if Annie had any tattoos.

"You're bossy."

"So are you. That's why you like me."

"True," she admitted, leaning over to kiss him. "Tell Jacob thanks again for last night."

Chay agreed and watched her walk away after she kissed Gracie as well. "Mama."

"Yup, your mama is going back to work," he said, gathering up their things. "Want to come to work with me?"

It had been on the tip of his tongue to call himself "daddy." But he wasn't Gracie's father. He was her uncle. Changing that relationship was going to require him to do some soul searching and heavy thinking. He was already leaning that way. Last night had changed a few things. Shown him that even though he felt he was protecting himself, he hadn't been.

He got to the National Parks ISB offices and made a

beeline for Jacob. He'd texted over the information he'd gotten from Ava and was ready to discuss it.

The baby strapped to his chest got a few smiles, and more than one person came over to say hi. Normally his gruff exterior kept most people at arm's length, but no one could resist Gracie's charm.

He caught Jacob up on the tattoo and the fact that Fern wasn't sure if she'd had it since she was a teen. The other man was just as interested in finding out what the rest of it was like. "I think Fern will shut down if we push her. This is going to be all we have until Ava gets her talking more about it."

"Agreed. But at least it gives us something to look for on other women. It's got to be trafficking. Are they using the women as sex workers or for porn?" Jacob asked.

"We could check arrest records. But usually officers aren't looking for tattoos."

"Yeah. And the sketch…it's not really enough to go on," Jacob said.

"I'll put it into the database and see if anything comes up. It doesn't look tribal," Chay said.

"I had that thought, too. What's your next move?"

"Figured we'd get the medical examiner to check Annie Ross. Maybe they took her as well and she escaped them?"

"Yeah, I like that. Keep me posted."

"I will. Ava and Gracie are going to stay with me for a few days until she gets a security system installed in her house. Do you still think the break-in is related to Annie?" Chay asked.

"Seems logical. I'm checking on the guy who stalked her in college just to rule that out, but honestly, he's in jail, so that doesn't seem to be connected," Jacob said.

"Well, if anyone comes for either of them, they'll have to go through me," Chay said, shaking the other man's hand as he got up to leave.

Jacob gave him a brief smile. Chay enjoyed working with the National Parks ISB, even though this was his first time working with the agency. Jacob ran a tight ship and had a good team around him.

Chay was confident that together they'd sort out what was going on and why Fern had been kidnapped. Something that he suspected would help Fern's recovery. She had to feel scared and vulnerable.

And Chay was determined that Ava and Gracie wouldn't experience that. He'd keep them up at his place for as long as he had to.

"Aponi Benally is here to see you," Darla said.

"Oh, send her back."

Ava made sure her desk was clear of all files and her computer screen saver was on. Aponi walked into her office a few minutes later.

"Hope you don't mind the drop-in. I was in town talking to Sassy about an exhibit she wants me to do."

"It's always lovely to see you. Want some coffee or tea?"

"I'm good for now." Aponi took a seat across from Ava. "I wanted to talk to you about Gracie. I know that you got visitation for Chay and me...will that continue once she is adopted?"

"I'm not sure. That is something that would have to be worked out through the courts with the family who adopt her. Right now there's no movement on that front until they figure out what happened with Annie Ross."

"That poor woman. I've reached out to friends in other

parts of Utah to see if they know anything about Annie or the baby's father. I wish we had a name or something to go on."

Ava did as well. She knew it would bring peace of mind to Aponi and Chay. "Did Chay's mom leave any type of correspondence behind?"

"Nothing. When we went to bury her, I was listed as next of kin," Aponi said, a glimpse of sadness crossing her face. "She was a troubled woman."

"What happen to your son... Chay's father?"

"Car accident. Chay was only six months old. Lucy came back here for the funeral with Chay. But they didn't stay. They had agreed that Chay would be raised away from the Navajo Nation. Both of them thought he'd have a better future," Aponi said.

Ironic that he'd ended up back there. Ava noticed that Aponi looked sad and maybe a little angry. "So Sassy wants you to have a show?"

"Yes. But my rugs aren't meant to be hung on walls. They are meant to be used and enjoyed. Like Gracie's blanket."

"Maybe. But the kind of weaving you do is highly prized. So many rugs sell online for a ridiculous amount of money, and they aren't authentic," Ava pointed out.

"Suckers should know better than to buy them online. You have to come to the source," Aponi said. "Festivals and exhibits."

"And silent auctions? My mom mentioned there were some Navajo rugs donated for the Colton Foundation fundraiser coming up."

"That part I don't mind. The weaves I put in the rug are to make the community stronger. Peace, acceptance... those are things the world needs right now."

"They do," Ava agreed. Her phone pinged.

"Go ahead and check it. I know you're a working woman."

"Thanks," she said. She hadn't wanted to seem rude. "That was Chay. He's on his way back. I'm going to be staying with him for a few days."

"Good—I'll get to see more of you and Gracie."

She was surprised that Aponi didn't ask any questions about her staying at Chay's. Like, did she think they were a couple now? Ava had no clue and no way to broach the subject without coming across as awkward.

The silence was a bit uncomfortable. More than likely just on her side. "Someone broke into my house. So Chay offered for me to stay with him until I can get a security system put in place."

"I'm glad you are staying with him," Aponi said. "I like you for him. But make sure it's good for you, too."

That was a bit too real for the moment. "I think he is. Do you see something I don't?"

Aponi didn't shrug or look away from Ava, keeping her gaze squarely on her face. "We all define ourselves in a certain way. You are someone who cares a great deal and wants to fix those around her. Chay doesn't need fixing—he's whole and complete. Make sure you remember that."

Ava's impulse was to defend herself, but Aponi hadn't meant any malice. Giving Ava a hug, she left her office. Ava sat on the edge of her desk, Aponi's words going through her head.

She was a fixer. As much as Ryan was a savior. They both had grown up children of wealth and privilege, aware that others didn't have the same leg up. For herself, Ava knew she looked out for others because she could.

Had she done that with Chay?

He texted that they were back at the hospital and waiting in the cafeteria for her again. A little thrill went through her at the thought of seeing them both. Her day felt long, probably because she'd had very little sleep in the last few days. But she couldn't make Chay into her oasis. She needed to find that peace for herself. No one wanted to be someone else's lighthouse all the time.

Right now she felt more vulnerable and unsure than she had in the last five years. That break-in, the feeling of being watched. This had to stop. But there were few clues as to who was taking women around the state of Utah. Even fewer clues as to what had happened to Annie Ross.

Keeping Gracie safe was Ava's number-one priority. But she also had to keep Chay safe. So not relying too much on him until he was ready for that. It was just a day ago when he'd canceled dinner.

The break-in had him feeling guilty. The last thing she wanted was a man who was with her because of something like that.

Closing down her computer, she grabbed her work bag and let the secretary know she was going to work from home for the next few days. She had some clients who preferred to do video calls than face-to-face meetings.

When she walked into the cafeteria and saw Gracie in Chay's arms, her heart felt too full. She got it. This was what she wanted. A family with him, the three of them. Gracie as their daughter, not a foster child. Chay as her partner. Not her reluctant boyfriend.

Chapter Sixteen

Chay followed her and Gracie out to the Navajo Nation and his house. She took her time driving; trying not to let the events of the last few days weigh on her was somehow easier because of him.

She hadn't lived with a guy, even temporarily, ever. She and Greg had had roommates when they'd been engaged and had spent the night at each other's apartments, but it had never just been the two of them. The way it was going to be with her and Chay.

Gracie had nodded off about halfway there, so she was alone with her thoughts. Last night she'd gone down the Daniel Wayne spiral immediately when she'd seen her home had been broken into. Understandable, given that he'd stalked her a lifetime ago.

It felt like she'd been a different woman when that happened. She'd also always thought nothing bad could happen to her in Dark Canyon. Her family was there. It was the one place where she knew most of the townspeople by name or sight. They didn't get a lot of tourists in the winter…which meant that someone would have noticed an outsider if they'd lingered in town with like either Fern or Annie.

Hitting the button for Chay's phone, she waited for him to answer.

"What's up?"

"I was just thinking that whoever brought Fern and Annie to town had to be familiar, you know? We don't get a lot of strangers this time of year," Ava said.

"Good thinking. I was already on that line of thinking. They didn't just stumble on that abandoned shack. Someone knew it was there," Chay said. "Narrowing down who it was hasn't been that easy, though."

"The cabin was so remote and on state land, right, not private?" she asked.

"As far as we can tell. But there are old hunting cabins and other ramshackle buildings that haven't been kept track of."

"I wonder when Fern was brought to the area. Was it in the dead of night?" Ava asked.

"Did you ask her?"

"She had a hood on and was drugged," Ava reminded him.

"But new details are emerging as she talks to you. The tattoo is interesting. Not sure if it's related, but we are going to look into it."

"No problem. As much as Fern doesn't want to relive everything, she wants those men who took her caught. I'm furious that it happened to her as well. That's not right."

"Nothing about what happened to her is," Chay said.

"Is that why you got into law enforcement?"

"No. *Bad Boys*."

"The movie franchise?" she asked.

"Yeah. I liked the idea of taking down criminals and being the good guy."

She could see that. They hung up, and a few minutes later she pulled into Chay's driveway. She was still smiling, thinking about him watching the Martin Lawrence and Will Smith movies.

Chay carried Ava's and Gracie's bags while she got the baby into the house. It didn't take them too long to get Gracie settled on her blanket playing while Chay went to the kitchen to make dinner.

"I'll help. I don't want to be a burden," Ava said.

"You're not a burden. I'm glad you're here. I made Crock-Pot chicken tortilla soup. So there's not much to do. We can eat on the couch so Gracie can keep playing."

"Perfect."

They made their bowls and soon were sitting close to each other watching Gracie play. It was really hard for her not to weave that fantasy she'd had for the last few days around them. Gracie mumbling, crawling, rolling over and playing with her feet while they sat next to each other talking about their days and eating dinner.

Her own parents loved each other deeply but were like oil and water. Dinner in their home growing up had been noisy and boisterous. Until this moment Anna hadn't realized how much she needed this peaceful kind of dinner.

"Aponi stopped by to see me today."

"Uh-oh," Chay said.

Ava smiled, as she guessed he'd wanted her to, based on his tone. "She's going to be donating a rug to the silent auction my mom is organizing. I think Sassy wants her to be part of an exhibit there."

"Good. I think her work deserves more attention."

"She's still thinking about it," Ava said. Wondering if she should bring up the personal stuff, too. But then she tried to figure out what she wanted from him if she did. Did she want Chay to say that he thought she was fine? Or that she needed to do some work? Definitely not the latter.

"That sounds like her. She is very private about the artist side of her personality. She likes that everyone loves her rugs and their quality but doesn't feel like it's about her…it's about the weaving and the practice, which has been around since the dawn of our people."

"That's fascinating," she said. "I'd love to know more about it."

"I'm sure she'll tell you if you ask her. I know some of it, but sometimes I zone out when she's talking about it."

"Chay! Shame on you."

"Tell me you always listen to everything your parents say."

"Okay, point taken. I do zone out sometimes… I'll ask her," Ava said.

They ate more of their soup, and when they were finished Ava was back to feeling awkward again. They'd slept together, but he hadn't asked her to stay with him because they were dating. He'd invited her because he wanted her to be safe, and possibly he'd felt guilty.

"So…what should we do now?" he asked.

"I think we have to watch *Bad Boys* so I can try to understand how they motivated you to become a cop."

"I never should have mentioned that."

"No, you shouldn't have, but you did. Also, do you have popcorn? I can't watch a movie without it."

"I have a box of the microwave stuff in the cupboard."

He went to fix the popcorn while she bathed Gracie and got her into her pj's. She gave her a bottle, holding her in her arms as the baby fell asleep. Chay joined her, holding the popcorn on his lap, his other arm around her.

Trying to be normal when he felt anything but was a struggle. Of course, having Ava and Gracie in his home was at once the best thing in the world and not. He felt like he was on some sort of repeat loop where his mind warred with his emotions. He wanted them both in his life, had spoken that to the universe, but he also was afraid that whatever was flawed or broken in him would show up.

Ava would see it and leave and take Gracie with her. To be honest, in his mind the two of them were a package deal, which he knew had no basis in rational thought, but who ever said feelings were based in reason?

"What are you thinking about?" she asked him.

"Nothing."

"Oh, you've definitely got something on your mind. Your face is so serious right now."

"I was thinking that rational thinking and relationships don't really go hand in hand," he admitted.

Gracie was solidly out like a light. Chay reached for her after putting the popcorn on the floor next to the couch. Ava handed her over. "Let me put her to bed first."

This conversation was the one they should have had yesterday instead of him dodging her. He wanted to talk this out. Most of his fears were alleviated when he took the time to get them out of his head. There was no way to every fix that abandoned part of him that felt if he'd been better at something, his mom would have stayed.

Because it wasn't rational.

But Ava was different. The situation with Gracie was more charged and complex than he wished it was. He had to sort this out so he could figure out if they were going to become more than what they were right now.

A couple who both cared for a baby who was only in

their care temporarily. Or…were there seeds of something more?

He put Gracie in her bed, dropped a kiss on her forehead and then tucked her in. The snow clouds he'd seen earlier had delivered, and steady flakes were falling around his cozy home.

When he got back to the living room, Ava had moved to stand by the glass door, looking out at the snow.

"It's so pretty," she said.

The non sequitur was her way of letting him off the hook if he didn't want to talk. He was beginning to read her and understand her. It was hard to separate Ava from the therapist she was. Her techniques that probably helped her patients also were employed in her daily life.

He got that. He could use a therapist. Maybe he should start his sessions up with Ms. Doogan again. But he hated to admit that he hadn't been fully healed. Would have to acknowledge that the last few years he'd been drifting in a haze. Not really living but more existing.

"It is," he said, coming up behind her and putting his arms around her.

She put her hands on his forearm, holding him lightly.

"You don't have to talk to me," she said softly.

"I want to," he admitted. There was a faint reflection of the two of them in the glass door. "I just… Let me spit it all out. I'm not looking for you to fix me."

"Good, because you are not broken."

"We are all broken," he said. "Even you."

He felt her finger stroking his arm. "You're so right. It's just easy to believe that I've patched over those pieces that don't quite line up."

"Same, which I was doing a damned good job of until you, Ms. Colton."

"Moi?"

"Yup." Oh, this was harder than he'd thought it would be. "A part of me just wants to let go of the caution and see where this leads, but the bigger part of me isn't sure. I think my parents might have been like that. And when my dad died, my mom was rudderless. It's like without her partner, she was lost."

She tried to turn in his arms, but he held her still. Not yet. He didn't want to see her face when he finished what he had yet to say.

"I promised myself I wouldn't hurt anyone the way she was hurt or the way she injured me. It was an easy promise to keep, because most people are put off by my gruff manner."

"But not me," she said, trying to turn again, and this time he allowed her. Her hands were on his cheeks, but he kept looking out the glass door at the snow falling. The flakes, so tiny, were accumulating and would be a good few inches in the morning. Just like these little emotions that Ava stirred in him.

He liked her smile.

No big deal.

She sassed him and made him hard with just a flick of her hair over her shoulder.

Also a tiny detail.

She was competitive.

She teased him about *Bad Boys*.

All these tiny snowflakes falling around him. A man who'd been used to a barren landscape and coping with it the only way he knew how. Building his house far from town. Making a life for himself where he couldn't really get too chummy with the other residents of the Navajo

Nation because he might have to arrest someone or give them a ticket.

Until Ava.

Falling around him and surrounding him while he wasn't paying attention. It was easy for him to pretend that he could ignore the feelings she stirred in him, but he hated to lie to himself.

He could no more ignore her than he would be able to drive to work in the morning without first shoveling out his truck.

He was busy trying to debate rational thought and emotions, but it was too late. Once emotion took hold, it was all over. Something that he wasn't sure how to proceed with.

TENSION SWIRLED AROUND her like the snow outside Chay's home. He was so brutally honest that she couldn't help falling for him that little bit more, which was dangerous. He wasn't like Greg, who she'd loved when she'd been young and had just the smallest bit of damage.

At almost thirty she had baggage. Lots of it. Chay did, too. They were both coming to each other battle hardened from their twenties, as most people did. Life wasn't all sunshine and happiness. She got that. She'd known it for a while now. But somewhere in the back of her mind was the belief that it should be.

Now she wasn't sure.

She wouldn't change one thing about Chay...maybe his stubbornness when it came to thinking of himself as a father to Gracie, but even that she knew was deeply rooted in his childhood, and she couldn't blame him for his reluctance.

No one wanted to be responsible for screwing up a little person's life...well, any person, really.

She got that more than he'd understand. She'd felt that way when she'd first been approached to foster.

But fostering was temporary. A nice, sweet spot where she could allow herself all the feels knowing that one day the baby or child would be in their forever home and she'd be a memory of a transition.

"That promise is one I know you can keep," she said to Chay. "You aren't your mom."

"Obvious, right? But there's still a part of me that can't shake the feeling that it's only because I haven't been around kids, haven't tried to have a long-term partner that I'm not."

"Oh, Chay. If only you could…" An idea popped into her head. "Turn and face the glass door again. Can you see yourself in the reflection?"

"I'd rather look at you."

She shook her head to keep from being distracted by that low, rumbly, seductive tone he used.

"First let's look at you."

"Are you therapy-ing me?"

"Maybe. Trust me?"

He nodded and then turned until he faced the glass door. She went to turn off one of the larger living room lights so they were bathed in a small pool of illumination. His reflection was clearer this way. He held himself still.

His jaw was tight, his muscles tense and his expression that serious, I-mean-business look that she knew so well.

"What do you see?"

"Myself."

"Stop it. When you look at yourself, what do you see? Is it your mom? Your grandmother? Your dad or some version that has little bits of them but is mostly you?" she suggested.

He was quiet beside her, and she stepped up next to him, realizing she might be pushing him way too far out of his comfort zone.

"I see a little bit of my mom in the way my eyes are and the shape of my nose. I see my dad in the freckles across my cheeks and Ryan in this tiny scar on the bottom of my jaw that I got when I tried to save him from a tree in the backyard," Ava said.

Chay took a long, deep breath. "I'm older now than my dad ever was. I have his hair, though, and his eyes. My jaw, I guess, comes from him, too. In fact I look a lot like him. On the outside I'm all Benally."

"And on the inside?"

"Grandmother, probably, and my mom. There are times when I shut down and retreat up here. I don't socialize at the station or even go out with friends."

"That's fair. My parents are both loud people, and there are times when I have to be alone."

"Yeah, that's good. But for me, I think about leaving like she did. I remember how she said there was no privacy on the rez. That's what she called this place. It always was a place to escape from."

Ava stepped around in front of him. "This place is your home. You can't convince me you think of leaving."

Trying to be nonchalant, he started to shrug, but then he shook his head. "I don't. The time I spent in Salt Lake was enough for me. I missed the Navajo Nation."

"One way you're different from her. This place feels like home," Ava pointed out.

"It does. The only one I've ever known."

"Dark Canyon is like that for me. College was nice,

and I really wanted to stretch my wings and show the world I was independent. But coming back here, I realized I didn't need to be out of Dark Canyon to do it."

"I'm glad. So what do you see?" he asked.

"I already told you."

"No, when you look at me," he said.

"Oh," she said softly. Suddenly she wasn't bossy, and the shyness that she'd never really acknowledged she had flexed its wings. "Well, I see your strength and these laugh lines around your eyes that let me know there is more to you than the stern expression you give when you are trying to get information."

"Stern? That's my serious don't-mess-with-me look."

"Oh, it makes me want to mess with you," she said.

"Yeah. How?" he asked.

She twined her arms around his neck, going up on her tiptoes and whispering what she wanted to do with him. Just thinking about it made her hot. He cupped her butt and lifted her off her feet. She wrapped her legs around his waist and brought her mouth down on his. Taking the kiss that she hadn't realized she'd been missing for what felt like a lifetime.

This was where she was meant to be.

That scared her, because independence had been the hallmark of these last few years. Living on her own despite the shadow of Daniel Wayne. But with Chay she knew she could be her own woman and be with him. There was nothing she wanted more than that.

Nothing except his body moving over hers in front of the fireplace while the snow fell around them.

Chapter Seventeen

Sleeping in Chay's arms was at once the most comforting and the most tempting thing she'd done in a long time. Gracie cooed and Chay went to get her, bringing her back to his bed after changing her.

"You two stay warm while I get the heat on and a fire going. There was something on the weather forecast about a blizzard... I thought we had a few more days before it was going to hit."

Snuggling Gracie closer to her, Ava reached for her phone. "Oh, there is a severe weather warning for our area. I need to check in on my parents and with work."

"Go ahead. You good to stay here?" he asked, putting on his uniform as he was talking to her.

"Yeah. You have to go?"

"I want to make sure we have everything set up, and I have to check on my grandmother," he said.

"Gracie and I will be here," Ava said.

Chay left a few minutes later, and she stayed in bed with Gracie as the little girl rolled around on the king-sized mattress. She texted her parents, who were both staying home from work today, and let them know she was going to be at Chay's until the storm passed.

Then she got up and got dressed. Taking a moment to nose around Chay's home. She'd seen the living room, kitchen and his bedroom, but there were a couple of rooms she hadn't seen.

One was a large mud and utility room with a shower off to the side. Opening the back door, she noticed it let out to the woods behind the house, and there were cords of wood stacked beside it. Getting her boots and winter gear on, she brought in enough wood to stock the woodbox and checked on Gracie, who was crawling around the living room.

In the utility room she found a battery-operated radio and some flashlights and candles. Gathering those things together, she placed them on the dining room table. She took a quick glance at the pantry and noticed that Chay had enough canned goods and dry staples to see them through a couple of weeks at least.

Looking in the fridge, she saw he had some meat and vegetables and put together the ingredients for a stew that could simmer most of the day. She got Gracie set up in her high chair and gave the baby some mashed apples that she knew she liked to munch on.

There was something so cozy about being in Chay's house. The storm looked as if it were getting worse, and she tried not to worry too much about him. He was capable and knew how to do his job and to stay safe. She knew this. Yet her heart raced as she waited to hear from him.

He messaged around noon to say he was almost done and would be heading home soon.

She called him back.

"Is Aponi coming with you?"

"No, she's staying with a friend. They are going to

tell stories and weave during the storm," he said. "Do we need anything at the house?"

"I found the radio and battery-operated lights. I've got a stew on and I brought in wood to stock the fireplace... so I think we should be good."

"What about Gracie?"

"I have enough baby food for her, and she can eat the vegetables you have here. I think we should be fine once you get home."

Home.

She hadn't meant to say it, but as soon as the words were out they felt right.

"I'm on my way," he said. "You two stay inside. The storm is getting pretty intense."

"We will. 'Bye."

"'Bye."

She hung up the phone, walking over to check on Gracie, who was done with her apples.

"Mama."

"Gracie."

More babbling that Ava didn't understand but knew that Gracie was starting to try to communicate. "Good girl. You ready to get down and play?"

Ava got her down and set her on the floor. The little girl took off crawling and laughing to herself until she got to her blanket, where she stopped to play with the board book that Ava's mom had given her.

Goodnight Moon.

The book was actually Ava's from when she was little. Her mom thought she should have touches of her own childhood around the children she fostered, which Ava knew was important. Giving those kids a sense of permanency.

She sat down next to Gracie and pulled her onto her lap, but the baby squirmed away and went back to her toys.

"Independent lady? I can respect that."

Gracie gurgled and smiled a bit. Probably a good idea that she didn't get too attached to Gracie, though she knew it was too late for that. She'd become attached the first time she'd held the little girl in her arms.

Now that she was here with Chay, the bond had deepened. Seeing a face so similar to his when she held Gracie, it made her...well, dream of a future with him. She'd sort of danced around that before, but now it was time to really focus and decide. They were going to be snowed in here for a few days at the least.

This time was a gift. A chance to see how they'd be as a family, which was what Ava wanted. She knew that Chay was leery of getting involved with her and Gracie long-term.

He was rolling with the flow and adjusting as his own past tried to pull him under, but the truth was she was there with him. She felt the same way he did. Scared to say she wanted a family of her own. Scared to risk it. But after the break-in the other night had stirred up old memories and wounds, she knew that she had to make a choice.

Let Daniel Wayne continue to control her future or shake him off and start to build the life she now knew she wanted. One with Chay and Gracie.

DRIVING AROUND MAKING sure everyone was prepared for the blizzard heading their way was different than the previous years. This time he was thinking about Gracie and Ava. His little family waiting at home for him. In the past he'd stay out on patrol because there was no one waiting at home. His boss had been clear that Chay should go home. He'd call him out if he was needed.

After making sure his grandmother had extra food, wood and blankets, he headed back to his house. For the first time he realized that it felt a lot like a home. His place had always been more of a sanctuary, but now it was both. A place to rest from the world and a home he saw himself sharing…was that true? Did he want to share his home with Ava?

The answer was an unequivocal yes. But he knew there would still be some steps back. He wasn't one to just barrel into things. Ava needed time as well. Like she'd said, they all had some form of PTSD from living.

He'd had some time to think about that today and realized just how deeply that had affected him. He'd always sort of just thought everyone else had their shit together. That other families were normal and not broken and messed up like his had been.

Other people had more than just a grandmother to rely on. Not that he'd really ever needed more than her. If he was only going to have one relative, he was glad it was her.

Which brought him around to Gracie. If she were adopted by a Navajo family, she'd be part of the bigger community in the same way his grandmother was. Chay had come back here too late to really feel settled in his soul, though he couldn't imagine living anywhere else.

He turned off the main road and onto the track that lead to his house. The snow was so thick now that he struggled to see, slowing his truck to only five miles per hour. Soon he saw the lights in his house blazing.

He wasn't sure how long the electricity would stay on, but he'd never seen a more welcome sight. As soon as he tromped up the stairs, the door opened. Ava, holding Gracie in her arms, held it for him as he walked inside and slammed it shut behind him.

"Dang, it's cold. You must be freezing," she said.

He kicked the snow off his boots and took off his shearling jacket, putting it on a hook.

"Mamama," Gracie said.

"Hey, little one," he said as they both moved into the living area.

Gracie squirmed to get down, and Ava let her. "Want some coffee? I just made a fresh pot."

"I'd love some. I need to check the generator in the garage and do a few more things before I can stay here," he said.

"Go on then. I did as much as I could think of. Do you need me to help?"

He shook his head and then went into the mudroom and checked that the emergency generator was connected before going into the garage and to fuel it up and get it ready for when they lost power.

The tribal police department had sent out a warning to residents not to use a generator in the house. The fuel-powered machines gave off carbon monoxide, which was deadly. More than once he'd gone to a home after an emergency situation and found the family dead from their own generator.

He could tell Ava was Utah born and bred, because she'd taken care of everything like a seasoned survivor. The wood was stocked up and all the supplies were ready for them to use. He noticed when he came back inside that she'd gathered bedding so they could sleep in front of the fireplace.

Gracie was nowhere to be seen when he returned. "Where'd Gracie go?"

"I put her to bed. She was getting sleepy. It is her nap time," Ava said. "I've got the monitor."

He noticed she had the app open on her phone. "What else do you need to do?"

Ava poured them both some coffee. "I'm meant to talk to a client this morning at eleven. I wondered if I could use your bedroom for that. Can you keep an ear out for Gracie?"

"I sure can," he said, noting that she had about fifteen minutes until her call. "Do you video chat with them normally?"

"Some of my clients. It's really down to preference. One of them will only talk on the phone. He doesn't like to see me or to be seen," she said.

"And you accommodate them all?" He hadn't really taken time to know the everyday part of her job.

"I do. My job is to help them get better," she said.

"I have some work to do, so I'll set up my laptop out here," he said.

"What are you working on?" she asked.

"Trying to see if Fern's tattoo is a known brand. One of the officers I've been speaking to said he noticed a tattoo on a girl they picked up for solicitation. It was like a brand. Sometimes gangs mark their women. Was just following up on a line of inquiry."

"Do you think that's why she was kidnapped, for sex work?" Ava asked him.

"Really, I have no clue. I'm trying to find something that makes sense," he said.

"Well, so far I haven't seen anything. But she's pretty heavily bandaged thanks to her wounds and the state she was found in," Ava said. "You could check with one of the nurses."

"Thanks. I'll make a note to do that," he said, and taking the mug of coffee that Ava had made him, he got to work answering emails and sending out inquiries. He could the sound of her voice in his bedroom and he realized that he could very easily get used to having her here.

He liked it. A lot.

AVA FINISHED HER session and then went to check on Gracie. It was such an ordinary day in spite of the storm raging outside. When she got back to the living room, Chay stood by the door where they had been last night.

"All good?" he asked.

"Yes. My other client postponed until next week, so that's it. How about you?"

"I'm monitoring the radio and if there's an emergency I might be called out, but the chief said I was good until the storm passed."

"Nice. What do you usually do during snowstorms?" she asked as he draped his arm over her shoulder.

"Watch movies, I guess. I don't have a routine," he said.

"What? That's not good. We always played rummy until a definitive winner was found," Ava said.

"Definitive? Like some kind of championship?"

"Yes. When we were little, Dad would fill up a coffee mug with snow and that was the trophy."

"Sounds prestigious."

"It really was. So I haven't been champ in a few years. How's your rummy?"

"Never played."

"What? You have been seriously deprived. It's a fun game."

"Says the woman who was a champion."

"Only against my parents and brother. And I'm pretty sure Mom and Dad rigged it so Ryan and I each won at least one championship."

"I play to win," he warned her. "Still want to do this?"

"Oh, hell yes. Do you have a deck of cards?" she asked.

"What would you do if I said no?"

"Get the emergency deck from my glove box." The grin on his face told her he was enjoying this.

Chay didn't often let his guard down, and she liked it.

"Lucky for you I have one deck. They are from the Universal Studios in California. My boss got them for me when he went there on a trip."

"Nice. Your boss here?" she asked as they both sat down at the kitchen table.

"In Salt Lake. Lawrence's wife insisted on one vacation a year to someplace new. So he'd grumble about it and then come back looking relaxed and tan. I think she might have been on to something."

"I think so, too. I pretty much use my vacation time for mental health days when I don't feel like working," Ava said as she shuffled the cards.

"I let it roll over until it expires," he said.

"We are a couple of chumps. We should make a pact to use our vacation days this year," she said.

"Together?"

That was a big one coming from Chay. Together? Why not? It wasn't like she could foresee herself not getting along with him. Even if they were just friends and the dating thing didn't work out. She knew she was still going to like him.

"Okay. Not until after we get Gracie sorted out."

"Sorted out…how is that going to work? Won't you miss her?"

"I will," Ava admitted. She quickly explained how to play rummy and then dealt them each seven cards. "I wouldn't have to miss her if the person who adopted her was a friend."

"I don't want to encourage you, but I have been thinking about her future," Chay admitted as he rearranged the cards in his hand.

"Her future with you?" she asked.

"On the Navajo Nation. The family she lives with will be a part of this community. I know Grandmother is going to stay close to Gracie. I think I will, too. So we could still see her."

Ava put her cards down in front of her. "I thought… don't you want more than to be some casual person in her life?"

"You said you wouldn't push."

"I lied. No one is going to be a better father to her."

Chay put his cards down, pushing back from the table, rocking his chair back up on two legs. "I didn't have a father."

"That's an excuse. You already love her."

"Do I?"

"Yes. You know it and so do I. You think about it. How will you feel if she calls someone else 'Dad' and not you?"

Chay opened and closed his mouth without uttering a word. "I don't know. But what if I mess up? Her future could be wonderful. It should be. That's what I want for her."

"Me, too. That's why I'm bringing up adoption again. To me you are the only one who could be her father. The one that she needs."

"I don't see it. I mean, you know I care for her, and having you both here…it's making me want a home in a way that I never really have before."

Ava went around and leaned against the table where he sat still rocked up on the back two legs of his chair. "That's how I know you are meant to be with her. You wouldn't feel strongly otherwise."

"You seem so sure, but where does that leave you?" he asked.

She hadn't really been prepared for him to turn the tables on her. "I…well, you and I are friends, so I'll still be in her life."

"Is that all we are? Friends?"

Ava chewed her lower lip, ready to dart back around the table when he took her hand in his. "Tell me, Ava. Show me the honesty that you pried from me. Do you want to just be my friend?"

"You know I want more," she said, the words coming out of her rapid-fire. "There is a part of me that wants this moment to last forever. You and me and Gracie isolated form the world by the snowstorm. Just us relying on each other and taking care of each other."

"But that's a fantasy. Not the real world."

"Exactly," he said. "Now you understand where I'm coming from. This would be such a sweet life, but it feels like a dream. And dreams don't last very long in the real world."

Chapter Eighteen

Chay was a bit moody, and they didn't finish the game of rummy. Instead he went to his office to work, even though he'd said he didn't have to. She got it. She knew she'd pushed too hard, but at the end of the day she'd do it again. Gracie woke up in a melancholy mood, just wanting a bottle and to cuddle with Ava, which Ava had no problems with.

Chay had had a point when he'd asked her if she was going to be okay with being on the outside of raising Gracie. She didn't think she was. That was part of fostering, and her parents and the social workers she'd talked to had been very clear that it was difficult not to get attached. And Ava had done a pretty good job up until now.

It would be easy to make an excuse for herself and say that it was all down to the fact that she was falling for Chay and Gracie was related to him. The two of them would be forever entwined in her mind and heart. So yes, she'd pushed to see how far she could go. See what it would take to break Chay.

He was so unbreakable when it came to everything. He rolled with whatever life threw at him. She knew it was because of his childhood. She got that he'd had grown up with a barrier around his emotions because that was the only way he would survive.

It was all well and good for her to be like, *trust me, this baby will bring you the family you've always wanted*. But the truth was she had no crystal ball. Chay was right to be cautious. Ava knew she could use some caution herself, but she wasn't built that way.

She finished reading *Goodnight Moon* and Gracie finished her bottle. Ava set her on the blanket while she stoked the fire and moved to the kitchen to wash the bottle. She heard the rumble of Chay's voice from the living room.

Peeking out at them, she saw he was down on the floor lying on his side next to the baby. He was talking to her, and she stared up at him with such rapt attention on her face, hanging on every word he said.

Pulling her phone from her back pocket, she zoomed the camera in and took a few photos of the two of them. This was why she'd poked at him about Gracie. Chay didn't see his own expression when he was around the baby, but the bond between them was already there. Already strong.

Ava had to back off and give him space to find that on his own—she knew that. She could do it, even if her instincts were at war with that course of action. She had to do it at work all the time. Everyone healed in their own time.

"Are you hungry?" she asked.

"Not really. Haven't done much today," he admitted.

"Me, either. Wish the snow would let up so we could go for a walk."

"Yeah, that would be nice," he said.

Her heart hurt a little as they exchanged pleasantries

like strangers. This was her work. This was what came of her pushing so hard at him. "I'm sorry."

"For?"

"What I said when we were playing cards." Apologizing wasn't enough. They'd had this discussion before, and each time he'd showed her his boundaries and she'd ignored him.

Going over near the edge of the blanket, she looked down at him and Gracie. "I have a lot of respect for you, Chay. I don't want you to think that I'm trying to force you into a situation. I just...when I see you two together, I feel like you are meant to be father and daughter. This little girl who has no one and the man who needs someone."

As soon as the words left her mouth, she regretted them. They were too real. Who wanted to hear that their vulnerability was out there for everyone to see?

"I...thank you. I do need someone. But my needs can't come before hers. I don't want to do something selfish and end up hurting her in the long run," he admitted. Gracie reached out and grabbed his finger, pulling it to her mouth to suck on it.

"That's always the hardest part in every decision, isn't it? Hoping that you made it for the right reasons."

"Never really knowing if you did," he finished. "Don't beat yourself up over it. You're pushing me, but I'm stubborn. You're never going to make me do something I don't want to. I might not like talking about it, but I know you are doing it from a good place."

The breath she hadn't realized she'd been holding exhaled in a long rush. She went to sit down next to him. He snagged his arm around her waist, tugging her off balance until she was sitting on his lap with Gracie in front of them.

She was happily mumbling something while she played with Chay's hands. Ava was overwhelmed again. Wanted this to be real so badly that she wasn't entirely sure what she was going to do when this ended. When Gracie moved on to her forever family and Chay... What was the future with Chay?

She'd spent most of her time trying to figure out how to convince him to adopt Gracie, never really thinking about what she truly wanted for herself.

"Want to try to teach me rummy again?" he asked. "I'd really love to kick your butt at it."

She nodded. Anything to get out of her head and try to find some feelings of normalcy in this world where it was just the three of them. This world that she wasn't sure she wanted to ever end.

She'd stay here with him if he asked her. But Chay wouldn't. The man who'd been abandoned and left behind was never going to ask anyone to stay with him. He wouldn't let himself be that vulnerable.

GRACIE WAS NAPPING AGAIN, and Chay was quietly working with a notebook and his laptop. The power had stayed on, but they both knew it was only a matter of time before it went off for good.

"What are you working on?"

"I'm trying to find a pattern to tie Fern and Annie Ross to the other women who've been reported missing across the state," he said. "You've given me some things that are helpful, but so far I can't find a link."

"What kind of link?"

"So far it's just missing women who have all aged out of foster care. Their backgrounds are all very diverse. The one thing that links Annie Ross to these other women is the fact that she was looking for a friend of hers who'd gone missing. Similar background to Fern's."

"Maybe Annie stumbled onto something and that's what got her being abducted and abandoned?" Ava asked.

"Yes. Have you been through all the stuff that came with Gracie? I wondered if there was something hidden in her bag or blanket. Maybe to explain why someone broke into your house."

Ava hadn't thought of that. "I mean, I haven't seen anything obvious. Let me go and get the bag. It was pretty empty when Marg got to the fire station to collect the baby. There's nothing in the blanket unless the weave holds a clue, which I think isn't really likely."

Chay rubbed his hand over his eyes and then shook his head. "No, that's not a thing."

Ava crept quietly into Gracie's room and retrieved the diaper bag. Emptying the contents on the table, she didn't find anything that she hadn't put in there herself. Not even in the lining of the bag, which was a little bit worn.

"Nothing."

"It was a long shot. Do you see many patients who came from foster care?" Chay asked. "Is there something I'm missing when I'm looking at this?"

"I only have Fern right now. In the past I have had a few foster care adults. Usually they come to me for help with adapting to a new relationship. I find the biggest thing is the struggle to accept anything permanent."

"Like me," Chay said.

"And me," she pointed out. "But my situation is different than yours."

"Yes, I've never felt physically threatened…not since I came to live with Grandmother."

"Were you mistreated?" she asked. She didn't want to

think of Chay ever being abused, but it happened. His mother was sort of a case study in someone who probably shouldn't have had a child.

"Sometimes. Usually my mom was so strung out she didn't know I was there. There were some men who treated me okay. Some them thought I was a nuisance."

Of course she wanted to comfort him, but Chay was so point-blank about it that she knew he'd processed his feelings around that a long time ago.

"I guess the one thing you have in common is that you don't trust easily. Why, then, are these women being taken?"

"If Fern had a brand on her, then it would indicate a reason why she was taken. Sex work or drug mule. Something to indicate that she was being trafficked. That's the most likely scenario for her being out this far."

Ava had wondered herself about that situation. She hadn't brought it up to Fern because the other woman was still so fragile and rebuilding her strength. The last thing that Ava wanted to do was worry her again.

But Fern was worried. She'd been afraid to go outside and sit in the sun. She hated that those men who'd abducted Fern still had so much power over her. "I hope you can figure this out."

"Me, too. It feels bigger to me than just one woman. Maybe I'm adding too much to it, but Annie Ross's death, your break-in. Feels like they are all too close together to be random."

"Yeah, that's what I was thinking....well, at first I was worried that my stalker was out of prison, but that's just because he's the only man to have terrified me."

"He's not, right? Jacob said he'd double-check," Chay said, trying to reassure her.

"Yeah, Jacob would have called if he'd heard anything different. I'm just saying that Fern or these other women who disappeared might have someone they were running from. Not Fern. She was settled in her job and her life. But maybe someone else. The woman you mentioned."

Chay rubbed the back of his neck and then went to get more coffee for them both. "Maybe. It feels like we are close to a breakthrough on this case, but I'm just missing something."

She smiled at him as she added sugar to her mug. "You'll get it. The snowstorm… I hope no one was being left like Fern was. Could you imagine a woman trapped and alone in this?"

"I can. I hope to God nothing like that is happening."

"Me, too," Ava said, rubbing her hands up and down her arms. It was so scary to think that men might be moving women around the state during a storm like this. It would give them cover, but it could also help expose them.

Gracie cried out, and Chay waved Ava to keep her seat. "I'll get her. You've been on baby duty all day."

"That's sort of my job right now."

"I know, but I like doing it, as you rightly pointed out. And you could use a break."

Ava sat back down and pulled her notebook closer to her. She hadn't brought any patient files with her, but she thought back over everything that Fern had told her. Was there something she was missing that could help Chay and Jacob figure out who had harmed Fern?

Or was she just hoping there was a hidden clue? There were some cases like this that went unsolved for years. Something that she knew was going to make it harder for Fern to recover.

THE GUSTING OF the wind and snow picked up, and the power flickered and went out completely. Chay had been expecting it long before now. Ava seemed nonplussed by it.

"I'll go turn the generator on. I think we should be warm enough in here."

"Do you have a kettle for the fireplace?" she asked.

"I do—it's in the cupboard near the back of the kitchen."

Gracie was on the floor with a wall of pillows to keep her safely away from the fire and from wandering too far while they both moved around to get themselves ready to be in the dark.

The generator would give them roughly sixteen hours. No telling how long the storm would last, so he'd use it sparingly. The wood that Ava had brought into the woodbox and the utility room would see them through a few days. So they would be set with heating and could use the fire to cook if need be.

Talking about the case with Ava had been nice. He'd always worked alone since returning to the Navajo Nation. Mostly because he had to figure it all out in his mind before it started to make sense to him. Right now, with the weather turning, he was thinking about Ava's worry that a woman could be trapped in this storm like Fern was.

It would be nice if they got a break, but he suspected the men who'd kidnapped Fern were staying safely inside. They weren't lazy, per se, but they definitely worked in a way that was easiest for them.

Coming back into the house, the thought wouldn't leave him. These women had all been targeted because they offered the least resistance. Something he'd considered early, but now it was making more sense. The foster system had no follow-up after eighteen; unless the women were arrested they wouldn't show up again. And if they were on their own or moving around trying to find a place to start over, no one would know they were missing.

Now, if they could just figure out why Fern had been taken. Human trafficking seemed logical, but without proof it was just another theory.

Ava had found the kettle and the cooking pot he had for the fireplace and set them on the kitchen counter. She was a good partner during the storm. In fact, she was a good partner most of the time.

He could easily see himself with her in the future. It no longer made him panic when that thought entered his head. He'd been irritated at her earlier, but now as he watched her moving through the living room getting things ready for the three of them, he wasn't. He saw instead the family she'd alluded to.

The one that she knew he'd wanted from his earliest memory. Taking nothing away from his grandmother, this was what he wanted for himself. People that were his in a way that had nothing to do with possession and everything to do with belonging. Ava and he understood each other. Didn't mean that it was ever going to be easy between them. At times she was going to keep pushing when he needed to retreat.

But he wanted to come back to her. He got that now. It was easier to just say that he was afraid and use that as an excuse, but the truth was without at least trying to be a father to Gracie and a partner to Ava, he'd never know if he could beat that challenge.

He'd never know if he was just like his mother or more than she'd been. Her fears had been different than Chay's.

He understood that now. It was something that he'd never faced before this.

"Chay?"

"Yes?" he asked, coming out of the hallway where he'd been watching her.

"Are you ready to have some stew for dinner?" she asked. "It's definitely done."

"Sounds good."

She got Gracie's high chair set up and put some cut-up vegetables that the baby could eat on the tray for her. Using one of the lanterns that Ava had gotten out earlier as a light, they sat at the table eating their dinner. It was so cozy together while the storm blew outside.

The sun had set, and with no lights in the backyard, it was hard to see what was happening. "The first winter I was here, we had a snow like this."

"Were you scared?"

"Yes. I'd only lived in California, and it didn't snow in L.A. At first I was fascinated by it, but then when it kept falling and the wind was howling... I didn't want my grandmother to know I was scared. I thought she'd send me away, so I was trying to be calm, but my hands were shaking."

The memory made him ball his hands into fists.

Ava put her hand over his, and he smiled at her. "Grandmother did the same thing. She told me a story of the storm and how it was blanketing the world, covering it carefully so that when winter faded, spring would be bountiful."

"That's beautiful," Ava said. "I love that story."

"Me, too," he admitted.

"My mom is a musician, so when the storm gets loud she likes to play something dramatic, like the fourth movement of Beethoven's Symphony No. 6. She'd play it as loud as she could, and we'd watch and listen. It was like being part of the storm instead of it hammering at our home."

"I like that. You seem very comfortable with the blizzard," he said.

"We have to be. It's part of our life out here, isn't it? Even Gracie is calm."

"Because we are. She knows she's safe as long as you and I are with her," Chay said.

Chapter Nineteen

With the power out and every topic of conversation exhausted, Ava was starting to feel the strain. Gracie had been good for the most part but, perhaps sensing her nerves, the baby had started to get restless. Nothing was satisfying her and she started crying.

"What's the matter, little one?" Chay asked, coming over and taking her from Ava. "Too much snow and darkness?"

"It is for me," Ava admitted, following behind Chay and Gracie. "I think I'm fine with a blizzard until the fun snacks are gone."

"We had fun snacks?" he asked her, deadpan.

"Oh, yeah, some really healthy fruit gummies and chocolate pudding cups," she said, naming the snacks she had put in Gracie's diaper bag before they'd come to Chay's last night.

"And I'm just now learning about them?"

"Honestly, you seemed too cool for the pudding cups," she said, feeling better just joking around with him.

"No one is too cool for pudding cups. I haven't seen any evidence of them in the recycling bin...that means you still have some. Let's see 'em."

"Maybe I don't want to share," she said, going to the food bag she'd packed.

"You like sharing. That's one of your core values," he said.

He wasn't entirely wrong. "How do you know that?"

"I'm an observant kind of guy—also, you keep pushing your way into my life. Hard to miss that you like sharing."

She fished out the pudding cups, which were still attached. Bending them back and forth she heard the satisfying snap as they broke apart. Trying really hard to be chill, but in this moment it was hard. Had Chay picked up on her frustration with the storm and the fact that she was moments away from losing it? She hoped not.

He was all cool with the storm—actually seemed to be thriving in it. It was like nothing fazed him. It didn't matter if the power went out or Gracie cried or if Ava was on the verge of a meltdown, Chay just rolled with it.

"Doesn't this bother you?" she asked.

"Not really. I mean, it's inconvenient. I had been saving *Bad Boys for Life* for tonight. You need more cop drama."

She couldn't help smiling at that. *Bad Boys* was fun, but what she'd really loved about watching it with Chay was how much he enjoyed it. Like when he'd grabbed her hand and said, "This part is the best." Stuff like that.

"I definitely don't need more drama. No one likes drama."

"Ah, that's true. But watching it play out on the big screen…that's not bad," he said.

He had a point. She handed him a pudding cup and then a spoon. "Watch this one, she likes to put her fingers in the pudding."

"That's because it's so tasty, right, bug?"

"Bug?"

He shrugged as he moved to the couch and sat down holding Gracie on one side.

"She needs a nickname."

"Sell it to me," Ava said as she sat on the opposite end. Then realized that Chay was going to feed some of the pudding to Gracie. She hurried to grab a bib and put it on the baby. "She's a messy eater. Now, about the nickname…"

Chay leaned back, peeling the foil from the top of the pudding cup. Scraping his finger over it, he held his finger out to Gracie, who grabbed it and shoved it in her mouth.

Making them both laugh.

"She's cute as a bug," he said. "That's it. Nothing more. What do you think?"

Bug…she wouldn't have chosen it, but it did suit Gracie. "I think it's perfect."

She concentrated on eating her pudding and not on pointing out that he was bonding with Gracie again. He'd said he'd consider adoption and Ava had to leave it at that.

"So where are these gummies you spoke of?"

"We can't eat them all at once," she said.

"We can. You said yourself the good snacks go first."

"You don't have any snacks in this house," she pointed out.

"Yeah, I tend to binge eat if I keep them around. I'm a sucker for anything dark chocolate," he admitted.

"Really? You seem so controlled. I wouldn't have pegged you for that kind of behavior."

He put his cup and spoon on the end table; Gracie was now chewing on her bib. "We didn't have money when I was with my mom, and I was always hungry. So when I got to grandmother's house, I wasn't sure the food would always be there. I'd eat as much as I could in case that was my last meal."

"Oh, Chay."

"It's fine. Grandmother always made sure there was extra food in the house so I'd learn that I didn't have to overeat, which eventually I did, but the junk food bingeing…that's stuck around."

That made her like him a lot more. He was so complicated and interesting and every detail he shared so matter-of-factly made her love him that much more.

And she did love him. She wasn't sure she was ready to say it out loud or admit it to anyone else. But the feelings were growing stronger and stronger every day.

"One summer we had strawberries in our garden. There were so many, and every day I'd go out and eat them off the plants. Just as many as I could pick. I made myself sick with it and broke out in hives," Ava said. "My mom is very practical. 'Well, now you know what happens when you give in to your greed.'"

Ava still thought about that when she was taking too much, wanting too much. She felt a little bit of warning when it came to Gracie and Chay. She wanted them as her family. It didn't feel greedy at all, but what she needed to be happy. That was always the thing that worried her. She remembered how joyous she'd been in college.

Independence had suited her and her classes had been challenging and rewarding. When she'd met Greg, it felt like her entire life was perfect and full. Then he'd died. She knew that fate wasn't out there watching her and balancing the scales of heartbreak and happiness, but there was another part of her that was wary of taking too much and losing it all again.

It was funny to watch Ava trying to stay centered as the night wore on. The pudding cups cracked him up. He wouldn't have pegged her as someone who liked those kind of snacks. But really, who could say what snacks anyone liked? He was addicted to Hot Cheetos, which was why he never bought them when he went to the grocery store.

Gracie was a little calmer now. Happily chewing on her bib while he watched Ava finishing up her pudding. She caught him staring as she licked the last bit from her spoon.

God, why was everything she did so sexy?

"The gummies?" he asked again, because truthfully he wasn't sure what else to do to distract her and him. If it was just the two of them, he'd take her to bed and make love to her until she was exhausted.

But they had sweet little Gracie.

"You're not giving that up."

"Nope. Also I think it might be time for a rummy rematch," he said. Knowing that they'd never really played. He could see that it was her affection for him and Bug that had her focused on trying to make them into a family. But he also knew himself and his limits.

Messing up with a kid wasn't like overeating Hot Cheetos. He couldn't just not show up for a few days. If he committed to adopting Gracie, he was going to have to be there on the tough days and the good ones.

Maybe because of his mom he wasn't one to leave anything. He took on the tough cases and was a loyal friend long after others had moved on. Once he committed, he was all in. That's why it was important for him to be very sure of himself before he thought about being Gracie's father.

Or Ava's man.

Though in his head, he couldn't picture his life without her. Might be too late on that one. Or a Hot Cheetos situation where he had to stop going to Dark Canyon… which would make adopting Gracie tricky. Because there was no way Ava was walking out of Gracie's life.

She got up and came back with two packs of natural fruit gummies. "These are healthy. Kind of defeats the entire good snacks thing."

Chay made a face.

"Healthy doesn't mean bad. They have real fruit juices, so I kid myself that these are part of my five a day."

He couldn't help laughing at the way she said it. "Or you could just have an apple. But no strawberries, right?"

Giving him a soft smile, she nodded. "Yeah, I have to limit myself to just one or two. But they are delicious. Here's the thing with these," she said, tossing him one of the bags. "I can eat as many of the strawberry-flavored ones as I like…there's only two per pack."

"Conducted a study on them?"

"It needed to be done. Plus, I was waiting for my oil to get changed. It's like when you sense there's more blue M&M's than the others and you make a bet with your brother. You gotta know what you're betting on."

"Sounds like you suckered your brother into a bet," Chay said.

"Only once. It's sort of his fault for being gullible."

"Or believing his older sister wouldn't con him," Chay pointed out.

"We were eight and six… I wasn't as sweet back then," she said as she opened her pack of gummies and dug into it.

He noticed she pulled out the two strawberry ones and set them aside.

"Saving the best for last?"

"Definitely. What about you?"

"Don't hate me, but they all taste the same." He poured a handful of them into his mouth at once. Fruit snacks didn't do anything for him, but he liked that Ava enjoyed them.

"That's so wrong, but I'll give it you. Some of them do sort of taste the same, and I think I'm sense remembering strawberries when I eat the red ones."

"I'd have to agree these don't taste much like real fruit." Gracie squirmed like she wanted to get down. So Chay put his snack down and took off the baby's bib before putting her back on her blanket.

They had made enough space for her to crawl with a pillow barrier, and the light from the fire illuminated her blanket area.

"Thanks," Ava said.

"For what?"

"Distracting me."

"No biggie. It helped me, too. There is always that moment in a storm when you feel like it's never going to end. That this is what the world will be from now on." It wasn't just storms that got him like that. Fall nights affected him that way, too, mainly because it had been November 5 when his mom had left him. That night he hadn't slept a wink, willing her to come back to him, promising that even if she brought another abusive boyfriend with her, he'd accept it. Be as good as he could be.

God, what a mess he'd been. Some days he felt like he'd left that messed-up boy in the dust, but most of the time he had to acknowledge that a big part of who he was had that boy at the heart of him.

"I'm glad. So, rummy. This time we're not allowed to talk about anything but pop culture stuff. Favorite movies, books and songs. That kind of thing. I'm not going to ruin another rummy game."

"You didn't ruin the last one. Things just got...intense. That happens around you," he said.

"I try not to let it," she admitted. "But if I see something, I've got to say it."

"Which is probably why you are a good therapist. So, favorite song?" he asked as she dealt the cards.

He learned she *loved* pop and R&B and that his favorite country artist was hit-or-miss for her. She teased him about *The Lord of the Rings*. She'd only read the books but hadn't been able to sit through the movies. He promised her she was missing out and invited her to a marathon when the blizzard was over.

Which she accepted.

"The Scholastic Book Fair started my addiction with reading. That and my mom would always buy us a book but not always a toy. So she made books appealing."

Books were a hallmark of his teen years. He'd learned more about the world from reading than he had from anything else.

"Grandmother took me to the library," Chay admitted. "I was behind when I first got here because my mom hadn't always made getting me to school a priority."

"I bet it was difficult at first," Ava said.

"Some, but the teachers were understanding and Grandmother used to teach me at night. I caught up with reading and math pretty quickly. She always said that as long as I could read, I could figure anything out. That's proven true."

Ava had already liked Aponi, but she loved her a bit more hearing that. Chay had mentioned that he felt like his grandmother had felt obligated to keep him, but that story right there showed she hadn't felt that way at all. She knew he'd only shared that because it was a deep-seated fear, like her own that she couldn't have too much happiness.

It wasn't rational, but it was still powerful all the same. "What's the first book you can remember reading that you loved?"

"Um... I guess it was Percy Jackson," he said. "He has a rough home life and school's not easy for him, but it turns out he's the son of Poseidon... I mean, I related on so many levels."

"I can see that. Are you trying to say you might be a demigod?" she tasted.

"I couldn't reveal it if I were. What about you?"

"Probably *Sisterhood of the Traveling Pants*. I didn't have a tight friend group like they did, but I wanted it. When I was reading that book it felt like... I did."

"Yeah, reading does that," he said. "I hope Bug likes reading."

"That's why I try to give her books to play with and read them to her," Ava said.

"Good plan. So...that's books and music and we've covered movies," Chay said as he won their second game. Ava had won the first. "What's next?"

"Hmm...sports? Except I'm not really into them. I mean, I watch the Super Bowl, but more for the commercials and halftime show," she admitted as she shuffled the cards and got ready to deal again.

"I watch them, but not fanatically. So we are pretty matched on sports," he said.

"We are, aren't we? Do you think we're compatible?" she asked. It seemed to her that Chay just fit all the missing parts of herself. But was she missing something? Love was blind. Ava knew that to be true from her own life as well as some of the sessions she had with her patients. But with Chay this felt...like nothing she'd experienced before.

She wanted them to be perfect together. To fit each other like a missing puzzle piece. Was that asking too much?

"On some things," he said. "But pop culture stuff isn't really a make-it-or-break-it thing. Even if you hate the *Lord of the Rings* movies, I still like you."

"Thanks. Even though you didn't have any snacks in your house, I still like you," she said with a wink.

"So I'm hearing you can be bribed with snacks?"

"Oh, hell yeah."

"Hands-down favorite?" he asked, picking up the cards she'd dealt him, but his mind wasn't on the game. His mind was her. On how easy it would be to lift her into his arms and roll her under him on the couch. To let his hands roam up and down her body while his mouth explored her neck. Gracie had dozed off, so it was almost as if they were alone.

"Bugles with spray cheese. My mom used to make them for us when we were kids," she said.

"You have the worst nutritional habits," he said.

"Don't knock it until you've tried it. What's yours?"

"Hot Cheetos."

She gave a shout of laughter. "I have bad habits. Those things—"

"Are delicious. I won't allow any slander against them."

"Sure, whatever you say," she said with a big grin on her face.

He couldn't resist her a moment longer. Moving carefully, he pulled her into his arms and onto his lap. She straddled him her hands on his shoulders, her center nestled against his crotch. Her breath smelling of chocolate pudding and coffee brushing over his face.

"You forfeit the game? That means I win two to one," she said.

"Fine," he said, tipping his head back as he pushed his hands into her hair. He drew her head forward until their mouths met.

The last thing he was thinking about was card games... but he was thinking about favorites.

That this might be his favorite blizzard ever. That Ava was his favorite woman as they fell to their sides and clothing was rearranged until his hands were on her bare flesh. He loved the sound of her muffled moans as she arched against him, loved the feel of her nails biting into his side as she moved them both until he could get inside her.

Loved the way she tightened around him and then called his name as quietly as she could as she came. He loved everything about this woman and knew that there was nothing that would stop him from claiming her as his. Not just temporarily, but forever. He needed Ava in his life.

With her by his side, he could see himself parenting Gracie and having the family he'd never really dreamed he'd find.

Chapter Twenty

Gracie woke first with a small cry, and Ava rolled away from Chay to pick her up. They were all sleeping on the living room floor. The fire, which Chay had banked before they went to bed, was still smoldering. Chay sat up, his hair sticking out on one side.

The storm seemed to have passed, but the world was covered in a white blanket. "I'll get the generator on so we can cook some breakfast and wash up. Then go and check the yard for damage."

"How are you going to get out?" she asked.

"Dig if I have to. The side door on the garage usually isn't too hard to shift the snow."

"I'll feed her and make us some coffee," she said.

He kissed her before getting up, and she watched him leave. Gracie was mumbling in her arms, and she looked down at her.

"What do you think, Bug?"

"Mamama."

Ava's heart was so full. She wanted to be Gracie's mom more than anything, but she wasn't sure that was going to happen. So instead she changed the baby's diaper and then dressed in warm clothes. She had heard the generator kick on and took Gracie with her into the bathroom to have a sink wash. She'd love a shower, but it was probably better to wait until the electricity was back on.

She braided her hair, meeting her own gaze in the mirror. She was buzzing with tiredness and a bit of excitement. Last night with Chay...it had been perfect. Who'd have thought that sheltering in a blizzard would be her dream date, but there it was.

Gracie continued her babbling as Ava took her back into the kitchen and got her high chair set up and fed her. She noticed that Chay had the makings of a breakfast casserole, and that would be something they could eat for lunch if they needed to, so she quickly pulled it together and put it in the oven.

She went to the garage once she had Gracie playing on her blanket and noticed that there was a slight path cleared form the side door. There was so much snow she wasn't sure if Chay was going to make much progress. He came back in on a gust of cold air, snow in his hair.

"Might have to try again later," he said.

"I think so. I've got a egg dish in the oven. Come in and warm up. What's your hurry to get out?" she asked as they went into the mudroom.

Chay got his outerwear off and then padded in his socks down to the kitchen, where he poured himself a cup of coffee.

"Not every household has generators, and some of the domiciles are older. I need to be able to check on everyone. The radio isn't going to work in this weather."

"Okay. After breakfast if you want I'll try to help you clear more snow."

"Thanks. How's the bug this morning?"

"Good. She ate well and now she's playing. How are you today?" she asked. "Last night…"

"I'm good. What about last night?" he asked.

"Just really enjoyed it," she said after a few moments. "I wouldn't mind being snowed in with you longer."

"If it was just us, I'd agree," he said.

But they both had people who needed them. And Chay was going to be itching to get out and check out the neighborhoods and make sure everyone was okay. He really cared about his people, which had led him to her to begin with. He didn't want anyone on the Navajo Nation to be harmed.

"If you can't get out today, what will you do?"

"There's nothing we can do. Now that the storm has passed, the snow will start to melt, which could be another problem. I'd like to get some of it shifted away from the foundation of the house. I do have some drainage built into the exterior, but not enough to handle this. I hope your place is okay," Chay said.

She hadn't thought of her little home since she'd been here. "Dad will probably go by and check on it. As soon as we get some kind of signal or electricity, I want to check in with them. I know they'll be fine, but still."

Chay nodded at her. "I need to check on my grandmother. I'm sure she's fine, but I'll worry until I hear her voice."

"Same. So we need to hear from our people and get ourselves out of this snow world. Did you ever read *The Lion, The Witch and The Wardrobe*?"

"I didn't, but I did see the movie. Are you thinking the Ice Queen did this?"

"No, I'm thinking of Turkish delight," she said.

He groaned. "Of course you are. What did you make for breakfast? It smells delicious and not like junk."

"It's a casserole with bacon, sausage, eggs and cheese. Figured we needed something hearty, and it will reheat easily for lunch."

She served them both breakfast, and they talked quietly while they ate. "You're a good partner in a disaster."

She flushed a little at his compliment. "Thank you. Even though I almost got cranky last night."

"Anyone would get cranky after sitting in the dark for hours with only the sounds of wind and snow hitting the house. Don't be so hard on yourself," he said kindly.

"You weren't."

"I was, I'm just able to hide it," he said.

"Because of your childhood."

"Yes. It's easier to act like nothing bothers me than to show how I'm really feeling," he admitted.

"All the time?" she asked, wondering if that was how he was with her. Was he pretending to feel something that wasn't there? Was she seeing something that she wanted to see?

"Mostly."

"Even with me?" she asked.

"In what way?"

"Were you pretending last night?" she asked.

He took her hand in his. "I'm never pretending, Ava. I just don't wear my emotions for the world to see. But I'm experiencing it all, and I'm never faking it around you."

THE RADIO CAME through just as the electricity was crackling back on. "Officer Benally? Chay, you there?"

"I'm here, Wes. We're good. Going to take me a while to get out of here. You?"

"The station and town are in the same shape. I'm getting a few officers ready to start going door to door to check on everyone. Lou has a plow fitted to the front of his truck, and he's gone to get the snowplow drivers and plow them out."

"Sounds like you're on top of things. I'll keep shoveling here, try to make it in as soon as I can."

"Great. Your grandmother's with mine at Aponi's house, and I just heard from them. They are fine."

"Thanks, Wes. I'll be in touch as soon as I'm on my way," Chay said, ending the radio call.

Knowing that his grandmother was fine was a relief. Now he needed to get out of the house to check on the rest of the town. Wes and the others would do what they could, but they'd been snowed in at the station and could use some rest.

When he came out to update Ava, she'd changed her clothes and had Gracie in her snow gear. "I thought we'd go outside and I'll help while Gracie plays in the snow."

"I won't say no to that. If we can get a path to my truck, I put the snowplow attachment on it yesterday," he said. "I can plow the drive in case you want to get out. I don't recommend driving back to Dark Canyon today. I think the roads are still going to be rough."

She nodded over at him. "I'll stay another night at least."

"Good. I like having you here." He turned to get his cold-weather gear on before she could respond. He wasn't looking for her to tell him she liked it, too. He just wanted her to know.

There were things he wished he'd said to his mom, so he tended to blurt things out when they entered his head. He did it with his grandmother all the time, and she was used to it. Ava probably wasn't. But he didn't want to have to explain it to her.

She sat on the bench next to him as he put his boots on and then handed Gracie to him while she got her boots on. Bug was snug in her snowsuit and kept smiling and drooling the slightest bit.

Chay put on his heavy winter coat and then the baby carrier and put Gracie in it facing outward. She kicked her little legs as soon as he got her in it. Ava put a winter hat on Gracie's head and made sure the baby was completely covered up.

"She can't stay out long," Ava reminded him.

"I'll keep a close eye on her. I'm not sure you should stay out that long, either."

"Agreed. Same for you, but you have that stubborn look in your eye like you're going to get the job done come hell or high water."

"Or high snow, as this case may be," he said, then kissed her, because he wanted nothing more than to stay in this house with these two. To cuddle under the blankets until Gracie fell asleep and then make love to Ava again. But there was work that needed to be done.

Chay wouldn't allow himself not to step up. The path he'd dug earlier was still there, but more snow had fallen. The six-foot-high bank wasn't easy to maneuver through. He caught himself cursing but stopped, not wanting Gracie to hear him.

"Why don't I take her for a little bit?" Ava suggested. He helped her put the carrier on and then went back to shoveling. He heard Ava behind him, working steadily to make the path he'd roughly carved easier to traverse.

Moving along the side of the house, he finally got to the front of it. His truck was parked behind Ava's in the driveway. He had a pretty good idea of the location in his mind. But he was also sort of winging it. There was so much snow it was impossible to tell if he was truly going in the right direction.

Then he remembered he had a compass on his phone. He'd just pulled it out to access it when Ava ducked under his arm, wrapping her arm around his waist. Gracie was looking up at him, and his heart stopped for a moment. He realized that this was all he needed. These two women at his side.

Blinking against the emotions that threatened to overwhelm him, he finally got the compass up.

"I think our vehicles are east of the house. Wanted to make sure we were going the right way." Explaining because he didn't want to talk about anything, afraid he'd just blurt out that he loved her and he wanted to spend the rest of his life with her.

"Okay. I'm going to take her back inside for about fifteen minutes or so to warm up and then I'll come right back. I can put her in the crib and bring you some coffee, if you'd like."

"Nah, I'm good."

"You're cold, but I'll let you be all macho for right now. I'll be back with a thermos later, though."

She hugged him and then turned, disappearing into the snow maze around the side of the house. Tipping his head back and looking up at the gray winter sky, he took a moment to thank the universe for sending Ava and Gracie into his life. Then he got back to work, slowly making his way, following the compass until his shovel hit the side of Ava's car. Ten more minutes and he'd be at his. He got to his truck and found the door locks were frozen, so he cupped his hand over the side to try to warm it up, knowing better than to go and get hot water to pour on it.

He got the door open and got inside the vehicle. The engine turned over easily, and he cranked up the heat. Soon he'd be able to check in on everyone and then when he came back he was going to make solid plans for the future with Ava.

THE PHONE LINES weren't working, but Ava was able to contact Ryan at the fire station via the radio. He reassured her that their parents were fine and that Dark Canyon was getting power back and the roads plowed. It was nice to talk to him since she felt so far removed from her normal life.

"Did you eat all your snacks before the power went out?" he asked her jokingly.

"No. I forgot about them, really."

"No way."

"I was busy with Gracie. I'll deny if you say it to her, but I don't know how Mom did this with both us. It's a lot more work than you'd guess."

Ryan laughed. "I'm not even surprised. How is it out there with Chay?"

"Good. I... I really like him, Ryan."

"I hear he's a good guy. Maybe we should get together in a couple of weeks," Ryan suggested.

"I'd like that. Did you go by the hospital to visit Fern?"

"Haven't had a chance yet, but I'm going to. I bet the storm wasn't easy on her."

"That's what I was thinking. If you can, and it's totally fine if you can't, would you bring her a balloon from me? Any one you pick out will do," Ava said, knowing her patient would find it comforting. If there was an easy way for Ava to get back to Dark Canyon she'd try to do it, just to see Fern.

"I'm not sure anyplace is open, but if I can't get one I'll tell her you wanted me to bring one. Will that do?"

"Yeah, thanks. Sorry I conned you with the blue M&M's when we were little and took your birthday money," she said.

Ryan laughed so hard she was sure that everyone in the fire house could hear him. "What brought that on?"

"Nothing...just realized I wasn't always the best sister back then." As an adult she was a little bit horrified at the routine meanness she'd exhibited toward her brother.

"It's cool. I stole it back from your room while you were sleeping. You were a heavy sleeper."

"You didn't."

"Yup. I told Mom that we counted them, and she told me she'd let you know a week or so earlier that there were always blues."

"She did. Glad you got your money back," she said.

"Not that we needed it as kids. Mom and Dad took care of everything," he said.

"So true. But the scales of justice are balanced," she said.

"Yup. Take care, sis. See you when you're back in town," Ryan said.

"You, too."

She got off the radio, feeling upbeat as she went around Chay's house setting it to rights. Putting away all of the supplies she'd assembled for the blizzard. Gracie was busy playing on her blanket. Once the pillow boundary was down, she'd been crawling all over the place.

A little bit Ava wasn't sure the little girl had realized there was more to the house than her blanket. She found her in the laundry room when she went in there to put the blankets they'd used overnight in the washer.

Scooping the baby up, she carried her back to the living room. Ava noticed the minute she set Gracie down the baby took off again. Laughing as Ava trotted after her.

They played like that for a good thirty minutes, which was tiring and reminded Ava she needed to get to the gym more often.

Finally Gracie showed signs of slowing down and getting tired. Ava gave her a snack and then laid her down for a nap.

She checked her phone for a signal, but there still wasn't one. She was anxious to know if Chay was okay. Would anyone think to let her know if he got in an accident? She doubted it.

They'd become close over the last few weeks, but their relationship was pretty insular. She'd just mentioned him to Ryan today. Though her mom knew she was seeing him. And Chay's grandmother, of course, but the wider community wouldn't.

She'd had a patient once who'd lost her high school boyfriend in an accident. They'd kept their relationship secret, so no one had known how deeply his death had affected her. It still affected her as an adult, which Ava and her patient worked on each week.

Chay was hard on himself about the past but also very accepting of who and where he was. It almost seemed as if it were easier for him to acknowledge his flaws than his strengths. But really, those flaws shaped his strength and made him stronger.

She heard the sound of an engine and hurried to the window, but of course there was just a mountain of snow there. Glancing at her watch, she realized Chay had only been gone a few hours. She'd thought it would be much later when he returned.

She hoped he was okay. Going to get her boots, she peeked in on Gracie sleeping in her crib before she went to the front door and threw it open.

The vehicle behind hers wasn't Chay's but looked vaguely familiar. Like that car that had sideswiped her the other day.

Stepping back toward the house as the door opened, she stumbled and tripped as the man got out of the car.

He was tall, but not as tall as Chay. He had thinning brown hair and his face looked older than his years as he came toward her.

Chapter Twenty-One

The storm had left a lot of damage and the snowplows were doing their best, but it was going to take time to get through the worst of it. Chay felt a twinge of anxiety thinking about Gracie and Ava at home by themselves, wishing he was with them. That was new.

As he did routine safety checks on the elderly and people with disabilities, he sat in the feelings. Let them surround him, realizing that his world had grown by two. It was nice. He had food and blankets and medical supplies. All of the officers had made it in, and they had divided up the town and were taking quadrants to inspect.

He'd gotten the one where his grandmother was; they all had people they wanted to check in on. All of the vehicles at the tribal police office were fitted with snowplows, so they were able to get into places that the town's plows hadn't reached yet. He cleared his grandmother's street and then started at the end to help shovel out a path from the doorway of each house to their vehicle.

Grandmother was happy to see him. She looked tired but well.

"How was it?" she asked him. Her friend who lived

next door was getting her stuff together so that Chay could get her back to her home.

"Not too bad. We lost power about midnight, I'd guess. You?"

"Same. I told Fiona that you had a generator set up for me. We fiddled with it, but decided the fire and candles were enough for us at first. Then it got really cold, so we went out there to try again," she said.

Chay wished he'd been with his grandmother. "Next time you both come and stay with me. I have plenty of space. Did you get it working?"

"I did. I even made sure to ventilate. Just a bit—the snow is coming in the garage when I went to outside to check on it," she warned him. "Not much."

"I'll take care of it after I get Fiona home," he said, hugging his grandmother tightly. She always seemed so indomitable, but she was getting older and would need more help from him. Something he knew he had to factor into raising Gracie. If he decided to apply to be her adoptive father, he needed to be aware that his grandmother was going to need more time as well.

Could he handle raising a child and caring for an elderly relative? He knew that was a question that many dealt with. He thought he'd be able to handle it. Especially with Ava by his side. But he had to be sure on his own. Life didn't come with guarantees. Plus, he liked contingencies, where he knew he'd be okay without anyone else.

"I'm ready. I'm leaving my loom for now," Fiona said.

"I'll bring it over once we get you settled. Grandmother, you wait inside."

Aponi gave him the side-eye. "Like I was going to wait out here."

He ignored her sass, offering Fiona his arm. He'd already shoveled out her house. He took her bag from her, putting it over his shoulder as he walked at her pace back to her home. Fiona's house was cold, but Chay got her heat working and made sure the appliances were all good as well. Then made two more trips, bringing her lap loom and some food that his grandmother wanted Fiona to have.

He worked at his grandmother's house getting the snow out of the garage and making sure the generator was turned off properly and stowed away.

"Were you alone during the blizzard?" she asked while they sat at her table with a cup of coffee.

"You know I wasn't," he said. She was fishing for information, and while he had no issues telling her about himself and Ava, the fact that she was being cagey made him want to do the same.

"You're hardheaded."

"So are you. We were good. Gracie dealt with it pretty well," he said. Then realized he wanted to talk about the baby. Ask the questions he had been trying to answer on his own. "Grandmother, I'm thinking about filing to adopt her. I know I'm probably the last man you'd expect to do that."

"You're not. I've seen the way you are with her. You love her. What did Ava say?" Grandmother asked.

"She's the one pushing for it. I haven't told her yet. I don't want to make a mistake that will affect Gracie. She's already had so much tragedy in her short life. We don't know who her father is, and the way her mom was found dead—that's going to impact her." Chay stated all of his fears. Wanted to make sure that his grandma knew he wasn't taking this decision lightly.

"Sounds like you'd be the best man to be her father.

You understand that situation better than most. And I'll be here to help you, as will Ava, I'm sure," Grandmother said.

"Yeah, she will be, but that's complicated, too. I really like her. But will I crack under all this? It's a baby, a girlfriend, commitment…"

"I bet you get even stronger, Chay. I've never met another person who handles adversity like you do. You get stronger, quieter sometimes, but always stronger. Those two will be lucky to have you and me if you decide to adopt. But I think you already know that. Why are you asking me about this?"

"Never hurts to get a second opinion from one of the wisest women I know," Chay admitted.

"I thought I was the wisest," she said smartly, but her smile beamed at him.

"Well…there is Ava. She's pretty smart—in a different way than you. She's pushy like you as well."

"That's why I like her," Grandmother said.

They laughed at that. His radio crackled.

"Benally. Jacob Colton is trying to raise you. Got to channel six to speak to him."

He switched channels.

"Benally here."

"Is Ava with you?"

"Yeah. She's at my place. What's up?"

"That's a relief. I just found out that Daniel Wayne is out on parole."

"Since when?"

"Two weeks ago. But you're with her, so that's good."

"She's at my place. I'm in town helping with the aftermath of the storm," Chay said. A rising sense of panic filled him. "I've got to go."

FEAR AND PANIC drove her to try to get away from him. Her mind was trying to make sense of the fact that he was here. He was coming after her.

Daniel Wayne.

How was that possible?

She struggled to get back into the house, her hands clawing at the door as she heard him behind her. His hand was on her wrist, grabbing her, knocking her off her feet. She hit the patio hard, pain shooting up her tailbone into her neck. She bit her lip to keep from crying out, not wanting to disturb Gracie.

Fear was coursing through her, and all the self-defense training she'd had after Daniel had started stalking her was a distant memory. She couldn't remember a single thing.

Panicking, she kicked out hard, but her foot bounced off his thigh. He grabbed her ankle and twisted it as he pushed her again. The strength in his push told her physically she was no match for him, but she wasn't just going to go meekly with him.

"Good to see you remember me," Daniel said. His voice was still so calm and warmly modulated. He'd never sounded like a monster, which she thought he should have.

"Who are you?" she asked. "I mean, you look familiar." She didn't want to give him the satisfaction of knowing that she'd never be able to forget him or the terror he evoked in her.

He kicked her hard in the stomach.

"Keep it up. I've been watching you and your...he's not your husband, but you two have a kid... I thought you were waiting for marriage," he said, dragging her to her feet by gripping her upper arm.

"When I was eighteen," she said. "Life was still so new. I didn't want to take a chance on having a child before I was ready."

"You are mine. You were always mine," he said, hitting her hard across the face. Her head flew back, and she hit the side of the house.

Pain exploded in her head; she saw stars. Daniel was in a rage.

"If I was yours, than why did you start seeing that other woman?" she asked. Her mind was frantically trying to come up with anything that would distract him enough that she could get away. Get inside the house and lock the door until Chay got here.

"You went to the cops. And they were making it difficult for me to see you," he said. "She understood what I was going through at first. I told her what a bitch you were. How you came onto me and then when I got serious, you pushed me away."

"Then she pushed you away?" Ava asked. "Maybe it's not her or me who were the problem."

He grabbed her hair in his hand, yanking her head back as he got in her face. His hot breath brushing her cheek. "Oh, it's you bitches. All that damned feminism making you think you don't need a man…but you know the truth. That's why you're shacked up with your baby daddy."

"I'm not shacked up with anyone," she pointed out. "I don't need a man."

"I'm sorry to hear that," he said. "In time you'll change your mind. You're going to need me more than ever."

Fear washed over her and she started struggling in earnest to get away from him, but he wasn't letting up. She had to talk him down. Distract. Acknowledge his pain and then get him to move around it.

"I was too young when we met, Daniel. I didn't know what I was looking for in a relationship. We had some good times," she said. "Remember the fall festival?"

All the truth, but also there had been something about Daniel that hadn't felt right. She hadn't really had an inkling of how off he was, but she knew that he wasn't the kind of man she wanted a future with.

"You were so young," he said. "The fall festival... I won you that stuffed—what was it?"

"A unicorn," she said.

"Do you still have it?"

"No," she admitted. "I didn't keep anything from those years."

"Too painful," he said, watching her like a hawk.

"Yes." She could honestly admit that it brought her pain and so much more when she'd looked at the items from their short dating life. She'd felt so silly and stupid for falling for a man who was so obsessive. He'd love bombed her big-time. Showering her with attention and gifts, and when she'd told him it was too much...things had turned sour.

"Where's your child? I think we should bring the baby with us."

"She's with her father. I'm just cleaning up the house," she said. Making up stuff. Gracie would be fine in her crib in the house. Safe and warm and far away from Daniel. "He'll be back soon. Have you seen him? He's big and muscly. You know he's a police officer."

"I don't like the police," Daniel said.

"You should leave now before he gets back," Ava said. She wasn't entirely sure that Daniel would do that. "You don't want to go back to prison, right? I won't tell him you were here."

"Ava, I'm not leaving without you. I'm here just for you," he said.

"I'm not going with you," she said. Prepared to do whatever she had to in order to stop him.

"I was afraid you'd say that." Lifting his hand, he hit her in the head, and this time when her head hit the porch she saw stars. Tingles spread through her entire body as she fell limply to the deck.

Vaguely she was aware of him lifting her over his shoulder. Her last thought was that he'd left the front door ajar.

CHAY'S FIRST INSTINCT was to run back to Ava. He was out the door with his grandmother on his heels.

"What are you doing?"

"Coming with you," she said, wrapping her scarf around her neck. "You're going to need me there if this guy shows up."

He started to argue with her but didn't want to take the time and having her by his side felt right. Her street was quiet, and the blanket of snow that still covered everything made the world look pristine. But it wasn't. He'd always known that. Somehow he'd fallen into this belief that things were all good since Ava came into his life.

"If you come with me, you have to do as I say. No going off on your own. Okay?"

"Yes. I would just sit here and worry, and I don't want you to have to call me and let me know what's going on," she said. "They're my family, too."

He hugged her for that. She locked her house, and he got her to his truck and inside. He radioed Wes to let him know what was going on.

"Wes, it's Chay. I'm heading back to my house. There's

a chance that a man who stalked Ava is in the area. I have to check on Ava and Gracie," Chay said.

"Understood. What's his name and description?"

"Daniel Wayne. I don't have a description, but you can probably get one from Jacob Colton. Send it to me when you have it."

"Affirmative. Let us know if you need backup."

"I'm sure they're fine—the storm would have hampered him getting to us," Chay said. That was the only thing that was keeping him from all-out panic. Neither Wes nor his grandmother said a word in response, which wasn't reassuring. It was like they didn't want to say anything to send him into overdrive. As if knowing Ava and Gracie were in danger wasn't his worst nightmare. Chay drove as quickly as was safe back to his house. As soon as he turned onto the drive, he saw the tire tracks. The ones that weren't his.

He'd always been practical, but he couldn't deny that his spiritual side warned him at times. Like when he'd known his mom wasn't coming back to the Navajo Nation. Right now he knew Ava was in danger. When he pulled up behind her truck, he saw signs of footprints in the snow. Just one set.

Not Ava's boots, which he could easily recognize from when they'd dug out the house.

His front door was open, and Grandmother was already starting to get out of the truck.

"Stay here. Lock the doors. I'm not sure if he's in there or not."

She nodded and closed her door. Chay radioed in that there was a break-in at his house and signs that someone else had been there. Palming his weapon, he got out of the truck. Moving carefully toward the house.

He avoided the tracks in the snow, knowing that he'd want to examine them later. Moving slowly and keeping low in case Daniel was already in the house...but the tire tracks made him believe that he wasn't. He had to confirm it, though.

On the front porch he knelt noticing some blood on the floor and some strands of dark reddiths hair. *Ava.*

He pushed the door open with his foot and swept the room with his weapon. It was clear. He moved farther into the house, hearing the sound of the baby crying. He wanted to rush to her but took his time, clearing the hallway and the bathroom before he got to her room.

Lying on her back, Gracie was crying for all she was worth. Arms and legs kicking, little face all squished up as she cried. He went to comfort her, using one hand to rub her belly as he talked to her.

"It's okay. I'm here now."

He left the baby in her crib to finish his sweep of the house, confirming it was empty. Holstering his weapon, he went back to Gracie and picked the little one up.

Still upset, she calmed when he hugged her to his chest. Ava was gone. Chay's heart was beating so hard that he had to take a moment to calm himself. Gracie's little hand on his shoulder helped him.

Looking into her brown eyes, he saw the future that he'd been afraid to take slipping away.

Pushing that to the back of his mind, he went out to his truck, giving Gracie to his grandmother while he radioed in what he'd found. Wes was dispatching some officers to come help with the search. His grandmother was in the house now with Gracie, making coffee for the men who'd arrive soon to help.

His radio in the house was crackling and he went to

answer it. Ryan, Ava's brother, was trying to get through to her.

"Ryan, it's Chay."

"Daniel Wayne is out of jail," Ryan said. "You have to let Ava know."

"She knows. He has her. I'm going to find her and bring her back."

"Where is she?"

"I'm not sure. He took her. I'm starting the search now," Chay said.

"Do you need some extra men?"

"Maybe later—right now I have the tribal police and Dark Canyon PD."

Ryan promised he'd talk to their parents. "Mom and Dad are going to want to come out there."

"You can stay at my place. My grandmother and Gracie are here."

He ended the chat and went out to the front yard where the tracks were. This time he studied them in more detail. Daniel was lighter of step going toward the house than he was coming back, which fit, since there was only one set of prints leaving. He must have knocked Ava out.

On foot he walked to the end of the drive. Since only his car had come in and out so far, he noticed the direction that Daniel Wayne had gone.

Chapter Twenty-Two

Ava came to in a panic. She was cold and her head hurt. Blinking quickly, she tried to take in as much as she could, but her vision was blurry. Opening her eyes she noticed that her feet were bound and her hands were tied in front of her body. She wiggled her fingers, which were numb.

Turning her head, she winced as needles of pain shot down her neck. It looked like they were in a long-abandoned shack or cabin of some kind. There was a small gas heater in one corner but not much else. The door opened, and she quickly closed her eyes as cold air wrapped around her and made her shiver.

No matter that she'd studied this type of behavior to get her degree, she couldn't be rational when it came to dealing with Daniel. Yet she had to be. Think of him as a patient.

Which was hard when she was in pain, scared and cold.

"I know you're awake, so stop pretending to sleep."

She took a deep breath and opened her eyes. He'd brought in a camp chair and was now sitting across from her. He had a gun held loosely in one hand and a thermos in the other.

"Why did you bring me here?" she asked.

Rage tightened his features. "You're the reason I was in jail. I want you to pay for what happened to me."

"I didn't put you in jail. The girl you assaulted did that."

"I didn't assault her. We were dating. You're allowed to have sex with your girlfriend," Daniel pointed out.

"Unless she says no," Ava said.

"Women like to play games, even you. Don't deny it."

Games? She'd never thought of any relationship that way. "Most people are careful when they are falling in love, Daniel. Maybe she just needed some space to figure out her feelings."

"I don't give a fuck what she needed. I wouldn't have been dating her if you hadn't broke up with me and then filed that restraining order." His voice rose on each word until he was shouting and standing over her. He kicked her, and when she cried out he smiled.

"You need to learn when to shut up."

"Why? We're not going to be together," she said, which just made him kick her again. She needed to get him away from her. Her side ached, and she wasn't sure he hadn't broken her rib with that last kick.

"We are," he promised her.

"What is it you want from me?" she asked. He looked like he might kick her again, so she brought her bound hands up to ward him off. "Make me understand it. I haven't seen you in years. I thought you'd moved on."

"I could never move on from you, Ava. You were my first love. Remember when we met on the quad? You spilled your raspberry tea on me and then laughed and promised to buy me a new shirt."

It had been a warm, almost summery day when they'd

been moving into their dorms. "I did. And I bought you one."

"No woman had ever bought me a gift before."

"That can't be true. What about your mother?"

"Left before I could know her," he said. "My dad said it was my fault. That if I hadn't been such a pussy she would have stuck around."

"That's probably not true. Your dad sounds like—"

Leaning down, he hit her to shut her up. Her jaw ached as she pulled herself back as far as she could from him.

"Of course you'd take her side. Bitches never own their shit. My dad wasn't all touchy-feely, but he was a real man. He raised me to be one, too."

Her mind was hazy with pain and cold. She really had no idea what to say to calm him down but was determined to keep him talking as long as she could.

"You are definitely a man."

"I know. I saw that wuss you dated after me."

"Greg?"

"Yeah. What was he? Like a science major?"

"Astrophysicist. He was studying for his PhD."

"Didn't get it, did he?"

"No, he was killed in a car accident," Ava said. Sweet, gentle Greg, who was the partner she hadn't known she'd needed. He'd helped her heal from the toxic relationship she'd had with Daniel.

"Was it an accident?"

"Yes. The cops said it was."

"Hit and run, right?"

Daniel knew too many details. She swallowed, hard watching him. "Did you do it?"

"I did. And I'm going to take care of the new guy in

your life and that brat of yours. If they'd been home when I got you, I would have shot them both."

Her heart raced with fear and anger at this man. He was so smug. He'd killed Greg without a thought for the other man's life. He'd killed Greg because of her. Ava knew there were no two ways about that. If he'd never dated her, Greg would be alive and studying far-off universes and black holes. Making discoveries. All gone because of her.

No way she was going to allow Daniel to ruin anyone else's life. Especially not Chay and Gracie. Ava would die in this ramshackle cabin with Daniel before she let him hurt either of them.

Pushing aside her pain and cloudy mind, she concentrated. The knots on her hands were tighter than the ones on her feet. Daniel had paced away from her, still going on about how he'd killed Greg. The planning he'd taken to make sure he knew Greg's routine.

Crying while she curled herself into a ball, bringing her feet closer so she could try to work the knot on the rope free. It was hard to see through her tears and she didn't realize how loud her sobs were until Daniel told her to shut up.

"He wasn't worthy of you."

"You aren't worthy of me," she said, unable to get free, but determined to get out of this cabin and put Daniel Wayne back in jail.

WES AND SOME of the other officers had arrived at his house. It was midafternoon, and there was another storm threatening on the horizon. In his mind everything became clear. He wouldn't return home without Ava. She was his entire world, but he'd been too afraid to admit it to her.

He'd acted like he had all the time in the world. One thing he should have realized was never the reality.

They all followed the trail of the car to a crossroads, where there were four paths he could have taken. There had been so much vehicular traffic that the track was obscured. Chay set up a command post at the intersection that would be in communication with the one he'd left his grandmother in charge of back at the house. She had Ava's phone and they were all hoping that once cell signal was restored, Aponi would be able to get a signal for Ava's smartwatch on the phone.

Chay wasn't waiting for that to happen.

They had the maps out and everyone was looking for any place where Wayne might take shelter. He had to see the snowstorm coming in the same as they did.

"I'm not going to ask everyone to stay out in the storm," Chay started. But this was his woman, and there was no way he was going home without her.

They had assembled six men who would help in the search. The rest of the force was handling emergencies in the town and helping people recover from the blizzard.

Chay was the second in command at the station, and his boss had put him in charge of finding Ava. Wes had come out to help, even though he'd been on duty for the last thirty-six hours straight.

"You don't have to ask. We're all here to find her. I think we need to work quickly. Lou remembers there were several hunting shacks dotted around the area," Wes said, clapping his hand on Chay's shoulder.

"Where were they, Lou?" he asked.

The other man leaned over the map they had spread

out on the hood of his truck. He pointed to an old trail that was marked with a thin line. If he remembered correctly, he'd seen it before. On the map he'd looked at of where Fern Hensley had been kept.

"Near as I can remember, about every six miles or so along here." Lou leaned over the map and drew his finger along it.

Chay continued tracking it, noticing that it lined up with the cabin where Fern was found. If they were similar, then he had an idea of what they were looking for. Something similar to the hiking cabins they had in Scotland.

The cabins had been built in the 1950s and weren't owned by any one person but were there in case a hunter or hiker got into trouble. No one monitored them, and as far as Chay knew no officer from the tribal police had been out to them in decades.

"The quickest way to handle this would be for everyone to try to target one cabin," Chay said.

"Agreed," Wes said.

"We'll all stay in radio communication and clear the cabins. Keep your eye out for signs of any recent inhabitants," Chay said, thinking that this investigation might show signs of other women trafficked into the area or rule that theory out. But his focus was on rescuing Ava. It had to be.

"We will."

They all headed out in different directions. Chay took the cabin the farthest from his property. He saw the other tribal police vehicles peel off every six miles until it was just him. The snow out here was thicker and the clouds overhead kept darkening.

He lowered the snowplow on the front of his truck,

driving in the direction that Lou had indicated the cabins were. The path was bumpy and the snow thick, making his progress slow. Frustrated, he turned his head, looking out the driver's window, and noticed tracks.

Was he seeing things?

He stopped his truck and got out to check it out. As he got closer, he realized that they were indeed tire tracks. Someone had driven over this path since the blizzard.

Getting back in his truck, he turned toward the tracks, plowing his way over until he was following the tire tracks. He kept his pace slow so he didn't miss anything.

The tracks veered to the left, as did Chay, slowing the truck to a crawl, scanning the horizon in the gathering darkness until he saw a vehicle parked in the distance. Not wanting to take a chance on alerting whoever was inside to his presence, he got as close as he felt safe and then radioed back to the checkpoint.

"Benally here. I found something. I'm leaving the truck and going on foot to check it out," he said, giving them his coordinates so they knew where to find him.

Then he silenced his radio and got out of his truck. His feet sank into the thick, cold snow. It was bitter out and a chill went straight to his bones. Fear for Ava kept him focused and moving steadily through the snow until he got to the car.

Kneeling near the bumper, he relayed the license plate back to Lou, who was manning the checkpoint.

"I'm going inside," he reported.

Pulling his weapon, he moved, keeping low to the ground. More snow started falling as he made his way to the one window. It was covered in some kind of cloth that only partially obstructed his view. Standing up quickly, he scanned the room, spotting Ava on the ground. She was crumpled into a ball.

He saw red at first, then took a really long breath so he didn't go in there and get them both killed.

It took a minute before he saw the man standing over her. He was saying something and looked like he was going to kick her.

THE DOOR OF the cabin burst inward like a gunshot. Ava's heart raced wildly as she saw Chay come into the room with his weapon drawn. Daniel turned toward him, lifting his gun. He fired off a wild shot, which brought Ava up to her knees.

Ava cried out to warn Chay. But he was already on the move, closing the distance between himself and Daniel. Daniel fired another shot that grazed Chay's arm, but he kept coming, hitting Daniel hard in the jaw. Daniel sidestepped him and leaned down over her, dragging her away from Chay and up to her feet.

The barrel of his gun rammed into her neck; it was hot from the bullets he'd fired and burned her. Scared, she wasn't sure what to do. She didn't want to die. She didn't want Chay to see Daniel kill her. But with her bound hands and feet, she was like a limp rag doll in his arms. She used her bound hands to try to punch him, but he cocked the weapon.

"Stop. Ava, if you move again, I'll kill you," Daniel growled against the side of her head.

She went still. "Let him go. Let him leave and I'll... I'll do whatever you want."

"Ah, that's sweet, she's pleading for your life. You know I killed the last man who thought he was going to marry her."

"We're not engaged," Ava said. "You don't have to kill him."

"I do. You'll say anything to save him. But I've seen your little family. I've been watching you for weeks now. I tried to warn you off visiting him with my car but you kept on," he said.

"Running me off the road was foolish. I reported your car to the National Parks ISB," she lied, wishing now that she had. But at the time it hadn't occurred to her that Daniel might be out of prison.

"Enough. I'm not debating this with you," Daniel said. Then he looked at Chay. "Leave now and she lives."

Chay glanced at her and then back at Daniel. Her heart was racing so hard she could barely breathe. But Chay was calm as he looked from her to Daniel. He had to be planning something, but what? His arm was bleeding from where the bullet had grazed his shoulder. His eyes were so calm. She'd never seen him this way before.

This was the protector that she'd always known Chay was. For the first time, she saw the police officer and why he'd been called to serve. His emotions were buttoned up, and he was calmly facing down Daniel.

And that was unnerving Daniel even more. He kept talking, spouting things about how he was the only one who was going to be with her. But Ava kept her attention on Chay.

It took her a moment to realize he was readying himself to lunge at Daniel. Her body ached and her ribs were making it hard for her to take a deep breath. Knowing it was going to hurt a lot, but that she had to give Chay an advantage, she made her decision.

Ava watched him and then decided to help the only way she could. She lifted her feet off the ground so Daniel held her entire weight. Jerked off balance, the gun pointed away from her.

Chay was on Daniel, knocking his gun from his hand as Ava fell to the floor. She crawled away from the two men. Chay had the upper hand, but Daniel was strong and wasn't giving up easily. Ava noticed Daniel was reaching for his weapon, and crawling as fast as her awkwardly bound body would allow her, she knocked it out of the way, but now she was close enough for Daniel to grab her hair, twisting it hard.

She cried out as Chay brought his foot down on Daniel's upper arm, crushing it under his weight. Daniel let go of her hair, moaning from the pain as Chay wrestled his arms behind his back and got a pair of handcuffs on him. She heard the sound of sirens as vehicles got closer to them.

Everything else was foggy as men entered the cabin, taking Daniel into custody. Chay's arms were around her, holding her gently and keeping her warm. He hadn't let her go since the moment that Daniel had been taken from the cabin.

Ava looked up into the face of the man she loved more than anything. She was still afraid that Daniel would get away from the cops.

"I was so scared he'd kill you or Gracie," Ava said. "He killed Greg. He was the one who killed him. We're so lucky you got him. Make sure he is watched."

"We are. That man is never going to hurt you again, Ava. He's not getting near Gracie," he said to her. She wanted to believe him. Chay had never lied to her, but she was in pain and couldn't stop crying.

"He almost got Gracie."

"But you saved her. You saved our girl," he said.

Our girl. She was their girl. Chay wanted her to be as well. As soon as her body stopped throbbing in time with her heart and her head cleared, she was going to tell him that they were getting married.

He tried to lift her, but she winced in pain and he laid her back down. "Where does it hurt?"

"Everywhere. I think he might have broken my ribs… I definitely have a concussion. I'm cold and tired," she said, feeling herself starting to fade. Now that Chay was here, she knew she didn't have to stay alert.

He wouldn't let anything happen to her. "Where's Gracie?"

"With Grandmother. She's safe."

"He thought Gracie was our daughter," Ava said.

"He was right," Chay said. "She is ours. And as soon as you are better, we are going to start the paperwork to make her ours."

Or that's what she thought he said. She sort of drifted in and out of consciousness after that. She remembered being transported to the hospital, but then it was all a bit black. She woke up two days later in a room not dissimilar to the one she'd been visiting Fern in.

Chapter Twenty-Three

Chay hadn't left Ava's side since they'd brought her into the hospital. Her parents and brother had been by. As had his grandmother, Jacob and a slew of other people who knew her. Ava was like that. Lots of friends who cared about her.

If he needed another example of how different they were, he'd gotten it, but the truth was he had enjoyed those visits. Had felt like he was part of her inner circle. Even if, for a loner, it had been a bit overwhelming at first.

Ryan had brought her a bag of M&M's—apparently she'd spoken to him about her long-ago deception. It had made Chay laugh to think of Ava apologizing for a childhood prank.

Gracie was sleeping quietly in his arms. He couldn't wait to share with Ava that he'd started the paperwork to try to adopt Gracie. Something that he knew would please her. But more importantly, he couldn't wait to tell her that he loved her. He'd been scared he wouldn't get the chance to.

When he'd seen Daniel Wayne holding that gun to her

head...that was something that Chay wasn't going to forget for a very long time.

Gracie's eyes opened up, and she made that little cry she did when she woke up. Chay stood up and sort of jostled the baby on his shoulder, trying that rocking move his grandmother had showed him.

"Shh...yazhi, Mama's sleeping and we don't want to wake her up," Chay said, making a circuit around the room. "She's had a rough few days."

"But she's safe now," Ava said from the bed.

"Mamam," Gracie said, turning her body toward Ava's voice. The baby had wanted to cuddle with Ava, but of course that hadn't been possible.

"Hey there," he said as she adjusted the bed and tried to raise it. Holding her arms out for Gracie.

He handed her the baby and then helped get the bed into a sitting position. "How are you feeling? Do you need me to ring the nurse?"

"Groggy, tired, I get why Fern doesn't like to be drugged. It's such a weird feeling. I'm thirsty, too," she said.

He got her some water and handed it to her so she could drink. "I'm sure you have some questions."

"Lots of them. How did you find me?"

"Lou remembered there were a string of old hunting cabins that ran along the edge of the wilderness. We divided them up. I choose the one farthest from the house, figured he was going to want to get as far away as he could before the storm hit again."

"I don't remember much of that. He knocked me out. I was so afraid he was going to get in the house and then kill Gracie and wait to kill you."

Her hands trembled and there were tears in her eyes. He wanted to hug her, but she had an IV hooked up and he wasn't sure how to get close without disturbing it. Leaning over, he squeezed her shoulder and dropped a kiss on the top of her head.

"He didn't do that. Thanks to you. How did you do that?"

"I heard a vehicle and thought it was you," she said. "I recognized the car as one that sideswiped me a few days ago."

"Something you never mentioned."

"I figured it was just some driver in a rush. That was the night I had the panic attack…guess it wasn't my imagination but really Daniel."

Chay wished she'd mentioned the car incident, but that was all in the past. Nothing he could do about that now. She was safe. Daniel Wayne was going back to prison and would stay there for a good long time.

"You're safe now," he said again.

She squeezed his hand, linking their fingers together. Gracie chattered her baby words, and for a few minutes they stayed as they were. A feeling of peace and happiness went through Chay.

"I'm still trying to deal with the fact that Daniel killed Greg. It's hard to think that he was watching me all that time. I guess he must have been keeping tabs on me. I should have known that. I'm a therapist. Behaviors like that are common," she said.

He sighed. "That's not your fault. You were in love and planning a new life. I don't think it's expected that you'd be worrying about an ex showing up."

"No, but I wish… I wish that I'd never gone out with Daniel," Ava admitted.

"But you did. The past... Not sure if this will help or not, but I realized that all the bad choices, decisions and circumstances that happened to me are out of my control. I spent a lot of time trying to rejig the past and make it so my mom would love me or even care about me. Nothing I could have done would have changed her," he said.

"It was the same for you. Daniel Wayne might have seen you walking across campus and gotten obsessed with you. Not going on a date wouldn't have kept him from your life. Then, who knows, he might have hurt more people than he has. It seems like if we'd made one different choice life would be better. But it would still be your life."

Ava's fingers tightened on his. Tears in her eyes again. "Thanks for saying that. If I was my own patient, I would say something similar. We can't change what happened..."

"Not today, but we can make a brighter future," Chay said. He wanted to tell her he loved her. To let her know that he was going to be by her side for their rest of their lives. That Gracie was going to be the start of their family. But he wanted to give her space to heal first.

Ava hadn't wanted to go back to her house after she left the hospital. Chay's house felt more like home to her now. But she wasn't sure she could just drop that on him without talking. After their discussion when she'd woken up in the hospital, she'd felt closer to him than ever.

Chay was clean shaven as always, wearing a pair of jeans that fit him just right and his sunglasses against the glare of the winter sun. The snowstorms had passed, and it now it looked so bright and beautiful out that it was hard to remember all the snow and trouble the storm had brought.

But there was a lot going on. Chay and Aponi had been keeping Gracie, which Marg at child services had no issues with. Everyone was going out of their way to make sure Ava was okay, which was nice, but it was too much attention. Not the kind she liked.

Chay told her that some people were waiting at her house, and she groaned. As much as she loved her family, she wanted to be alone with Chay. There were things she wanted to talk to him about. She needed to tell him she loved him and find out if he felt the same. She'd hoped now that she was out of the hospital and away from nurses and doctors who kept coming into her room she could make that happen.

"What?" he asked as he turned toward her subdivision.

"Who is there?" she asked. She wasn't ready to see all her Colton cousins and aunts and uncles. They'd all been to see her in the hospital, which she appreciated, but today she wanted something quieter.

"Your parents, who I couldn't tell not to come. Ryan's working, but he will stop by later. Aponi and Gracie."

She was looking forward to seeing everyone. Her mom and Aponi got along really well. Of course, her mother was sure she was going to get Aponi to donate more than one blanket to the silent auction. Her mom was persuasive, but Aponi was pretty stubborn when she wanted to be. She'd have to really believe in the Colton Foundation to change her donation.

"That's not bad. I'm just. I feel gross and I don't... I don't want everyone looking at me like they pity me," she admitted. Also she still had some guilt for bringing a man like Daniel Wayne into her life. But Chay's words rang in her mind, reminding her that she had no control over how Daniel felt or behaved.

"No one pities you," Chay said, sounding so reasonable that it made her a little bit crankier.

Her heart filled with love for him. This man made her feel like she was special. Not just Ava Colton, therapist, foster mom and sister. Like who she was at her core was important. It meant more than she could put into words. He'd been great the last few days. Everything she asked for, he'd given her. He was taking care of Gracie like she was his biological child. Honestly, it felt like she was getting a glimpse through a mirror at her life, but she was active in it.

They were getting closer to her house, and she realized that the last thing she wanted to do was be surrounded by their families until she knew where they stood. "Can you pull over for a minute?"

"Sure," he said, signaling and then finding a safe place to pull over. "What's up?"

"What's up? Wow, so much. I'm not sure where to start, but I've had a lot of time to think while I was in the hospital and... Chay, how do you feel about me?"

He quirked his head to the side and raised both eyebrows at her. "I love you."

The breath went out of her and she blinked a bunch of times. Had he just said?

"You love me."

"Yup. Was going to tell you sooner but figured you needed time to get over your guilt—"

She undid her seat belt as he was talking and threw herself into his arms, hugging him so tightly. Tears fell freely down her face. "I love you, too."

"I was hoping you would say so, but you know it wouldn't change how I feel about you."

Of course it didn't. Chay was solid—always. He'd learned so many lessons from that six-year-old who'd been left behind by his mom. God, she loved this man so much.

Kissing him again, she put her hands on either side of his face, pulling back. "I. Love. You."

She dropped kisses on his face with each word.

"Me, too. I want you to marry me," he said.

"Shouldn't you ask?"

"I could, but we both know you're going to say yes."

"I am. And what about—"

"Gracie? I think we should apply to adopt her. We're the only family she's known, and we will get justice for Annie Ross and keep her mom alive for her," Chay said. "She's going to have questions, and I want to make sure she gets her answers when she's older."

"We definitely will," she said.

A few minutes later they were at her house, Chay's hand in hers as she walked to the front door. Remembering how irritating he'd been the first day he'd come to see her. "You were such a pain about Fern."

"Good thing I was or we wouldn't be together now," he said.

Laughing together, they went to spend the afternoon with their families. Ava felt a kind of peace she'd never experienced before. She tired easily, but she didn't want the afternoon to end. It was the first time she realized that she was fully present in the moment. The fear that Daniel had planted in her and losing Greg had been a shadow over her everyday life.

Knowing that Daniel was back in jail and slowly coming to terms with Greg's death was helping her. But she knew the real reason for her happiness was right in her arms. Chay held her and she held Gracie. There was nothing more she needed than this.

* * * * *

COMING SOON!

We really hope you enjoyed reading this book.
If you're looking for more romance
be sure to head to the shops when
new books are available on

Thursday 26th March

To see which titles are coming soon, please visit
millsandboon.co.uk/nextmonth

MILLS & BOON

FOUR BRAND NEW BOOKS FROM
MILLS & BOON MODERN

Indulge in desire, drama, and breathtaking romance – where passion knows no bounds!

OUT NOW

Eight Modern stories published every month, find them all at:
millsandboon.co.uk

LET'S TALK
Romance

For exclusive extracts, competitions and special offers, find us online:

- **f** MillsandBoon
- **X** @MillsandBoon
- **◉** @MillsandBoonUK
- **♪** @MillsandBoonUK

Get in touch on 01413 063 232

For all the latest titles coming soon, visit
millsandboon.co.uk/nextmonth